LIFTPORT

The Space Elevator—
Opening Space to Everyone

Edited by
Michael J. Laine
Tom Nugent
Bill Fawcett

Meisha Merlin Publishing, Inc.

Liftport

Published by Meisha Merlin Publishing, Inc.
PO Box 7
Decatur, GA   30031

Editing by Michael J. Laine, Tom Nugent and Bill Fawcett
Interior layout by Lynn Hatcher
Cover art David Mattingly
Cover design by Kevin Murphy

ISBN: Soft Cover 1-59222-109-2

http://www.MeishaMerlin.com
First MM Publishing edition:

Printed in Canada
0 9 8 7 6 5 4 3 2 1

ACKNOWLEDGEMENTS

Nearly 40 authors and contributors are writing for this book, each with their own vision of the project, each with their own understandings of how it will work. This is a very large project and the simple fact is we don't even know all the questions, let alone have all the answers—yet. That means there are parts of this book that are not consistent. Rather than condemning the authors and the project, please recognize that this is a vital part of the process. We are in a phase of constant re-assessment, re-imagining, and revision. That should be expected for a project of this size and complexity. We don't even want a rigid, final plan until late 2007. Until then, every assumption is open to vigorous debate and skepticism. The technical parts of this book reflect that reality.

And, with that in mind, my first acknowledgements go to you, the readers of this book. My LiftPort Team and the authors worked very hard to make this available to you. If you have questions—and you should, once you've finished this book—please consider yourself 'invited to get involved'. And the most important thing I have to say to you is "thanks!" for your interest, enthusiasm, and vitally important at this stage—thanks for your curiosity.

Brad—for showing me what is possible.

My Family—for your support and notable absence of "the voice of reason"

To the Families of my Team—for your willingness to "let" your loved ones participate in this adventure. You've given up a lot of time with your family so that we could pursue this.

To my LiftPort Team—for putting up with a guy who makes a lot of mistakes, has unreasonably high expectations, demands long hours, total dedication and has very little money for paychecks and bonuses you so richly have deserved. Thanks for rising to the occasion and working hard to build something great. We have a long ways to go, but we wouldn't be this far along without your talent, creativity and dedication.

To our Investors—For having the courage, vision, and resolve to commit to a project that has a lot of risk, and just might - if we are all very lucky and very skilled - make a pile of money and help change the world.

Children of Team LiftPort—I want you to know that your moms and dads want to give you an enormous gift, the biggest gift a parent can give a child—the solar system, and a better world to grow up in. Their work on this project is tangible proof of their love for you.

E, C, J, M-L—I'd like to build this for your families. I want the very best for you and yours.

I appreciate all of you and all that you've done. Further, I understand and appreciate all that you still have left to do. Let's get to work.

—Michael Laine

LIFTPORT

The Space Elevator— Opening Space to Everyone

Edited by
Michael J. Laine
Tom Nugent
Bill Fawcett

TABLE OF CONTENTS

Our Next Great Leap: The LiftPort Space Elevator Book Introduction
by
the LiftPort Staff

IN 1405, EMPEROR ZHU DI of the Ming Dynasty commissioned hundreds of graceful Chinese junks to explore the world. Fifty years before European travelers arrived there, the Chinese navy explored the Indian Ocean and even reached Africa. Within one hundred years, however, it was illegal to build or even ride on a Chinese ocean-going vessel. Due to political wrangling and bureaucratic malaise the Ming Dynasty lost a great opportunity to better their society and expand their horizons.

In 1969, the United States of America successfully established a human presence on the Moon. Neil Armstrong, the first person to step foot on an extraterrestrial body, marked the moment with his unforgettable words "One small step for man, one giant leap for mankind." Within three years, however, that human presence had been withdrawn and we have been stuck circling in low Earth orbit ever since. Due to political pressure and poor bureaucratic decision-making, humanity wasted the efforts of the Apollo program and the benefits it could have provided for this increasingly crowded globe.

With those two lessons in mind, the time has come for humanity's next "great leap." We can once again reach out from our cradle of life and begin exploring the Universe around us. However, this time we have the ability not only to access space, but to remain in space as well. This ability to colonize our solar system will be provided by the Space Elevator.

The Space Elevator, in its contemporary form, is composed of an extremely strong ribbon stretching from an ocean-going platform up to a counterweight 100,000 kilometers (62,000 miles) in space. Autonomous climbing robots, known as "Lifters," haul cargo and passengers up the ribbon into space. Ground based lasers will beam power to the Lifter's solar panels, thereby providing energy for the lifter motors.

All of this technology currently exists in one form or another, save for the ribbon. However, recent advances in materials science have indicated a ribbon with the strength to stretch 100,000 kilometers into the sky can be built. Carbon nanotubes are a unique molecule that, if bonded appropriately, could provide the necessary strength and weight characteristics for a Space Elevator. While there are still many engineering hurdles to overcome before construction begins, there are no physical reasons why a Space Elevator cannot be feasibly constructed using current and near-term technology.

Besides technical hurdles, the Space Elevator faces many financial, political, legal and social challenges as well. Current estimates to develop and build the first Space Elevator put its cost at around $10 billion. To put this number in perspective, a large bridge may cost $1-4 billion, hydroelectric dams cost $4-7 billion, one space shuttle launch costs $1 billion, and the Big Dig project cost $15 billion.

In the political arena, as of the time of writing, there has been no vocal support from any national leader in the United States of America (currently home to most Space Elevator developers). There is no legal precedence or regulatory framework for a Space Elevator anywhere in the world. There is no "Office for Space Elevator Construction" and therefore obtaining the necessary licenses will be difficult. Finally, the general public, has a limited understanding of the system and what can be achieved with it.

What could a Space Elevator mean for our world? Ultimately, the Space Elevator will provide safe, inexpensive and reliable transportation into orbit. And it will do so on a daily basis. The very first Space Elevator could lower the price to orbit from thousands of dollars per pound today, to four hundred dollars per pound.

With the current estimate of four hundred dollars per pound, many space activities now financially impossible become quite feasible. Initially, solar power satellites and huge communications arrays will be launched. These will encourage a greater exchange of ideas and provide clean, renewable energy to the globe. As time advances, orbital retirement homes and hotels will be developed. Travel to the Moon and Mars will become much easier. Eventually, space-based industry and manufacturing will develop, and activities like asteroid mining might become commonplace. With the reduced launch costs and increased safety provided by the Space Elevator, one's imagination is the only limiting factor as to what humanity can accomplish in space.

There are several major misconceptions regarding the Space Elevator that must be addressed. These are: falling ribbons, Space

Elevator destinations, the state of the rocket industry and how the structure "stands up" without falling. All of these topics are covered in detail in other chapters of the book, but they are so common that they will be briefly covered here as well.

The ribbon, if it were to break, would not cause destruction and havoc on a global scale. Earlier NASA studies defined the Space Elevator as a tower-like structure that, if it were to fall, would shower hundred-mile long rigid beams onto the poor planet below. The design being discussed most readily today (and coincidentally also the result of a NASA-funded study by Dr. Bradley Edwards) is actually a much more flexible ribbon design. If this ribbon were to tear, most of it would be flung out into space while the part that fell would almost entirely burn up in the atmosphere. The part that survived reentry would flutter down to the ground with all the speed of a falling newspaper.

When the Space Elevator is discussed in popular culture, it is often described as an elevator to the moon. This is incorrect. While it is true that the Space Elevator will greatly reduce the complexities and fuel required to leave Earth orbit, it will not offer direct service to any other planetary body, except for the Earth itself.

While the Space Elevator may make Earth-to-orbit heavy-lift rockets obsolete, there will be a great need for rocket engines to propel to destinations beyond the area adjacent to the Elevator ribbon. One will need a rocket to change orbits, go to the Moon, to Mars or the asteroids. Therefore, the Space Elevator will not wreck the current aerospace industry. In fact, it will greatly increase the revenues of current rocket/space companies.

The basic physics behind the Space Elevator are quite simple to understand. Imagine a person holding a string with a ball on the end. As the person swings the ball above their head in a circle, the string becomes horizontal. Now imagine that the Earth is the spinning person and the string is the Space Elevator ribbon. As the Earth turns, centrifugal acceleration pulls the ribbon outward, and gravity pulls it inward to the Earth. With a properly designed Space Elevator, these two forces balance one another and the structure stays taut for robots to climb. Therefore we can see that the Space Elevator does not so much as "stand up" from the Earth as it "hangs" from space and is "pulled out" by centrifugal acceleration.

As previously mentioned, the nation most actively pursuing Space Elevator research is the United States. As of this writing, there was no on-going official government funding for Space Elevator research either in the United States or elsewhere. However, there are several commercial and non-profit entities pursuing direct Space Elevator research and literally hundreds of institutions (governmental, academic, commercial and non-profit) pursuing research that will aid Space Elevator construction.

LiftPort Group is currently on the forefront of Space Elevator development. LiftPort is pursuing high altitude robotics and carbon nanotech research, as well as setting the legal, financial, social, and political foundations for Space Elevator construction. LiftPort has a policy of international public inclusion because we feel that such a large project cannot be built without the support of many people throughout the globe. For more information about LiftPort Group, please see the list of resources at the end of the book, or just go to www.liftport.com.

The Spaceward Foundation is a not-for-profit organization whose flagship project is Elevator 2010. The Elevator 2010 Challenge is an "X-prize like" competition to promote Space Elevator awareness and technology development. Please see the accompanying chapter from the Spaceward Foundation's Ben Shelef.

THERE ARE TWO broad categories of development for the Space Elevator: technical, and non-technical. Technical development encompasses numerous hardware challenges (carbon nanotube ribbon construction, laser power beaming, long-duration robotics, and more) and analytical challenges (e.g., orbital debris monitoring and avoidance). As important as the technical considerations are, though, the space elevator won't be built without hard work in the non-technical fields, namely the political, financial, legal and social arenas.

There is only one piece of space elevator technology that has not yet been demonstrated in one form or another—the ribbon material. Luckily, hundreds of labs (government, commercial, and academic) around the world are attempting to harness the strength of carbon nanotubes for material science applications. And existing research is already making great progress on producing stronger materials made with carbon nanotubes.

The basic laser, robotic and power beaming technologies required for the Space Elevator currently exist. These technologies, however, must be refined, scaled up, and integrated correctly so as to serve the purposes of the Space Elevator. Again, LiftPort Group has made significant strides in Space Elevator-specific robotics technology. LiftPort has a working Lifter prototype and has tested their Lifter numerous times. The Spaceward Foundation, a not-for-profit organization, has established the Elevator 2010 competition to promote power-beaming, ribbon material, and robotics development necessary for the Space Elevator.

The biggest challenges to Space Elevator construction will be in the non-technical areas. Therefore, LiftPort Group is leading the way in marshalling social, financial and political support for the project. LiftPort has organized a Finance division to begin raising funds for the Space Elevator and other space infrastructure projects. LiftPort is reaching out to key political, government and military officials in order to garner their support early on for the project. Finally, LiftPort Media is appealing to the general public for support by popularizing the Space Elevator via books, DVDs, educational curricula and technology demonstrations.

There is much to be done, however. At the time of writing, the Space Elevator had no vocal political support and was just beginning to penetrate the mainstream consciousness of the United States (despite Dave Barry and Jay Leno joking about the project, many people still don't know what a space elevator is). Internationally, some space enthusiasts know about the project but otherwise it is relatively unknown. LiftPort has received requests of inquiry from some very high-placed military officials and, after a successful set of demonstrations, elected officials are beginning to take notice as well. As for the general public, it is hoped this book becomes the tool that truly makes the Space Elevator a household term throughout the world.

This book is organized into two types of articles, interleaved with each other. The first type of article is non-fiction and covers the basic technical, financial, legal, social and political requirements of the system. Each chapter is written by an expert in the field and the reader is encouraged to visit any website links they provide in their attached biographies.

The second type of article is science fiction. There are many stories outlining the possibilities and implications of Space Elevator construction for the whole world. After reading this book, LiftPort would just like you to be aware that there are many ways to continue your journey and get involved with the Space Elevator project. Please see the last chapter of the book (conveniently titled Further Information and How to Get Involved) to find out how you can learn more about the project and support the organizations developing the Space Elevator.

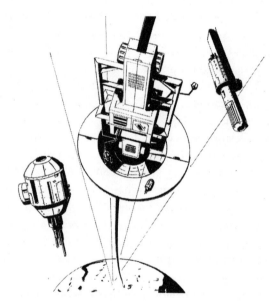

The following paper was first published in 1981 in *Advances in Earth Oriented Applied Space Technologies*. It is reprinted here with the author's permission.

THE SPACE ELEVATOR: 'THOUGHT EXPERIMENT', OR KEY TO THE UNIVERSE?
by
Sir Arthur C. Clarke

ABSTRACT—The space elevator (alias Sky Hook, Heavenly Ladder, Orbital Tower, or Cosmic Funicular) is a structure linking a point on the equator to a satellite in the geostationary orbit directly above it. By providing a 'vertical railroad' it would permit orders-of-magnitude reduction in the cost of space operations. The net energy requirements would be almost zero, as in principle all the energy of returning payloads could be recaptured; indeed, by continuing the structure beyond the geostationary point (necessary in any event for reasons of stability) payloads could be given escape velocity merely by utilising the 'sling' effect of the Earth's rotation.

The concept was first developed in detail by a Leningrad engineer, Yuri Artsutanov, in 1960 and later by several American engineers quite unaware of Artsutanov's work. All studies indicate that the idea, outrageous though it appears at first sight, is theoretically feasible and that its practical realisation could follow from the mass-production of high-strength materials now known as laboratory curiosities.

This paper is a semi-technical survey of the rapidly expanding literature of the subject, with some speculations about ultimate developments. Whether or not the Space elevator can be actually built, it is of great interest as the *only* known device which could replace the rocket as a means of escaping from the earth. If it is ever developed, it could make mass space travel no more expensive than any other mode of transportation.
Piotr Jagodzinksi

INTRODUCTION

WHAT I WANT to talk about today is a space transportation system so outrageous that many of you may consider it not even science-fiction, but pure fantasy. Perhaps it is; only the future will tell. Yet even if it is regarded as no more than a 'thought-experiment', it is one of the most fascinating and stimulating ideas in the history of astronautics.

This paper is essentially a survey; in the unlikely event that it contains anything original, it's probably wrong. Your complaints should be addressed to Director-General Roy Gibson, who is responsible for getting me here.

What's in a name?

First of all, we have a severe problem in nomenclature. It is very difficult to talk about something, until people have agreed on its name. In this case, we have an embarrassingly wide choice.

The Russian inventor used the charming 'heavenly funicular'. American writers have contributed 'orbital tower', 'anchored satellite', 'beanstalk', 'Jacob's Ladder'—and, of course, 'Skyhook'. I prefer 'space elevator'; it is euphonious (at least in English) and exactly describes the subject.

Historical

As usual, it all began with Tsiolkovski—specifically, with his 1895 paper 'Day-Dreams of Heaven and Earth'[1]. During his discussion of possible ways of escaping from the earth, he considered the building of a high tower, and described what would happen as One ascended it. I quote:

'On the tower, as one climbed higher and higher up it, gravity would decrease gradually; and if it were constructed on the Earth's equator and, therefore, rapidly rotated together with the earth, the gravitation would disappear not only because of the distance from the centre of the planet, but also from the centrifugal force that is increasing proportionately to that distance. The gravitational force drops. . . but the centrifugal force operating in the reverse direction increases. On the earth the gravity is finally eliminated at the top of the tower, at an elevation of 5.5 radii of the earth (36000 km).

'As one went up such a tower, gravity would decrease steadily, without changing direction; at a distance of 36000 km, it would be completely annihilated, and then it would be again detected. . . but its direction would be reversed, so that a person would have his head turned towards the earth. . . .'

Tsiolkovski then calculates the height of similar towers on the Sun and planets, but his comments—at least as I read the translation ('it would be excessive to discuss how possible these towers would be on the planets' he suggests that he does not regard the concept as a serious practical proposition. And of course he is quite right: it would be impossible, if I dare use such a risky word, to construct *free-standing* towers tens of thousands of kilometres high. If Tsiolkovski failed to mention the alternative solution, it may be because he was concerned only with the first steps away from earth. And the space-elevator is completely useless in the pioneering days of astronautics, unless you are lucky (?) enough to live on a very small, rapidly spinning planet.

Nevertheless, it is interesting to find how high a tower we could build, if we really tried. In early 1962 the Convair Division of General Dynamics carried out a feasibility study, to see if very high towers would be of value for astronomy, high altitude research, communications and rocket launching platforms [2]. It turns out that steel towers could be built up to 6 km high, aluminium ones up to almost 10. Nature can do just as well; it would be cheaper to use Mount Everest.

However, we now have much better materials than steel and aluminium in the form of composites, which give both high strength *and* low density. Calculations show that a tower built of graphite composite struts could reach the very respectable height of 40 km, tapering from a 6 km-wide base. I dare not ask what it would cost; but it's startling to realise that, even with today's technology, we could build a structure *100 times* as high as the world's tallest building.

But the geostationary orbit is a thousand times higher still, so we can forget about building up towards it. If we hope to establish a physical link between Earth and space, we have to proceed in the opposite direction—from orbit, *down*-wards.

That it might be useful to hang a long cable from a satellite must have occurred to a great many people. I myself toyed with the idea in 1963 while preparing an essay on comstats for UNESCO, published next year in *Astronautics* [3]. At that time, there was still considerable uncertainty about the effects of the time delay in satellite telephone circuits; some thought that it might have proved intolerable in ordinary conversation.

Although we should be duly grateful to Nature for giving us the geostationary orbit, one can't help wishing, for INTELSAT'S sake, that it was a good deal closer. So I wondered if it would be possible to suspend a satellite repeater 10000 or more kilometres below the 36000 km altitude that the law of gravity, and the Earth's rotational speed, has dictated.

Some desultory calculations soon convinced me that it couldn't be done with existing materials, but as I wanted to leave the option open I wrote cautiously: 'As a much longer-term possibility, it might be mentioned that there are a number of theoretical ways of achieving a *low-altitude, twenty-four hour satellite*; but they depend upon technical developments unlikely to occur in this century. I leave their contemplation as "an exercise for the student"!' In 1969, 6 years later, Collar and Flower came to exactly the same conclusion in a J.B.I.S. paper 'A (relatively) low altitude 24-h satellite' [4]. To quote their summary:

'The scheme for launching a twin-satellite system into a 24-h orbit with the inner satellite relatively close to the earth's surface is theoretically possible, although with the materials currently available no operational advantage would result. New materials now being developed, however, if used to the limit of their strength, could result in a system that considerably improved communication efficiency. Even with materials that are strong enough and light enough many problems exist. Static and dynamic stability investigations would need to be made, and temperature effects allowed for. In the design of the system, means of deployment and of minimising meteorite damage would in particular need careful consideration.

'The final conclusion is that while theoretically possible, the twin satellite system is impractical at the present time, but will show ever increasing promise as new, strong, light materials are developed.'

Incidentally, Collar and Flower did mention that it would be possible for the cable to reach *all the way down to the Earth's surface*, though they did not elaborate on this point, and were apparently unaware of earlier work in this field. For it now appears that at least half a dozen people invented the space elevator quite independently of each other, and doubtless more pioneers will emerge from time to time.

In the West, the group that got there first consisted of John Isaacs, Allyn Vine, Hugh Bradner and George Bachus, from the Scripps Institute of Oceanography and the Woods Hole Oceanographic Institute. It is, perhaps, hardly surprising that oceanographers should get involved in such a scheme, since they are about the only people who concern themselves with very long hanging cables. Very long, that is, by ordinary standards; but in their 1966 letter to *Science* [5] Isaacs *et al.* discussed a cable over *three thousand* times longer than one to the bottom of the Marianas Trench, a mere 11 km down.

Their brief but very comprehensive paper made the following points:

The cable would have to be tapered, and would have to be spun out in both directions simultaneously—that is, towards the Earth and away from it, so that the structure was always balanced around the geostationary point. One would start with the smallest possible cable—perhaps with a minimum diameter of only a few thousandths of a centimeter—and the lower end would have to be guided down to earth by some kind of reaction device. Once the initial cable had been established between stationary orbit and the point on the equator immediately below it, it could be used to establish a stronger cable, until one of the required carrying capacity was attained. In principle, it would then be possible to hoist payloads from earth into space by purely mechanical means.

Now, you will recall that, as one ascends Tsiolkovski's hypothetical space tower, gravity decreases to zero at stationary orbit—*and its direction then reverses itself.* In other words, though one would have to do work to get the payload up to the geostationary position, once it had passed that point it would continue to travel on outwards, at an increasing acceleration—falling upwards, in fact. Not only would it require no energy to move it away from earth—it could *generate* energy, which could be used to lift other payloads! Of course, this energy comes from the rotation of the earth, which would be slowed down in the process. I have not attempted to calculate how much mass one could shoot off into space before the astronomers complained that their atomic clocks were running fast. It would certainly be a long time before anyone else could notice the difference....

Isaacs *et al.* go on to say:

'In addition to their use for launching materials into space, such installations could support laboratories for observation of conditions in space at high altitudes; they could resupply energy or materials to satellites or spacecraft, collect energy or materials from space and the high atmosphere, support very tall structures on the earth's surface, and others. There is no immediate limit to the total mass that could be retained near the l-day orbit by such a cable.'

Isaacs *et al.*, discussed only briefly the obviously vital question of possible materials, listing amongst others quartz, graphite and beryllium. The *total* mass, with the best material, of a cable strong enough to withstand 200 km h^{-1} wind forces, turns out to be surprisingly low—only half a ton! Needless to say, its diameter at the earth and would be extremely small—one five-hundredth of a centimetre. And before anyone starts to spin this particular thread, I should point out that the material proposed is quite expensive. I don't know what the market quotation would be for half a ton of—*diamond.*

The first reaction to the Isaacs paper came some three months later [6] when an unlucky American scientist fell into a neat dynamical trap. He was not the only one to do so, apparently; but James Shea was unfortunate enough to have his letter published. The objection he raised was ingenious and so apparently convincing that he stated flatly: 'The system is inefficient as well as mechanically unsound and *theoretically* impossible.' (My italics.)

Shea's paradox can best be appreciated as follows: Consider the payload to be sent up the cable, when it is resting on the equator at the beginning of its journey. Obviously, because of the Earth's spin, it's actually moving eastwards at about 1700 km h^{-1}.

Now it is sent up the cable—*how* it is, is for the moment, unimportant—until it reaches the geostationary orbit, 36000 km above the Earth. It is still exactly above the point from which it started, but almost six times further from the centre of the Earth. So to stay here, it must obviously move six times faster—about 11000 km h^{-1}. How does it acquire all this extra tangential velocity?

There's no problem when you consider the analogous case of a fly crawling from the hub out along the spoke of a spinning wheel. The wheel is a rigid structure, and automatically transmits its rotational velocity to the fly. But how can a flexible cable extending out into space perform the same feat?

The explanation may be found by looking at one of mankind's simplest, oldest and most cost-effective weapons—the sling. I wonder if Goliath's technical advisers told him not to worry about that kid with the ridiculous loop of cloth—it couldn't possibly transfer any kinetic energy to a pebble. If so, they forgot that the system contained a rigid component—David's strong right arm. So also with the space elevator. Its lower end is attached to the 6000 km radio of the Earth—quite a lever.

Having easily refuted this criticism, Isaacs & Co. were now in for a shock. More than a year after their letter had appeared, *Science* printed a lengthy note [7] from Vladimir Lvov, Moscow correspondent of the Novosti Press Agency, pointing out that they had been anticipated by a half a decade. A Leningrad engineer, Yuri N. Artsutanov, had already published an article in *Pravda* which not only laid down *all* the basic concepts of the space elevator, but developed them in far greater detail.

This 1960 paper, which may turn out to be one of the most seminal in the history of astronautics, has the unassuming title 'Into the Cosmos by electric vehicle'*. Unfortunately, it has never been translated into English, nor have the extensive calculations upon which it is obviously based yet been published. The summary that follows is therefore based on Lvov's letter.

Artsutanov's initial minimum cable, constructed from materials which already exist but which have so far only been produced in microscopic quantities, would be able to lift two tons, would have a diameter of about one millimetre at the earth's surface, and would have a total mass of about 900 tons. It would extend to a height of 50000 km—that is, 14000 km beyond geostationary altitude, the extra length providing the additional mass needed to keep the whole system under tension. (The weight, as it were, on the end of the sling.)

But this is just a beginning. Artsutanov proposed to use the initial cable to multiply itself, in a sort of boot-strap operation, until it was strengthened a thousand fold. Then, he calculated, it would be able to handle 500 tons *an hour* or 12000 tons a day. When you consider that this is roughly equivalent to one Shuttle flight every *minute*, you will appreciate that Comrade Artsutanov is not thinking on quite the same scale as NASA. Yet if one extrapolates from Lindbergh to the state of transatlantic air traffic 50 yr later, dare we say that he is over-

---

* Artsutanov's own translation is: 'Into space with the help of an electric locomotive' (See Acknowledgements).

optimistic? It is doubtless a pure coincidence, but the system Artsutanov envisages could just about cope with the current daily increase in the world population, allowing the usual 22 kg of baggage per emigrant...

Lvov uses two names to describe Artsutanov's invention: a 'cosmic lift', and a 'heavenly funicular'. But a funicular, strictly speaking, is a device operated by a rope or cable —and we may be sure that the space elevator will not hoist its payloads with the aid of moving cables tens of thousands of kilometres long.

One would have thought that this correspondence, in one of the world's leading scientific journals, would have triggered a large scale discussion. Not a bit of it; to the best of my knowledge, there was no reaction at all. This may be because the Apollo project was then moving towards its climax—the first moon landing was less than two years away—and everyone was hypnotised by big rockets, as well they might be.

But the idea must have been quietly circulating in the U.S.S.R. because it is illustrated in the handsome volume of paintings by Leonov and Sokolov *"The Stars are Awaiting Us"* (1967). On p. 25 there is a painting entitled 'Space Elevator', showing an assembly of spheres—hovering, I am pleased to see, over Sri Lanka—from which a cable stretches down to the earth. Part of the descriptive text reads as follows:

'If a cable is lowered from the (24 h) satellite to the earth you will have a ready cable-road. An "Earth-Sputnik-Earth" elevator for freight and passengers can then be built, and it will operate without any rocket propulsion.'

Rather surprisingly, there is no reference to the inventor. Sokolov's original painting, incidentally, has been acquired by my insatiably acquisitive friend Fred Durant for the National Air and Space Museum, which by now must surely have the world's finest collection of space art (and space hardware).

The next major development was not for another *eight* years. Then Jerome Pearson of the Flight Dynamics Laboratory, Wright-Patterson Air Force Base, invented the idea all over again and published the most comprehensive study yet in *Acta Astronautica* [8]. His computer search of the literature had failed to turn up any prior references, and in view of the indexing problem I'm not surprised. How would you look up such a subject? Pearson called it an 'orbital tower', and presumably never thought of telling his computer to hunt for 'sky-hook', which might have located the *Science* correspondence.

I speak with some feeling on this, because for 2 years I was solely responsible for indexing *Physics Abstracts*, and you'll find some very strange entries round 1950. But the problem is insoluble, unless you can do retrospective re-indexing. When a new phenomenon is discovered, you may not even know how to *classify* it, let alone what to call it (after all, we're still stuck with X-rays, after almost a century□).

Pearson's 1975 paper was the most thorough study of the project yet published, and emphasised one of the space elevator's most important characteristics. Like a terrestrial elevator, it *could be used in both directions*. Returning payloads could be brought back to Earth without the use of heat-shields and atmospheric braking. Not only would this reduce environmental damage; it would mean that virtually all the energy of re-entry could be recovered, and not wasted as is the case today.

This characteristic makes the space elevator unique—at least, until someone invents anti-gravity. *It is a conservative system.* If, as would probably be the case, electrical energy is used to lift payloads up the elevator, and the mass flow is the same in both directions, incoming traffic could provide all the energy needed to power outgoing traffic. In practice, of course, there could be the inevitable conversion and transmission losses, but they could be quite small.

In this and subsequent papers [9] Pearson was the first to go into the dynamics of the system, discussing the vibration modes of the structure due to launch loads, gravity, tides etc. He decided that none of these, though important, would cause any insuperable problems. Indeed, I have suggested elsewhere that they could even be used to advantage [10].

Pearson has also located at least three other independent originators of the concept [11], though none prior to Artsutanov's 1960 paper. From now on, at least, further re-invention is unnecessary; however, as we shall see later, novel and often surprising extensions of the basic system are still appearing.

THE PROBLEM OF MATERIALS

THE VERY MINIMUM requirement for a space elevator is, obviously, a cable strong enough to support its own weight when hanging from geostationary orbit down to earth, 36000 km below. That is a very formidable challenge; luckily, things are not quite as bad as they look because only the lowest portion of the cable has to withstand one full gee.

As we go upwards, gravity falls off according to Newton's inverse square law. But the *effective* weight of the cable diminishes even more rapidly, owing to the centrifugal force* on the rotating system. At geostationary altitude the two balance and the net weight is zero; beyond that, weight appears to increase again—but *away* from the Earth.

So our cable has no need to be strong enough to hang 36000 km under *sea-level* gravity; allowing for the effects just mentioned, the figure turns out to be only one-seventh of this. In other words, if we could manufacture a cable with sufficient strength to support 5000 km (actually, 4960) of its own length at one gee, it would be strong enough to span the gap from geostationary orbit to Equator. Mathematically—though not physically —Jacob's ladder need be only 5OOO km long to reach Heaven…. This figure of 5000km I would like to call 'escape length', for reasons which will soon be obvious.

How close are we to achieving this with known materials? Not very. The best steel wire could manage only a miserable 5O km or so of vertical suspension before it snapped under its own weight. The trouble with metals is that, though they are strong, they are also heavy; we want something that is both strong and *light*. This suggests that we should look at the modern synthetic and composite materials. Kevlar (Tm) 29, for example [12] could sustain a vertical length of 200 km before snapping —impressive, but still totally inadequate compared with the 5000 needed.

This 'breaking length', also known as 'rupture length' or 'characteristic length', is the quantity which enables one to judge whether any particular material is adequate for the job. However, it may come as a surprise to learn that a cable can hang vertically for a distance many times greater than its breaking length!

This can be appreciated by a simple 'thought experiment'. Consider a cable which is just strong enough to hang vertically for a hundred kilometres. One more centimetre, and it will snap….

* My brief apologies to purists for invoking this fictitious entity.

Now cut it in two. Obviously, the upper 50 km can support a length of 50 km—the identical lower half. So if we put the two sections side by side, they can support a *total* length of 100 km. Therefore, we can now span a vertical distance of 150 km, using material with only 100 km breaking length.

Clearly, we can repeat the process indefinitely, bundling more and more cables together as we go upwards. I'm sure that by now you've recognised an old friend—the 'step' principle, but in reverse. Step *rockets* get smaller as we go higher; step cables get bigger.

I apologise if, for many of you, I'm labouring the obvious, but the point is of fundamental importance and the rocket analogy so intriguing that I'd like to take it a little further.

We fossils from the pre-space age—the Early Paleoastronautic Era—must all remember the depressing calculations we used to make, comparing rocket exhaust velocities with the 11.2 km 5' of Earth escape velocity. The best propellants we knew then—and they are *still* the best today! —could provide exhaust velocities only a quarter of escape velocity. From this, some foolish critics argued that leaving the Earth by chemical rocket was impossible *even in theory*[13].

The answer, of course, was the step or multi-stage rocket—but even this didn't convince some sceptics. Willy Ley [14] records a debate between Oberth and a leading German engineer, who simply wouldn't believe that rockets could be built with a mass-ratio of twenty. For Saturn V, incidentally, the figure is about five hundred.

We escaped from earth using propellants whose exhaust velocity was only a fraction of escape velocity, by paying the heavy price demanded by multi stage rockets. An enormous initial mass was required for a small final payload.

In the same way, we can achieve the 5000 km 'escape length', even with materials whose breaking length is a fraction of this, by steadily thickening the cable as we go upwards. Ideally, this should be done not in discrete steps, but by a continuous taper. The cable should flare outwards with increasing altitude, its cross-section at any level being just adequate to support the weight hanging below.

With a stepped, or tapered, cable it would be theoretically possible to construct the space elevator from any material, however weak. You could build it of chewing gum, though the total mass required would probably be larger than that of the entire universe.

For the scheme to be practical we need materials with a breaking length a very substantial fraction of escape length. Even Kevlar 29's 200 km is a mere 25th of the 5000 km goal; to use that would be like fuelling the Apollo mission with damp gunpowder, and would require the same sort of astronomical ratio.

So, just as we were once always seeking exotic propellents, we must now search for super-strength materials. And, oddly enough, we will find them in the same place on the periodic table.

Carbon crystals have now been produced in the laboratory with breaking lengths of up to 3000 km—that is, more than *half* of escape length. How happy the rocket engineers would be, if they had a propellant whose exhaust products emerged with 60% of escape velocity!

Whether this material can ever be produced in the megaton quantities needed is a question that only future technologies can answer; Pearson [8] has made the interesting suggestion that the zero gravity and vacuum conditions of an orbiting factory may assist their manufacture, while Sheffield [15] and I [10] have pointed out that essentially unlimited quantities of carbon are available on many of the asteroids. Thus when space mining is in full swing, it will not be necessary to use super-shuttles to lift vast quantities of building material up to geostationary orbit—a mission which, surprisingly, is somewhat more difficult than escaping from Earth.

It is theoretically possible that materials stronger—indeed, vastly stronger—than graphite crystals can exist. Sheffield[15] has made the point that only the outer electrons of the atoms contribute, through their chemical bonds, to the strength of a solid. The nucleus provides almost all the mass, but nothing else; and in this case, mass is just what we *don't* need.

So if we want high-strength materials, we should look at elements with low atomic weights—which is why carbon (A.W.12) is good and iron (A.W.56) isn't. It follows, therefore, that the best material for building space elevators is—solid hydrogen! In fact, Sheffield calculates that the breaking length of a solid hydrogen crystal is 9118 km—almost twice 'escape length'.

By a curious coincidence, I have just received a press release from the National Science Foundation headed 'New form of hydrogen created as Scientists edge closer to creating metallic hydrogen'[16]. It reports that, at a pressure of half a million atmospheres, hydrogen has been converted into a *dense crystalline solid at room temperature*. The scientists concerned go on to speculate that, with further research—and I quote—"hydrogen solids can be maintained for long periods without containment".

This is heady stuff, but I wonder what they mean by 'long periods'. The report adds casually that 'solid hydrogen is 25 to 35 times more explosive than TNT'. So even if we *could* make structures from solid hydrogen, they might add a new dimension to the phrase 'catastrophic failure'.

However, if you think that crystallitic hydrogen is a tricky building material, consider the next item on Dr. Sheffield's shopping list. The ultimate in theoretical strength could be obtained by getting rid of the useless dead mass of the nucleus, and keeping only the bonding electrons. Such a material has indeed been created in the laboratory; it's 'positronium'—the atom, for want of a better word, consisting of electron-positron pairs. Sheffield calculates that the breaking length of a positronium cable would be a fantastic 16,700,000 km! Even in the enormous gravity field of Jupiter, a space elevator need have no appreciable taper.

Positronium occurs in two varieties, both unfortunately rather unstable. Para-positronium decays into radiation in one-tenth of a nanosecond—but orthopositronium lasts a thousand times longer, a whole tenth of a microsecond. So when you go shopping for positronium, make sure that you buy the brand marked 'Ortho'.

Sheffield wonders wistfully if we could stabilise positronium, and some even more exotic speculations are made by Moravec [17]. He suggests the possible existence of 'monopole' matter, and hybrid 'electric/magnetic' matter, which would give not only enormous strength but superconductivity and other useful properties.

Coming back to earth—or at least to this century—it seems fair to conclude that a small cable could certainly be established from geostationary orbit down to sea level, using materials that may be available in the near future. But that, of course would be only the first part of the problem—a mere demonstration of principle. To get from a simple cable to a working elevator system might be even more difficult. I would now like to glance at some of the obstacles, and suggest a few solutions; perhaps the following remarks may stimulate others better qualified to tackle them.

DEPLOYING THE CABLE

THE SPACE ELEVATOR may be regarded as a kind of bridge, and many bridges begin with the establishment of a light initial cable— sometimes, indeed, no more than a string towed across a canyon by a kite. It seems likely that the space elevator will start in the same way with the laying of a cable between geo stationary orbit and the point on the equator immediately below.

This operation is not as simple as it sounds, because of the varying forces and velocities involved, not to mention the matter of air resistance after atmospheric entry. But there are two existing technologies which may provide a few answers, or at least hints at them.

The first is that of submarine cable laying, now considerably more than a century old. Perhaps one day we may see in space something analogous to the triumphs and disasters of the *Great Eastern,* which laid the first successful transatlantic telegraph cable— the Apollo Project of its age.

But a much closer parallel, both in time and sophistication, lies in the development of wire-guided missiles. These lethal insects can spin out their metallic gossamer at several hundred kilometres an hour. They may provide the prototype of the vehicle that lays a thread from stationary orbit down to earth.

Imagine a spool, or bobbin, carrying some 40000 km of filament, a few tenths of a millimetre thick at the outer layers, and tapering down to a tenth of this at the core—the end that finally reaches Earth. Its mass would be a few tons, and the problem would be to play it out evenly at an average velocity of a kilometre a second along the desired trajectory. Moreover, an equivalent mass has to be sent outwards at the same time, to ensure that the system remains in balance at the stationary orbit.

My friend Professor Ruppehas investigated [12] the dynamics of the mission, and concludes that it can be achieved with modest mass-ratios. But the mechanical difficulties would obviously be formidable, and it may well turn out that material of such tensile strength is too stiff to be wound on to a spool of reasonable radius.

Sheffield [18] has suggested an alternative method of installation which I find—to say the least—hair-raisingly implausible. He proposes constructing the entire space elevator system in orbit, and then launching it towards the earth, grabbing the lower end when it reaches the equator! The atmospheric entry of a few megatons dead weight, which must impact within metres of the aiming point, seems likely to generate a lot of opposition from the environmentalists. I call it 'harpooning the Earth', and would prefer not to be near one of the Poles if it's ever tried out.

CHARLES SHEFFIELD AND *THE WEB BETWEEN THE WORLDS*
by
Kim Stanley Robinson

IN 1989, WHEN I began my novel RED MARS, I was living in Washington D.C. Soon after my arrival there, I had been invited to lunch by Charles Sheffield, and quickly we established a tradition of meeting for lunch about once a month, with Roger MacBride Allen, to get out of the house and discuss science, science fiction, and the issues of the day. So when I talked to Charles and Roger about my Mars story, Charles suggested that I introduce a space elevator to my scenario, as being an ingenious and practical method of lifting lots of weight out of a planet's gravity well, easier established on Mars than on Earth.

After that lunch I read up on space elevators in Charles's novel *The Web Between Worlds,* and in Arthur C. Clarke's *The Fountains of Paradise,* and in some technical papers Charles lent to me. I could see it was a really good idea; if humanity were to attempt the inhabitation of Mars, or really do anything substantial in space, a robust lift mechanism like an elevator would be a huge help. Also, in story-telling terms, the concept was still fairly obscure and under-utilized, despite the introduction of the concept to the science fiction community by Sheffield and Clarke in the late 1970s, in novels they wrote at the same time, without being aware of what the other was doing. The obvious appeal of the concept, in terms of real-world practicality, visual appeal, science fictional "sense of wonder," and plot possibilities, convinced me that it had to be included in my story.

A space elevator is only practical when its planetary terminus is located near the equator, and on Mars the equator crosses the rim of the crater of Pavonis Mons, the middle the three great "prince volcanoes" on Tharsis. So I decided to locate my terminus there, even though the extra twenty-seven kilometers of altitude was insignificant when compared to the total length of the cable; it still seemed to me that it would be a location attractive to new Martians. The view from the rim would be spectacular, and the city that would spring up around such an important link to the home planet, would surely become a major city. Naming that city Sheffield was an obvious thing to do, honoring not only Charles's introduction of the idea to fiction and his help to me in writing about a cable, but also making a small joke in a secondary reference to the city of Sheffield in England, where a famous ironworks was experiencing a scandal involving their manufacture of an extremely long metal tube for Sadam Hussein, who evidently wanted the component to help him build a kind of Jules Verne long-barrelled cannon, a very different kind of long metal object.

The asteroid anchoring the upper end of my cable I named Clarke, as only seemed fair, and later Sir Arthur told me he was pleased to see that. He was a strong supporter of my novel when it was published. I never heard much from Charles in reaction to my naming the base city Sheffield, but I see that he must have had the opportunity to revise the appendix to *The Web Between Worlds* at some later point, for in the version published here he briefly mentions the reference, with his typical dry wit about the town's destruction when the cable falls.

This cataclysm of a falling space elevator seemed to me to be a logical progression of my plot; a revolt breaks out in which forces are struggling to free themselves from Terran control; the space elevator is the strongest link in that control. So down it came.

Here too Charles was a big help to me. I still remember the startled look in his eyes when I asked him at one lunch—If the cable were to fall, which way would it go? He did not answer immediately, but got back to me later, with a sheaf of calculations he had printed out from his computer; Charles was the principle space scientist at the satellite company Earthsat, and his calculations were never casual. All the details of my catastrophe followed what he told me his calculations had indicated would happen, given my initial conditions.

Later, when I read that Phobos is only a few million years away from slowing down so much that it will fall to the Martian surface, it occurred to me that Phobos too could be a base used to control Mars, and thus might be another danger to my rebels, so at some later lunch I surprised Charles again with a further question: How much would you have to slow Phobos down to make it crash? I could see by his expression that he thought I had a dangerously destructive attitude toward the glories of the solar system, but this amused him as well. Back he came the following month with another thick sheaf of computer print-outs, the pages not yet separated. In an engineering sense he seemed pleased; it could be done. And so I did it.

By the time I got around to asking him what it would take to cast Deimos out of its orbit, he was beyond being surprised by any question I could ask him. A third time he came back with the necessary calculations in hand. He liked doing that kind of work for his own science fiction; and he liked helping other writers too.

Inevitably I could never include all the detail he provided me, but I was pleased to think that the descriptions I wrote were backed up by real calculations. I still have those computer print-outs, treasured gifts and mementos of Charles's analytic mind and generous nature.

The fall of the elevator cable at the end of *Red Mars* became one of that novel's signature scenes, and is remembered well enough, I have heard, that when space elevators are discussed, it often gets brought up as illustrating a serious danger. This is unfortunate. In the book I made the cable thicker than it had to be, precisely in order to increase the magnitude of the destruction when it was brought down; and I had it constructed by people who built in the mechanism of destruction, in case they ever found they needed it. Also, the crash occurred when the Martian atmosphere was so thin that it could not burn the cable up before it hit the ground. All these were aspects of the particular plot and history of my novel, and not generalizable dangers that would be incurred by every space elevator one might postulate or build.

Indeed, even in my novel the fallen cable (which in falling does not do enormous damage in any case) is replaced by another one, and later in the story, people construct one on Earth too. These function perfectly, and become an indispensable part of the story of humanity inhabiting the solar system.

It seems to me they are a natural and almost inevitable part of any robust history of humanity in space. And the rapid improvements in materials science, foretold by Charles in his own book, means that in reality the cable itself will be so light that it would not represent a danger to anyone on the ground, even in the extremely unlikely event of a fall; if it dropped through Earth's thick atmosphere it would burn up harmlessly, like an elogated shooting star. So the scene in *Red Mars,* though I am still quite happy with it as a scene in a novel, does not represent a danger that should be part of any serious objection to proceeding with the construction of a space elevator in the real world, either on Mars or on Earth.

The obvious advantages of a space elevator more than outweigh any potential dangers, either real or fictionally exaggerated. I hope that space elevators get built on Earth, on Mars, and anywhere else there is a gravity well that we want to get out of. Really it's a case of the sooner the better, because if it were to happen, it would be one of the best signs we could have of a healthy human civilization, extending our reach to the solar system's resources, and thus taking some environmental pressure off poor Mother Earth. And if it ever happens, I hope the builders will name one of the tether points Sheffield, in honor of one of smartest and kindest people I have ever known. I miss him.

This is chapter seven in *Web Between the Worlds*, a novel by Charles Sheffield. He and Sir Arthur C. Clarke both wrote their space elevator novels about building the space elevator in 1979 without either knowing the other had done so. Guess it was just a great idea whose time had come.

HOW TO BUILD A BEANSTALK

EITHER REGULO HAD somehow furnished the study with exactly the fittings that Rob had seen in the room where Rob first met him, or he took the whole thing with him from place to place. There was no mistaking the curious pink-topped desk, with its flanking wall displays, video cameras and output terminals. The dark red carpet was the same, and the internal lighting was held to its familiar subdued level. Only the gravity was noticeably different, lower here than at the station in Earth orbit. Atlantis could not tolerate the rotation rate that significant centrifugal gravity would require.

Regulo was seated behind the big desk. He watched while Rob stared around him, reading his reaction.

"You see, now I'm no better than a tortoise," he said. "I carry my house about on my back. Costs a little, but it's worth it for the convenience. Old dogs don't like new kennels. Come on in and sit down, Merlin. Welcome to Atlantis."

Rob moved to the chair that the old man indicated. His weight on the seat was barely perceptible, no more than a fraction of a kilogram. He looked at Regulo, shocked again by the sight of the ravaged face with its seamed and corroded features. Then he pushed that thought to the back of his mind. Regulo had a big pile of documents sitting in front of him, and a curious expression of suppressed glee shone in his bright eyes.

"Got your work on the beanstalk design," he said gruffly. "Ready to talk about it, or do you need time to settle down?"

Apparently Regulo didn't intend to indulge in social patter about the length of the trip from Earth. That suited Rob. He wanted to get to the real meeting as much as Regulo. He nodded. "I'm ready."

"Good." Regulo patted the stack of materials in front of him. "I pulled my old work out of the files. All done a long time ago, back before we could even mass-produce high-load graphite whiskers, never mind the doped silicon stuff that we've got now. You'll see it soon enough"—Rob was leaning forward in the seat—"but first I'd like to hear what you have to say. Do you think you could build me a beanstalk?"

"I can build it." Rob's voice was confident as he pulled out his own design notes. "That's the least of my worries. First of all, I can speed up the Spider. Two hundred kilometers a day of extruded cable will be no problem; maybe we can do a bit more than that. I can make it work with doped silicon instead of graphite, that's a minor change. That gives us a load-bearing cable that can take over two hundred million newtons per square centimeter. I used a design diameter of two meters for the bottom end, but you can make that any value you choose. There will be a little bit of a taper as you go up, but it's very small. The cable is only five percent thicker at geo-synchronous altitude than it is at the ground tether."

Regulo was nodding, his eyes fixed on Rob's. "What load will it take with that diameter?"

"More than I ever see us needing. About two-thirds of a billion tons at the bottom end. I wouldn't expect that you'd ever want to haul anything more than a few hundred thousand tons up to orbit at one time, or bring it down to Earth. Actually, I can't see us needing even a tenth of that, but I'm following your advice and thinking big."

Darius Regulo was nodding happily, drinking in Rob's words and numbers. He was in his element. "I started out my design with a one-meter base diameter when I did it. Either way, it ought to give us more capacity than we'll expect to use; but I've found that whenever you build in a capacity, you somehow get to use it." His eyes seemed to capture and focus the dim light of the room, shining cat-like at Rob through the gloom. "So far, our thinking matches. What problems have you found?"

"Four main ones. Only two of them are really engineering." Rob consulted his notes, then leaned back and began to tick off points on his fingers. "First of all, *where* do you construct it? The obvious way would be to start out at synchronous orbit and extrude cable up and down simultaneously, so you keep a balance between the cable above and below you, with gravity and centrifugal forces matching.

"But I suspect you know as well as I do that you can't operate that way. The structure is unstable until you actually get it tethered down on Earth at one end, with a thumping great ballast weight pulling it out beyond synchronous orbit at the other end. If you start building from geosynch, once you have a good length of cable extruded the structure becomes unstable. Small displacements in position grow exponentially. So that's problem number one: you can't build it at synchronous orbit, the way you'd like to. And that leads to question number one: where do you build it?"

"Do you have an answer?"

"Of course. But let me go on. Problem number two raises another question of how you build, but it involves different issues. Where do we get the power and materials? I calculate that we'll be putting something together that masses about three billion tons. It would only be a quarter of that if we went to your design of a one-meter bottom diameter, but either way it's a huge amount of material. I don't think you realize how much power it takes to operate the Spider. So where will we get it?"

Regulo stared down at the desk in front of him. "Are you asking me? I hope not. I could tell you, but I'm hiring you to give me solutions, not tell me difficulties."

It was hard to know how serious he was in that comment. Rob nodded and said, "I'll give you answers. But first let me finish the statement of the problems. There's one more engineering question. We have to tether the beanstalk at the lower end, and we'll need something like a billion tons to give it the tension that we need. So what do we do about earthquakes? We need some way of making sure that the tether can't be shaken loose by a natural disaster. We have to include storms, too, though I'm convinced we can handle that with local weather control. I checked with Weather Central, and they would be willing to take responsibility for that one; but earthquakes are another matter.

"One more problem, then I'm done. We'll be stringing a few billion tons of cable up from the equator out beyond synchronous orbit, and we'll be putting drive trains, passenger cars and cargo cars all the way along it, going up and down. Add all that together, and you have a hefty piece of work. What would we do if the beanstalk were to break, way up there near synchronous orbit?"

"We can build in ample safety factors."

"Against natural events, maybe." Rob shook his head. "That's not what worries me. What about sabotage? Suppose some lunatic gets on the beanstalk with a fusion bomb? We'd have a three-bil-lion-ton whip, cracking its way right round the equator. You can imagine what that would do when it hit the atmosphere. It would have more stored elastic energy than I like to think about, and it would be falling from thirty-odd thousand kilometers out."

Rob paused and looked at Regulo, who seemed not in the least disconcerted by the prospect of a collapsing beanstalk. He was star-ing up at the ceiling now, and thoughtfully tapping his pile of papers. "Are you proposing that as an engineering problem, Merlin?"

"No." Rob leaned forward. "We both know there's no good engineering solution to sabotage. But I still think that this is the issue that decides whether or not we can ever build your beanstalk. We have to convince other people that the risks are worth taking. How do we sell them on the idea that the benefits outweigh the risks?"

There was a smile of pure pleasure on Regulo's face. Rob's words seemed to delight him.

"You're the right man for this job," he said. "You've got your finger on the real problem. The engineering is the fun, eh, but the real problem is going to be the permits? Is that what you're telling me?"

"Of course. It's the same with every big engineering project. Somehow we have to persuade them back on Earth that they should let us go ahead, even with a small risk of sabotage."

Regulo had leaned over the desk and rubbed his hand at one part of it. "If I didn't have an answer to that one, I'd never have called you in the first place. See that sign?"

He tapped the glowing desk top with a thin finger, where the familiar sign ROCKETS ARE WRONG gleamed red on the surface.

"That's a true statement for four or five different reasons. You just have to pick the argument that serves your purpose at the time. I talked over the risks of this with the environmental control people back on Earth. I told them that we have a basic choice to make. We can go on with chemical and radioactive pollution, year after year, from the rockets that we are using now. That's not a *risk* of damage to Earth and the environment, it's an absolute stone certainty. And they know they don't have the clout to stop it. *Or* we can switch to a system that's completely non-polluting, with a tiny and controllable chance of having an accident."

Regulo chuckled and shook his head. "They weren't sure, but you know that the safest thing for a bureaucrat to do is to say no to everything. If I'd left it there, they'd have vetoed us. So I told them that the chance of an accident went up or down, depending on the level of the monitoring operations. They would need to create a new security department, one with a high level of funding. New jobs, new facilities, new equipment. Naturally, the money for that would come from the builders of the beanstalk—us. And naturally, the funds would go to them. Did you ever see a bureaucrat when he sees a chance for a little empire-building? Anyway, here's your permit."

He pulled a document from the pile in front of him.

Rob stared at it in amazement. "A permit to build a beanstalk?"

"To build three of them, if we choose to. If you're going to ask at all, why not ask for a lot? I suggest we think of the first one as having a Quito tether point. That's where I have the best franchises."

Regulo suddenly stared sideways at the TV cameras pointed toward the desk. He seemed satisfied with what he saw, and turned his attention again to Rob. "Now then, I've given you help on that one. What about your solutions for the others? How do you propose to build it?"

"Let's start with *where.*" Rob glanced briefly at his notes, then tucked them away into his pocket. "We have to perform the construction well away from Earth, and we ought to choose a stable point that's not too far away. I'm proposing that we go to L-4, where we have an existing labor pool to draw on if we need it. There's a decent-sized solar power satellite there, too, and we'll need the SPS to run the Spider—unless you have other ideas?"

Now he looked at Regulo, deliberately waiting a moment before he went on, "All right, so we extrude the whole thing up there at one go: load-bearing cable, synchronous drive motors all the way along it to move the cars up and down, and superconducting cables to feed power into those."

"The Spider can do all that?" Regulo showed surprise for the first time since the conversation had begun.

"That, and more." Rob felt easier. Up to this point of the meeting Regulo seemed to have thought of and improved on everything that Rob could suggest. Now at last there was something Rob could do that the other man couldn't.

"Maybe Corrie already mentioned to you that the Spider has a biological component," he went on. "It's a lot more adaptable than any ordinary piece of hardware, so changing the fabrication plan as the materials are extruded is no big trick. Originally, I wanted it flexible to handle things like tapering supports for bridges without my needing to re-program. Now it turns out the versatility will come in useful here."

"Aye, Cornelia did mention the bio thing." Regulo rubbed at his face with a thin, veiny hand. "Did she tell you just how much we fooled with that damned design, and never once sniffed at a bio-combine system? Maybe it's time I went back for a technology refresher course."

"You seem to do pretty well." Again, Rob couldn't tell if Regulo was being serious. His facial abnormalities distorted every expression. "So far, I haven't managed to come up with anything better than your designs. But let me keep going. We get to the point where we have a hundred thousand kilometers of load cable, with power cables and drive attached to it, up near L-4. We need one more thing apart from a powersat, and that's a ballast weight. It has to be a big one. It provides the tension in the load cable and balances the tether. We can't attach the ballast until we make contact with the tether, so the ballast weight will be flying around the Earth in its own orbit.

"We fly the beanstalk in, and curve it down to make contact with the tether point—at Quito, if we decide that's the best place for it. We'll have to curl in to atmospheric entry along a spiral approach from L-4. The ballast weight swings up and contacts the end of the cable at the same time as the tether end comes in to ground contact—and we'd better not miss that tether, or the whole thing will be off like a slingshot, past the Moon and on its way to God-knows-where. I've checked the timing, and I don't think we have any real problems. The inertia of the system works both ways—you have time to do things. But changing direction or speed is almost impossible unless you have a *lot* of time to work with."

"We won't miss the catch. I'll be down there to hold and tether it myself if I have to, and damn what the doctors say."

Regulo's face was full of resolve. Rob wondered suddenly just what the doctors *did* say. If anything, the old man looked worse than at their first meeting. How much of Regulo's body was covered with the terrible deformity that marred his face?

"All right, my lad, what are your other worries?" Regulo broke into Rob's train of thought. "I agree with you, the fly-in from L-4 or L-5 will get around most of the problems of stability. I'll always take a situation with dynamic stability over one with static stability, any time. What are you suggesting for the transport system itself? How many cars, how big, how fast?"

"I'm designing for six hundred; three hundred going up and three hundred coming down. There will be a continuous drive arrangement from a set of linear synchronous motors running up and down the entire length of the beanstalk. I've chosen a nominal load for each car of four hundred tons." Rob pulled out his notes and glanced at them again for a moment. "You might want to think about this, see if you agree with me. If you do, it provides us a carrying capacity of about two hundred and forty thousand tons a day. It sounds a lot, but it's completely negligible compared with the mass of the beanstalk itself. Long term, we'll have to keep the upward and downward movements pretty well balanced or that will affect the stability, but we have nothing to worry about on a day-to-day basis. As you'll see from my numbers, with even spacing of the cars we'll have a velocity of about three hundred kilometers an hour. That's respectable for travel up through the atmosphere and not high enough to cause aerodynamic problems."

"Hold it." Regulo held up his hand before Rob could continue. "So far, we've been running along on just about the same design lines. Take a look at my calculations, and you'll find that they parallel yours remarkably closely. But if you're wanting a two-meter diameter load cable, then I'd suggest that we go for a bigger shipment rate. Why keep the weight of the cars so low?"

"It's your money." Rob shrugged. "If you're willing to spend more, that's no problem for the design. I can increase the load. But I sized the carrying capacity to fit with a fifteen-gigawatt supply system, because that's what we'll get with an off-the-shelf powersat. We could use a couple of them, or even a custom-made job, but the total cost will go up."

"Don't worry about that, finance is my department. Let's have a daily carrying capacity, up or down, of a million tons. That's a nice round number, and there's no point in spoiling things for a few riyals. You never know, some day I may want to ship a few million tons of salt up here. Cornelia says she's getting tired of the taste of freshwater fish."

That *was* a joke, it had to be. Rob looked at Regulo closely, but still the facial expressions offered no clue. After a moment, he shrugged. "A million tons. Fine, I'll design for that. Everything else stays the same except the size of the cargo carriers. I think we ought to keep the passenger carriers small, that gives us a more flexible service. I'll just arrange to have more of them, and time them to run more frequently. Let me dispose of one more problem, and I'll save the tough one for last. Earthquakes. I'm proposing a really simple-minded solution. Instead of a fancy sort of tether, I suggest that we pile a billion tons of rock on the bottom end of the beanstalk. It won't matter how much the ground moves about, there will still be all the anchor that we need."

"No argument with that. Simple solutions usually beat any others." Regulo again tapped his own pile of papers. "I thought just as you did. No point in making it hard if you can make it easy. All right, what's your other problem? So far we seem to be doing well."

"Materials." Rob pulled a single sheet of calculations from his notes. "We need a few billion tons of silicon and metals, and we need it close to the L-4 location where we'll be doing the main construction. Where will we get it? I'm relying on you for an answer, because obviously it can't come from Earth. An asteroid, of course, and we move it to where we want it. But which asteroid?"

TECHNICAL ISSUES
BASIC SPACE ELEVATOR PHYSICS
by
Dr. John LoSecco

John LoSecco is a professor of physics at the University of Notre Dame. He was educated at Cooper Union and Harvard University before spending time on the faculty of the University of Michigan and Caltech. His research interests are in particle physics, astrophysics and cosmology. He has contributed to the discovery of the neutrino mass, the observation of neutrinos from a supernova from outside of our galaxy (SN1987A), the discovery of CP violation in beauty mesons and evidence for exotic mesons. He has searched for dark matter, magnetic monopoles, proton decay, quark-gluon plasma and cosmic neutrino point sources.

IF YOU TIE a weight to the end of a string and spin it about your head fast enough, the weight will spin in a horizontal plane. This is the fundamental idea behind the space elevator. In the space elevator the spinning is provided by the natural rotation of the Earth.

In the case of the weight on a string, you will feel a large tug outward if you spin it fast enough. But as the weight slows there will be less of a tug outward. If it spins slowly enough the path will droop from the horizontal plane. You may also notice that the longer the string, the slower you must spin it to keep it horizontal.

For the space elevator, the natural tug outward on a spinning string is offset by the weight of the string. In the ideal case the two balance each other exactly. In practice, one would firmly fasten the bottom edge to the Earth and use the rotation of the top end to keep the whole length under tension. In order to achieve this balance, or slight tension, at the very slow rotation rate of the Earth would require a long uniform string of about 144,000 km (89,500 miles) high. It is simplest to position the structure at the Equator so that the directions of the weight and the outward pull due to the Earth's rotation are aligned. By locating a substantial mass at the upper end, this length might be reduced. But it must always be greater than 35,800 km (22,300 miles).

Most space elevator designs have a non-uniform mass distribution along the string. A non-uniform design is dictated by engineering considerations. The space elevator will not have a uniform tension throughout its length. This is similar to the design of tall buildings. The lower part of the structure of a tall building must be strong enough to hold up the weight of the entire structure above it. But near the top it does not need to be nearly as strong since there is very little weight to support. Think of the Eiffel tower, with a massive support structure below, flowing to a graceful pinnacle at the top. In a space elevator the point with the most tension will not be at the bottom but at the height of 35,800 km.

A satellite launched into a stable orbit at an altitude of 35,800 km above the Earth's surface has an orbital period (the time for one revolution about the Earth) equal to one sidereal day. So the satellite appears fixed in position relative to the Earth. These so called geosynchronous orbits are useful for communications satellites, in particular broadcasting satellites due to the fact that they never move below the horizon for the region of their coverage. Satellite dishes aimed at them do not need to be adjusted since the satellite and the ground dish rotate at the same rate. Once the dish is aligned it does not need to move to track the satellite.

Satellites launched into stable orbits below the geosynchronous altitude will move faster than the Earth. From the ground they appear to move to the east. Those launched into stable orbits above this altitude will move slower than the Earth and will appear to move west. In the space elevator the upper westward moving part is attached to the lower eastward moving part. Forces transmitted through the structure result in uniform motion of the whole object. Neither the upper nor the lower portion are in a stable orbit by themselves. Stability comes about by forces that are transmitted through the structure. These forces hold the lower portion up and the upper portion is held down. Without the stabilizing forces, the upper portion would fly off into space.

Transmission of these forces is the major challenge to the construction of the space elevator. As for most structures, the forces needed to stabilize them depend on how heavy they are. Lighter objects require less force to keep them stable. So the space elevator must be constructed of very high tensile strength materials with very low mass. In fact the trade off of mass and strength means that the optimal design would not be a uniform string from the surface of the Earth to the top but, to minimize mass, a "string" whose size is optimized to withstand the tension through it at that point. Near the surface of the Earth it would not have to support much weight so it could be rather thin. But at the geosynchronous orbit height it would have to be strong enough to support the net weight below it.

Constructing stable structures is an important part of the practice of civil engineering. A critical part of such construction is a design that transfers all of the forces throughout the structure. Bridges and skyscrapers are examples of the art of civil engineering. Such objects are stable when all the internal forces are balanced and the weight is transfered securely to the ground. The weight is balanced by tension in support wires or by pressure on a support column or a wall. A weakness, a force imbalance, in any part of the structure can lead to catastrophic failure.

Dynamic stability is also of concern for many structures. If you pluck a guitar string the vibration persists for a long time. It is eventually damped out as sound radiates from the string. In a space elevator any deflection will propagate along the structure and be reflected back down from the top. Very little of the vibrational energy will be dissipated since the string can not radiate sound into space. Wind and other disturbances can feed energy into the structure. If this energy is not dissipated the size of the vibrations can grow with time, ultimately destroying the structure. To deal with this problem the ground mounting must be designed to drain vibrational energy from the structure, similar to the way earthquake tolerant skyscrapers are constructed.

While the dynamics of the space elevator are dominated by the Earth's gravitation and rotation, both the Moon and the Sun will exert tidal influences on it. The structure must be carefully designed to avoid resonances near the periods of the Sun and Moon, or these small regular perturbations will multiply and grow to dangerous amplitudes.

Once a space elevator is in place, one could move objects into space by "walking" them up the string (via robotic lifters). But getting them into space is not quite the same as getting them into orbit. An orbit is a stable configuration. An object released from the space elevator would simply fall to Earth if released too low, or fly away from the Earth if released too high. In between, an object would go into an eccentric orbit. Only objects released at the geo-synchronous altitude would remain in place. Since such a spot is likely to get crowded any space launch mechanism based on a space elevator would need to include an additional propulsion source to move stably away from the release point.

Construction of a space elevator requires a great deal of energy. This is perhaps no surprise since we are all aware of the spectacular power of a rocket powered space launch. During construction energy must be expended for two purposes. It requires energy to overcome the gravitational pull of the Earth. Since the materials used in the construction (most likely) start out on the surface of the Earth they must be lifted into place. In addition to the energy re-quired to lift the materials, they also must gain speed to stay over the same point of the Earth. An object at rest at the Equator of the Earth is actually moving at a speed of 1674 km/hr (1046 miles/hr). To stay over the same point on the ground an object at a higher altitude must travel a longer distance in the same time. For example at an altitude of 35,800 km the speed must be 11,030 km/hr to stay over the same ground point (and 39,400 km/hr at an altitude of 144,000km). So energy must be spent lifting materials from Earth and accelerating them to the correct speed to move with the rest of the elevator. The amount of energy required depends on the actual design. In particular it depends on the mass distribution along the length. The higher the mass the more energy that is needed.

In raising or lowering objects along a space elevator one must also deal with a force perpendicular to the elevator. A static elevator only has forces directed along its length. But an object moving up or down will experience the so called Coriolis force. This "force" is an artifact of the rotating reference frame of the elevator. It is a reflection of the need to increase the horizontal speed as one moves upward (or decrease it when moving downward) to stay on the elevator. In terrestrial elevators the horizontal force needed to keep the elevator moving straight is provided by the elevator shaft. Some means must be provided to cancel this effect when lifting objects on a space elevator. The Coriolis force is proportional to the radial velocity so it can be reduced by raising or lowering the object more slowly. For most reasonable speeds it is small.

The Coriolis force plays a role in terrestrial weather patterns. As air rushes north in the northern hemisphere, it moves closer to the

Earth's axis of rotation but it is going too fast for this smaller radius so it also flows east. If it flows south, in the northern hemisphere, it will be pushed west. As a consequence one sees clockwise weather patterns in the northern hemisphere and counterclockwise ones in the southern hemisphere.

The basic physics of the space elevator is essentially the physics of a uniformly rotating reference frame, the Earth. In such a situation the normal rules of Mechanics can be supplemented with the addition of two forces. The forces are artifacts of the non-inertial nature of the reference frame, since it is accelerating. One force points away from the Earth's axis of rotation. So on the Equator it directly opposes gravity and can be arranged to just balance it. The other force comes into play while an object is moving closer or further from the axis of rotation. This force plays a role during the construction of the space elevator and in the process of using it to transport objects up or down.

There is no physical limitation to the construction of a space elevator. But there are still many engineering issues to be addressed before a stable structure could be usefully deployed.

TRIBUTE
by
Todd McCaffrey

ANNOGI FLOATED IN Observation Room Four staring blindly out of the viewport to the blue Earth below.

Clutched tightly in her hand was a small strip of paper. She had read it twice and still could not believe the words written on it. Words that, at age ten, she should not have been able to read— words stored on the station's computers that should have been kept from her for eight more years.

But Annogi was station-trained, station-bound, clever; and Tanuro was the head of station security. Tanuro had adopted her when she was three, just after her mother had died.

Annogi wondered why Tanuro had adopted her. He never seemed to smile, was never satisfied with her work, was always angry with her failures. Yet his adoption of her had solved a very difficult problem for the space elevator; because Tanuro was the head of security and his job demanded that he be at the top-end station much of his time, he could provide Annogi with the zero-gee quarters that her body had grown accustomed to in the months after her mother's death.

Annogi looked down, past the bottom of the viewport, past her hand with the clenched slip of paper, to one of the many pictures which lined the walls of the Observation Room.

The face which smiled back at her had blue eyes and blond hair, not the dark eyes and jet-black hair that was mirrored back at Annogi in the viewport. The only feature Annogi had in common with her mother was a thin smattering of freckles across her nose.

'Amanda Brown. She died so that others may live, May 5th 2025.' Annogi didn't need to read the caption to know what it said. She thought idly of linking in to the station's computer network to call up a video of her mother, then shook her head and pulled the earpiece which doubled as a holographic display out of her left eye and slid it into the top pocket of her shipsuit.

Images of her mother disturbed her. They were different from her memories. And all her happy memories were hidden behind the last frightening minutes of her time with her mother.

Annogi knew that her mother had volunteered to work on the space elevator. In fact, Amanda Brown, former astronaut, had been in retirement when the elevator was first funded. She had become an artist and writer, chronicling the adventures in space of herself and so many others.

When the chance came to take residence in the space elevator, to draw, photograph, and scribe about the new project and its impact on Earth, Amanda had grabbed at the chance. Annogi knew this because Tanuro had told her.

Amanda had spent almost all her time in the Observation Rooms. She had helped select the pictures that adorned the walls of Observation Rooms One through Three. No one had ever thought that there would be pictures in Observation Room Four.

Observation Room Four was a special room, even now. This was the room chosen above all the others for inaugurations of presidents, premieres, prime ministers, and even kings. From this vantage point the world had no boundaries, save that brilliant blue band between the cold of space and the life-giving atmosphere.

The space elevator was more than just a place from which to understand man's place as caretaker on the Earth. It was a place of new beginnings.

Here was the doorway to the solar system. Where before the cost of moving into space was impossible, now it was achievable. Where before Mars and Venus were mere points of light, now they were home to growing numbers of scientists, explorers, technologists, and colonists.

Here also was the doorway to Earth's healing. Where before solar satellites were the thing of fiction, now they were commonplace. Factories in space were being constructed that made marvels never seen before, and produced goods that would cost hundreds of times more to make on Earth —all without polluting the fragile homeworld.

Bases on the Moon, Mars, and Venus also provided invaluable insights in to how to husband the Earth itself; for what kept life alive on the airless Moon could be applied to making life less polluting on the bountiful Earth.

So Amanda had sat in the various Observation Rooms, floating cross-legged, her sketch pad and colored pens strapped to her with Velcro or floating in hands' reach nearby while Annogi played with toys and goggled at the glowing Earth below.

Often Tanuro would stop by to talk. Amanda's behavior with him was strange, it seemed to little Annogi almost like a game of hide-and-seek—Amanda would smile and talk animatedly, then Tanuro would say something and Amanda's smile would fade and she would become silent. Annogi taught Tanuro hide-and-seek one day after asking about it, and Tanuro would often play the game with her, so much so that Annogi became adept at finding all the nooks and crannies of the station.

At that time Annogi had wished that Tanuro was her father. Amanda had always refused to talk with Annogi about her father, insisting that he was a good man and that she would tell her when she was older, that it was not the right time. Annogi could never understand that and often cried when her mother would tell her that she could not see her father for dinner.

"Your father does not know about you," Amanda had explained once. "I chose to have you by myself. You are my star child. It was my choice; he never knew."

Annogi learned about sperm donors and artificial insemination years after Amanda's death. It took her two more years to learn about DNA typing and another year to gather the nerve to break the station's security systems, worrying all the while that security manager, not-father Tanuro would discover her.

Tanuro had visited them several times when they were not in the Observation Rooms. In fact, Tanuro had dined with Annogi and Amanda just the night before the accident. When Amanda had put Annogi to sleep that night, she invited Tanuro to participate.

"She looks so Japanese," Tanuro said. "No one would ever think she wasn't my daughter."

Why would they ever worry about that? Annogi had wondered muzzily to herself at the time.

Amanda had laughed and shaken her head. She shushed him, pushed him out of the cramped room with her hand, gave Annogi one last kiss goodnight, turned out the lights and had left.

But Annogi had not fallen asleep straight away. Tanuro's comments had got her wondering about her father again. So she was still awake when their voices rose loudly and the front door was opened and Tanuro left, his voice full of sorrow. Annogi couldn't remember the words they'd said but she wondered if their argument had contributed to the disaster of the next day.

The day certainly hadn't started like a day for disaster. Amanda seemed a bit withdrawn but her smile for Annogi was as bright as ever, perhaps even brither.

"We're going to draw today, would you like that?" Amanda had asked Annogi over breakfast. Annogi liked that.

They set up in Observation Room Four. Just before lunchtime, a group of strangers came in and crowded around the viewports.

Annogi frowned at them because Amanda frowned at them. Amanda saw Annogi's frown and smiled at her.

"Maybe this is a good time for lunch," Amanda said, starting to gather in her floating pencils.

In that instant, Annogi's world changed.

It would take nearly a year to finally discover what had caused it but the large bolt, which slammed into the Observation Room, did not hit one of the walls. If it had, maybe the worst that would have happened would have been a loud bang that startled everyone. Instead, the bolt hit one of the viewports with such force that it shattered both the outer and inner panes. Its size and speed were so great that it continued through into the room and started bouncing like a deadly missile off the walls—and through the suddenly terrified people.

Amanda, with years of astronaut training, was not terrified. It was her actions that saved everyone else in the room. She forced them through the hatch, forced Annogi into the arms of one of the wailing women, and closed the emergency hatch. She would have gone through it, but as it slowly closed the bolt ricocheted into her head.

Annogi screamed and yelled for her mother and struggled to get back to the hatch, to open it for she was a smart girl and even at three knew how, only to find herself restrained, held tightly—in the arms of Tanuro.

In that moment Annogi hated Tanuro. She hated him more when he seized her struggling body and squeezed it tightly against his, keeping her head on his chest. Annogi remembered wondering for a moment if Tanuro had been hit by the flying bolt too, for as she screamed and yelled into his face she could see all color and life draining out of it, as if Tanuro were turning to stone before her eyes.

Annogi broke out of Tanuro's tight grip when another group of station personnel arrived and fled. She knew the station so well that it took even Tanuro six months to track her down. By then her body had grown too accustomed to microgravity; she could not return to Earth. So Tanuro had adopted her.

It was years before she realized that Tanuro had been watching her mother die, still tormented by the flying bolt, and that Tanuro had held her, Annogi, instead of donning a spacesuit to rescue Amanda from the now airless Observation Room.

It was still more years before Annogi realized that even as Tanuro had cradled her against him, Amanda had been too long without oxygen and had become just as dead as the bolt that had killed her.

But by then Annogi was too accustomed to hating Tanuro to say anything to him.

So Annogi decided to track down her real father. She would ask him to raise her, forgetting that years in microgravity had banished her from Earth forever. It didn't matter to Annogi; she would be rid of Tanuro.

And now she had her slip of paper, now she knew.

A noise from behind her startled her and Annogi turned to see someone enter the Observation Room. It was a teenager, and something about the way he moved caused Annogi to turn her body, reach into her pocket and put her earpiece into her far ear. She brushed her hair over the earpiece, hiding it.

The boy was blond-haired and blue-eyed. Something about him seemed familiar but he moved like an earthling, not a spacer.

He was older than her, Annogi realized. Not really a boy at all, in fact. In his mid to late teens, he was not yet shaving or had very soft facial hair. He still had the look of a youngster about him; that was why Annogi had first thought of him as a boy.

They spoke at the same time.

"What are you doing here?" the boy demanded.

"Are you lost?"

Annogi waited for the boy to respond. She'd seen enough television to expect that they would both burst out in laughter but she had no real friends her own age.

"You should leave," the boy told her. His voice was full of tension and anger. Annogi realized that he kept his back to her and that he was holding something with one hand behind his back. His nerves left him shaking, and Annogi caught a glimpse of a handle dangling behind him.

An axe? Annogi wondered. But where could anyone get an axe on the station? And just as soon as she asked the question, Annogi had an answer: at any of the fire posts in the station. There was one just outside the elevator that came up from earthside.

Those fire posts were all alarmed. Annogi knew because her 'father' was the head of security. But Annogi also knew how to deactivate those alarms. Clearly the teen must have done the same, or the fire alarm would be blaring all over the station.

Aside from fire or catastrophe, there was only one use for an axe—destruction.

A rush of terror set Annogi's heart. I cannot fear, she told herself. She took a deep breath and let it out slowly, letting her fear go with it as Tanuro had taught her.

She saw that she could escape through the airlock, that the teen had actually left room for her to do so.

No. I choose differently.

"Hi," she said looking up at the teen who towered above her, "I'm Annogi, who are you?"

As she spoke, she walked toward the boy, not so close as to spook him but close enough that it would be hard for him to strike her with the axe.

As she looked up at him, and saw him glance nervously down at her, then out the porthole, Annogi knew that wasn't his intention.

TANURO NAKASHIMA STARED at his computer screen in anger and amazement. How had she done it?

When he'd checked the computer logs in the morning, Tanuro had noticed the record of abnormal activity. His suspicions aroused, he spent the rest of the morning tracking the activity down—and discovered that Annogi had hacked the station's security system. She had broken into the system's time-locked database and had read several files—files that Tanuro could not access himself—and had then meticulously covered her tracks.

In fact, as Tanuro discovered, Annogi's intrusion would have been completely undetected except that someone else accessed the same part of the database at nearly the same time—someone who was permitted under the time-lock protocols.

This person had used the protocols as a springboard for a hack into the security system's innards. As Tanuro followed the hacker's assault he became more and more nervous. The hacker had accessed engineering data on the station. The hacker was looking for physical weaknesses in the station. He was looking for the one place where he could destroy the station—and the space elevator.

"Security Alert Level Two," Tanuro had called calmly on the security network. He was calm because he was trained that way; he was calm because he willed it; he was calm because panic would accomplish nothing.

Level Two meant that an assault on the station was possible. Throughout the station, airtight doors were sealed, inspections increased, non-essential personnel assigned to the next free elevator—either up or down.

Tanuro returned to his pursuit of the second hacker. In fifteen minutes he had located the source of the assault. In twenty minutes he had a name—Chris Halleck.

Chris Halleck was an intelligent teenager, just turned eighteen. Eighteen. The number caught Tanuro's attention. Chris' eighteenth birthday was yesterday. The boy was now a man, was able to vote, to stand on his own and—what else?

Tanuro frowned in thought. Why would someone use his eighteenth birthday to hack into a liftport station's security system? Why not hack at a younger age, when the penalties for such intrusions were so much lower? What Halleck had done was a felony, he could lose all the privileges he'd just earned.

Eighteen, Tanuro mused. Legal age.

Of course!

Tanuro's fingers flew over the keyboard as request after request streamed into the security system. Each answer brought another query until finally Tanuro understood.

And when he did, calmly, for there was no room for panic, Tanuro hit the emergency button.

Chris Halleck was a test-tube baby. His mother's ovaries were infertile, so his father's sperm was combined with that of a donor's egg to produce a healthy baby boy. Healthy in body but not in mind. Tanuro's quick scan of the boy's records portrayed a loving childhood which was shattered by his birth-parents' divorce when he was fourteen. At fourteen—no coincidence—he tried to commit suicide. His school records displayed the decline in grades Tanuro associated with an increasingly bitter and depressed youth.

At age eighteen, Chris was allowed to know the identity of the egg donor.

The egg donor was the famous hero and astronaut, Amanda Brown.

Tanuro tapped into the UN population database and waited while it determined the location of Christopher Halleck, aged eighteen.

"It's alright, there's nothing to worry about," Annogi's voice piped up over the security channel. Tanuro frowned, wondering why his adopted daughter would so wantonly flaunt station protocols—he had taught her better.

Tanuro's eyes widened in sudden apprehension—he *had* taught her better.

"Security Alert Level One," Tanuro announced softly, raising the safety guard on a button that he never expected to use and pressing down upon the button.

"The station is under attack," he added. Tanuro swallowed hard and took a deep steadying breath. Annogi was his daughter; he knew her, he heard the message in her words and knew that she had told him that there was nothing to worry about. He would trust her.

"An agent is in place and will affect apprehension."

An agent. His daughter.

Tanuro took another deep steadying breath, forcing his heart to calm down, telling himself that his panic would do nothing for his daughter—for Amanda Brown's daughter—yet all the while memories of Amanda's death, toddler Annogi's screams and Tanuro's breaking heart pounded inside his skull.

CHRIS HALLECK JUMPED when the flashing alert light strobed and the alert sounded.

"It's alright, there's nothing to worry about," Annogi said both to him and to her open station microphone.

"What is it?" he demanded, his voice harsh, breath jagged.

"Security test," Annogi replied calmly. She glanced over at the hatch and saw that it was closing. She looked back at the teen, hiding her relief in another question, "Do you have the time?"

When the blond boy looked at her incredulously, Annogi continued, "They do random tests but I've been trying to find a pattern."

"A pattern?" the boy repeated dully.

"Sure," Annogi replied with a shrug. "I'd like to avoid getting caught out when there's a test going on." She gave the boy a conspiratorial look and leaned closer, whispering innocently, "Sometimes I like to sneak away from my father. With these security tests, he notices when I'm missing.

"I don't like to get in trouble, do you?" she finished, looking right up into his eyes.

Reluctantly Chris shook his head.

Annogi smiled at him. Her smile was genuine, she was well within his reach, well within the arc of any axe swing. The teen would now have to step back if he wanted to strike at her, a motion that would give Annogi plenty of advance warning. In fact, anything the teen might want to do with the axe would require him first to move away from her.

"Is this your first time on the station?" Annogi asked, glancing toward the flashing lights.

Chris nodded.

"I figured," Annogi said. "They run the tests so often that even regular tourists notice pretty quick."

"They do?"

"Sure," Annogi said, gesturing to the ports on the outer edge of the Observation Room. "Space is right there and you never know when there might be another accident—"

"This is where Amanda Brown died, isn't it?" Chris asked suddenly, staring around at the pictures lining the walls.

The question startled Annogi. She nodded reflexively. Chris' jaw tightened at her response and he moved the axe from behind his back.

"What are you doing with that?" Annogi asked, feigning surprise. Her eyes narrowed. "Did you steal that?"

"Yes," Chris told her.

"You set off the alarm?" Annogi asked, eyes wide. She knew better, knew he must have disabled the alarm. That told her that he had spent a lot of time planning. But she asked the question because she needed him to continue to underestimate her. She could tell that he saw her as harmless, a little girl.

And she was. Both harmless and a little girl. Trapped in Observation Room Four with a deranged teenager.

"Turn your weaknesses into strengths," Tanuro had told her long ago. Annogi had never understood that—until now.

"No," Chris said, "I didn't. I got past the alarm system."

"What are you going to do with the axe?"

"You should leave," he told her, gesturing toward the door with the axe. "If you close the door, it'll act as an airlock."

"An airlock?" Annogi repeated. She looked at the axe, asking in the role of a little girl, "Are you going to use that here?"

"My mother died here," Chris told her in a flat tone. He gestured again to the door. "They watched her die from the far side of that airlock.

"Now I'm going to die here, too," he finished solemnly.

"Amanda Brown?" Annogi asked, her act forgotten in her shock.

"They say her picture is here somewhere," Chris said, glancing around at the pictures placed below the viewing portals. "She died because—"

"Because there was a stray bolt which breached the viewport," Annogi finished for him, her voice as flat as his. Startled, Chris glanced down at her. The memories came back, the images of Tanuro as his face turned to stone replayed in her mind, only now, at ten, Annogi could see that Tanuro's stone-faced look was because his heart was breaking. He had loved her, Amanda Brown. And he had watched her die. Annogi blinked rapidly to clear the tears of compassion which threatened to flood her. How was Tanuro feeling now, with Amanda Brown's daughter in the same situation?

The slip of paper in Annogi's back pocket was suddenly immensely more important than it had been minutes before.

"I was going to visit her the week after," Chris continued, ignoring Annogi. His face took on the image of a happy eight year-old. "I was all ready to see my real mom."

"I was three," Annogi said. "I was in the Observation Room."

"You were?" Chris asked, suddenly aware of Annogi once more. "She saved you?"

"Yes," Annogi said with a sob she couldn't control. She caught his eyes with hers, her tears suddenly rolling down her face. "Our mother died to save me."

"Our mother?" Chris repeated. His blue eyes were troubled as her words registered.

Annogi withdrew the slip of paper from her back pocket. She kept her thumb over part of it, on purpose, but extended it to Chris, her other hand reaching for the axe.

"Our mother," she said again, her voice firm once more as she grabbed the axe, "would not want this room, of all rooms, harmed. She gave her life for it."

Chris didn't even notice himself relinquishing the axe as he read the printout.

"And she wouldn't want you hurting yourself, either," Annogi added, sending the axe spinning slowly away from them. She turned back to face Chris. "And I don't want you hurting yourself, either, brother."

"Brother?" Chris echoed softly.

Annogi nodded and moved away from the viewport, gesturing at the picture below.

"I often come here," Annogi told him a little shyly. Chris looked down at the picture and crouched down beside Annogi, suddenly smaller than she was. She looked down at him and gently touched his shoulder. "I was mad all these years, angry that she was gone, that I had nothing left to remember her by—"

"You too?"

Annogi nodded. "But I'm not angry any more."

"No?"

"No," Annogi replied firmly. She gestured to the viewport and the stars beyond it. "She left me everything to remember her by. She left us this spaceport, the elevator, and she left what she loved most of all—the stars."

Still crouched, Chris looked out the viewport over Annogi's shoulder. He could see the brilliant blue Earth below and above he could see the faint twinkling of uncountable stars.

"We can't take that away from her, Chris," Annogi said. "Clear?"

"Clear," Chris agreed, looking up at his little sister.

TANURO OPENED THE airlock. With a glance behind to indicate that the follow-on security officer should retrieve the axe, he kicked off to the two children huddled by the viewport.

No, not children, Tanuro corrected himself. Either of them.

The import of the past twenty minutes weighed down upon him. His ten year-old daughter had disarmed a full-grown man with only her words.

Annogi saw him and turned to follow his glide toward them. She touched Chris gently on the shoulder and pointed at Tanuro.

"This is the man who raised me after our mother died," Annogi said as Tanuro reached them. Tanuro nodded in recognition, his heart frozen by her words. Annogi saw his reaction but continued to Chris, "He is the head of station security. He is a just man. You broke a number of station rules by what you did; you'll have to accept the consequences."

Chris nodded in acceptance, his face grim.

"But I'll ask him to understand that you are my brother," Annogi said. "And I'll come visit you if I can."

"If you can?" Chris repeated.

"My body adapted to zero-gee," Annogi explained, "I can't go earthside."

"Will you call me?"

"Of course," Annogi replied with a grin. "We have a lot of catching up to do." She turned to the viewport for a moment. "And there are all those stars."

Chris nodded, his eyes bright with the light of the stars. To Tanuro he said, "I'm ready."

Tanuro nodded brusquely and gestured to two security men who led Chris away.

When they were alone, Tanuro turned to Annogi. "I am very proud of you."

"I hacked into the security system," Annogi confessed, pulling the slip of paper once more from her pocket. "I wanted to know who my real father was."

"So you can live with him?" Tanuro asked, his voice devoid of emotion. Once again the images of Amanda Brown's death floated in his eyes.

"Yes," Annogi said. "Always and forever."

"Very well, it shall be as you wish."

"This is his name," Annogi said, handing him the slip of paper. "He is my real father."

"He is a lucky man," Tanuro admitted, taking the paper from her.

"No, I am," Annogi said, flinging herself into Tanuro's arms and hugging him fiercely.

Tanuro was shocked and dismayed but he instinctively hugged Annogi back, even while trying to read the name on the paper. And when he did, he gave a heartfelt sob and clutched her all the more tightly, tears flowing for the first time in seven years as the rock that was his heart finally melted once more.

The name on the paper was Tanuro Nakashima.

The Deployment of the Space Elevator
by
Timothy Cash

Mr. Cash was born in South Bend, Indiana in 1952 and received a BA in Physics and Mathematics from Indiana University in 1977. He invented three space tether transportation systems in 1997 and a tether propulsion system in 2004. He has done engineering work for the NASA Shuttle program (Experiments Engineer), and the International Space Station (Tiger Team). He also has experience as a Field Engineer for Security in Iraq AOR. His expertise is in the engineering and manufacture of extremely long cable systems for undersea, aerospace and telecommunications applications. He has had a keen interest in space exploration his whole life. He has a wife named Rachel and two children. His personal website is: http://www.angelfire.com/fl5/tjctjc/

LIKE MANY OF the greatest works of humankind, the assembly of the Space Elevator will be complex and time-consuming, but the result will be elegant. It will take several years and billions of dollars, but ultimately will result in a system that will provide great benefits to humankind. I have outlined the basic steps of deployment below. The references (tables and most of the calculations) cited below are derived from Dr. Bradley Edwards' design for the Space Elevator, in addition to the latest new launch vehicle studies from NASA and the major Aerospace contractors.

SE System Assembly from LEO
Several rockets are launched to low earth orbit (300 miles), carrying an "anchor" satellite or counterweight. The counterweight is assembled and transferred to geosynchronous orbit (GEO), from where it ascends to 100,000 km (62,000 miles) as a ribbon made from a carbon nanotube composite fiber is deployed. The ribbon floats towards the Earth's surface, where it is attached to an ocean-based platform at the equator. The SE counterweight system maintains its position on orbit by virtue

of a balance between the centripetal force of the counterweight and the gravitational forces on the downwards deployed ribbon. A minimal ribbon is initially deployed from space. A much stronger multi-thread ribbon structure is built up by lifters (elevator cars) powered by ground-based lasers that deploy additional ribbon filaments as they climb up the initial ribbon from the surface.

The ribbon is precision wound on the spool and deployed when it reaches GEO. The end of the ribbon is terminated into a unique device with multiple capabilities:

Maintain proper orientation,

Prevent torsion or twisting of the ribbon,

Provide acceleration in any given direction through a small monopropellant system.

As the ribbon is deployed from GEO to Earth surface, there is a balance between forces derived from the angular momentum of the closed ribbon/deployment system and gravity gradient torque derived from ribbon velocity and angle to the vertical. The local gravity gradient torque maintains the correct angular velocity and orientation for the deployment system. The first kilometer of the initial ribbon deployed is the most unstable. As the length of deployed ribbon exceeds one kilometer, the forces become more stable and ribbon deployment can proceed at any feasible rate. The gravity gradient torque will then keep the ribbon vertical. The deployment system must possess the ability to dampen ribbon oscillations. As the ribbon is deployed, gravitational acceleration varies along the ribbon's deployed length. This causes a change to the apparent mass distribution and forces an increase in angular momentum in order to maintain the center of mass of the system at geosynchronous orbit during deployment. This is accomplished by the application of continuous thrust to the spacecraft, since the geosynchronous altitude for the center of mass depends on the amount of ribbon deployed. An initial ribbon length of 100,000 km was chosen in order to have the capability of reaching the inner solar system and to give a favorable ribbon to counterweight mass ratio of 1.364.

Launch Vehicle/Upper Stage Considerations

Several choices for the launch vehicle and upper stage propulsion systems were considered. The components must be lifted to LEO, assembled, and the entire system boosted to GEO due to the fact that no heavy lift launch vehicle exists to place the entire system into geosynchronous orbit direct from Earth. In addition, an upper propulsion stage is required to boost the system to its final altitude beyond GEO. The Space Shuttle and Delta-4 Heavy are the only existing launch vehicles capable of placing sufficient mass into LEO to accomplish the SE mission profile. The use of the Space Shuttle is no longer possible due to existing launch commitments for the International Space Station; and scheduled retirement in 2010. The National Aeronautics and Space Administration (NASA) is chartered by President Bush to design the infrastructure necessary for a return to the moon and the future exploration of Mars. The initial NASA internal study document is called the Exploration Systems Architecture Study (ESAS). The study compares the heavy lift variants of the EELV (Delta-IV and Atlas V) to a Shuttle Derived Vehicle (SDV) for unmanned heavy lift vehicles. The SDV outperforms the EELV variants in payload lift capability (100 or 120 Ton vs. 50 to 85 Ton) and has an existing infrastructure base to build upon, but launch vehicle availability is further out in time. If we assume the use of an EELV variant or NASA's new heavy lift vehicle, then the 186 metric Tons of ribbon, spool, propulsion system, associated payout hardware and fuel will be optimally launched into orbit on as few as two Heavy Lift Vehicles, each with a cryogenic upper stage and the development cost paid for by others. There are several advantages to this:

The number of launches is optimized (two for an SDV or EELV variant, four for the existing EELV).

On-orbit splicing is avoided.

The schedule can be shortened (EELV variant), or optimized for lower cost (SDV).

The number of required lifters is decreased.

The deployment schedule is shortened several weeks, thus decreasing the overall risk of serious meteor damage.

The heavy-lift versions of the Space Shuttle are called the Shuttle-C, capable of lifting approximately 100 tons to LEO, or the "in-line" booster, capable of lifting 125 Tons to LEO. The "in-line" booster would mount payloads on top of the booster and feature a cluster of SSMEs on the first stage, enlarged Solid Rocket Boosters (SRB), and would mount the SE payload package on a cryogenic upper stage. It could lift about 125 tons to LEO, and is estimated to cost $540 million per launch. The heavy-lift booster would be ready for flight by 2018. With minor modifications, the Delta 4-Heavy could deliver about 50 tons to low Earth orbit with solid boosters and modifications to both the main engine and upper stage. A payload to LEO greater than 50 metric tons would require much more extensive EELV variant vehicle modifications and a new launch pad and infrastructure. Any payload to LEO above 100 metric tons would require building what Boeing considers a next-generation Delta with bigger engines and a wider first stage and new production and launch facilities.

An upper propulsion stage is required to boost the SE system from LEO to GEO. There are several alternative options for upper stages:

Advanced chemical propulsion systems.

Electric propulsion systems.

Thermal propulsion using thermal energy (solar or nuclear) to heat a working fluid which then expands through a nozzle.

A Centaur cryogenic chemical propulsion upper stage was studied in addition to older but proven technology based on MMH/ NTO hypergolic fuels. A cluster of seven Centaurs, in addition to several of the hypergolic thrust units are required to get the full system to GEO and impart the required angular momentum as the ribbon is deployed and moved outwards from GEO to endpoint. This is a prohibitive weight penalty on the launch vehicle. The thrust of thermal propulsion systems falls in between chemical and electric, so the trip times are in between as well. Development and integration of a thermal propulsion system would be more difficult than a chemical or electric system because the technology is not as mature. A new upper stage electric propulsion system was studied, the Magneto-Plasma-Dynamic (MPD) system. The MPD is the largest and most efficient of all electric propulsion methods. Significantly higher Specific Impulse (Isp) can be obtained, but thrust levels are low, and trip times are long (trip times on the order of 30 days as compared to hours for chemical propulsion). Due to maturity, the development of an electric propulsion orbit transfer vehicle (OTV) would be relatively simple and is the best choice for an upper stage. Since the trip time for an all-electric propulsion upper stage is on the order of 30 days, it may make sense to provide a boost with a small chemical rocket to optimize trip time. Trade-off studies using a flight-scale MPD system as the upper stage indicate a reduction in orbit change timeline from one year down to 150 days, and a reduction in the required number of launch vehicles down from eight to four (or two). The size of the initial ribbon can be doubled and the complexity, cost and risk of constructing the system further reduced due to the improved propulsion system.

Energy is expended during the initial climb up the elevator using lifters with guide wheels in contact with the ribbon. One analysis determined that the energy required to climb the space elevator from the ground to GEO would be H"60 MJ/kg. We can recapture up to 90% of the hypergolic fuel system mass if the energy from regenerative braking (as the ribbon is unspooled) was used in an electrically powered propulsion system (MPD) as an alternative to maintaining cable velocity by using an electric motor. Thus, the weight savings for an MPD electric propulsion system are optimized further yet.

Trajectory Changes and Fuel Management

The delta-v method of computation will be used to optimize the fuel remaining when the spacecraft arrives at the end point (63,170 km) and the ribbon touches down on Earth. There are four trajectory changes required in the ribbon deployment sequence: The first three to get into GEO and the fourth is the ribbon deployment maneuver as the spacecraft is moved from GEO out to its end point. The "delta V" of required fuel is calculated given the mass, and the angular momentum is computed when the system arrives at GEO and again when the ribbon touches the ground. The moment of inertia for each small piece of ribbon and spacecraft are then computed and added together. The combined moment of inertia and angular velocity are then multiplied to arrive at the final angular momentum. The difference between initial and final angular momentum will be equal to the torque supplied by the MPD propulsion system. At the time when the spacecraft arrives at the end point, the end of the ribbon will be deployed by centripetal force as a result of being tied down to a mobile platform at sea. This imparts the rest of the angular momentum required as the ribbon deploys to its full length.

Laser Beam Time & Power Delivery Considerations

Another system requirement is to optimize the duty cycle of the laser beam on the lifter's solar cells (the amount of time period the deployment satellite will be in view of the laser beam). If an initial orbit of 300 km is assumed, then the laser-deployment satellite viewing angle is 17.24 degrees, and double that (34.48 degrees) for the entire viewing arc. This is only 9.6% of the entire orbital time period of 96.6 minutes, or 9.25 minutes of power beam time for the first orbit from one station only. This angle gets wider as orbital altitude increases, with a correspondent increase of beam time and orbital period. The fuel flow rate of the MPD system is known, so the new velocity is calculated for the next higher orbit to arrive at the new orbit beam view time. If we assume multiple power beaming stations, we can bring the total time to get from LEO to GEO down from 481 days to between 126 and 137 days, plus 71 more days to end of mission. If the MPD is designed to run at a lower Isp at end of mission, the post GEO maneuvers would be shortened from 71 days to 45 days and the trip to GEO would be shortened from 137 days (three stations) to 91 days.

Ribbon Design Considerations

The initial ribbon deployed from orbit is about 1 micron (0.00004 inches) thick, tapering from 13.5 cm (5.3 inches) at the Earth to 35.5 cm (14 inches) wide near the middle (GEO) and has a total length of 100,000 km (62,000 miles). The initial small ribbon under tension can support 3,970 pounds (1,800 kg) before it breaks. After the initial ribbon deployment, the next step is to build the ribbon outwards in width to a size more useful for carrying larger payloads. This is done by sending lifters one way up the initial ribbon with additional epoxy and ribbon so that they will build the ribbon out in the width dimension. The lifters will terminate their trip at the far end and serve as additional counterweight mass. For each lifter that ascends the SE, the ribbon is 1.3% stronger. It will take 2 years and

230 lifters to construct a ribbon capable of supporting a 20 Ton lifter with a 13 Ton payload.

First/Future SE Considerations

The primary use of the first SE is to place spacecraft (payloads with kick motors) into orbits ranging from LEO to geosynchronous or those orbits thrown outwards from earth orbit to the moon or other planetary destinations. The first SE could produce comparable capacity space elevators along the equator every 200 days, or elevators with an extended capacity of 1,000 Tons, roughly the size of a shuttle orbiter in a few years. The larger capacity space elevators could be used for construction and supply of large manned space stations at GEO or missions to the moon, mars, and beyond. All these capabilities are achieved at a cost per kilogram far less than current launch vehicles. The Space Elevator will be the most important project of the 21st century.

REFERENCES

NASA Exploration Systems Architecture Study *http://exploration.nasa.gov/acquisition/cev_procurement3_lite.html*

"The Space Elevator A revolutionary Earth-to-space transportation system" NIAC Phase 1 Report by Dr. Bradley C. Edwards *http://www.spaceelevator.com/docs/472Edwards.pdf*

"The Space Elevator NIAC Phase II Final Report" —March 1 2003 Dr. Bradley C. Edwards, Eureka Scientific *http://www.spaceelevator.com/docs/521Edwards.pdf*

"The Space Elevator, A revolutionary Earth-to-space transportation system" by Dr. Bradley C. Edwards and Eric A. Westling; ISBN 0-9746517-1-0 *http://amazon.com/o/ASIN/0974651710/*

"Space Elevators An Advanced Earth-Space Infrastructure for the New Millennium" compiled by D.V. Smitherman, Jr. Marshall Space Flight Center, Huntsville, Alabama NASA/CP—2000—210429 August 2000 *http://flightprojects.msfc.nasa.gov/pdf_files/elevator.pdf*

"Boeing and Lockheed Martin Push Separate Designs for Possible Moon Missions" by Brian Berger; Space News Staff Writer *http://www.space.com/spacenews/businessmonday_050613.html*

THE HERMIT OF THE SKIES
by
Mike Resnick & Paul Crilley

THEY CALLED HIM the Hermit of the Skies. Very few people knew his real name, and even less cared. He was a legend to some, a hero to others, a joke to a few.

And a major problem to the government.

RAQUEL ACTIVATED HER vidphone.

It was Byron, her immediate superior. He was bald, he was pot-bellied, he really needed a trip to the dentist—but she liked his smell. Even from 200 miles away, he reeked of money.

"Got a job for you," he said, getting right to the point as always.

"Let me guess: it's the Hermit of the Skies."

"How did you know?" He sounded genuinely surprised.

"I keep hearing about him on the news. No one else knows what to do with him, so I knew that sooner or later it would get kicked up to our department. My question is: why me? You've got forty people working for you."

"The truth? You're bright—"

"Everyone who works for you is bright," she interrupted.

"And you're non-threatening," he concluded.

"What's so important about being non-threatening?" asked Raquel.

"You know the story. The spacers think he's some kind of good luck charm. He's been living up there on that ribbon all by himself for twenty years. It's time to pull it down and build a new one—but they can't until he agrees to come down."

"He doesn't own it. I don't understand why the government can't just condemn it, go up there, and take him down?"

"The people won't stand for it. The press loves him. There have actually been threats, ranging from strikes to the dismemberment of certain select government officials. This guy is a symbol, and word from on high is that he's got to come down of his own free will." A pregnant pause. "That's where you come in. I always thought you were pretty good at sapping men's wills."

"You're making me sound like a floozy instead of a negotiator!"

"Be whatever you want. Just get him down."

EXACTLY NINE HOURS AND twelve minutes later, she was sitting in a small carrier on her way up the sixty-two-thousand-mile ribbon. She'd caught the sub-orbital shuttle from Paris and arrived at the tether base in Micronesia within two hours. Byron had already cleared everything for her, so all she had to do was climb into the lift and she was off.

She studied a holograph of the Hermit—his less than impressive name was Wilbur Melville—and then began studying his dossier. It read like a fiction book, or better still, a collection of tall tales. It was amazing how little the government actually knew about him. There was just the tiniest handful of facts—age, height, weight, birthplace, ID. This was followed by the bulk of the material, a recounting of the legends that had sprung up around him in the past two decades. He was a reclusive millionaire. He was the exiled president of a small Balkin state. He was a professional athlete who'd been caught accepting bribes to shave points. He was carrying the deadliest contagious disease on record, one to which he himself was immune, and had given up everything he had known back on Earth so as not to infect anyone else. He was a military deserter. He was a contract killer who had rebelled at shooting a child and was hiding from the Syndicate.

There were more. Twenty years was more than enough time to build an impressive set of legends, even contradictory ones.

AFTER AWHILE HER attention started wandering, and she put the dossier aside and watched a holo entertainment, then took what was to be a brief nap that lasted until she came to a jarring stop.

"Stand up," said a disembodied voice.

Raquel got to her feet.

"Now turn around."

"Who are you?"

"You know who I am. Turn around, please."

She did as she was told.

"OK, you're clean—no weapons, no diseases. State your business."

"I want to talk to you."

"Okay, I'm listening."

"I'm uncomfortable talking like this, and I'm feeling a little claustrophobic in the carrier," she said. "Won't you please let me come in?"

"It won't do you any good."

"It'll get me out of *here*," she replied. "That'll be enough."

There was a long pause, and finally the door slid open.

"All right," said the voice. "Come in."

Raquel stepped through the doorway and into Melville's quarters. There was a parlor, and behind it she could see a small kitchen. There was a room to the left, doubtless a bedroom.

Melville stood at the center of the parlor. The difference between him and his holograph was shocking. His thick brown hair was white and thin. His athlete's body was emaciated. His once-prefect teeth were no longer very white or very straight. Only his eyes seemed the same, blue and piercing.

"Please sit over there, Miss—?" he said, indicating a chair.

"Raquel Cordero," she replied.

"Miss Cordero."

She sat down and he seated himself across the room from her, passing a couple of closer chairs.

"I don't bite," she said.

"I've been up here for twenty years," he replied. "I don't know what I'm still immune to and what I'm not."

"A reasonable precaution," she said. "I approve."

"Thank you," he said sardonically. "Now get your pitch over with, and then you can go home."

"My pitch?" she asked innocently.

"You didn't come here to just visit a recluse you've never met before," he said. "The government sent you to threaten or cajole me into coming back down. You'll be wasting your breath, but the least I can do is hear you out after you took the trouble to get here."

"Suppose *you* do the talking."

Melville looked surprise. "Me?"

"I work for the government," she admitted. "And they've asked me to try to convince you to leave. But I can't do that until I know why you stay here. So I thought perhaps you could help me to understand."

"I don't think I can," he said.

"You can't tell me why you stay up here?"

"Oh, I can tell you why—but I don't think I can make you understand."

"Try me."

He gestured to a polarized viewport. "There they are."

"There *what* are?" she asked, puzzled.

"The stars."

"I don't want to seem dense or insensitive, but couldn't you see the stars while you were on Earth?"

"Yes," he replied. "But I'm closer to them now."

"Is *that* what this is all about?" she asked, frowning.

"That you're 60,000 miles closer to stars that are still billions of miles away?"

"That's only part of the answer," he said placidly, walking to a different viewport. "Come look through this window and tell me what you see."

She got up and walked over to the port he indicated. "That's the Earth," she said.

"Right."

"What's your point?"

"I'm not on it or of it any more."

"You're right, Mr. Melville," said Raquel. "I don't understand."

He signed deeply. "I told you, you wouldn't."

"But I'd like to." He stared at her for so long that she became very uneasy. "Is something wrong?"

"I'm considering." He continued staring at her for another minute, then nodded his head. "All right," he said at last. "What the hell. I ought to tell *somebody* before I die—and make no mistake about it, Miss Cordero. I will die up here, even if it's by my own hand."

He crossed the room and sat down next to her.

"I thought you were concerned about germs and diseases," she said.

"It occurs to me belatedly that it doesn't really matter *when* I die, only *where*."

"You sound like you *want* to die."

"No living thing wants to die, Miss Cordero," he said. "That's one of the dirty little tricks Nature plays on us."

"Has it played many on you?"

He shook his head. "A few. I don't eat sweets, I'm not overweight, and I'm a diabetic. I don't drink wine or eat organ meats, and I have gout. I breathe only the purest, scientifically-processed air, and I have asthma. I'd say God's a bit of a practical joker, wouldn't you?"

"I never looked at it that way," said Raquel.

"Well, one can't really blame Him for amusing Himself."

"Has this something to do with why you stay up here?" she asked.

"Not a thing, Miss Cordero," said Melville. "We were just having a conversation, and you made an observation that required an explanation."

"I didn't mean to distract or offend you," she said quickly.

"I know you didn't," he said apologetically. "It's been a long time since I sat down and talked to a *person* instead of an electronically-projected image. I'm out of practice. You came all this way to learn why I won't go back with you, and here I am talking about other things."

"That's all right," she said. "I find it interesting."

"Do you?" he replied. "That's curious. I don't think I'd find a recitation of *your* physical ailments interesting." He sighed. "Or maybe I would. When you've been alone this long, you don't always remember how to respond."

"But surely you've spoken to other members of the government," said Raquel.

"They wore uniforms, and they didn't *converse*—they *demanded.*" Suddenly he smiled. "I guess you're what they use when intimidation doesn't work."

She returned his smile. "When I asked why I got this assignment, I was told that I was non-threatening."

"Maybe they knew what they were doing," he admitted. "I find I'm perfectly comfortable talking to you."

"Then let's talk."

"The simple truth is that I'm here because it is the one place where I know I am free. When I was a boy I wanted to reach the stars, but my vision's not very good, and I have other ailments, and I didn't qualify for the space program, so this is my compromise with my dreams."

"You were free on Earth," said Raquel.

"Oh, yes, I was free on Earth," he said bitterly. "I was free to marry, and have children, and have a home."

"You sound less than sincere."

"Not at all," said Melville. "I had all those freedoms. I had three lovely daughters. If you stay long enough, I'll pull a holo of them on the computer."

"Do they visit you here?" asked Raquel.

"No."

"Aren't they speaking to you?"

"They aren't speaking to anyone. Two of them were killed by friendly fire in the Uraguay policing action, and the third was raped and killed in the park not a block from her house. Her husband committed suicide a year later. They were very much in love."

"That's terrible!" said Raquel. "Did they ever find the killer?"

"They never found any of them."

"There was more than one?"

"All my daughters were killed. I asked the army to find out who killed the two in Paraguay. They wrote back that it was an honest mistake and no one was to blame and the case was closed."

"That must have been very hard on your wife."

"It would have been, if she'd been alive for it," answered Melville. "She died when the girls were teenagers. Bad flu shot." He paused. "Thirty-six men and women died from that vaccine. The courts eventually fined the drug company fifty thousand dollars. If you divide it evenly, that means they put a value of fourteen hundred dollars on my wife." He smiled bitterly. "The army was much more generous. They decided each of my daughters was worth a whole six thousand dollars. The insurance company was still fighting against paying off on my third daughter when I decided I'd had my fill and left."

"I'm surprised you didn't kill yourself."

"I considered it," he said. "But the more I thought about it, the more I realized that *I* hadn't done anything wrong. Why should I make *their* lives easier by ending my own? So I came up here. Maybe I can't reach the stars, but I'm going to live and die as close to them as I can."

"You ran away," she said. "If you want to change anything, you have to stay and fight."

"Tell me how to change my wife's and daughters' deaths, and I'll come back."

"You have to fight to see that it doesn't happen to anyone else."

"Let them fight their own battles," he replied. "I have no one left to sacrifice for the good of society." He nodded toward the window. "They can do anything they want down there. I've washed my hands of them. This place may not be much, but it's free and it's mine."

"It isn't, you know," said Raquel. "The government owns the ribbon, and I suspect they own this structure too."

"Not if possession is still nine-tenths of the law."

"I don't know that it ever was," she replied. "I think it's just a folk myth, rather like yourself."

"Like me?"

"Everyone's heard of the Hermit of the Skies. You wouldn't believe how many legends have sprung up around you."

"Good God, why?" asked Melville. "I'm just an old man who turned his back on everything he found objectionable and chose to live up here on the ribbon."

"No one knows why you're here, only that you are—and that you're so popular that the government hasn't had the guts to forcibly remove you."

"I haven't done anything to make myself popular," he said, puzzled. "I've stayed up here and kept to myself."

"Didn't you ever wonder why the spacers stop by and give you food? You're their mascot, their good-luck charm."

"I never wanted to be anything like that," said Melville, clearly disturbed. "I'm just a man, nothing more, doing what he thinks is right."

"Do you know how rare that is in this day and age?" she asked.

"The world down there has taken away everything I've ever cared about. I don't want revenge. I don't even want to make it right. I just want them to leave me alone." He paused. "I'm nothing special. I'm not a mascot or a charm; I've given up the battle. That's hardly something to brag about."

"You can't always choose what you represent to others," said Raquel. "They call you a mascot or a charm, but deep down I think they view you as a hero."

"Some hero," he said bitterly. "I lost everything."

"Remember the story about the gambler who played in a card game that was crooked because it was the only game in town?" she said. "You had the guts to walk away from the table."

"And now you're here to get me back into the game."

She was silent for a long minute. "I don't think so, Mr. Melville."

He started at her curiously.

"I think you've been dealt enough dirty cards. I'll stay here long enough for them to think I'm making an honest effort, and then I'll go back and tell them I couldn't convince you to come down. They can route air traffic *around* the ribbon."

"You mean it?"

She nodded her head. "I mean it. Hell, it's just a ribbon."

"Thank you, Miss Cordero."

"While we're waiting, have you got any coffee?"

After he'd made it, and showed her some holographs of his wife and daughters, and they'd spent what Raquel considered enough time to convince Byron she was doing her damnedest to talk him down, she contacted him on her pocket computer.

"How's it going?" asked Byron the instant he saw her image.

"You can't win 'em all," she replied, doing her best to look exhausted and disappointed. "He's staying."

"That's unacceptable."

"That's what I told him. He's staying anyway."

"That ribbon *has* to come down, damn it!" snapped Byron. "Tell him he's got twenty-four hours to reconsider."

"It won't help, Byron," said Raquel. "His mind's made up."

"You tell him if he's still there in 24 hours, we're coming up and pulling him out of there."

"Come on, Byron—he'll know it's a bluff."

"The hell it is! I just got the word from the top: that ribbon's coming down."

Byron cut the connection.

"Do you think they mean it?" asked Melville, looking worried.

"I don't know," answered Raquel. "I doubt it. He knows the consequences."

"Consequences? What consequences?"

"The spacers will go on strike, and there will be protests outside every government office all around the world."

"Because of *me*?" he asked disbelievingly.

"I told you: they care about you."

"The protesters—what will happen to them?"

She shrugged. "The security police will break a few heads, and use some chemical agents to pacify the crowds."

"How big a crowd?" he asked. "How many crowds?"

She sighed. "I don't know. Lots, I suppose."

"It would be unrealistic to assume that some protesters won't die, wouldn't it?"

She frowned, trying to see where this was leading. "Probably."

"And the spacers—I know they bring back diamonds and rare earths and the like, but they also bring back that substance they found in the asteroid belt that's used for treating leukemia?"

"Yes."

"So if I stay up here, dozens, maybe hundreds of people will die, and some leukemia victims won't get the medication they need?"

"It's possible," she said carefully.

"I know it's possible. Is it *likely*?"

"Yes, it's likely."

"I can't have all those people dying because of me," said Melville.

"Does that mean you'll come back down with me?" asked Raquel.

"No," he said. "I will never live on Earth again."

"Then I don't understand."

He got up and walked to the hatch door. "I wonder how long it takes to fall 62,000 miles?"

"You're crazy!"

"Do you really think so?" he asked curiously. "I don't *feel* crazy. For a moment I felt defeated, but now—now I feel *elated*. Think of what it must feel like, to fall almost forever, to stay in the air for hours and hours, to soar through the skies like a bird!"

"Birds don't land the way you're going to land."

"To be free—to be *really* free for a few hours—don't you think it will be worth it?" A gentle smile crossed his face. "Or do you think my life up here is so fulfilling that I can't bear to part with it?"

"You'd rather fall the length of the ribbon than live on Earth?" she asked. "Don't forget: you'd be treated as a hero. The spacers and the others would never let the authorities do anything to you."

"I will not try to find common ground or reach an accommodation with a world that took everything I loved from me!" he said with his first show of temper.

"You'd really rather die?"

"I told you before: no living thing wants to die," he said.

"Certainly I don't want to. But neither do hundreds of misguided men and women who have this misguided view of me as some kind of hero. I won't have them on my conscience."

"So you're just going to open the hatch and jump?"

"That's right," he said. "And thank you for playing along with my fantasy."

"You're fantasy?"

"About falling endlessly," he said. "We both know I'll burn up as I enter the atmosphere, and I'll be dead from cold and lack of air long before that happens. But I like to imagine myself floating all the way down, truly free for the first time." He put his hand on the hatch release. "You'll have to close this right after I leave, or I won't be the only one to freeze in the airless cold of space."

"I will." She stared at him. "I wish I had your courage. Or your convictions."

"You wouldn't enjoy the way I came by them, Miss Cordero," he said.

And then he was gone.

She closed the hatch. She toyed with trying to follow his flight through the viewport, but she knew that he was already too far away for her to make his figure out, and that she wouldn't see him again until he briefly illuminated the sky as a fireball.

She sat and thought about what he had said, what he had suffered, what he had finally done to prevent others from suffering. It made his life—which she had previously thought of as isolated, irresponsible, even half-mad—seem somehow more meaningful than her own, with all her citations and commendations.

Finally, after another half hour, she contacted Byron.

"What's up?" he asked. "Did he change his mind?"

"So to speak."

His image looked visibly relieved. "Then he's coming down?"

"He's already on his way."

"That's fantastic!" he enthused. "There should be a bonus in this for you."

"It's a little early for bonuses and celebrations," said Raquel.

"Oh?"

"Yes," she said. "It turns out that there's still someone up here who refuses to come down."

"Who?"

"Me," said the new Hermit of the Skies, breaking the connection.

The LiftPort Anchor Station:
Where the Space Elevator Journey Begins
by
Rudolph Behrens

Rudolph Behrens is an experienced engineer with a background in all areas of engineering, plus finance, sales, marketing and management. Most recently he was president of Pumpcom, an innovative consulting engineer firm. Rudy began his career with Worthington Corporation, a large and varied manufacturer of turbo-machinery. During his time as District Engineer-Philadelphia, he increased the companies parts and service sales from $25,000 annually to $1,200,000 annually in 16 months. In addition to his business acumen, Rudy has extensive engineering experience. He worked out a temporary solution to keep the core cool during the Three Mile Island Accident, and has been Published in the ASME Journal three times.

Rudy is a graduate of Rutgers University with a double major in Mechanical-Aerospace Engineering and Economics on an Air Force ROTC scholarship. He is active in several community groups, operates a small hydroponic farm, is a life-long aerobatic pilot and is fluent in American Sign Language.

AS THE OLD proverb said, 'A journey of a thousand miles begins with one step'. It can now be said 'a trip to the stars begins with a ship'. The Space Elevator anchor point, contrary to popular belief, will not be on land. It will be on a revolutionary ship in the middle of the Pacific Ocean. The anchor platform will be known as a "liftport." Just as an airplane ride begins at an airport, a space elevator ride will begin at a liftport. This article will discuss the basic design of the first liftport and will go on to describe what life might be like once the space elevator has been operational for several years.

Specifically, the liftport anchor site will be about 2,500 (4,024 km) miles south of San Diego and 1,000 (1,610 km) miles west of Quito, Ecuador. This site was chosen for its benign weather and the fact that there is minimal cloud cover. Initially, the design of the anchor station was based on a converted oil rig (very similar to Boeing's SeaLaunch platform) but further research showed the ocean currents in the desired anchor area were quite strong. The design was modified to become a very large ship, specifically 600 feet (183 meters) wide and 900 feet (275 meters) long.

Here passengers assemble for their ride into space. Facilities much like any airport are available such as food service, hotel rooms, baggage handling and so on. The base is a semi-catamaran/SWATH hull that acts as the ground floor of the space elevator. Yet the great vessel does not 'hold' the entire ribbon's mass. That would be extremely difficult, given that the ribbon's mass is 890 tons. For a ship to counter the mass of the elevator ribbon would require a huge vessel. No, the ribbon is essentially in equilibrium. Almost as much of its mass is below the geosynchronous point as is above it, and thus, the base ship merely waits at the bottom, holding the ribbon down against its small upward tension. The ship can easily handle the stabilizing forces that may be needed.

Being 'the ground floor' is the ship's primary function. It does this in several ways. First of all, it uses powerful thrusters and sophisticated positioning systems to continuously adjust its position. While compensating for wind, currents, storms, waves, and the movements of the elevator ribbon itself, the ship must move in such a way as to maneuver the ribbon's position to help it avoid orbital debris. Gas turbine engine-generators, enough to power 126,000 homes, provides power for the ship, the thrusters, and the ribbon winch devices.

The ship might be made from some of the same carbon nanotube fibers as the ribbon, to save weight. A lighter, stronger ship has more room for passengers, freight, fuel, spare parts, water purifiers and all the other necessary equipment to operate the space elevator. However, the liftport won't have to stockpile all of its supplies onboard. Fleets of robot ships will process the surrounding sea into fresh water, fuel and food. Flights from land will contain mostly passengers, freight and some repair parts.

When passengers enter the superstructure they will find the promenade deck. Here they will check in to their rooms to wait 48 hours for their lifter to depart. The base ship is therefore a small hotel, with rooms, dining, recreation and health facilities. Since the journey to orbit takes several days, food service is needed in the lifters. It is hoped the food will be better than most airline food, but probably won't be quite as good as cruise ship cuisine.

The next morning the elevator car touches down. There are only twelve hours until the next lifter touches down so there is a lot to do before then. The first thing is to use the gantry to move the passenger module away from the ribbon and its lifter "locomotive." It is moved to the service area where it is replenished with food, water, compressed air and emergency power supplies. Next, the safety inspectors go over every inch of the exterior and test all the systems and their back-ups. Only then are the lifter and its passenger module cleared for transfer to the UP side of the ribbon. Had it failed inspection a spare lifter would have been brought up from storage.

After the safety inspection, the scene becomes more familiar. Just like any airport or train station, luggage is loaded, the ascent crew begins preparing staterooms and passengers begin boarding.

What will be their whole world for the next few days is very spacious and comfortable. The passenger module has ten levels, oriented vertically like an apartment building. The lowest level is the machinery deck, while the upper is the flight deck (the name is a hold over from airlines). The crew resides in the level below that, so the passengers have seven levels for staterooms, a grand salon, and a main observation lounge.

First-class tickets include a stateroom, while general tickets include a seat much like a recliner in your living room. General ticket seats will have a sleeping curtain to provide a modicum of privacy. All passengers have the choice of taking meals in the dining room or taking meals to go.

The grand salon is a bit of Earth in space. The windows are small and the focus of the room is on the décor, which tends to be plush and cozy, somewhat like a large country house. Those passengers with some doubts about space travel spend most of their time here, either reading or socializing.

The main observation lounge is, as the name suggests, the opposite of the salon. Here the windows are huge and the lighting is kept low so you have a near perfect view of the spectacular vistas outside. It will most likely be one of the most popular places on the passenger module. Some people spend their whole trip in it, leaving only for meals.

An observer may write this in their journal one day about the Space Elevator liftport:

"I was standing by the rail as the transport plane touched down. It was a clear night and 'the ribbon' was visible overhead where the light from dayside reflected off it. I looked up. The elevator was still an hour away from touch down but if I followed the glow of the upper ribbon downward I could make out the lights of the car against the starscape. On nights like this it, literally, looked like a stairway to the stars.

"The 'Kalidhasa' had been at Earth-base Station for six months now and would be replaced by the "Vannevar Morgan' in a few days. Then we would be in port for six months for repairs, refit, training and shore leave.

"Ever since L5 stations opened the place has been like a 20th century train station. I watched the passengers entering the terminal. Most were colonists, giddy at the idea of their first trip to space, but I saw one or two old spacers, obviously on the way to Midway station to repair a satellite."

While the preceding was fictional, such is how a journey to space may begin sometime in the near future. For all the sophistication of the space elevator, it does begin with the oldest of human vessels, a boat. It is this boat that will ferry humanity to the stars.

This is an excerpt from T*he Fountains of Paradise* by Sir
Arthur C. Clarke.

THE BILLION-TON DIAMOND

IN THE LAST seven years, much had been done, yet there was so much to do. Mountains—or at least asteroids—had been moved. Earth now possessed a second natural moon, circling just above synchronous altitude. It was less than a kilometer across, and was rapidly becoming smaller as it was rifled of its carbon and other light elements. Whatever was left—the core of iron, tailings, and industrial slag—would form the counterweight that would keep the Tower in tension. It would be the stone in the forty-thousand-kilometer-long sling that now turned with the planet once every twenty-four hours.

Fifty kilometers eastward of Ashoka Station floated the huge industrial complex that processed the weightless, but not massless, megatons of raw material and converted them into hyperfilament. Because the final product was more than ninety percent carbon, with its atoms arranged in a precise crystalline lattice, the Tower had acquired the popular nickname "the Billion-Ton Diamond." The Jewelers' Association of Amsterdam had sourly pointed out that (a) hyperfilament wasn't diamond at all, and (b) if it *was*, then the Tower weighed five times ten to the fifteen carats.

Carats or tons, such enormous quantities of material had taxed to the utmost the resources of the space colonies and the skills of the orbital technicians. Into the automatic mines, production plants, and zero-gravity assembly systems had gone much of the engineering genius of the human race, painfully acquired during two hundred years of spacefaring. Soon all the components of the Tower—a few standardized units, manufactured by the million—would be gathered in huge floating stockpiles, waiting for the robot handlers.

Then the Tower would grow in two opposite directions—down to earth and simultaneously up to the orbital mass anchor, the whole process being adjusted so that it would always be in balance. Its cross section would decrease steadily from orbit, where it would be under the maximum stress, down to earth; it would also taper off toward the anchoring counterweight.

When its task was complete, the entire construction complex would be launched into a transfer orbit to Mars. This was a part of the contract that had caused some heartburning among terrestrial politicians and financial experts now that, belatedly, the Space Elevator's potential was being realized.

The Martians had driven a hard bargain. Though they would wait another five years before they had any return on their investment, they would then have a virtual construction monopoly for perhaps another decade. Morgan had a shrewd suspicion that the Pavonis tower would merely be the first of several. Mars might have been designed as a location for Space Elevator systems, and its energetic occupants were not likely to miss such an opportunity. If they made their world the center of interplanetary commerce in the years ahead, good luck to them; Morgan had other problems to worry about, and some of them were still unsolved.

The Tower, for all its overwhelming size, was merely the support for something much more complex. Along each of its four sides must run thirty-six-thousand kilometers of track capable of operation at speeds never before attempted. This had to be powered for its entire length by superconducting cables, linked to massive fusion generators, the whole system being controlled by an incredibly elaborate, fail-safe computer network.

The Upper Terminal, where passengers and freight would transfer between the Tower and the spacecraft docked to it, was a major project in itself. So was Midway Station. So was Earth Terminal, now being lasered into the heart of the sacred mountain. And in addition to all *this*, there was Operation Cleanup.

For two hundred years, satellites of all shapes and sizes, from loose nuts and bolts to entire space villages, had been accumulating in earth orbit. All that came below the extreme elevation of the Tower, at *any* time, now had to be accounted for, since they created a possible hazard. Three quarters of this material was abandoned junk, much of it long forgotten. Now it had to be located, and somehow disposed of.

Fortunately, the old orbital forts were superbly equipped for this task. Their radars—designed to locate oncoming missiles at extreme ranges with no advance warning—could easily pinpoint the debris of the early Space Age. Then their lasers vaporized the smaller satellites, while the larger ones were nudged into higher and harmless orbits.

Some, of historic interest, were recovered and brought back to earth. During this operation, there were quite a few surprises—for example, three Chinese astronauts who had perished on some secret mission, and several reconnaissance satellites constructed from such an ingenious mix of components that it was quite impossible to discover what country had launched them. Not that it now mattered a great deal, since they were at least a hundred years old.

The multitude of active satellites and space stations, forced for operational reasons to remain close to earth, all had to have their orbits carefully checked, and in some cases modified. But nothing could be done about the random and unpredictable visitors that might arrive at any time from the outer reaches of the solar system. Like all the creations of mankind, the Tower would be exposed to meteorites. Several times a day its network of seismometers would detect milligram impacts; and once or twice a year, minor structural damage could be expected.

Sooner or later, during the centuries to come, it might encounter a giant that could put one or more tracks out of action for a while. In the worst possible case, the Tower might even be severed somewhere along its length.

That was about as likely to happen as the impact of a large meteorite upon London or Tokyo, which presented roughly the same target area. The inhabitants of those cities did not lose much sleep worrying over this possibility.

Nor did Vannevar Morgan. Whatever problems might lie ahead, no one doubted now that the Orbital Tower was an idea whose time had come.

THE SPACE ELEVATOR RIBBON
by
Dr. Arthur Smith

Arthur Smith received a PhD in physics from Cornell University in 1991, in the theoretical study of non-crystalline materials. He published several papers in the early 1990s based on quantum mechanical calculations of the properties of fullerenes and inter-calated graphite compounds. Most recently Arthur has been working as manager of the database group for the research journals at the American Physical Society, and has volunteered as an active space advocate with the National Space Society.

THE SPACE ELEVATOR will be one of the most challenging construction projects ever built. This is not because the project is large in a material sense—the first ribbon would weigh less than a loaded semi-trailer. The challenge comes in the fact that this ribbon is stretched over a length of 62,000 miles, is very thin, and has to support itself.

Gravity decreases with the square of distance from Earth's center, making the job a little easier. Even better, the countering acceleration due to Earth's rotation increases with distance, so that the two cancel out at geosynchronous orbit (22,236 miles above sea level). Taking the two factors together, the length of ribbon on Earth's surface that weighs as much as the net pull of the same thickness cable for the space elevator is about 2,900 miles (4,700 km); the decrease in gravity saves us almost a factor of 8 in required strength.

Within the ribbon, forces are balanced between the gravitational force pulling the whole ribbon towards Earth, and the effective centrifugal force from rotation, which is strongest at the outermost end where the cable moves fastest. Pulling in opposite directions, these lead to tension in the ribbon that must not exceed the material's yield strength, the maximum force (divided by cross-section area) before the material starts to stretch and break. Yield strength is typically measured in metric units of pascals (Pa). For a material with a density the same as water (1 metric ton per cubic meter) the 4,700 km effective length implies a tension of 47 billion pascals, or 47 GPa. Higher density materials would need higher yield strengths than this to be able to build the elevator with such a constant-width ribbon.

This is a huge number. Steel typically has a yield tensile strength under 1 GPa, although thin high-tensile (and high-carbon) steel wires have been made with strengths up to 4 GPa. The best titanium alloys can only handle slightly over 1 GPa, and these metals are 4 to 8 times as dense as water. Kevlar is a bit closer to what we need - it can have yield strengths as high as 4 GPa, and a relative density less than 1.5. Carbon fiber materials have been made with strengths as high as 6 GPa. But all these materials are still more than a factor of 10 weaker than we need to build the space elevator. What can we do?

One option is to taper the ribbon, making it thicker in the middle and thinner at the ends, reducing the ratio of weight to area. With the right shape, in theory, a material of any tensile strength could work. However, as you lower the material strength the ratio of area at geosynchronous orbit to ribbon area near the ground grows exponentially. For steel that ratio becomes at least 10 to the 30th power, so a ribbon just 1 atom across at ground level would have to be thousands of miles in diameter in orbit. Even for Kevlar the area ratio is about a hundred million, so a 1 millimeter diameter cable on the ground would need a 10 meter cable in orbit to support it. Including a safety factor of two doubles the strength requirement and greatly exacerbates the exponential ratios.

In his 1978 novel "The Fountains of Paradise" which introduced the space elevator concept to popular thought, Arthur C. Clarke speculated that the problem could be solved with a fictional "diamond hyperfilament" material that had the required strength, based on the well-known strength of diamond. The element that forms diamond, carbon, was long known to have a second form, graphite, with very different material properties. Carbon is also at the heart of the huge variety of organic compounds that sustain life on Earth; the key property of the element that makes these different forms possible is that each atom is able to bond with up to four neighbors, but is also happy making fewer, stronger bonds, if necessary.

In diamond, the carbon atoms form a three-dimensional interlaced network, with each atom bonded to exactly four neighbors. This structure strongly resists being deformed, leading to diamond's very high strength. In graphite, the carbon atoms form two-dimensional sheets where each atom is linked to three neighbors in a network of interlinked hexagons, like chicken wire. The bonds in these sheets are even stronger than the bonds in diamond, but they rest on one another with no covalent bonds between layers. This makes slippage easy so that graphite, rather than being immensely strong, is often used as a lubricant.

In recent years, scientists have found ways to take advantage of graphite's strengths through the manufacture of carbon fiber composite materials. In carbon fibers the atoms are arranged in the same interlocked hexagonal sheets as for graphite, but these sheets are twisted and bent around one another and combined in a random arrangement that prevents the sort of sliding around that happens with crystalline graphite. As a result, carbon fiber composites are among the strongest known materials.

In 1985 Kroto, Smalley and Curl discovered a new form of pure carbon, one that had been theoretically predicted but never before observed. By replacing some of the hexagons in a lone graphite sheet with pentagons, a closed surface can be made. The smallest of these is a 60-carbon near-spherical molecule, which the discoverers named "buckminsterfullerene", and nicknamed the "buckyball". Techniques were quickly developed to make buckyballs and other "fullerenes" in quantities large enough to be visible; it was soon found that they are actually a common component of soot and are produced in small amounts when wood is burned.

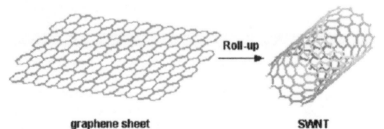

graphene sheet   SWNT

In 1991 a new class of related pure carbon materials were found by Iijima: "buckytubes" or "nanotubes". These are essentially graphite sheets rolled up to form a cylinder, with semispherical "buckyball" caps on either end. In many cases several graphite sheets seem to be rolled up one inside the other, producing what are called multi-walled nanotubes.

There are many slightly different varieties of even the single-walled tubes, depending on the orientation of the hexagons relative to the axis of the cylinder and how tightly they are wound around that axis. The electrical properties depend strongly on these details—some nanotubes are extremely good conductors, better than any ordinary metal, while others are semiconductors or insulators. Tube diameters also depend on these parameters, but are generally on the order of 1 nanometer (nm)—hence the name. Nanotubes have already found a myriad of applications within the burgeoning field of nanotechnology.

Measurement of the yield strength for individual nanotubes has been difficult because they are so small; theoretical predictions go as high as 300 GPa, though 100-150 GPa is a more likely limit. In the lab, strengths of as much as 65 GPa have been measured for individual single-walled nanotubes. Further, nanotube density is only 1.3 times that of water, so in principle a continuous nanotube would be capable of supporting its own weight from geosynchronous orbit, without any taper at all. A material has finally been found that can more than meet the requirements to build a space elevator!

But we will probably not be able to build space elevators from single molecules 62,000 miles long. The longest single-walled nanotubes grown so far are a few centimeters in length, produced by catalytic chemical vapour deposition over a period of about an hour. At that rate, even with no other limitations on length, it would take thousands of years to grow nanotubes long enough.

That means we must somehow capture this immense single-molecule strength in some sort of composite matrix, so that bulk fibers can be formed and grown to meter or kilometer length, and then linked together into the ribbon. This sort of materials problem has been tackled before, but accomplishing it with nanotubes is still a huge challenge.

WORK ON THIS challenge has progressed substantially in the past decade. Nanotube composite fibers as long as 100 meters have been created. The best measured tensile strengths, however, are still only a few GPa, but researchers seem to be convinced that composite strengths close to the limits for individual nanotubes are possible in the long run. Joining these fibers together to make the final ribbon is a similar problem at a larger scale. The tensile load has to be transmitted between fibers at different positions on the ribbon over the length of their overlap, through bonding materials that are weaker than the individual fibers. Several designs for this have been considered; joining aligned fibers with "tape sandwiches" every meter or so may be sufficient.

So we should soon have a material made of nanotube composite fibers, bonded into a 100,000 km ribbon, that may meet the strength requirements to build our space elevator with only a modest taper ratio. What other constraints are there on this ribbon?

The need for a taper dictates increasing area with height (up to geosynchronous orbit)—the details, including a safety factor, are complicated by the decrease in gravity. The area increases fastest near the Earth end, and is close to constant for thousands of kilometers near geo-synchronous orbit. Given ribbon area at any particular height, the ideal cross-sectional shape is then constrained by the hazards that threaten to sever it.

The bulk of the elevator ribbon is above the atmosphere, where the worst threats come from natural micrometeoroids and man-made orbital debris. Natural and artifical objects larger than one centimeter in size can be actively tracked and the structure moved out of the way to avoid any that are projected to come too close. At orbital speeds, space debris impacting a thin ribbon would just punch right through, leaving a hole only slightly larger than the dimensions of the debris (more if the impact is at a shallow angle). Since we want the elevator to survive without breaking for decades, at least one dimension of the ribbon must be more than a few centimeters across. Adding a curve, wave, or bend to the ribbon then further limits the damage from debris striking at very shallow angles.

Rockets available today can carry, at most, about 20 tons to orbit in one launch. That constraint means that the first full ribbon, deployed from orbit, will have a mass no more than that (assuming a single launch), or at best no more than a small multiple with splicing. With a density of 1.3 tons per cubic meter, that means total ribbon volume would be 15 cubic meters (or possibly 30-60). Over 100,000 km length the average cross-sectional area is then 0.15 square millimeters. Making the ribbon 15 cm wide to avoid micrometeoroid damage then leaves it just 1 micron thick on average, a width to thickness ratio of 150,000.

The other threat to our elevator ribbon comes in the first portion of its length, within Earth's atmosphere. With such a wide and thin ribbon, wind loading can add significant stress over the first 20 miles or so. Fortunately, the micrometeoroid threat is much reduced within the atmosphere, and the length in question is relatively short - the simple solution here is to minimize the area facing the wind by bringing the width and thickness closer to equal. For example, we could force the ribbon to 1.5 cm by 10 micron dimensions within the atmosphere, leaving a width to thickness ratio of just 1,500.

Other hazards at intermediate altitudes would also require specially fabricated ribbon segments. For example, reactive atomic oxygen in the outer reaches of the atmosphere would require a protective coating to prevent having the ribbon deteriorate too quickly. The heaviest layer of space debris is in Earth orbits below about 1000 miles, so a stronger, wider ribbon in that section may be necessary.

Nanotube materials should make the space elevator possible, but there's still a lot of work to do. Developing strong enough composite fibers may be just a few years away, or may take much longer than we expect. The final detailed ribbon design will depend on these fiber properties and hazard mitigation considerations - as far as possible, we want to ensure that the first space elevator we build is successful and able to be in service for a long time.

HIGH SPACE
by
John Helfers

ORBITING THREE HUNDRED miles above Earth, Jeremy Swift Waters racked his brain for the perfect words to sum up what was about to happen.

Hoping for inspiration, he pushed out of his ergonomic chair and floated over to a thick, double-paned window that gave him a spectacular view of the world below. Even though the laboratory he was in moved through space at a constant rate of 27,000 kilometers per hour, he always saw the same part of the planet—the west coast of South America, and the bright blue Pacific Ocean next to it. *In the next half-hour, we're going to make history*, he thought.

After fourteen years of effort, setbacks, and triumphs, including the private space station built by a consortium of companies around the world, the now multi-national corporation Liftport was about to complete its singular achievement—launching a carbon-composite nanotube ribbon that would form the slender backbone of the conglomerate's first space elevator. The ribbon would be ejected from its holding facility in space and fall to earth, where it would be securely anchored to Liftport's ground station, a large floating ship stationed near the equator in the Pacific Ocean, several hundred miles off the coast of Ecuador. Robotic climbers would then begin the long journey up to the geosynchronous-orbiting counterweight, reinforcing and thickening the ribbon until it would be able to support the actual space elevator module itself, which would then be able to carry equipment, and even humans, into orbit at a fraction of the cost of launching a rocket.

The device promised to revolutionize how the world thought about space. Other businesses were already looking to sign on for future hotels, research facilities, even a sightseeing company that pitched a crazy idea about advertising "the ultimate bungee jump" over the planet itself. Jeremy didn't think that one was ever going to get off the ground, pun notwithstanding.

But all that was years in the future. Right now, the entire program depended on what Jeremy and others, both on the surface and in space, were about to oversee—the launch of the ribbon from its assembly point to the ground station. Everyone at the company and its satellites was watching what was happening on the station where Jeremy and his team would do everything in their power to that insure the ribbon launch went smoothly. Many were comparing the feeling of anticipation to what the engineers at NASA must have felt just before they launched their first satellite into orbit back in 1958.

Along the way, someone on Liftport's board of directors had gotten the idea to create a "ribbon's-eye view" of what the fiber would see as it came down to earth, broadcasting it over the web in real time. The board had approved inserting a small camera into the weight at the bottom of the ribbon, affectionately called the "sinker."

The engineers on the space station overseeing the launch would be the first ones to get a look at what the world would see as the space elevator became a reality. Many of them were mavericks in their fields, and had signed on to this project because they had wanted to bring space to everyone, or just to be a part of the company that proved it could be done. Jeremy, however, had another reason for being here, one that went back to his childhood more than twenty-five years ago...

* * * * *

THE NEW YORK *forest baked in the relentless July summer. Jeremy sat in the shade of a pine copse, waiting for the heat to dissipate. Waiting for his father to drink himself into unconsciousness. Waiting in the vain hope that he will somehow, some way, get himself out of this backwoods nowhere.*

A vehicle approaches in the distance, its rattling growl indicating that its muffler is more for decorative than anything. Jeremy knows that sound. Rising to his feet, he waits at the side of the road.

A battered, rusty red Ford pick-up pulled over, and his Grandfather regarded him with deep brown eyes nested in a web of fine wrinkles. His hair is worn long, like many of their relatives, but he never ties it back, preferring to keep it under control with a battered cowboy hat.

"Come on, it's getting dark, and I want to show you something." No hello, no how you doing. Straight to the point. Jeremy smiled as he got in, wishing again that Grandfather had been his father, instead of the weak shell of the man that dragged them out here from New York City when Jeremy had been an infant.

They drive in silence for several miles, Jeremy not wanting to say anything, and Grandfather not prying. Finally the boy couldn't contain his frustration any longer. "I hate this place. I hate everything about it. I'll never understand why

Dad brought us here. I hate the forest. We're not Mohawk that live in longhouses anymore. I mean, this is the 20th century, for crying out loud!"

"Your father has—different views on many things," Grandfather replied. "He felt we should uphold the traditions of our forefathers."

"Are you serious? Back to the woods? What's out here for us? You knew better. You were smart enough to adapt, to change with the times. You didn't go chasing something that doesn't exist anymore. What's wrong with him?"

"Your father went looking for something that didn't exist, that hasn't existed for decades. That he hasn't found it is what's slowly killing him. Unfortunately, he's also dragging all of you down with him."

"Why didn't he ever go into construction, working the high steel, like you?"

"Your father always hated the city. He said once it encroached on what was the land's spirit—his people's land. When he couldn't take it anymore, he left. I came with because I was done with that part of my life, and I had a feeling that he—and the rest of you—would need all the help he could get. Looks like I was right."

"I'll never understand him." Jeremy shook his head. "I mean, it's 1992, not 1892. We have to move forward, not backward."

"Your father chose his path, just as I chose mine." Grandfather poked Jeremy in the chest. "Yours, however, is still out there somewhere."

"I'll never be like him, that's for sure. I'd leave all of this behind tomorrow, if I could," Jeremy said.

"I'm sure you'll get your chance, but you'd better prepare for it." Grandfather's eyes narrow as he looks at Jeremy. "You don't want to end up like rest of our people, do you?"

"Of course not." Jeremy shakes his head, his black hair falling across his eyes/

"Then you need to start making sure now that doesn't happen."

Grandfather turns the truck onto a side road. Out in the northern part of the state there is little but forested hills interspersed with meadows; no lights, buildings, no cars, just endless thick, dark forest as far as Jeremy could see, with pink and red rays of light being swallowed by the horizon. They come to a small field, and Grandfather pulls the truck over.

"Why're we stopping? I've already seen enough of this to last me a lifetime."

Grandfather pushed his door open. "Humor an old man, then." He hopped out, walked to the front of the truck and climbed on the hood, sitting over the ticking engine. Jeremy rolled his eyes and followed suit, hoisting himself up alongside. They sit there for a few seconds, then Grandfather pointed with a skinny, wrinkled finger.

"Look up."

Jeremy did so, and saw the universe arrayed before him. The night was perfectly clear, and he saw not only the stars, but more of the cosmos then he had ever seen before. The stars filled the night sky; from dim, pale ones to bright dots that glow like airplane lights. Swirls of pale vapor streamed between the constellations in purple-white tendrils, creating a heavenly panorama that stretched everywhere he looked.

Jeremy didn't say a word, he just stared up in awe. His grandfather remained silent beside him, letting his grandson absorb the sight.

"It's—it's beautiful," the boy finally said.

"When I used to walk the steel in New York in the 1940s, some nights I would come back to the site when no one was around and climb up as high as I could, to the top most girders. Usually I'd look out over the city, see the people running around thirty or forty stories below me. But my eyes would always look upward eventually. Now, around New York City proper, it was too bright to see anything, but when the Northeastern Blackout of '65 hit— not the more famous one of '77, mind you—I knew I had the a chance I might never get again."

Jeremy's grandfather took his hat off and rubbed his eyes. "My company was working on the U.N. plaza buildings at the time. I was stuck in the city any way, so I walked back to the site and took the freight elevator up to the roof. When I walked out, I saw something fairly similar to what you and I are looking at right now. I spent several hours there, until the power came back on in Brooklyn around 11 p.m. Of course, that was during the space race, and right then I knew we were going to reach the moon, just like Kennedy had wanted. That was as close as I was going to get to the stars, and that was fine for me. When your father came out here, I came with and rediscovered the stars all over again."

Grandfather looks over at Jeremy. "I don't expect you to understand your father's decision. Some of the choices he's made, I don't understand too well either. I wanted my son to have the chance to do more than I ever could. Since that doesn't seem likely now, I'm wondering what you would do with that same chance if you got it."

Jeremy tore his gaze away from the universe and regarded his grandfather. "If someone gave me a chance to get out of here and do something with my life, I wouldn't waste it."

* * * * *

AFTER THAT, JEREMY and his grandfather came out to the woods several times each summer to look at the night sky. Grandfather told Jeremy of the Mohawk legends that pertained to the skies; for example, the three stars that make up the handle of the big Dipper were actually a trio of hunters chasing the Great Bear that had marauded their village for months. Jeremy had absorbed all of it, while taking all of the advanced math and science classes he could in school, trying to prepare for the rest of his life.

When Grandfather had passed away four years later, he had left everything to his grandson in a trust fund to pay for the college of the boy's choice. By that time, Jeremy knew what he wanted to do, and there was only one place to do it: the Massachusetts Institute of Technology.

Ah, -hsotha, if only you could see me now, Jeremy thought. *I'm on the ultimate high steel. High space, even.*

A loudspeaker came to life in the station's control room. "Launch countdown is go at T-minus five minutes and counting. Space anchor systems are all online and go for launch. All systems, initiate final procedures checklist."

Each man and women bent over their monitors, ensuring that every triple-checked system was reviewed one last time. Jeremy was no different, pushing off the wall to float back to his seat. His responsibility was to oversee the computer system that would be adjusting the fiber-optic camera in the small, aerodynamic chunk of aerogel-filled ablation tile that would absorb the heat generated as the ribbon fell through the atmosphere to the surface. Even though the camera would be only a few millimeters from thousands of degrees, the insulating aerogel would completely block any transfer, allowing the camera to transmit its images safely around the world.

Jeremy continued his final checklist, confident that everything was progressing according to their schedule, but going over it one last time. The eyes of the world were upon them, and every engineer and scientist on the ground, at the connection point, and in space felt the pressure to ensure that the ribbon launched without a hitch.

To Jeremy, this kind of pressure was nothing new. During his time at MIT, he had thought he was going to split a dozen different ways under the strain of his Space Systems Engineering final project...

* * * * *

JEREMY FLUNG HIMSELF into the old chair in the office of his graduate studies professor. "We cannot solve the spin-induced artificial gravity problem. Every equation we try to proof falls outside the human comfort zone. Even factoring in the data from the recent tests on the Mars Biogravity Satellite, we still aren't any closer to a solution. My project is going down the tubes fast."

His professor, Choi Jung Hun, looked up at him from behind his ancient L-shaped desk. "Yes, I've reviewed your status reports, and am concerned by the lack of progress. So how are you going to fix this problem, Mr. Swift Waters?"

"I have no idea." Jeremy ran both hands through his tangled hair. "We've been trying to advance any physical aspect of it for weeks now, but either run into unacceptable force factors or cost infeasibilities. Our current business plan is running seven million over budget. I don't even know if this is worth it, what with the advances the Chinese have made in the last decade. Maybe we should just outsource our space program, like everything else."

"You know you do not believe that," the diminutive astrophysics professor said. "After all, you of all people do not have the luxury of failure."

Jeremy frowned. "Says who? I could bail out on the whole thing right now. Doesn't sound like a bad idea, either."

"You could, and sacrifice your years of effort and struggle, thereby perpetuating the myth of the lazy American."

Jeremy looked hard at him for a moment. "Thanks, Prof. For a second, I thought you were going to say 'Native American.'"

"Indeed, the thought had crossed my mind, but then I would be agreeing to the stereotype you are considering propagating yourself." Choi turned in his chair and looked out the window at the light traffic on the Charles River. "You know, even though many nations have made scientific advances that have outshined America's, thousands still hunger to come here and research, experiment, exchange ideas. Even in this age of virtual reality, I believe that there is nothing like actually being on the United States, that it invigorates the faculties, broadens the horizons, expands the thinking. For this nation is, in my opinion, the only one that has fostered that spirit of exploration and invention ever since it was founded. It has been a haven for nonconformists, free thinkers, iconoclasts. No matter what is being done elsewhere in the world, many still look to America as the forefront of science and technology, even as less and less of its population take an interest in the sciences, replaced instead by foreigners and outsourcing."

Jeremy couldn't believe his ears. "Wait a minute, you're not playing the race card, are you?"

"No, I do not need to, as that has already happened in many ways. The graduating population of MIT this year will have a higher concentration of Asian and Asian-Americans students than ever before. Talk about propagating a stereotype, eh?" The professor clasped his hands behind his head and chuckled.

"But when we have the chance to bring you, an original American here through much hard work, then we as a university, and I as your professor have more than a vested interest in seeing you succeed in your chosen field, and cast off the legacy that many of your people have been unfortunately reduced to in the last century."

Jeremy stiffened in his chair, that last remark hitting a bit too close to home as he thought of his father.

Upon seeing this, Choi leaned forward. "I hope that I have not caused any offense."

"No, no, none taken. I must confess that I hadn't really thought of it that way in the first place. Being the first member of my family to go to college was enough of an achievement for my relatives."

"But only if you are the first person to drop out of college. I remember you telling me about your grandfather, and the goals he had for you. You are so close to achieving them that I—and, if I may, he—would be sorely disappointed if you were to give up now."

"Well, I'm not ready to throw in the towel just yet. So, any advice on our brick wall?" Jeremy asked.

"Like many starting graduate teams, yours has chosen to tackle the entire elephant. Step back, and concentrate on an aspect of the problem that looks most feasible to solve. While it is certainly attractive to try and create a solution to the problem as a whole, that happens so rarely that it is almost unheard of. Instead, it is through the achievements of teams making incremental progress over years, and even decades, that pay off in the long run. I suggest that you revise your project to solve one aspect of the artificial gravity problem, and go from there."

* * * * *

JEREMY PAUSED FOR a moment as he remembered just how close he had been to actually quitting MIT at the time. He had gone back to his team, and, amid much grumbling, convinced them to revise their project requirements and concentrate on a less far-reaching goal. Their system of room and hall markings on a proposed space station to help orient humans on independent space stations, while not nearly as groundbreaking as conquering the problems inherent in creating artificial gravity itself, did have a practical, real world applications right away, and indeed had even been used in the space station Jeremy sat in right now.

The loudspeaker clicked again. "Final countdown to ribbon launch commencing. All systems are nominal."

Jeremy looked around at the men and women waiting for the next part of history to be made. All systems were green. "Roger that, we are go with final launch countdown," Jeremy replied, sitting poised over his monitor, ready to act should any kind of malfunction necessitate it. *This has to work the first time, it just has to,* he thought. Sure, Liftport would recover if the ribbon launch malfunctioned or failed, but the media beating it would take would prove embarrassing at best, and crippling at worst. *We'll make it happen.*

The final seconds ticked away, and when the countdown reached T-minus zero, Jeremy watched the sinker burst from the space anchor in a glittering spray of particles. The micron-thin, ten-centimeter wide ribbon unreeled from the anchor station without a hitch, prompting a brief round of cheers from the station crew, but Jeremy knew this was just the beginning.

'Pacific Control, this is Top Floor, the ribbon has launched, and is beginning its descent into the atmosphere." With those words Jeremy pressed the monitor button that would activate the ribbon camera feed. He caught a brief glimpse of the planet stretching out below, then a red-orange glow crept in from all around the camera lens as the sinker heated up in the atmosphere, obscuring the view completely.

"Pacific Control, this is Top Floor, the sinker is midway through the troposphere, and is currently on target. ETA in twenty-three minutes." *It does take a while to unreel 31,000 miles of nanotube fiber ribbon,* he thought. *Like dropping the longest needle in the world into a blue haystack.* The "target" was a ten-square-mile radius around the ground station. Even though the site had been chosen for its prevailing calm airflow, there would be some unavoidable drift as the ribbon plunged through the atmosphere; so heavy-duty, oceangoing tugboats had been rented to recover the sinker if necessary and to tow it back to the station, where it would be secured.

The minutes ticked by, with calm voices all around Jeremy updating the speed and trajectory of the ribbon as well as the status of the anchor station and weather conditions at the ground site. Suddenly the orange glow on his monitor flickered and receded, and he saw, along with the rest of the world, the broad blue expanse of the Pacific Ocean below as the sinker and ribbon descended further into earth's atmosphere.

"Pacific Control, this is Top Floor, sinker has penetrated the mesosphere, and is now fifty-eight miles above your location. Visual sighting in three minutes." Due to the earth's rotation, the ribbon wouldn't fall straight down, but arc across the sky before coming to rest in the ocean. Jeremy alternated watching the spectacular view as the sinker drew close to earth with monitoring the feed and speed of the ribbon as it unwound. By now they were more than three-quarters of the way there, and the scene taken in by the unblinking eye of the camera was incredible: endless blue ocean stretching to the horizon and growing larger and larger with each passing second. And then, Jeremy spotted a tiny speck still dozens of miles below—

"Pacific Control, this is Top Floor, we have you on visual. All systems are functioning green. ETA eight minutes." Jeremy said. Windows on his monitors winked open at him, informing him of the status of the anchor station and everything else, all currently operating at optimum capability.

Jeremy turned his head to look at everyone in the shuttle, a conglomeration of races, genders, ages, all coming together in the pursuit of a single vision; to find someway to bring mankind closer to the stars on a daily basis. Now, in a few short minutes, Liftport was about to do just that.

It was then that Jeremy realized what his grandfather and his professor has been saying during those conversations long ago: naturally, that they wanted him to succeed for himself, but also that he was part of a bigger process, the American tradition of progress and discovery. Choi's words came back to him; *America is the only nation that has fostered a spirit of exploration and invention ever since it was founded.* This was no different. When that ribbon was attached to the Pacific Control base, it would usher in a completely new age of space exploration that eventually even a middle-class family could afford. It had the potential to rekindle the interest in space that had been lost by the American public over the past half-century. And it would catapult the country to the head of the pack of nations that were driving ever outward, reaffirming that, although the grand old nation would always would have its problems, it could still accomplish what any of its citizens set out to do, not just for themselves, but for the world.

Jeremy heard the soft chime signaling that the sinker was about to splash down. The guidance system had steered it to within three hundred meters of the station, and a tug was already on its way to intercept the ribbon as it plummeted toward the ocean's placid surface.

Jeremy keyed his mike. "Impact in five...four...three...two...one. Pacific Control, this is Top Floor."

Right at that moment, he knew exactly what to say, and broadcast the beginning of a new era to the world: "The future has landed."

THE LIFTER: THE SPACE ELEVATOR'S ROBOTIC WORKHORSE
by
Ben Shelef

Ben Shelef is currently on the forefront of Space Elevator development as the director of the Spaceward Foundation. Mr. Shelef is branching out from his engineering roots to establish the Elevator 2010 Competitions. These X Prize-like competitions are intended to publicize the Space Elevator project while simultaneously working to find solutions to robotics and ribbon-based technological challenges. The first competitions will be held in September 2005 and cash prizes will be awarded. To learn more about Mr. Shelef and Elevator 2010, please visit www.elevator2010.com.

WHEN DESCRIBING THE Space Elevator concept to the uninitiated, we always take great care to point out that unlike the elevator you take to reach the office, in the Space Elevator the ribbon (not a cable!) does not pull the elevator cars up. Rather, the ribbon is fixed, and the elevator cars travel up it, using their own electric motors to make the climb. Which is the reason, of course, that some people call them climbers. We prefer to call them lifters because "you lift cargo" and "climb by yourself!"

A good way to think of a lifter is as a vertically moving, powered-from-below solar car. A regular solar car travels on a flat road, and is powered by the sun (you knew that!). A Space Elevator lifter, on the other hand, travels straight up a ribbon, and is powered by an intense light beam that we shoot up at its underside from the surface of the earth.

Beam Me Up, Scotty!
Transferring the power using a light beam is actually a pretty clever trick. While the lifter carries its own motor with it, it does not have to carry a huge fuel tank or an even bigger battery bank—these stay on the earth and power the ground station that is transmitting the beam. Remember how a rocket, when taking off, is only 5% payload? Well with the Space Elevator design, the payload weighs 60-75% of the vehicle—easily a 12-fold improvement!

Below is an illustration of a lifter climbing the ribbon and receiving the beamed laser power.

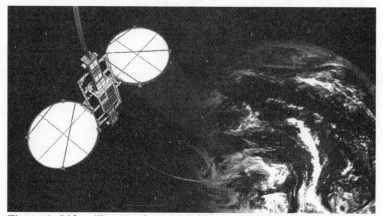

Figure 1: Lifter illustrated, with ribbon and light beam

We are often asked why we used beamed power instead of conventional solar power. The answer is simple—solar light is just not concentrated enough. The required light beam has to be about 10 times more concentrated than sunlight. This is an intensity that won't cut through steel (or ribbon), but also not something you want to stand in.

We are also often asked about microwave beamed power. Microwave power is often mentioned as part of solar satellite power transmission, but it requires a relatively small transmitter and a very large collector—which is desirable in the case of earth-to-space power transmission, but is undesirable when the collector is part of the vehicle.

Lastly, we often get asked—why not just carry a small power plant on the lifter? This seems to be more desirable the larger the lifter gets. The problem with carrying a power plant is the very large amount of heat rejection we need to accommodate. The rules of thermodynamics state the only way to make a power plant efficient is to make its exhaust temperature as low as possible. These rules also state the only way to radiate heat away in an efficient way is to make the exhaust temperature high. Since low is the opposite of high, it turns out that a power plant needs more radiator weight than it can lift—and so cannot carry a power generator on board.

Lifter Anatomy 101

A Space Elevator lifter is composed of the following subsystems:

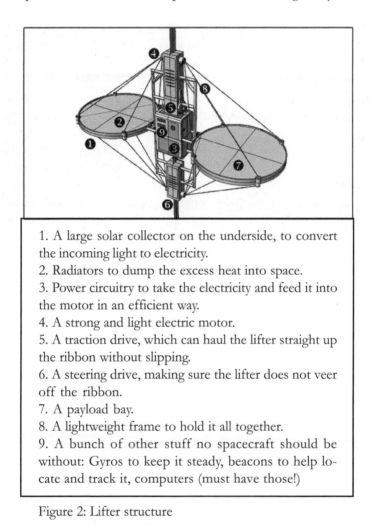

1. A large solar collector on the underside, to convert the incoming light to electricity.
2. Radiators to dump the excess heat into space.
3. Power circuitry to take the electricity and feed it into the motor in an efficient way.
4. A strong and light electric motor.
5. A traction drive, which can haul the lifter straight up the ribbon without slipping.
6. A steering drive, making sure the lifter does not veer off the ribbon.
7. A payload bay.
8. A lightweight frame to hold it all together.
9. A bunch of other stuff no spacecraft should be without: Gyros to keep it steady, beacons to help locate and track it, computers (must have those!)

Figure 2: Lifter structure

Our baseline lifter weighs 20 tons, about the weight of a large truck. The lifter travels up the ribbon at a relatively slow speed—less than 200 miles per hour. (Yes, we said "slow"—remember we have to cover 25,000 miles on the way to GEO—that's a travel time of more than 5 days!) Even so, hauling 20 tons straight up at 200 miles an hour takes motors as powerful as a train's locomotive.

Feeding these power hungry motors with electricity takes a very large solar pane—the solar collectors for our baseline design are about 15 m [45 feet] in diameter. Luckily, this structure does not need to withstand the loads of a rocket launch, and so can be made relatively light weight—otherwise, it would have ended up weighing more than our entire 20 ton vehicle.

Folks familiar with the solar collector will be right to point out at this time that solar cells (we will start using the more correct term photovoltaic cells) are not 100% efficient, and so will heat up. Using monochromatic light (which is a fancy way to say "pure color" light) we can make the cells work efficiently, and make sure they reflect unused light. This makes the task of "dumping" the excess heat more manageable.

Efficient state-of-the-art power supplies, working in tandem with a lightweight rare-earth magnet based motors then transform the electrical power into mechanical motion. This motion is then transferred to the traction drive—a set of mechanical rollers that grab the ribbon and pull the lifter up.

The frame of the lifter is a unique structure. Unlike regular spacecraft that are typically rigid and compact, the lifter is a "flimsy" structure. We already noted that it does not have to withstand a rocket launch, and we only intend to unfurl it once it leaves the atmosphere, so it only needs to support its own weight in one gravity—the image above illustrates the type of structure we are envisioning—not quite your typical rocket ship.

This line of reasoning affects the payload bay too, since it does not have to protect its cargo from hypersonic aerodynamic flows or fiery re-entries. Rather than have a shuttle-style double-door closet-like bay, the lifter has an open bay that can accommodate large and bulky payloads, such as long beams, or large inflated structures.

The rest of the components mentioned above are pretty standard for a spacecraft. The gyroscopes make sure the lifter does not twist about the ribbon (the spaghetti-ball effect....) A good beacon is necessary so that the ground station can take good aim at the lifter and illuminate it well. Computers are, well, we're not really sure why an elevator should have AOL, but it's a sign of the times—if refrigerators have one, we think a Space Elevator lifter should probably have a computer as well.

Are We There Yet?

Since the lifters travel using a mechanical traction device (a set of fancy rollers actually) their speed along the ribbon is pretty limited—definitely no more than 200 miles per hour—very slow in cosmic terms. The reason the lifters achieve the very large speeds required to stay in orbit (more than 5 miles per second!) is that as they move outwards, they describe ever-larger circles around the planet, and always take exactly 24 hours to complete each circle.

When a lifter travels out 25,000 miles, its speed around the planet becomes enough to stay orbital. At that point if the lifter lets the ribbon go, it will float weightless right next to it—it is in orbit. We can now calculate how long it takes to get to orbit—25,000 miles, 200 miles per hour—125 hours, 5.2 days.

Being a Lifter—it's a one way trip, baby.

For the foreseeable future, space transport is going to be an "upwards only" business—the amount of return cargo will be relatively limited compared with the upwards traffic necessary to support the large scale construction projects that the Space Elevator will enable. For this reason, it will not make financial sense to bring back the lifters after they reach the top of their climb.

Rather than simply discard them, we need to look closely at the anatomy lesson we just covered.

Each lifter is great asset: a good photovoltaic array, electronics, motors, and light-weight structures—nothing that cannot be used in building space-borne structures. We therefore expect to engineer the lifters from scratch to have a second life as an integral part in a GEO space station, solar power satellites, or any of the other applications described in this book.

Power optimization

A funny thing happens to a lifter every time it goes to space. When launched, a lifter weighs its full weight. (Unlike a rocket, where due to the high-gee acceleration, a 1-ton piece ends up weighing 5 tons or more.) As the lifter ascends the ribbon, its rotational speed starts balancing out gravity (which is itself decreasing as we pull away from earth) and the lifter becomes more "orbital". At 3,000 km (2,000 miles) out, the lifter already weighs less than half it own weight, and at 6,000 km (4,000 miles) it weighs a quarter. During the rest of the trip, the weight drops to practically zero. This drop in weight means that the load on the power system (photovoltaic cells, electronics, motor) gets lighter and lighter as we go.

For this reason, if we make the lifter weigh only 75% of the ribbon capacity, we can launch a second lifter after the first one has traveled (approximately) 6,000 km, or a quarter of the way up.

The above discussion puts us in a bit of a dilemma—should we make the power system strong enough to carry the lifter at full speed as we start the climb (thus making it unnecessarily heavy for the rest of the trip) or should we make it lighter and therefore travel at slower speeds in the beginning of the trip (thus increasing the amount of time before we can launch the next vehicle)?

This is just one example of many situations where the economics of the Space Elevator system affects the design of its components—after all, we're not just trying to reach space, but build a system that enables a large scale space economy.

The atmospheric section

The first 50 miles or so of travel happen inside the bowl of soup that we call the atmosphere.

While representing only 50/25,000 = 0.2% of the trip, the atmosphere completely changes the rules of the game for the Space Elevator and its lifters.

Wind, for example, becomes a major factor. The photovoltaic collector is a huge sail, and even a very moderate wind will break it (unless of course we make it very sturdy, and therefore heavy, which we will regret for the other 99.8% of the trip.)

Same goes for the ribbon—it is fine to have our tether in the form-factor of a sheet of paper when we're in space, but where there's wind, it is probably much better to bunch it up into its equivalent 1/8" diameter wire form. In such a case, it will become difficult to climb using rollers that are designed work with a flat ribbon.

For these and other reasons, the lifter will most likely begin its ascent in a folded-up form. Rather than making the lifter negotiate the first 50 miles of tether, the ground station will perform a 50-mile reel-in operation, and then simply attach the lifter in a "dormant" state, with a folded photovoltaic array. The ground station will then unreel the ribbon back out, and allow the lifter to "float" up with it. Once the lifter clears the atmosphere, it will unfurl its photovoltaic array, power up, and start climbing.

Lifters to Mars

The last aspect we want to cover regarding lifters is their added role for solar system exploration.

As mentioned above, when the lifter gets to GEO its weight approaches zero, and it becomes orbital. If the lifter were to continue climbing and cross GEO, it will start to feel reverse weight, and start "falling" outwards. The further away from GEO, the stronger this pull is. For an outside observer, it will seem that the lifter is hanging on to dear life while being swung around in circles around the earth.

When it is far enough away from earth, and when the timing is just right, the lifter can separate from the ribbon, and be flung outwards with enough speed to escape the Earth's gravitational field, on a trajectory that will take it relatively close to the Moon or Mars.

INTO THE BLACK
by
Janny Wurts

WHERE WORDS FELL short, wonder commanded. At least, Merrick Alverson never tired of experiencing the moment when the space-lift arose from the earth. Today, the outbound pod was the co-op's new showpiece, a light frame geodesic bubble, paned with transparent panels that offered a spectacular panoramic view.

Alverson adjusted the mike on his headset. "Standing by for up-lift," he affirmed to the ground crew. "On your mark, engage the cable."

The live shudder of the decking under his feet let him sense the moment as the locking gears meshed. Home base's response crackled through his ear-piece. "Cable engaged, Mick," Alice said in her whiskey grained alto from ground station. Alverson could picture her: muscular long legs propped on the console, with shoes kicked off to expose her pink toes, and the habitual coffee mug printed with lipstick, snugged in a cynical hand. Her style of sharp language and penetrating wit had earned her the closet nickname of 'Nosy Alice.' "Pod 5, you are go," she declared by routine. "All green for your lift at six hundred hours."

Alverson smiled. "Bon voyage, baby," he whispered.

A test pilot tamed by a wheelchair injury, he unfolded crossed arms, shot the cuff of his jumpsuit and threw the lever that engaged the crawler. Gears meshed with the lift engine. His self-satisfied smile split into a grin. Alverson never tired of watching as his parcel of passengers caught their breaths, infused with delight by the first upward surge as the bubble thrust into motion. The electric machinery made scarcely a sound. Powered by microwave, with secondary batteries for cabin power under the floor deck, the pod rose on the carbon-based ribbon that linked to the orbital station twenty-five thousand miles out.

Alverson rechecked the satellite scan. A clear morning above with a variable, light crosswind: no cu-nims or dangerous windshear disturbing the troposphere. Last night's front had weakened. The threatening dip in the jet stream had shifted. Alverson projected no difficulty above. The lift would be calm, by all the numbers an uneventful, clear ride. He retested the stabilizer vanes, then adjusted their attitude to deflect any buffeting gusts, while the ground fell away underneath.

The fuzzed lights of home station dissolved into mist as the pod climbed above the predawn gloom and broke through, under a gunmetal sky streamered with neon-pink cirrus. All instruments showed green. Smooth as a water drop riding a filament, the pod accelerated through the wisped upper cloud layer and emerged into sunlight at six thousand feet.

The passengers gazed downward. Some murmured in awe. Most were exhilarated, though the pregnant matron who clutched at the arm of her banal husband seemed a touch nervous. Near term, dripping diamonds, she'd have married the fashionably rich, whose latest chic fad was to give birth in null gravity. Since her type would frown at his roving eye, Alverson smothered his impulse to wink. The ease of the ride would soon reassure her. This ascent was a light-weight pod bearing folk with paid tickets—not a bare-bones container with perishable supply, or a 'heavy' that crept up by robotic control and transferred linked modules of space cargo. As an operator hired to bus-drive the tourists, Alverson savored the slice-of-life variety attracted by space-faring opportunity.

Beside the expectant parents, today's payload included a wide range of individuals.

The ascetic fellow with the shaved head and yellow robes likely would be climbing up to high orbit to meditate. Beside him, a crisp, blonde doctor in white was escorting an elderly client to null gravity for an experimental study on hip fracture regeneration. Only the academic in the tweed coat, hunched over his laptop, looked bored enough to be a regular. Alverson pegged him as a comet astronomer, space-bound to study the Oort cloud on the second extra-solar mission.

The two women with bent heads, consulting on satellite phones would be cutting-edge industrial scientists—either nano-technicians, or active-form biogeneticists. Both carried sealed containers, checked into baggage below. They would be pursuing highly reactive experiments, too sensitive or dangerous to risk earth-bound, against the threat of escape contamination.

Mankind's myriad frontiers marched ahead, but did not exclude the mundane. Today's pod also carried a maintenance hand, returning from leave-time on earth. The eighth passenger was a serious, crop-haired young boy, fidgeting in sneakers and a school blazer. Either he'd be a student who'd won a national science fair prize, or a brat dispatched for joint custody with a space-based parent. A divorcee's kid, if his destination became the low orbit waystop. Brainchild destined for scholarship, if he stayed through the second, or rode the full distance to the last platform that launched the solar-wind ships and interplanetary shuttles from high orbit.

Alverson liked to bet with himself: today, his odds opted for brain-child.

Earth dwindled below. By habit, he surveyed the instruments as the pod soared above the last layers of cirrus and entered the stratosphere. No anomalies presented. The cold air conditions, with almost no wind, changed rapidly as the pod crossed the warm belt of the ozone layer. Then the temperature plummeted again. Ice crystal formations of nacreous cloud feathered past, with a brief buffet of windy turbulence. The passengers had settled, some absorbed by the view, while the experienced ones opened up palm links or reading. Cabin pressure was green, with oxygen engaged.

Auxiliary to the microwave dish, that powered the lift into space, Alverson deployed the graceful wings of the solar panels, which unfurled like flower petals from the pod's base and locked into extension. The back-up batteries were healthy, and charging in the thinned air and strong sunlight. Alverson stretched. He'd pour coffee, shortly. Shaping up as a pleasant, fair-weather run, he felt content, until a falling object clanged into the dome strut overhead, and bounced, clattering, off one of the polymer view plates.

"What the—!" Alverson muttered, shot straight in his chair. One glimpse, snatched as the item rebounded off the pod; his pilot's reflex already engaged, Alverson cupped the mike on his headset. "Ground station? We've got somebody upstairs." Lightning hands busy, he reversed the logged data on the pod's topside camera, then played forward one frame at a time. No time, even to swear under his breath, as the object popped up on his view screen. "Whoever, whatever," he told Nosy Alice, "there's a Swiss army knife cut loose from topside and headed your way under free fall."

Disbelief and obscenities rattled the earpiece. Then, "Damn you Mick! That's so ridiculous, the joke's not even funny!"

"No such," Alverson stated, voice kept low to keep from alarming his passengers. "Alice, I'm serious." He added, no trace of the provocative drawl he used when he pulled someone's leg, "I've run the front cam's data-feed backwards and confirmed. Check my logged transmission. We had a snag loosely wrapped on the ribbon. Our crawler's vibration shook the string free, and the jetsam just bounced off the bubble."

Scarcely mollified, Alice drew breath and wound up again. "Some hoaxer probably——"

"From *above* us?" Alverson snapped her off short. "No light-wit pranker would choose to try his high jinks *up the wire!*" He turned his head, spoke fast, since his passengers were stirring, unsettled and murmuring. "Don't worry, we're not damaged. The pod's specialized panels are specifically hardened to withstand the impact of small meteors."

The comet researcher knew better, of course. As well, the brain-boy dressed in the school blazer was too sharp to swallow the platitude. "But mister! Meteorites burn as they enter the earth's upper atmosphere. I saw a jackknife tied to a string, attached with a carabiner."

"I saw the same." The comet researcher affirmed, by astute observation and his trained eye for snapshot impressions of deep sky phenomena.

"Alice!" barked Alverson. "Did you catch my drift?"

She did. Smart when it counted, she also grasped the whacked logic: a mountaineering tool used to rig ropes had to be the lost gear of a climber. "Unholy hell, Mick, you've *got* to be kidding."

Yet the madcap assumption made chilling sense. Why not, when the mightiest peaks on the planet had become the paid playground for eccentric tourists? What frontier remained for a cutting edge sport, renowned for its breed of macho extremists? Some hardy, self-determined adventurer *would* aspire to be first to achieve mankind's unassisted ascent into space.

The white-noise pause in the headset extended. Since Nosy Alice was never the type to be chasing stunned thoughts before words, she'd have paused the connection to mobilize the ground crew. If not in position, the next pod in line would be loading for lift. A scant margin at best, before the climber's free-falling possessions could be imbedding themselves in the ground pad, or maybe hammering an unlucky service vehicle pulled up for duty alongside.

Any silence from Alice would have been a precedent worth noting, if Alverson hadn't been forced to sort through the problematic repercussions himself. A stunt on this scale would require tight planning. In fact had to have been arranged with keen foresight, if only to broach the security surrounding the lift station. The daredevil who challenged this frontier must be prepared to survive extreme altitude. He'd need oxygen, pressure suit, sophisticated wind and thermal protection, not to mention a means to escape the danger of becoming chewed to shreds in the lift gears, as rising pods overtook his position.

On second thought, and perhaps not a mistake, the mad man may have timed his ascent ahead of the new pod with the fancy overhead view. Since the lift might have to be stalled to avoid him, Alverson started precautions.

"Attention, everyone! Please stay in your seats. Make certain you lap belt and shoulder harness stay fastened and firmly adjusted."

The deep space research guy was already in step, leaned over to assist the arthritic granny, while the osteopath checked the placement of the straps on the lady with the near-term pregnancy. Alverson scanned the instruments. The pod approached an altitude of thirty-five miles, well into the mesosphere. Here, eddies off the belt of the jet stream often caused a rough ride. Though last night's changing weather had moved the flow of worst turbulence farther north, a pause here was nobody's picnic.

The headset crackled. "Mick? We're sending a spider. Your nutcase is real, unfortunately."

Alverson could not shake his sense of tight dread. "The spider team's primed for search and rescue?"

"Standing by, but for body recovery, more like." Insensitive without even thinking, Alice resumed, "The story gets worse. Security's collared a dumbshit in a van with a satellite phone dish who claims he's the climber's associate. The guy lost contact with his buddy three hours ago. He's been too frightened stiff to own up and call the authorities."

"Well, at least now the jet stream won't interfere with him," Alverson murmured, cranked taut. The old, binding rage clamped a knot in his gut, *that this mess should happen on his watch!*

He resisted the urge to slam a fist into the atrophied legs on his chair, while his pilot's integrity kept an infallible eye, tracking the instruments and the outside wind speed. No red-line reading troubled him yet. All the same, he packed in the solar panels then deployed the secondary wind vanes to deflect severe buffeting. The jet stream could travel up to three hundred miles per hour, a killer force made worse by wind chill as the outside temperature plummeted to minus sixty degrees Fahrenheit. He could not be too careful, where an unstablized pod threatened a kink in the ribbon.

But today, the damaging winds of the upper atmosphere had already thrown their monkey wrench in the works. Alverson spotted the obstruction on the wire ahead, just a moment before the eagle-eyed kid shouted the news through the cabin.

"Mister, look! There's somebody in a pressure suit dangling above us!"

"Thanks, son, I see him." Alverson felt the strain of every raised voice, each pointing finger, and the sharpened gestures, from behind, that expressed mounting concern. The trapped person ahead needed hardcore search and rescue, not a man whose trial term of employment was arranged by a disabled veterans' program. Yet Alverson had been a performance-grade pilot, far too well-trained to take pause for the foundation that had launched him as their star project. His foremost concern should be the pod and its occupants, not a trespasser fouled by an accident.

Alverson disengaged the lift gears, and set the limpet clamp, stopping the pod on the wire. "How long for that spider?" he barked through his mike. "We've encountered the climber. He's hung up, and apparently unconscious."

The zoom on the forward cam showed the figure, swinging limp on a waist sling from his makeshift tether. The odd mess of pressure clamps he had used to scale the ribbon winked in the strong sun, scaled with a white coat of rime ice. Metal, no doubt, that had picked up condensation in the warmth of the stratosphere and then failed as accumulated condensation crystallized in the frigid temperatures.

The climber might have been able to compensate had he not been thrashed by the vicious force of the wind when the jet stream changed course through the night. He wore a suit pack strapped with oxygen tanks. A second arrangement of clamps and pulleys secured a bulky, towed sled that carried his net of auxiliary supplies.

Ground station's instructions came through Alverson's headset. "Clamp your pod, Mick. Stay put and wait. The spider should reach you within half an hour. The onboard crew are coming equipped to tackle the problem." The short, poisoned pause cut deeper than pain, or the humiliation of crippling injury. "Keep your passengers calm, Mick. That's your only priority."

Alverson locked his shaking hands to keep from tearing the headset off, straightaway. *Do nothing.* The downside order challenged the grain of free initiative, not to mention his humane integrity. *Wait for the spider.* Fritter away what narrow margin remained, never based on the slim chance the senseless adventurer might still be alive—but as the forced shortcoming of a paraplegic pod operator, who could not be asked to perform his hale function. Even worse, the low words exchanged at his back, that surely condemned him for the same shortfall.

More than bitterness prompted a muffled curse. Alverson surged forward to unclamp the pod, hardly stopped by the urgent touch that closed over his shoulder.

A protest from the passengers, Alverson presumed.

He twisted around, primed for an explosive argument. Eye to eye, he met the female doctor who had, against orders, unclipped from her seat, and crossed the pod's cabin to confront him. Under crisis, she was no longer the demure blonde with the sweet bed-side manner.

"You're going up anyway?" she challenged.

"Yes!" Alverson snapped.

She smiled back with the same, fierce conviction. Alverson sized up a healer with steel nerves, her affirmed avocation to stand firm in the breach against even desperate odds.

Nor was her rebellion an empty commitment. "You think the climber may still be alive?"

"Probably not," Alverson admitted, unflinching. Yet her caring deserved his honest answer; and his unruly fingers already eased the hydraulic that fastened the limpet clamp. "Only a suicidal idiot would seek his thrills this way. But even the craziest explorers have families. Maybe a sweetheart and kids. His folks surely deserve to be given the benefit of the doubt. Once, I was a young fool in trouble. Why shouldn't this one be granted an outside chance?"

"We're all with you on that," the doctor replied. She gestured to the others. "The comet researcher has an EVA suit. Since his custom-fit can maneuver more readily than your standard issue stocked for evacuation, he's asked whether you can access the hold to get at his baggage."

Alverson ripped off his headset, astonished. "The escape airlock's underneath us," he warned. "We're still under the influence of earth's gravity, and not fashioned with the outside handholds that equip the spiders. We do have a tether wire. Brave as your man is, the dome's polymer and ceramic struts won't make his effort at rescue an easy ticket."

A brisk, thumbs-up signal flashed from behind. Apparently the researcher was quite aware of the pod's limited emergency resources.

Not only that, the other passengers were pooling what resources they could bring to bear on the problem.

"We might fashion a makeshift shepherd's hook," the station technician suggested. "I've got cutting tools, and a knack for design. If your pod's equipped with a telescoping ladder, I could rework that to snag the guy's tether."

"All right! I'm with you." Alverson pointed. "There's an access hatch to the baggage hold, there, in the floor. Is the school kid willing? He's small enough to squeeze through and unstrap the tie-down rigging. If the case is too bulky, he can unpack below and probably push the suit through."

The wealthy father-to-be was already on his knees, helped by the yellow-robed Hari Krishna to muscle the ring pulls and raise the hatch.

Alverson re-checked his instruments, uncrimped the limpet and re-engaged the lift gears. Then he crept the pod upward, while delivering a swift stream of instructions. "We're powered by microwave. Not harmful, except that your man will have to clamber over the topside dish. The focal point won't fry him, if I turn the orientation away from the beam from the satellite. But we'll be without full power for the duration. Our secondary solar panels and batteries are limited. They can handle the cabin life support, but not drive the lift engines. Once I open the downside airlock, we're going to lose heat pretty fast. Things could become unpleasantly chilly. Since the backup system isn't efficient enough to give us a rapid recovery, you people need to worry about hypothermia."

The doctor shrugged. "My elderly patient's equipped with spare blankets."

"Use them," said Alverson. "You can also take the sheets of thermal foil packed for the emergency canopy, in the hold."

From underfoot, the dropped headset squawked. "Alverson! Alverson, damn it! You've got that pod *moving!* Your strict orders were to hold position and stand by for the crew on the spider! If one of your passengers should come to harm—"

Alverson retrieved his discarded earpiece, shamefaced. The situation had escaped all the protocols: half his passengers were already down the metal gangway, deploying the wire tethers, and assisting the suited-up researcher into the emergency airlock. The shared impetus of the impromptu rescue was already beyond his recall, even if he had wanted to toe the line issued by home station.

While the dropped headset yammered, the grandmother across the cabin waved off its tirade and chuckled. "As if they think we were tame sheep in the first place, to venture off into space."

Alverson laughed. "I don't think ground station will buy the idea that I was subjected to mutiny." His sensitive fingers nursed the controls, edging the pod upward until the dome gently nosed into the climber's sled and lashed net of supplies. He fastened the limpet clamp. "Though I'm glad you agree that I'm risking my position for a worthy cause."

"You won't be fired," the pregnant wife snapped. "Parts of this station are privately funded. Our family business runs pods that need operators. We'd be pleased to have your experience."

"Thank you, ma'am, but I hope that's not necessary." Alverson eyed the wind speed and tweaked at the vanes. The pod shuddered anyway. Stationary and exposed to turbulence, this was scarcely the place for a scenic stop. Or a paid passenger's unlicensed excursion that could too easily compound into a wider disaster. Not pleased to be party to sending a second man into jeopardy, Alverson mopped his brow. He tried not to hang on the forward display that showed the inert adventurer, haplessly dangling. Whatever crazed impulse had brought him up here, Alverson could not dismiss him.

"No putting the brakes on human enterprise," he murmured, then powered up the airlock controls, and punched the pod's intercom.

"All ready," he announced. "Warn the man in the suit that the wind speed's variable. I'll shelter him with the vanes as I can, but he should link up with the double strength tether. If the doc and her crew aren't planning to scrub, proceed with the rescue at will."

"No faint hearts, here," the doctor responded. Seconds later, the pod shuddered again. The light that signaled the airlock's cycle flickered from green through yellow to red.

Alverson blinked stinging sweat from his eyes. All his concentration and skills were now bent toward trimming the tabs on the wind vanes. Thirty five miles was too low for null gravity. The suited man inching upward to hook in the one dangling would be nursing precarious balance, at best.

The pod shuddered, hard. Alverson swore, dancing delicate fingers over the joysticks to swing the vanes in position to compensate.

He was not alone in concern, under pressure. Aware of the high stakes, the woman who looked like a nanotech specialist spoke up in steady encouragement. "I'm station security, escorting a gene researcher carrying sensitive biological samples. I've been in ground contact by satellite phone. You should know that the victim you're trying to help has a name. Allen Henry Fitzgerald has a young wife, a mother, and two toddlers at home. Whatever uncertainties you might be feeling, they are blessed by your courage this minute."

"Thanks," said Alverson through his clamped teeth. He nursed the vanes, riveted, and forced his stopped breath through the muffled series of thumps that would be the outside man, scaling the dome. He could not turn, to look. If the microwave dish provided secure handholds, it also obscured the camera. Which was just as well, since the whip-lashing crosswinds kept Alverson fully absorbed without direct view for distraction. A small mistake now meant the spider's crew would be forced to divide their resources. Two injured victims would not be readily forgiven, once the press probed into the story.

A flash of movement in the forward camera——then a bump, as the climber's supply net scraped its way down to the dome. The comet researcher had lengthened its tether, a smart move that would act as a ladder for his descent. He would be above, then, now reaching the hook to drag the unconscious man into reach.

Changing the tether, tying in a pod wire, then cutting the home-grown gear free: no easy feat, wearing pressure suit gloves, and without a spare hand to use tools. Alverson kept his eyes glued to the wind gages, more than glad he did not have to watch.

The doc's voice on the intercom did not jar his touch as he jockeyed to hold the pod's attitude. "Alive. We're confirmed. The victim's unconscious, but breathing."

Alverson snatched up the headset. "Ground, to the spider's crew. Prepare to take on a live victim."

He could not hold back his sigh of relief as he saw the comet researcher use good sense and lower the man down ahead. More bumps as the victim was drawn into the pod, and the rescuer still topside tied himself in on the struts on the microwave dish. He had a good suit, and adequate air supply. Secured, he would wait for the spider.

The lights to the air lock cycled again, which meant the station maintenance guy had borrowed a bulky emergency suit, and made use of the baggage grapples.

Soon afterward, the doctor's prognosis came through. "Tell the med team en route: we have severe hypothermia, a dislocated shoulder, and frostbite in several fingers, where a loop in the tether cut circulation. My patient's not conscious, but he should pull through under prompt handling. How long for that spider?"

"Fifteen minutes," ground station responded.

Alverson relayed the message into the hold. Though he longed to take pause in near tearful relief, the wind vanes still commanded his pilot's reflexes. A snatched glance at the forward camera's screen showed a white-suited hand, outstretched from the strut of the dish. The comet man, now an injured man's hero, was sending a cheery thumbs up.

Alverson found he was able to speak. "There are chemical heat packs in the emergency first aid locker," he said, in case the enterprising doctor had not yet rummaged and helped herself. Then, through the headset, he importuned Nosy Alice. "Call the man's wife. Look for her listing under Allen Henry Fitzgerald, and let her know that her husband is under emergency medical treatment."

POWERING A SPACE ELEVATOR
by
Dr. Jordin T. Kare

Dr. Jordin T. Kare is a former astrophysicist (Ph.D., University of California at Berkeley, 1984) who evolved into a designer of advanced space technology at the Lawrence Livermore National Laboratory. He has led programs to develop laser-powered launch systems and miniature reusable launch vehicles, and is a two-time Fellow of the NASA Institute for Advanced Concepts. Since 1997 he has been an independent consultant to the aerospace industry and government, designing satellites for food (and the occasional beverage). He lives in Seattle with his wife, two cats, and a large collection of obsolete electronics.

POWERING LIFTERS ON a space elevator is a challenge. It takes about 50 megajoules of energy, or 15 kilowatt-hours, to pull a kilogram (2.2 lbs) up the ribbon from the ground to geosynchronous altitude. Carrying an engine and fuel won't work: even the most energetic chemical fuels, such as liquid hydrogen and liquid oxygen, burned in an ideal 100% efficient engine, only produce about 4 kilowatt-hours per kilogram. Batteries, flywheels, and other ways to store energy are all worse than chemical fuels—and you can't even throw them overboard once you've extracted their energy.

Nuclear fuels—uranium and plutonium—contain far more energy than any chemical fuel. No one has built a lifter-sized nuclear power plant, but it's certainly possible: some Russian satellites have carried small nuclear reactors. They only produced a few kilowatts of electricity, but megawatt-sized spacecraft power plants have been designed. The payload—including people—could be towed on a cable a few kilometers below the lifter mechanism, insulated by distance from the reactor's radiation. The biggest problem with a nuclear lifter is that an accident could be catastrophic: a broken ribbon, or even a broken lifter, could drop a reactor into the atmosphere anywhere around the equator. Nuclear-powered lifters will probably have to wait until space elevators are well-proven, low-risk technology.

If we rule out nuclear power, how about solar power? The best solar panels used on satellites generate about 100 watts per kilogram of panel in full sunlight, enough to lift themselves up a ribbon in 150 hours. But satellites in zero-gee can easily have moveable solar panels that turn to face the sun, while a lifter would probably have fixed panels which, averaged over a day, only produce about 60% of their peak power. Near the ground, where we need power the most, solar panels would be in Earth's shadow half the time. Plus, of course, a real lifter couldn't be all solar panel!

If half the lifter mass were solar panels, it would take roughly 25 days for a lifter to climb to geosynchronous altitude, compared to less than 5 days for a lifter that could travel at a steady 320 km/ hour (200 mph). So solar-powered lifters would be slow, and short on cargo capacity. They'd also be *very* expensive if they used current satellite-type solar panels, which cost several hundred dollars per watt. Fortunately, lifter panels could probably be much cheaper, since they don't have to fold up, or survive being shaken around in a rocket launch, or be guaranteed to last for 10 years.

Can we supply power along the ribbon with electrical conductors? Ordinary copper wire would be far too heavy. A twenty-ton lifter climbing at 90 meters per second (200 mph) needs 1.8 megawatts of drive power. A household extension cord that can carry about 1.8 *kilo*watts (15 amps at 120 volts) weighs around 100 grams per meter; a mere 200 kilometers of such cable would weigh 20 tons. Of course, you'd really use a much higher voltage than 120 volts—but even at 120 kilovolts, it would still take a current of 15 amps to transmit 1.8 megawatts, and a cable for that would need at least as much copper as our extension cord, and a *lot* more insulation.

Low-temperature superconductors, the kind used in superconducting magnets for MRI machines and particle accelerators, can carry thousands of amperes per square millimeter without any electrical resistance loss. Two thin threads of superconductor could carry power the length of an elevator ribbon—but only at liquid-helium temperatures, around 4.7 K (4.7 degrees above absolute zero). Alas, there's just no way to keep them that cold.

So-called high-temperature superconductors, made from complex materials like yttrium barium copper oxide (YBaCuO) can work at 50 to 80 K. That's still pretty cold, but it's possible to keep things that cold in space if they're shielded from the sun and the warm Earth. Unfortunately, a thin space elevator ribbon can't afford the mass for sun-and Earth-shades. Also, high-temperature superconductors can't carry as much current as low-temperature ones; with the best materials today, 20 tons of superconductor might just barely carry a few tens of amperes the length of a space elevator.

There are other problems, too. For example, if the conductors are bare, they will be shorted out over a few kilometers by the weakly-conducting plasma that is everywhere in space. If the conductors are insulated, not only will they be much heavier, but there's no easy way for a lifter to make contact with them. Massive space elevators of the future may use superconducting power cables to run their lifters, but it just doesn't look practical for first-generation elevators.

(Using the elevator ribbon itself as a conductor has been suggested, since some forms of carbon nanotubes are highly conductive, but unless we're lucky enough to find a form of nanotube that is both super-strong *and* a high-temperature superconductor, there's not enough cross-section in a space elevator ribbon to carry a useful amount of power.)

That brings us to the best way, so far, of powering lifters—a completely weightless "extension cord" in the form of a laser beam. There are three pieces to a laser power beaming system: a big laser on the ground, a telescope (and other optics) to transmit the beam, and a receiver on each lifter. We'll start at the end with the receiver, and work backwards.

The easiest way to turn a laser beam into electricity is with photovoltaic (PV) cells—semiconductor devices that convert light to electricity. Solar cells are one type of PV cell, designed to work best with sunlight. For a laser receiver, we'd use "laser cells" made of a single layer of silicon or gallium arsenide, like most solar cells, but with optical and electrical properties tweaked to give the best efficiency at the laser wavelength. (Some modern solar cells use two or three layers of semiconductor, each layer capturing a different part of the sun's spectrum for greater efficiency; that doesn't help with single-color laser light).

Good laser cells can convert 50% to 60% of the laser beam power to electricity, compared to 20 to 30% efficiency for solar cells. Less of the power that falls on them turns into heat, so they can handle more power than solar cells without getting too hot.

Laser cells can generate perhaps 5000 watts per square meter. With a 90% efficient electric motor, we'd need about 400 square meters of cells to power a 20-ton lifter. That's a 24-meter (80 foot) diameter circular array, which is big—several times bigger than the solar panels on the largest current satellites—but not unreasonable. It would weigh about 2 tons.

To focus the laser beam on the receiver array, we need a sizeable telescope, sometimes known as a beam director. The size of the telescope is set by diffraction—a fundamental physical limit—and here we'll use one equation:

$$d_t = 2 \, R \, l \, / \, d_r$$

The diameter d_t of the telescope is proportional to the range R that we need to transmit over, times the laser wavelength l, divided by the receiver diameter d_r. (You'll often see slightly different values like 2.44, in place of the 2 in this equation; the exact value depends on how you define the "edge" of a fuzzy, blurred-out beam). We know R: 36,000 km for geosynchronous orbit. We also know what wavelength—what color of light—we want to use: the most efficient PV cells work best with wavelengths of 0.7 to 0.8 microns in the near infrared, just a little longer than the longest wavelength we can see, Using $l = 0.8$ microns and 24 meters for d_r, we get $d_t = 2.4$ meters. That's a good-sized telescope, but well within what we can can build (and afford); the biggest astronomical telescopes today are 8 to 10 meters in diameter. In practice, we'd want a bigger telescope, perhaps 5 meters, to allow for other effects that spread the beam, including jitter (vibrations in the telescope) and imperfections in both the laser beam and the telescope.

Turbulence in the atmosphere will also spread the laser beam, typically by about 10 microradians. That's 10 meters of beam width for every 1000 km of range, or 360 meters at geosynchronous orbit, which is far too much for us to tolerate. Fortunately, astronomers have learned how to compensate for such turbulence. They measure the turbulence hundreds of times per second by looking at light coming downward through the atmosphere, and distort a special "adaptive" mirror in precisely the right way to correct for the atmosphere. Astronomers have to generate the downward light by scattering a laser beam off the upper atmosphere, but we can simply put a small down-pointing laser on each lifter.

Occasionally, a laser beam will be blocked by clouds, and the lifter it's powering will have to pause for a while. While we can minimize that by picking sites for the laser that have mostly clear weather, we will eventually want to have more lasers than we have lifters, at sites far enough apart so they have different weather. That would also keep the lifters moving if one laser has a problem or needs repairs.

Not all of the power coming out of the laser will get to the lifter. Some will be absorbed or scattered by the atmosphere; even the clearest air scatters some light. A little will be absorbed or scattered by the telescope mirrors. Some will miss the edges of the receiver, especially at long range where diffraction and other effects make the edges of the beam fuzzy. Overall, we will do well if two-thirds of the laser power gets to the receiver. If the receiver itself is 50% efficient, we need 6 megawatts of laser power to drive our 20-ton lifter:

6 MW laser power
x 0.67 (transmission efficiency)
x 0.5 (receiver efficiency)
x 0.9 (motor efficiency)
= 1.8 MW drive power

Unfortunately, there are only a few kinds of laser that work in the right part of the near infrared, and right now none of them can produce anything close to 6 megawatts. The highest-power lasers, built for military testing, have power levels around one megawatt —the exact numbers are classified—but work at wavelengths where standard photovoltaic cells don't work at all. The closest is the Chemical Oxygen-Iodine Laser (COIL) which works at 1.35 microns; the U.S. Air Force is developing megawatt-class COILs for its AirBorne Laser (ABL) to shoot down short-range ballistic missiles. Also, these high-power military lasers can only run for a few seconds or minutes at a time, while a Lifter-powering laser will need to run for days on end.

The laser we'd like to use for the Space Elevator is called a Free Electron Laser, or FEL. FELs work by firing a beam of electrons between two rows of magnets. The magnetic fields make the electrons wiggle side to side as they travel—the magnet assemblies are even called "wigglers"—and when electrons wiggle, they emit light. If the electron beam is dense enough and high enough in energy, the light and the electrons interact to produce a concentrated, single-wavelength beam. FEL's can be tuned to any wavelength by picking the right beam energy and wiggler dimensions, although shorter wavelengths are harder. They're reasonably efficient (up to 20% or so) and run on electricity, with no expensive chemicals or dangerous exhaust. So far, though, the biggest FEL (at the Department of Energy's Jefferson Laboratory) only puts out about 20 kilowatts, at a wavelength near 5 microns. Oh, and that 20 kilowatt laser has cost about $30 million to build; at that rate a 6 MW laser would cost $9 billion!

FEL advocates are confident they will be able to build large, efficient, short-wavelength FEL's much more cheaply once the bugs are worked out in the research lab, but FEL's have been around for 20 years or so, and progress has been slow so far. Fortunately, there are now alternatives to the FEL, some of which look much easier to build. We'll just mention one of these: the Diode Pumped Alkali vapor Laser, or DPAL.

The DPAL is one of several kinds of lasers that start with arrays of semiconductor diode lasers —high power versions of the lasers in laser pointers and CD players. Diode lasers convert electricity to light very efficiently, and they can run continuously for thousands of hours. They're also cheap—as low as $10 per watt today, and getting cheaper. But individual diode lasers put out at most a few watts of power. Arrays of diode lasers can put out kilowatts or megawatts, but not in a single tight beam, so they can't transmit power directly to a lifter, except perhaps for its first few kilometers of travel. For longer ranges, diode arrays have to "pump" some other material, which generates a single intense beam. Until recently, this material was a solid rod or slab of glass or crystal, which worked fine for lasers up to a few thousand watts (although at a wavelength of 1.06 microns, a little too long for PV receivers). But for higher power lasers, the rod or slab would get too thick to be kept cool, and would overheat or crack.

In the DPAL, invented in 2003 by researchers from the Lawrence Livermore National Laboratory, the second material is vaporized rubidium or cesium (both alkali metals) mixed with helium and some other gases. Since it's a gas, it can flow through the laser head and then through a cooling system. Only a laboratory-sized test DPAL has been built at this writing, but it works just as predicted from theory, and it looks like DPALs as large as a few megawatts will be possible soon. Conveniently, DPALs produce just the right wavelengths for PV receivers—0.695 microns for rubidium, 0.795 microns for cesium.

If we just can't get a good laser at the right wavelength for PV cells, there is another option: we can use the laser beam as a simple heat source to run a turbine and generator. The flat PV array on the lifter would be replaced by a large concave mirror that focuses the laser energy onto a heat exchanger. Fluid—probably a mix of helium and xenon gas—would be pumped through the heat exchanger, gets hot, expand to drive a turbine, and then cool off in a large radiator and return to the pump. These systems, called dynamic power systems, aren't quite as efficient as laser-driven PV cells, but they don't care what the laser wavelength is.

There's much more to powering lifters than we've talked about here. For instance, we will want to store a little energy on board the lifters, perhaps in a flywheel, so the lifter won't abruptly stop if the laser beam is briefly interrupted. We'll need a way to get rid of the energy produced by a descending lifter without overheating its brakes —and no, we can't somehow pipe that energy to an upward-bound lifter, or at least not easily; see the problems of power cables discussed up above. If we do use laser power beaming, and we want to put the lasers on mountaintops far from the elevator anchor, we'll need a way to get the lifters up the first few hundred kilometers until they can "see" the lasers, and we'll have to worry about airplanes and satellites flying through the laser beam. But if we can get a good, cheap (well, not exorbitantly expensive, anyway) laser, be it FEL or DPAL or something else entirely, laser powered lifters are the way to go.

THE COUNTERWEIGHT:
THE "OTHER" SPACE ELEVATOR ANCHOR
by
Blaise Gassend

Blaise Gassend is a PhD candidate at the Massachusetts Institute of Technology. In 2001 he graduated from the Ecole Polytechnique in France. Then in 2003, he received a Masters degree from MIT in Electrical Engineering and Computer Science. He has done research both in computer hardware security, and in femtosecond lasers. His interests include rocket engine design, Space Elevator ribbon dynamics, underwater hockey and SCUBA diving. Visit his website at http://blaisegassend.com

IN THIS CHAPTER, we look at a very important part of the space elevator: the counterweight. The counterweight is basically a large mass attached to the far end of the space elevator ribbon. Its main purpose is to keep gravity from pulling the whole structure down. In what follows we shall attempt to answer the key questions about the counterweight: why it is necessary, where it is located, what it is made of, and how it is used.

Role of the Counterweight

The space elevator is only possible because of a subtle balance between gravity and centrifugal force. Gravity is the force that keeps you pinned to the Earth, preventing you from floating up into the sky; most people are familiar with gravity. Centrifugal force is a bit trickier. Most people have encountered it while driving fast around a sharp curve. It is the force that pushes you sideways towards the outside of the turn.

For the space elevator, centrifugal force arises because of the Earth's daily rotation around its axis. On the equator, it pulls objects straight up. You probably haven't noticed this force yet because at ground level, it is dwarfed by gravity. Farther from the Earth, this is no longer true. As you move away from the Earth, always staying above the same point on the Equator, gravity gets weaker, while centrifugal force gets stronger. About 36,000 km (22,000 mi.) up, the two forces balance out. There is as much upward pull as downward pull, and you just float in place. This is where geosynchronous satellites live. They stay in a fixed place above the equator, at just the right altitude for gravity and centrifugal force to cancel out. Satellites like this are said to be in geosynchronous earth orbit (GEO).

Unlike a satellite, the space elevator extends over a wide range of altitudes, starting from the ground and reaching far into space. If the elevator is less than 36,000 km (22,000 mi.) long, gravity exceeds centrifugal force everywhere, and the elevator is pulled down along all its length. It can only remain standing as a tower, with the bottom holding up the top. A tower into space would have to be incredibly massive to avoid buckling and collapsing. Structures that are held up by the top like the space elevator cannot buckle, allowing them to be much lighter. However, to stay up, a space elevator has to be longer; long enough to extend past GEO. That way, at the top of the elevator, centrifugal force exceeds gravity, creating a net upwards force.

Simply extending beyond GEO is not sufficient in itself to keep the elevator up. For the elevator to stay upright, the total upwards force along all its length must exceed the total downward force. For this to happen in practice, it is usually necessary to place a big mass at the very top of the elevator —where the upwards pull is greatest. This big mass is what we call the counterweight. The counterweight isn't necessary on all space elevators. Depending on the tapering of the ribbon, centrifugal force acting on the ribbon above GEO can be sufficient to keep the elevator up. For example, an untapered ribbon about 150,000 km (93,000 mi.) long wouldn't need a counterweight. From now on, we shall stick to so-called uniform-stress elevators that use the ribbon material's strength most efficiently, and which are tapered; they always need a counterweight.

A Giant Sling

You can imagine the space elevator as a giant sling. The Earth is holding on to one end of the sling and rotating around its axis. The counterweight on the other end of the sling is pulling outward, keeping the ribbon taut enough to be climbed.

The similarity with a sling would be even more striking if the elevator was ever to break. The counterweight and the part of the elevator that is attached to it would be flung far out into space. The longer the elevator, the farther it would go. In current plans, the elevator is long enough that, in the event of a break, the counterweight would leave the Earth's gravitational influence completely and become a satellite of the Sun. For all practical purposes, if the elevator breaks, it is completely lost. This is actually an advantage because the top part of the elevator, with its heavy counterweight, is guaranteed not to fall back to Earth. Nor can it stay in orbit where it might collide with other assets, particularly other space elevators. When it is built, the space elevator will probably include multiple redundant ribbons near its base, where breaks are most likely, to prevent the counterweight from ever being completely disconnected from the ground.

The sling effect can be turned into a big advantage for solar system exploration. If a payload is attached high enough along the space elevator and released, it will be flung out into space. This is a cheap way to start a voyage to the planets. Which planets can be reached this way depends on how long the elevator is.

Elevator Length

We have already seen that the space elevator has to extend beyond GEO to hold itself up. It seems natural to wonder how much past GEO it should extend. For space systems, an important criterion is mass, so one might wonder what length has the lowest mass. It turns out that, as the counterweight is moved farther from GEO, the total mass of the elevator decreases. This may seem paradoxical, since a longer elevator has a greater ribbon mass, but it is easy to explain: as the elevator gets longer, the outward pull on the counterweight increases, so less counterweight mass is needed to keep the elevator up.

In theory, the lightest elevator would be infinitely long. In practice however, an infinitely long elevator would not work. This is primarily because the elevator uses a tapered ribbon. Beyond GEO, the ribbon keeps getting skinnier as you move up. If the ribbon is much skinnier at the top of the elevator than at GEO, you start to run into problems because of the way disturbances move along the elevator.

Recall the last time you threw a pebble into a pond. First you see a splash as the pebble enters the water. Then you see rings of waves moving slowly away from the place where the pebble hit the water. The disturbance caused by the pebble created some waves in the pond. The same thing happens on a space elevator ribbon. If the ribbon gets jolted, for example by a lifter that releases a satellite, the jolt creates a wave that propagates up and down the ribbon.

However, the size of this wave can change as it propagates, if the cross-section of the ribbon changes. A wave that starts at the equator may initially be very small, but as it propagates upwards and the ribbon gets skinnier, the wave becomes bigger to conserve energy. If the ribbon becomes too skinny, the wave ends up being big enough to snap it. Because of this effect, the ribbon's cross-section shouldn't vary too much across the length of the elevator, which effectively means that the elevator shouldn't be too long.

The moon provides another reason to limit the elevator's length. As the elevator gets longer, the moon's gravitational influence on the elevator increases. The force exerted by the Moon on the elevator varies on a daily basis as the elevator rotates with the Earth, as if the moon was rhythmically plucking the elevator ribbon. This plucking is very near a resonance frequency of the elevator, so it tends to create large oscillations in the ribbon. The longer the elevator, the closer it gets to the Moon, and the worse this problem becomes.

The current design calls for the elevator to be about 100,000 km (62,000 mi.) long, less than a third of the way to the Moon. With this length, the ribbon cross-section at the counterweight is more than half the cross-section at GEO, so we need not worry about small disturbances becoming too large as they propagate. Moreover, a payload dropped from the end of the elevator can reach Venus, Mars, and the asteroid belt, and nearly reach Mercury. Finally, for a 20 T (44,000 lbs.) payload, the mass of the counterweight is about 650 T (1.4 million lbs.), holding up 890 T (2 million lbs.) of ribbon.

What to Use as the Counterweight

That's a pretty heavy counterweight we need at the end of the elevator! What should all that mass be? There are many possible answers. Someday, perhaps, the counterweight will be a space station. The gravity in the station will mainly be due to centrifugal force. Inhabitants of the station will weigh half of their Earth weight, and will stand with their head towards the Earth, and their feet pointing at the stars. The low gravity will make the station into an interesting location for a hospital, a hotel, or a research lab. I look forward to spending some time at the counterweight hotel some day, but for the first elevator we need to focus our efforts on getting the minimum useful space elevator up. All the glamour will come later.

When science fiction writers build a space elevator, they often build it from an asteroid. First they go out to the asteroid belts and pick a nice carbonaceous asteroid. Then they move it into an orbit around the Earth, set up a factory on the asteroid to produce ribbon material, and unroll the resulting ribbon down to Earth. The remains of the asteroid are finally used as the elevator's counterweight.

This romantic vision is needed to build a massive elevator with the infrastructure to support high speed magnetic levitation transportation to orbit, but seems unlikely with our current level of achievement in space. Fortunately, Dr Edwards has shown us that a much lighter space elevator is possible. One that can be entirely built with materials launched from the Earth—at great expense, but with technology that already exists. In this context, it is good that the counterweight is just a big mass. It doesn't have to do anything special. To keep things cheap, we will just build the counterweight out of all the spare junk that we have to put into space anyway to get the elevator built.

The very first counterweight will be the remains of the spacecraft from which the initial space elevator ribbon was deployed. On it you will find many derelict items: the spools around which the initial ribbon was wound; the magneto-plasma-dynamic (MPD) thrusters that maintained the elevator in a geosynchronous orbit as the ribbon was deployed; the fuel tanks and solar panels that powered the MPD thrusters; the mechanisms that slowed down the ribbon as it was fed out towards the Earth; the radiators that dispersed the energy that was released during deployment; the communication, navigation and guidance devices that kept the initial spacecraft oriented in space and in touch with ground control; and finally, the structure that keeps the spacecraft together.

Later, as the space elevator is built up to its full 20 T (44,000 lbs.) capacity, the counterweight has to be built up proportionally. During build up, hundreds of construction lifters will climb the ribbon laying new ribbon as they go, each strengthening the elevator by a few percent. As the elevator ribbon gets wider, the counterweight has to be made heavier to hold it up. The lifters are used for this purpose. Each one climbs to the top, and shuts down, contributing its mass to the total mass of the counterweight. By the time the elevator is fully built up, the counterweight will be a cemetery of construction lifters parked one below another under the initial spacecraft. An orbital junkyard, tasked with the critical mission of keeping the space elevator standing.

A Prime Location

It seems likely that once the space elevator has been completed, the reduced cost of access to space will cause a sharp increase in space activity. The location of the counterweight has a number of unique features. It has about half of Earth-normal gravity. It is readily accessible via lifters. It is geosynchronous (i.e. it always stays above the same place on the Earth), but is much higher than any geosynchronous satellite, and therefore it can see more of Earth's surface. It is at the end of the elevator, where it won't prevent lifters from going by. At some point people will want to make use of this piece of prime real-estate.

The good news is that this is easy to do. To put something up at the counterweight, you just send it up along the elevator and park it at the counterweight. To avoid increasing the counterweight mass, you then jettison one of the old pieces of junk that are up there. Since most of counterweight is initially old lifters, it is relatively easy to jettison the counterweight mass a bit at a time. Some care is nevertheless necessary when releasing a lifter. Indeed, if the lifter is simply released, it will "fall" straight up and hit other lifters or the initial spacecraft.

The main point is that the counterweight doesn't have to remain a junkyard forever. It can be progressively transformed into a location of considerable economic activity. Initially, it may be used for simple scientific experiments, or for communication purposes. Later, more ambitious projects like the counterweight space station will become possible.

The Counterweight and Space Elevator Dynamics

For the most part, we have discussed the space elevator as if it is a rigid structure. This is only approximately true. In fact, the elevator can undergo many different motions around the idealized rigid configuration we have been considering: it can swing North-South or East-West like a giant upside-down pendulum, it can bob up and down like person on the end of a bungee jumping cord, and waves can propagate up and down its length. There are also twisting motions, but they have hardly been studied so far. Engineers classify motions by their period, or how long it takes for the motion to repeat itself.

Because of these motions, the counterweight will continuously be moving around. It will mainly follow the swinging and bobbing motions, and be impervious to all the shorter period waves. Most of the waves that reach the counterweight will simply get reflected back towards the Earth. The motion of the counterweight will be fairly elaborate because each motion has a different period. The North-South swinging has a period close to 24 hours. Swinging in the East-West direction is slower: once every few days. Bobbing up and down occurs every few hours. Seen from the Earth, the counterweight will be slowly and rhythmically moving about on the end of its 100,000 km (62,000 mi.) long leash.

This motion is perfectly acceptable as long as it doesn't get too large. How large is too large? Nobody knows for sure yet, but for a structure this long and flexible, a 1,000 km (620 mi.) motion isn't much of a problem. What will cause this motion? Many things. Sudden changes in solar wind will cause the elevator to start swaying. The gravitational forces from the Sun and Moon will be particularly effective at stirring up North-South swinging with a period near 24 hours, but they will also cause some 12 hour period Up-Down and East-West motion. The wind will generate a lot of short period waves. Lifters starting and stopping and debris avoidance maneuvers by the liftport will also contribute.

Calculations made so far suggest that perturbations like a change in solar wind could cause oscillations with an amplitude of 100 km (62 mi.) in the elevator. These perturbations are difficult to predict. But for debris avoidance, ground controllers will need to know the position of the elevator to within a few kilometers. Therefore, they will need to track the position of the elevator, and in some cases control it. These detection and actuation activities can occur in one of four places: the liftport, the counterweight, the ribbon and the lifters. Which locations are most appropriate is currently the object of much speculation.

The counterweight can certainly be used to observe the elevator's motion. It can be equipped with a radar retro-reflector allowing it to be easily tracked from the Earth. This should give good information about the swinging and bobbing motions of the elevator, and a bit of information about the large period vibrations it is undergoing. This information could also be gathered by measuring accelerations and forces at the counterweight. To get access to information about shorter period waves running along the ribbon (periods less than an hour or so) takes more effort. Indeed, the counterweight is made up of many construction lifters parked along the top of the ribbon. The shorter period waves will be reflected by the lowermost lifter. So to detect them, sensors have to be placed on that particular lifter.

Similarly, the counterweight can be used to help reduce motion in the elevator. The brute force approach would be to use thrusters to push the counterweight in a way that counteracts the elevator's motion. Unfortunately this would require a constant supply of propellant. Reeling the ribbon in or out in synchrony with the elevator's motion is a cheaper alternative, inspired by children using their legs to get a swing moving, but it may not be strong enough to have much effect on the elevator. Finally, the way the ribbon is attached to the counterweight can be used for damping. With a rigid attachment, waves are perfectly reflected by the counterweight. If the ribbon is held via suitably selected shock absorbers, waves that reach the counterweight can be completely absorbed. As with sensing, shorter period waves can only be controlled properly from the lowermost lifter.

Clearly, the counterweight can play an important part in controlling the space elevator's dynamics. However, I would argue against using it, except as a radar reflector. Indeed, most of the detection and actuation that can be done at the counterweight can be done just as well at the liftport. The only exceptions are the accelerometer based detection and the thruster based actuation, which are of dubious value anyway, the former being superseded by radar tracking, and the latter needing propellant. If functionality can be placed either at the liftport or at the counterweight, it should always be placed at the liftport for ease of construction and maintenance. You don't want to repair a faulty damper at the counterweight if that damper could have been placed on Earth! If for some reason the elevator really needs to be controlled from the top, that functionality would best be implemented from the bottommost lifter only. That way even the shorter period oscillations are accessible, and the functionality can easily be restored in the event of a breakdown by sending up a new bottommost lifter.

Conclusion

This concludes our discussion of the counterweight. As we have seen, its main purpose is to hold the space elevator up. It can also be used to help control the elevator's dynamics, but it may be unwise to place such important functionality out of reach of easy repair. For the first elevator, the counterweight will be made of assorted equipment —mainly construction lifters —left over from the deployment process. As the space economy grows, this dead mass will progressively be replaced by more useful equipment and facilities, and someday, perhaps, a vacation resort with an unforgettable view!

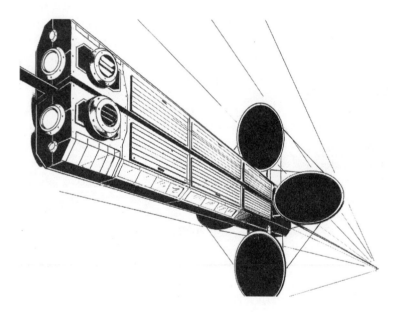

BASIC FACTS—an email exchange between:
Jody Lynn Nye and Michael Laine

JLN: First, how high up will the living platform be?

ML: The Platform is going to be about 22300 miles up in a geo-synchronized orbit.

JLN: How large do you anticipate it to be?

ML: At the beginning, the living platform is going to be quite small, but within five years, I expect it to be about as big as a midsized office building. In another ten years, it's going to get very large: big enough for about 100 people to live and work there on a daily basis. After 30 years, there should be enough space for tens of thousands of people to live, work, and play on the living platform. Also, eventually there will be more than one of these. In the early days, there will just be one and it will be used as a deployment station for solar satellites, it can be used for crystal manufacturing, electronics, research, and it could even be a "jump-off" point for the moon, mars, and eventually deeper into space. In the more developed days of the project, the platform will be used for just about everything, including housing, entertainment, storage, hospitals and retirement centers.

JLN: How wide will the ribbon be when it is able to accommodate the elevator car, the Lifter?

ML: The ribbon will be 3 feet wide at first, for commercial use, but will eventually grow to be 5-8 feet wide when we start transporting heavy-lift cargo.

JLN: How large will the Lifter car be? I know you told me how long the ribbon itself will be, but I can't recall the precise figure.

ML: The car will be 140 feet tall, 70 feet ide. http://www.liftport.com/gallery/Concepts_Lifter that should be a good link to Nyein's concept art of the lifter. The actual living area of the lifter is really about half the total size, because most of the width is the solar panels. Its actually just a tall thin 'box' that the people will stay in, while traveling back and forth. Some people have described it like living in a motor home, for a week.

JLN: Do you have a guess on what the price per kilogram will be to transport cargo? Ballpark, in the tens, hundreds, thousands of dollars?

ML: Well, we've got 62,000 miles of ribbon to construct, and that will be a little expensive. Our goal price that we are estimating is $400/pound. That price will change over time, but that is the goal that we are reaching for.

JLN: What is the assumed weight capacity that the engine will be able to raise on the ribbon?

ML: The weight capacity will be 20 total tons (5 tons of cargo, 7 tons of infrastructure—the remainder is excess capacity and safety margin), and the Elevator will make 200 trips per year. The goal is to eventually have four elevators. The second will be the same as the first, and the third and fourth systems will be able to take 100 tons of cargo per day. There will be two "up ribbons" and two "down ribbons," 2 light capacity fast lifters and two heavy capacity slow lifters.

GOING UP?
by
Jody Lynn Nye

"BUT, MOMMY, I don't want to see Grandpa!" Leon Sanchez said in a whiny, singsong voice. He sat on the floor of the Elevator with his back against the viewing window. He jabbed savagely at the controls of his handheld game with his thumbs. "Shut up and—"

"If you tell that joke one more time, I'm taking away your electronic game," his mother, Elisa, sighed. She tapped her foot and peered down at her fifteen-year-old son with the mix of empathy and exasperation of any mother. "You wanted to come along."

"Only because you said the alternative was staying with Uncle Cisco," Leon said, resentfully.

"That was very nice of Frank," Elisa said, who never used the Hispanic form of anyone's name, like that was going to change who they were. "He was looking forward to having you stay while we visit Papi."

"Yeah, so I could babysit Maria Leona and Tati. That's sure a vacation."

"Your cousins adore you!" Elisa groaned. "Fine, play your game. But you are missing the experience of a lifetime!"

"It'll look the same coming down as going up," Leon muttered.

The trip up had taken almost seven days already. By the end of the first day, Leon had explored the entire Space Elevator car, including the control center, and there was nowhere left to go. A week, a whole week of his precious vacation wasted! When they said the car would be traveling over 125 miles per hour, that sounded fast, but you could hardly tell the car was moving! It would have been more exciting in a real elevator. At least there he could have had the fun of pushing all the buttons and seeing the annoyance on the faces of the other passengers, or racing the car up a flight or two on the stairs. Here the 'floors' were farther apart (his dad droned on endlessly) than the distance from New York to Moscow. He didn't want to go to any of *those* places, either.

The trip to Quito had been cool, he thought. He paused while the game made fake explosion noises and registered the new level he had attained. His family had stopped over in the Galapagos Islands and gone out on the rocks with a naturalist to look at birds and lizards. In freshman year he had done a paper on the blue-footed booby. Got an A for it, too, or he would have, if Selana McCartney hadn't said he had copied off her notes. Could he help it if she left them in the encyclopedia? Still, it had gotten him interested in the islands. Darwin had stopped off there in his ship, the *Beagle*. Old Darwin had gotten to see thousands of things that no one else had ever seen before. And what was Leon going to see? Nothing. Trillions of miles of nothing. And some old people. Maybe he should have stayed home with Uncle Francisco.

His parents kept trying to tell him that the journey was the important thing. That, he thought with a superior sneer, was what adults said to you when you had to endure something boring that you couldn't get out of. They made it sound like you were gaining a worthwhile experience.

Outside the window, the bright glow of Earth looked like a scene out of *Star Wars*, with the constellations beyond tiny pinpoints of light on a black background, now that the car had ascended above the atmosphere. He had long ago stopped looking out. The only thing that kept him from going out of his mind was the entertainment. Side screens were spaced around the observation room in between the huge floor-to-ceiling plexiglass windows. They showed endless commercial announcements for the attractions on the platform station, punctuated by brief news broadcasts in five or six languages, full-length movies and television shows, different on each screen to suit different tastes. Though there was on-demand video and audio programs in their cabin, Leon hovered around the side screen in the observation lounge that he had staked out as 'his' territory, the one that showed horror movies and situation comedies. There were a few other teens on the transport, but they were traveling together and didn't want to hang out with him.

The smartly uniformed steward came by and touched Elise on the shoulder.

"We're going to be arriving very shortly. Please go back to your seats and stay buckled up until the doors open."

"Is it going to be bumpy?" Elise asked, nervously.

"No, ma'am," the steward smiled, "but when this car stops moving, you'll be in zero gee. We don't want everyone hitting inertia, then the ceiling."

Leon laughed. It was the first funny thing anyone had said to him. Privately, he was looking forward to trying out no gravity. He heard the astronauts threw up when they first tried it, and he vowed he wouldn't, to the extent of eating no breakfast. He had to admit that low blood sugar was part of the reason he was cranky. Curiously, he followed his mother back to the assigned seats that they had hardly occupied since they left the Terminal a week before.

"Is this awesome?" his father, Miguel, demanded, a grin stretching from one side of his thin face to the other. He was already strapped in, but his fists were clenched in anticipation. "I can hardly wait. In a minute we're going to lift off!"

Leon sighed. Were all parents such an embarrassment? "Yeah, right."

Miguel wasn't going to be deterred by his offspring. "Strap in! Yeah, look on the screen. It's coming really soon."

The LiveCam monitors spotted around the elevator 'car,' as the crew referred to it, alternated showing the face of the Earth below them and the platform above. Tying both images together was the black polymer ribbon eleven yards wide and one micron deep—was it really that thin? —that was the track on which the car ran. He had been disappointed that they weren't going all the way out to the top of the ribbon, 62,000 miles up. You couldn't go that far on Earth, no matter what direction you flew.

At first, the Earth had been huge. Leon found it interesting, for about the first hour. Since the elevator's track was tethered in the waters off the western coast of South America, the view never changed, except to recede away from them, very slowly. It took a few days before the platform began to come into view, and it grew from a tiny, square speck, also very slowly, into a bigger square. Leon couldn't work up any enthusiasm for arrival at a station that had been in sight for ages. It was like Jacques Cousteau pretending for the TV cameras that he was surprised the *Calypso* had arrived in Antarctica, which was like only three thousand miles across. Now the upper view was full of detail like hatches, lights, big white numbers, and some tiny floating specks. Were those little moving things people?

All of a sudden, the side screens stopped showing movies. There was a collective groan from the passengers, but it died away as a siren sounded. A deep announcer's voice echoed over all the speakers.

"Ladies and gentlemen, please pay attention to your cabin stewards as we go through instructions for safe locomotion in zero-gee."

The uniformed men and women moved to strategic points around the observation center, and began to demonstrate swimming movements. Leon kept his chin lowered, but watched very closely under his eyelids.

"...There are handholds in easy reach on every surface of the station. Pull yourself along. You'll come to find that it's easier than walking. You've all had personal instruction on how to use the toilet facilities, which is the hardest thing to adjust to in space, but please feel free to ask any one of the station staff if you need help with anything. And if at any time you feel uncomfortable or distressed, any of us will be happy to assist you. And now," the announcer said, portentiously, "we welcome you to the LiftPort platform."

All the stewards, smiling broadly, floated up into the air like genies rising out of a six-pack of bottles. They clapped their hands, and the passengers, enchanted, joined in.

"Welcome!" they shouted.

"Am I in space, Bernard?" a woman's voice asked petulantly. "It doesn't feel like I'm in space. Whooops!"

Leon felt the floor under him seem to drop away. His hands and knees rose of their own accord, as if he was lying in a pool of water. His mother and father fumbled with their shoulder harnesses. Miguel looked more thrilled than Leon had ever seen him.

"Come on, Leon!" Elisa called, holding out a hand to him. "Join us!"

Trying not to seem too eager, Leon tucked his electronic game away and unclicked his buckle. He crossed his legs and put his hands behind his head, as if it was no big deal to attain a state of null gravity. No air sickness at all. He rose gently out of his chair, keeping a casual expression even though inside he was thrilled to pieces. *Take that, John Glenn*, he thought.

"Look at the big shot," Miguel laughed. He grabbed Leon's arm and began to windmill his other arm and legs toward the exit, towing his son behind him. "Come on, let's go see Papi!"

They swam out into the arrival hall. No gravity meant that there were no neat ranks of friends and relatives awaiting the carload of visitors. Instead, people filled the air like flakes in a snowglobe. Leon scanned the bobbing faces for the one familiar one somewhere in the crowd, worrying that he wouldn't recognize his grandfather after almost two years. Suddenly, a pair of feet upward, and Leon found himself nose to upside-down nose with Elisa's father, Roberto Leon Milagro de Fuentes.

"Leonito!" The old man grabbed him around the head and gave him a fierce hug. "Look how big you are!"

"Papi!" Leon shouted. "Papi, I missed you!"

He forgot all about his fifteen-year-old dignity, and kicked at the air until he was facing the same direction as the old man. He gave him a fierce hug. Then, conscious that his parents were watching, he let go and floated a little way back. "Wow, you look good, Papi."

The old man's eyes crinkled. "I feel good, Leonito. And look at you! What's this with the hair?"

Leon's hand went up self-consciously to the gelled spikes. "All the guys are wearing it like this."

"So you have to do what they do? Never mind. I'm happy to see you. There's my little girl!"

With incredible dexterity, the old man shifted orientation again and propelled himself toward Elisa and Miguel. He gathered them up in a big hug, which was just as well, because Dad kept spinning around, unable to stabilize himself in one direction.

"Papi!" Elisa was as surprised as Leon when she got a good look at her father. "You look so well."

"This is the best thing I ever did, except marry and have you babies," Roberto said. "Miami can't compare with this. Come and see my apartment!"

PAPI KEPT TALKING all the way down the long corridor and up the elevator, or was it out? Leon made his way as his grandfather did, using U-shaped handholds set in the walls to propel himself, and to hang onto when the capsule-shaped lift gave them a temporary taste of gravity.

"This whole section is the retirement community, and it's a fantastic place, let me tell you. When I sold my two-flat, everyone said I was crazy to move up here. I tell them every day that they're wrong."

He glanced at Leon, who was listening to every word. "You'd be proud of me, chico. Your old grandfather was the first to sign a lease in this complex. I'm a trendsetter. Now I get to tell all the sexy grandmas on the Internet, come and visit me, I live near the moon. And a couple of them came up already. Nothing worked out so far, but it has been fun."

Mama blushed at this reference to Papi's sex life. No one ever wanted to think of their parents doing it. Now that Leon thought about it, he didn't like the idea, either.

"You look like you feel good, Papi," Elisa said, hastily changing the subject.

"I feel terrific. I don't hurt any more. The pressure is gone. I love floating around like this. It's like swimming all of the time, and never having to take a breath."

"Aren't you afraid to be up here?" Miguel asked the question that monster trucks with winches couldn't have hauled out of Leon, even though he was dying to ask it. "It's just that one little cable, not even as wide as a road." Roberto shook his head.

"No, it's wonderful. I think I was afraid the first night I slept up here, thinking it would all collapse in the night, or go spinning out into space, but after that I just loved it. There are such good people up here, so interesting, and they always have lectures. Hey, listen, I'm taking a college degree in science. You have to come back to my graduation. But I have to write a paper, and I'm not so good at that."

"Yes, you are," Leon declared stoutly. No one got to diss his grandfather, not even Roberto himself.

His grandfather laughed and pinched Leon's cheek. He took out a little device like a garage door opener and pointed it at an oblong door. A little red light went on above the handle.

"How do you like that?" he asked, pushing the door open and ushering his guests through. "We've got practically free electricity, so everything is electronic."

"Does it ever cut out?" Miguel asked.

"There's backups on backups, and generators in case of emergency," Roberto said, "but I've never heard of them going on in two years I've been up here."

Leon looked around the one-bedroom apartment curiously. The bedroom had no bed in it, only a contraption like a cross between a quilt and a fishing net in between a pair of light fixtures screwed to the wall. A jointed arm with a TV screen attached to it was folded against the wall 'above' it. The kitchen had a little re- frigerator and a convection oven, and a closed plastic bubble with hand-sized holes at waist height. The living room, if you could call it that, was an oval cylinder, padded all around, with handles and a couple more nets, plus a few cabinets. A huge curved screen no thicker than his hand was attached to the wall near a big round porthole. "There's hardly anything in here."

"There's not much I need," Papi said. "If I want movies, I can watch movies. If I want to read books, there are millions of books in the computer system. Magazines, too. If I want to write letters or work on my homework, I use the computer keyboard that straps to my thighs. The phone system is built in the walls. Exercise equipment is in the gym down the hall. I work out every day. I have pictures from home, and a few little things, but the cargo allowance even for new tenants was not too much. It costs a fortune to haul anything up here, and everything has to be hauled up, of course. But you see that you hardly even need furniture. It's all padded, but that's good, be- cause the ventilation system goes all the time, and it's very loud."

"What's this?" Miguel asked, examining the bubble in the kitchen.

"That's the sink. Everything has to be covered so water doesn't go floating out. You put your arms through the holes and it keeps it all in when you wash dishes. You should hear the vacuum system going when you empty the sink. Like a tidal wave."

"Uh-oh," Elisa said. "What about—?"

Roberto grinned. "You get used to it. So, how's Francisco? He keeps saying he's going to come up here and see me."

While the adults talked, Leon toured the little apartment, and amused himself rebounding off the walls and seeing how much English he could get caroming from corner to corner. Pretty soon even that novelty wore off, and he fetched up near the porthole. Earth was straight up out of the window. Same view he had been seeing for a week. He let out a sigh.

The adults suddenly woke up to the fact that he was there.

"Why don't you go explore for a while, Leonito," Papi said. "Here, take my station charge. Get yourself a snack. We'll meet you, say, six o'clock in The Orbit Restaurant for dinner. Level 8. Anyone can tell you where it is."

As dearly as Leon loved his grandfather, he hated to listen to boring talk about relatives. He took the proffered card and clambered out of the little apartment like a monkey fleeing jaguars. Back in the public area of that level, he started poking around in open doors. When he told them how he was going to be spending his summer vacation, his school friends had been divided between disbelief and jealousy that he was going up the space elevator. Yeah, what he ought to do was bring them some kind of souvenir, something that they could only get up on the platform. That would give him a mission while he waited for his folks to come out and meet him for dinner.

Most of the places he glanced into were very grown-up oriented, serious offices with computers and busy people talking into phones. If the people happened to look up and see him, they smiled. Leon fled along to the next doorway.

He spotted what looked like a cool boutique with a round door and spacescapes on the black glass wall. Leon pulled himself inside. There weren't any sales clerks in the room, just a couple of dudes with clipboards and a woman looking into a gigantic telescope.

"The storm is five minutes west of Cuba, on a heading north-northwest at 142.7 miles per hour," the woman said.

One of the guys made a note on a computer notepad, then looked up to see Leon. "Hi, there," he said. "Want to have a look?"

"Uh, sure," Leon said. What the hell? He peered into the eyepiece, and saw a big hunk of gray cotton with a hollow dot in the middle, moving slowly away from the skinny, brown, single parenthesis in the middle of the blue-gray ocean. "Is that really Cuba?"

"Yes, sir," the first man said.

"What's the cotton thing?"

"Hurricane Harmilda. Category four. This is the Liftport office of NOAA. There's no better place in the world to watch the weather. Cool, huh?"

Leon leaned back for a moment and looked at them. They looked so happy. Were they really that thrilled, or was it a put-on for the kid? "I guess so. Do you know where the gift shop is?"

The two men looked at one another. "There's one on level 1, next to the lifter terminal, but there's shops on a few other levels. Try the directory next to the elevators."

"Thanks."

The elevators didn't stop on every floor, Leon discovered when he tried to punch 2 and 3. A short man in a white jumpsuit, who was the only other passenger at the moment, smiled.

"They're building a platform there for the joint NASA/ESA mission to Mars. Gonna be off limits for the next couple of years."

"That's bogus," Leon said savagely. The fierceness of his response sent him floating backward in the car. He grabbed for a nearby handhold.

The man shrugged. "Plenty of other places to look at. If you go out to the end of level 15, you can watch the shuttle leaving for the moon. I think there's one going this evening."

"How come you think I'm a visitor?" Leon challenged him.

"Because I'm the youth activities coordinator," the man said, with a grin. "I haven't seen you before, and I meet pretty much all the kids your age. My name's Ed Ikhito. The video arcade is up on 17, under the dome. We're starting a Galaxy Crash game tournament tomorrow. You should come and join up."

"Maybe." Leon didn't say another word. He waited for the doors to open, then hauled himself out deliberately in the opposite direction the man went.

The gift shop was crowded with visitors, but Leon found it a huge disappointment. Leon found a meager collection of books, in print and on CD-ROM, but his friends weren't the reading kind. A small screen on top of a rack of videos for sale showed the construction of the cable and platform. Since it had been worldwide news for years, he figured all of his friends had seen about every minute there was of any documentary. The postcards were hoky, and all of the souvenirs like pencils, snow globes, notebooks, decorative rubber erasers and toy spacemen with light-up LEDs had all been made in Taiwan or India, just like the souvenirs he could buy in almost every tourist trap on Earth.

"What have you got that comes from here?" Leon asked the attractive girl hovering behind the counter.

"You can have your picture taken with Earth," she suggested. She gestured toward a big glass bubble in the wall that showed the black cable with the planet behind it. A camera on a tripod stood at hand. *Get your picture taken with Earth!* an overhead suggested. "I can arrange it so you're floating in the middle of the photo. It looks really cool." She indicated a wall full of color images of happy tourists mugging it up for the camera.

"How much?"

"Fourteen ninety-five," the girl replied, pointing to the small print on the sign.

Forget that, Leon thought brusquely. They wanted too much for something that some of his homeys were going to insist was faked anyhow. All he had to do to take a similar picture in real gravity was to jump in the air just before the shutter clicked.

"What have you got that I can bring home to my friends?"

The girl smiled at him apologetically. "I'm sorry, but this is all we have."

"No moon rocks? No asteroids? No stamps?"

"We have no natural resources," the girl said. "I've got some leftover pieces of the polymer that makes up the cable."

"Let's see those."

She pulled out a drawer and brought him a flat box with an acrylic display top. To his dismay it contained nothing but pieces of a dull black rubbery substance. Leon looked so disappointed that the girl opened the container and fished a couple out. "Here. Take them. I know they don't look like much, but believe me, they're unique."

Leon muttered his thanks and stuffed them into his pocket.

Suddenly, all the lights went out except square white lights in the corners of the room and yellow LEDs outlining the door. In the corridor, red lights began flashing, and a siren wailed.

"Attention, please. Everyone report to emergency stations. I repeat, everyone report to emergency stations."

Leon let out a yelp and started to look for someplace to hide. The platform was under attack. He *knew* Papi shouldn't have come to live here!

The girl behind the counter unbuckled herself from her harness and swam over to Leon. She grabbed his wrist. He shook her off.

"Come on," she said, her face dyed blood red by the emergency flashers. "It's just a lifeboat drill. It happens every week. Follow me."

Leon was still shaking badly, but he kicked at the air and grabbed for the door frame the way he saw her do. She coaxed him toward a big door outlined in orange lights, through which crowds of people were pouring. Beyond it the eternally cheerful crew members were handing out gray, wrapped packages and directing people further in.

"What's that?"

"The assigned lifeboat for this part of the level. This is just a way to make sure we're all safe. It's like being on an ocean liner. Haven't you ever had to do life jacket drills on a boat?"

"Yeah, but—"

"Nothing to it, I swear," the girl assured him. By that time they were sailing into the opening. A man in uniform took him by the wrist and pushed a parcel into his arms.

"This is your emergency environment suit. Don't put it on unless ordered to do by the captain," the man said, briskly but with a smile. "Go on back there. Let everyone else in."

Since it was still in zero gravity, the big, orange-painted room had no seats but lots of hand-holds. Leon pulled himself within a few feet of the nearest crowd and held on while others filled in around him, all holding on with one hand and clutching their environment suits with the other.

It's just a drill, he kept telling himself. It's just a drill. Nothing like this ever happened to him in South Bend!

But nothing was going wrong. Most of the people around him were talking and laughing. A few businessmen in suits with their ties floating over their shoulders were looking at their watches with pissed expressions. It was all so business-as-usual for them that Leon started to relax. He figured out right away who lived up here and who were visitors. The latter were the ones looking scared. At that moment he decided he wasn't going to let anyone else peg him as a visitor. He'd handle this. If his Papi could do it, he could, too!

That thought was the one that worried him while he waited for the capsule to finish loading and listened to the cheerful guy in the uniform making his long speech about what to do in a emergency. If this had been for real, he didn't like the idea of being separated from his family. What if they needed him, and he wasn't there to help? They could be a million miles apart in no time!

Calm down, he thought, tightening his fist on the plastic covering of his environment suit. Papi knows all about this.

The capsule he was standing in juddered suddenly, and a loud *honk! honk!* came from the speakers. It must be detaching from the platform. He didn't want to be there any longer. It was just too much out of his control. No, they weren't detaching; the capsule door just shut, and they were floating on their tether against the side of the platform. In a moment the door opened again, and all the lights were back.

A kid his own age nudged him in the ribs. Leon almost socked him one with the wrapped suit.

"Hey," the boy said, brandishing his own parcel. "Isn't it good they've got a plan?"

Leon shook the tension out of his shoulders. "Yeah. Yeah, it is."

HE DIDN'T FEEL like looking at anything else after that. He went up to Level 8 and literally hung around The Orbit Restaurant until his family met him. The tables were arranged around the walls of a hollow sphere. The hostess guided them to a table way up and to the left of the door. They strapped themselves to it with belts around their waists. Both top and bottom surfaces were covered with Velcro so one could sit at it facing either way. A friendly server in a jumpsuit sailed over and took their drink orders. From finding it the hottest marvel in the universe only hours ago, Leon had come to be annoyed with zero gravity.

Miguel grinned at him. "You find anything for your friends?"

"No," Leon said flatly, trying to stave off further parental queries by using his most sullen expression. It didn't work. It never did.

"What did you think of the lifeboat drill?" Elisa asked.

"What about it?" Leon glared at her. Elisa shook her head, with that aggravating Mom-smile. "All it did was tell me this whole thing is stupid. It's a big empty box hanging off the Earth on a *shoestring.* There's nothing up here at all."

"You're wrong, Leonito," Papi said, patiently. "There's *ideas* up here. Knowledge don't weigh nothing, but it's the most important thing in the world. Here you only have what you bring with you, but this place gives you ideas. Even I have had some. Like I told your folks a little while ago, I'm talking to the scientists about making us old folks more comfortable. They listen. They involve us. I participate in a bunch of tests that some guys from a company that makes ergonomics are doing. They called for volunteers, and I signed up. We're testing braces to keep people from hurting their backs when they sleep. Pretty good, huh?"

"They're using you as a guinea pig," Leon said darkly.

Papi clicked his tongue. "It's not like that. It's fun! I've had some good ideas, too. We're part of a scientific community. It's not just warehousing us up here, like it might be in an assisted living community back down there. We matter. We have value. It's because we lived so long that maybe we'll live even longer. How about that for nothing? It's been a while since I felt this good, either my body or my mind, and it's because I feel needed. There are old folks here who just want to float around and do nothing. That's their privilege. They earned it. But that's not me, you know that. I have to get into the community. It's a fresh start. Space is plenty big enough for all of us."

"But my friends won't understand *concepts*," Leon complained.

"Maybe they should try. This is the future up here, Leonito. It's not about things, it's about ideas. I don't mean there's nothing you can share with your friends, but it's more of what you can express to them than what you can give them. This is when ideas are more important than objects. Up here there's no us and them, because we all need each other. I've been reading a lot of stories, old stories, where they talked about what we're doing right now, out here in near Earth orbit. Do you know how that makes me feel? All my life I watch people pass me by. For once I'm part of something fantastic and new, people look up to me. Literally. I think it makes me a better person. I'm thinking of the whole world, not just my little family, and I like it. You can be part of it. Open up to it. Don't try to drag us down. Follow us. Maybe if you try, you'll invent something new that will let us reach even farther out. I think about God a lot. I used to think God had only to do with the things on Earth, but from here I can see that it's only one of His marvels."

"I'm not ready for this kind of future," Leon said. "When we had to go into the lifeboat, I felt so helpless. There's no air out there! I felt like I was going to suffocate. All I want to do is go back down to the surface. Right now. This is all too far ahead for me."

"No, it's not. I know you like I know myself." Papi pounded his chest proudly. "Just open yourself up to it. It's a little scary at first, I know. You don't remember what it was like to learn to walk, but how about when you learned to ride your bike? There was that moment when Miguel running alongside you had to let go, and you had to trust yourself, even though you didn't really know what was going to happen. It was scary, but it was good at the same time, yeah?"

Leon looked at him with a dawning sense of understanding. "It's like that, huh?"

Papi crinkled his eyes at him. "Just like that. Every time you try something new. It's a little dangerous, but, hey, so is life. There. That's my philosophy for the day. Let's eat."

New philosophy firmly in hand, Leon accepted his bubble of cola from the server and, after the first disastrous glug, experimented with drinking it in small sips so it wouldn't try to escape out of his nose. There, he thought. One small step.

Ed Ikhito floated up to their table. "Hiya, kid. Find what you're looking for?"

"No," Leon said.

"Leon's afraid his friends are going to hassle him because he can't find any souvenirs," Elisa said brightly. Leon wished he could sink through the floor. "He wants to bring them something to let them know about his trip up here."

"A lot of people get disappointed about that, Leon," Ikhito said. "Maybe what's up here is just for you. Your friends will simply have to envy your experience. I wanted to remind you about the tournament tomorrow afternoon. Come on and join us. It's up under the observation dome. We've got our own telescope. You can monitor the Perseids on your own computer screen while you're playing."

"Oh, that sounds awesome, Leon!" Elisa exclaimed, with a pleased look at the man.

"Okay, maybe," Leon said, gruffly. It sounded pretty good, if there weren't any catches. "Can I e-mail my friends on this computer?"

"Sure enough. We've got broadband. They can even join in the game, if they're good enough." Ihito gave him a conspiratorial grin.

Leon caught Papi looking at him. He began to get an idea that this whole space platform experience was something that could include him, even if he wasn't totally in control of it. There were a lot of familiar things, and, well, he could get used to the rest. Some of his ancestors had crossed the Great Plains, and they didn't even have air conditioning. Space, the final frontier, wasn't that it?

"Okay," he said.

"That's great!" Ikhito said, kicking off. "With you, that'll make an even seventy-five entrants. See you then!"

The lights went down. Leon looked around in alarm, thinking it was another lifeboat drill, but strobes started flashing and spotlights began to swirl around an area in the center of the restaurant. Music boomed out of hidden speakers. All over the restaurant people began to detach themselves from the tables and swirled into the middle, where they started to gyrate in every direction like tadpoles escaping from a net.

"They're dancing!" Elisa squealed. "Oh, come on, Mike, let's dance!"

Miguel unhooked his belt and held out his hand to his wife. "My pleasure."

Papi watched them as they kicked their way out to the happy crowd. Leon waited until they were far enough that no one else could hear him, and leaned close to the old man.

"I miss you, Papi. Aren't you ever going to come home?"

Papi shook his head. "This is my home, now, Leonito. I'm comfortable. They even think it could enhance our lifespans, maybe a long way. I'd like that, to maybe see the next century. How about that, eh? You can see the future from here, that's what they're always saying."

Living another whole century? Leon thought. His precious grandfather might never die! The big hollow box began to sound more interesting. "Hey, maybe when I'm old I'll come and live here, too."

Papi leaned over and gave him a strong hug around the head. "You do that, Leonito. I'll do my best to be here to greet you." He raised his drink bulb and tapped it against Leon's. "We'll share our future."

"It's a deal," Leon said, taking a good sip. He felt as effervescent as the soda. "To the future."

CONSTRUCTION AND OPERATIONAL HAZARDS TO THE SPACE ELEVATOR

by

Robert Carlson

Rob Carlson is a scientist who works at boundaries. A Princeton-trained physicist interested in technology of all kinds, he devotes much of his current research and writing to biology and is working on a book exploring the future of biology as technology. Rob is a Senior Scientist in the Department of Electrical Engineering at the University of Washington, was recently a Visiting Scholar in its Comparative History of Ideas program, and is a Senior Associate at Bio Economic Research Associates (www.bio-era.net). Rob's current passions revolve around conceiving and developing new technologies that enable rapid understanding of biological phenomena and provide a basis for engineering synthetic biological systems. He has co-developed several patented technologies to detect and quantify small amounts of proteins in complex mixtures, and is now working on new fabrication techniques to build microdevices for basic research and clinical diagnostics. His home on the web is at www.synthesis.cc.

CLIMBING A NARROW ribbon of carbon seems a tenuous means of reaching for the stars. Like the horse hair suspending the sword over Damocles' head, reminding him of the precarious nature of political power, the thin thread of the Space Elevator will constantly remind us of our fragile freedom from Earth's gravity well. The primary argument for building the elevator can be derived in a few lines on the back of an envelope; the energy cost of putting 1 kg in geosynchronous orbit on the elevator is approximately 1% the cost using rockets. We then must determine whether the 100,000 km long structure is theoretically plausible to build and operate.

Even in theory, the sheer size of the elevator inspires both awe and fear in the form of unknowns that appear overwhelming at first glance. Fortunately we have accumulated many person-years of operational knowledge of the environments the ribbon will experience. Moreover, all of the technology required to build the elevator has already been demonstrated, save the completed ribbon itself. This means we can apply existing engineering know-how to evaluate whether the elevator is a feasible project and what risks may arise during construction and operation. And the ribbon is far from being "unobtanium". There appears to be only one known material suitable for building the ribbon, carbon nanotubes (CNTs). The amount of progress made in understanding both the construction and properties of long carbon nanotubes is quite remarkable given our mere 15 years of experience. Many critical properties of the ribbon, and its constituent adhesives and CNTs, can already be measured or estimated.

Still, the history of human engineering and construction is full of hubris confronted by physics. The devil is definitely in the details for this project. The few engineering details available come largely from two NASA Institute for Advanced Concepts (NIAC) reports and a book, all written by Dr. Bradley Edwards.

The purpose of this chapter is to explore what could go wrong with the deployment and operational plans, and what might be done about it. Much of those plans are determined by the seemingly unavoidable requirement of launching an initial full-length ribbon and then lowering it from orbit to the Earth's surface. As related in [1-3], the deployment strategy appears a happy confluence of economic and design factors. The numbers, remarkably, work out quite nicely.

Asking why we should bother with the Space Elevator in the first place requires comparing potential risks and benefits of the elevator with current launch technology. There are two important questions for the long run: 1) What dangers to cargoes, the planet, and its inhabitants are common to the elevator and other launch technologies, and 2) What significant novel and specific dangers do the elevator or its components pose?

There is insufficient space here to fully address these questions, and what follows is but a brief sketch.

Launch and Construction

The current plan for getting the initial ribbon into orbit involves up to five launches of Delta IV rockets, or an equivalent system, with the components of the deployment craft distributed amongst them. The components would be designed for rapid assembly on orbit.

The risk at this stage is equivalent to that for standard flight operations; e.g. loss of a booster and its cargo of components. As a hedge against loss of a cargo flight, as much of the deployment craft as possible should be constructed using components used in the fleet of lifters. The cost of insuring these launches should be no different than any other large satellite launch, and perhaps less since there will be no tricky solid- or liquid-fueled upper stage aboard. On arrival at low earth orbit (LEO), the cargo craft should be stationed in a parking orbit near the International Space Station (ISS), there to be unpacked and assembled by astronauts during a short mission.

A simple strategy for managing the risk of the human launch is to use tried and true Russian craft, with the astronauts staying at the ISS for the duration of the mission. The ISS has already hosted tourists, at a few tens of millions of dollars per person, though supporting a construction crew engaged in spacewalks could add considerably to the cost. However, a few temporary residents engaged in a commercial endeavor should neither unduly tax the ISS systems nor be difficult to arrange.

From Low Earth Orbit to Deployment Orbit

The current "reference design" relies on electric propulsion to get the deployment craft from Low Earth Orbit to an altitude where the ribbon will be unrolled. Power will be provided via lasers on the surface, a system that is already being tested. Electric propulsion is low thrust, and therefore slow, but it also probably involves extremely low risk. Moreover, there are no moving parts, no need for careful control of a slow propellant explosion, and no fear of a rapid propellant explosion.

Unrolling the Ribbon

Once the ribbon starts its decent to the surface, time is the real enemy. No environment along the length of the ribbon could be called benign. The survival time of the deployed structure is a strong function of its size (a small ribbon is quite vulnerable), and a fully robust ribbon would be too massive to deploy all at once with current rockets. Edwards suggests managing this risk by launching a small ribbon, likely to survive for months to a year, which will be built up through the addition of material from a series of several hundred robotic lifters. Thus we are stuck biting our nails until the ribbon is of sufficient size to survive its varied environmental challenges.

From this point on, operational and construction hazards are identical. These hazards are many-fold, but fortunately some progress can be made towards quantitatively assessing risk. Based on measurements made on the Long Duration Exposure Facility (LDEF), historical weather patterns, long human experience with wind loading of structures, and active control of ribbon motion to avoid obstacles, Edwards calculates that the elevator can be built with a reasonable engineering safety factor.

A summary of the arguments made in [1-3] for specific hazards are as follows:

Lightning

Because CNTs are excellent conductors, the ribbon will be the world's longest lightning rod. While CNTs have a high melting temperature and would themselves likely survive a strike, the epoxy or tape cross members may suffer damage, and the effects of current through a surface layer of rainwater are not presently amenable to estimation. The best solution to this problem is to locate the elevator in a region where inclement weather is historically minimal. The reference anchor station, 1500 km west of Ecuador, has been measured to be remarkably free of thunderstorms and lightning strikes.

Natural Meteors and Man-Made Objects

Objects of different sizes may collide with the ribbon. The effects of a collision depend both on the size and the speed of the object, and different strategies will be employed to deal with each.

Near Earth objects smaller than 1 cm in diameter are primarily natural meteors, while man-made debris constitutes the majority of objects larger than 1 cm. The flux of natural meteors through Earth orbit is a relatively well-measured quantity. In addition, U.S. Space Command currently tracks debris larger than 10 cm in diameter. Plans are being made to improve the resolution of tracking systems to 1 cm, and several stations with this capability are included in funding estimates for the elevator. Below this size limit, objects are not easily observable and impacts will occur at a predictable and unavoidable rate. The ribbon simply must be robust to such collisions. The ribbon must thus be constantly inspected and repaired, which will in any event be required by the constant wear and tear of the lifters.

The ribbon will be moved to avoid collisions with objects large enough to track that may cause significant damage. Because the elevator will share orbits with existing satellites, which have right of way, the ribbon must also be moved to accommodate them. This will be accomplished by moving the anchor platform to alter the orbital motion of the ribbon.

Wind Loading

The small fraction of the ribbon in the lower atmosphere will be subject to wind loading. The wind velocity required to break a relatively weak, ~1 km long section of a thin, wide CNT ribbon is estimated to be just over 30 m/s. Low altitude winds of this magnitude are so rare at the proposed anchor location they have never been measured there. Building in an additional safety factor can be accomplished by using thicker, narrower ribbon in the section vulnerable to winds, and by reducing the ratio of epoxy to CNT, thereby reducing the cross-sectional area of the ribbon. While the specific properties of a composite ribbon have yet to be determined, it appears the structure can be made robust even to winds in a category 5 hurricane, though such storms never approach the anchor location due to its proximity to the equator.

Atomic Oxygen

Oxygen molecules in the upper atmosphere are split by incident radiation. The resulting individual oxygen molecules are highly reactive. Experience from the LDEF suggests that the carbon-epoxy composite ribbon will be subject to etch rates of up to 1 micron per month, though the CNTs should be much more resistant than the epoxy. Coating the ribbon with a thin metal layer may significantly reduce the etch rate, but this layer would be under constant mechanical stress due to the passage of lifters. In the end, considerable experimentation will be required to determine the best combination of design factors to limit the etching of the ribbon.

Electromagnetic Fields and Radiation Damage

A 100,000 km long ribbon will pass through the Earth's magnetic field, and will be exposed to varying degrees of both ionizing and non-ionizing radiation along its entire length. Potential electrical currents induced in the ribbon by relative motion though magnetic fields are so small, and the conductivity of the ribbon so large, that very little Joule heating will occur, on the order of one milliWatt at maximum. Whatever heat is generated will be radiated so rapidly as to not increase the temperature. The ribbon should be similarly robust to radiation, with studies of epoxy/carbon fiber composites suggesting lifetimes of at least 1000 years.

Induced Oscillations

The elevator will be the largest structure on this planet by far, which means it will be subject to the largest mechanical perturbations we have ever seen. Wind will induce a hum (though far below the range of human hearing), the passage of the lifters will contribute energy to the ribbon, and the bottom of the ribbon will be moved to avoid collisions or rare inclement weather; each will excite normal modes of the world's longest string. Fortunately, these are problems human engineers are familiar with. Because we know the mass density of the ribbon and the tension in the ribbon, and we can choose its overall length, Edwards suggests that the design aim for a lowest normal mode of about 8 hours. This is far enough from the pumping frequencies of the sun and moon, due to their motion relative to the earth, that their impact will be minimal. It is likely that the only oscillations of note will be induced intentionally to avoid objects in earth orbit.

Environmental Impact

In the event the ribbon is severed, several scenarios are possible. If the break occurs near the anchor, the lower section will gently flutter down and fall in the ocean and could probably be reeled in for reuse or disposal, while the upper section will slowly drift into a higher orbit. If the break occurs further up, we are faced with the prospect of tens of thousands of kilometers of ribbon wrapping itself around the Earth's equator. Science fiction images of massive structures traveling at supersonic speeds are completely off base. The mass density of the ribbon is quite small, less than paper or thin metal foil, and the upper reaches should be moving fast enough to burn up upon reentry. So what happens if many kilometers of CNT, epoxy, and tape are incinerated in the atmosphere? Very little, according to initial calculations. For a low altitude break, Edwards estimates that only about 3000 kg of material would be deposited in the atmosphere, likely as fine dust, and would contribute a small fraction to the dust that falls from space every year. If the entire initial ribbon burned up on the way down, it would still provide less than a 10% increase.

We can also compare the effects of losing the ribbon through combustion in the atmosphere with material deposited there due to launches of large rockets and the Space Shuttle. The Titan IV exhausts 500,000 kg of burned propellant on the way up, while the

Shuttle exhausts closer to 2,000,000 kg of propellant during launch. Losing an entire 20-ton capacity ribbon in the atmosphere (an unlikely event) would contribute only 890,000 kg. It is clear from these numbers that consistent use of the elevator would prevent a vast amount of atmospheric pollution from launch debris and burned propellant. The effects of this sort of pollution can be appreciated from a paper that appeared in *Nature* examining the environmental effects of suspending of commercial air traffic, and the resulting atmospheric source of water vapor and exhaust, following 11 September 2001. The study found that cloud cover was strongly affected across North America, and that the diurnal temperature difference increased by almost two degrees Celsius[4]. Similarly, particulates from rocket exhaust nucleate ice crystals that form clouds in the upper atmosphere[5]. A 20-ton elevator operating at full capacity would prevent 100 million kg of exhaust and debris being put into the atmosphere[3], mitigating a considerable amount of pollution. Depending on the international political environment of the day, and on the negotiating skills of the commercial operators of the elevator, this gap might be traded or sold to polluting countries or corporations for an additional revenue.

No discussion of risk in a large-scale construction project would be complete without addressing the issue of insurance. In particular, the fact that CNTs are viewed as "nanotechnology" could be problematic, even though CNTs are a component of soot produced naturally in forest fires. (It is not yet clear how the mass of CNTs in the ribbon compare with the mass of naturally occuring CNTs.) A recent report from Swiss Re suggests it will be difficult for companies to receive indemnification for nanotech products until the effects of those products on people and the environment are better understood[6]. It is also unclear how insurance companies will assess risk due to terrorism and the constant traffic up the elevator of explosive rocket fuel for orbital positioning of payloads.

The Space Elevator may be the most audacious technological opportunity of the next century. It will certainly compete for the title of grandest construction project in history. We have much to learn before embarking on the effort, but at least it appears unlikely fall down on the first day.

1.Edwards, B., *The Space Elevator: NIAC Phase I Final Report.* 2002.

2.Edwards, B., *The Space Elevator: NIAC Phase II Final Report.* 2003.

3.Edwards, B. and E. Westling, *The Space Elevator: A revolutionary Earth-to-space transportation system.* 2003, Houston, TX: BC Edwards.

4.Travis, D.J., A.M. Carleton, and R.G. Lauritsen, *Contrails reduce daily temperature range.* Nature, 2002. 418(6898): p. 601.

5.Platov, Y., S. Chernouss, and G. Kulikova. *Classification of Gas-Dust Formations from Rocket Exhaust in the Upper Atmosphere by Scale and Dynamics.* in *Physics of Auroral Phenomena.* 2002: Russian Academy of Science.

6.http://www.swissre.com/INTERNET/pwswpspr.nsf/ fmBookMarkFrameSet?ReadForm&BM=../vwAllbyIDKeyLu/ ULUR-5YAFFS?OpenDocument.

This is another excerpt from *The Gardens of Paradise*
by
Sir Arthur C. Clarke.

THE END OF THE LINE

NO WONDER THEY called it the Trans-Siberian Railroad. Even on the easy downhill run, the journey from Midway Station to the base of the Tower lasted fifty hours.

One day it would take only five, but that lay two years in the future, when the tracks were energized and their magnetic fields activated. The inspection and maintenance vehicles that now ran up and down the faces of the Tower were propelled by old-fashioned tires gripping the interior of guidance slots. Even if the limited power of the batteries permitted, it was not safe to operate such a system at more than five hundred kilometers an hour.

Yet everyone had been far too busy to be bored. Professor Sessui and his three students had been observing, checking their instruments, and making sure that no time would be wasted when they transferred into the Tower. The capsule driver, his engineering assistant, and the one steward, who made up the entire cabin staff, were also fully occupied, because this was no routine trip. The "Basement," twenty-five thousand kilometers below Midway—and now only six hundred kilometers from earth—had never been visited since it was built. Until now, there had been no purpose in going there, since the handful of monitors had never reported anything amiss. Not that there was much to go wrong, because the Basement was merely a fifteen-meter-square pressurized chamber—one of the scores of emergency refuges at intervals along the Tower.

Sessui had used all his considerable influence to borrow this unique site, now crawling down through the ionosphere at two kilometers a day toward its rendezvous with earth. it was essential, he had argued forcibly, to get his equipment installed before the peak of the current sunspot maximum.

Already, solar activity had reached unprecedented levels, and Sessui's young assistants often found it hard to concentrate on their instruments; the magnificent auroral displays outside were too much of a distraction. For hours on end, both northern and southern hemispheres were filled with slowly moving curtains and streamers of greenish light, beautiful and awe-inspiring—yet only a pale ghost of the celestial firework displays taking place around the poles. It was rare for the aurora to wander so far from its normal domains; only once in generations did it invade the equatorial skies.

Sessui had driven his students back to work with the admonition that they would have plenty of time for sightseeing during the long climb back to Midway. Yet it was noticeable that even the Professor himself sometimes stood at the observation window for minutes at a time, entranced by the spectacle of the burning heavens.

Someone had christened the project Expedition to Earth— which, as far as distance was concerned, was ninety-eight percent accurate. As the capsule crawled down the face of the Tower at its miserable five hundred klicks, the increasing closeness of the planed beneath made itself obvious. Gravity was slowly increasing, from the delightful less-than-lunar buoyancy of Midway to almost its full terrestrial value. To any experienced space traveler, this was strange indeed: to feel *any* gravity before the moment of atmospheric entry seemed a reversal of the normal order of things.

Apart from complaints about the food, stoically endured by the overworked steward, the journey had been devoid of incident. A hundred kilometers from the Basement, the brakes had been gently applied and speed had be halved. It was halved again at fifty kilometers; as one of the students remarked: "Wouldn't it be embarrassing if we ran off the end of the track?"

The driver—who insisted on being called pilot—retorted that this was impossible, because the guidance slots down which the capsule was falling terminated several meters short of the Tower's end, and there was also an elaborate buffer system, just in case *all* four independent sets of brakes failed to work.

And everyone agreed that the joke, besides being perfectly ridiculous, was in extremely poor taste.

HOW SAFE IS THE SPACE ELEVATOR?
by
Edward Greisch

Mr. Greisch was born on July 20, 1946, in Patuxent, Maryland. He received his B.S. in Physics in 1968 from Carnegie-Mellon University. He went on to receive seven more years of higher education including Army graduate training in Quality Control, Reliability and Maintainability [QRM]. He is well-versed in both Physics and QRM methodology including probability and statistics courses required to understand safety. Physics is a highly mathematical science. This kind of training is necessary to overcome the emotional instinctive irrational thinking that untrained people do, especially on the subject of safety. Mr. Greisch has two adult children.

Astronaut Safety

THE SAFETY ASPECTS of the Space Elevator will be explored in this article. The Space Elevator will be compared to the Space Shuttle (currently the only human-rated heavy-lift launch vehicle) with regards to crew recovery in case of a catastrophic failure. Also, the perennial question of "What if the Space Elevator ribbon falls?" will also be answered in this chapter.

Until now, astronauts on the Space Shuttle have had a 2% chance of not coming back alive. That is one of the design specifications of the Space Shuttle and is the statistical truth for other spacecraft as well. The Space Elevator changes everything. The Space Elevator will be comparable in safety to other normal human activities such as driving a car or riding in an airliner. There are two basic reasons for this:

1. On the Shuttle and other rockets, you ride a pillar of flame into space. A rocket in action is a controlled explosion.

2. The shuttle and other re-entry vehicles hit the atmosphere at 18,000 miles per hour. At that speed, friction between the air and the vehicle heat the outer surface of the vehicle to high temperatures. The temperature of the front of the shuttle is high enough to melt the shuttle structure if heat shield tiles are missing.

The space elevator avoids both of the above dangerous situations.

1.The Space Elevator is powered by electric motors as opposed to volatile rocket fuels. We all own numerous electric motors and we know that electric motors are safe. Most household appliances contain electric motors. Since the Space Elevator will not be powered by explosive fuel, it is inherently safer than rocket-based space access systems.

2.The Space Elevator exits and enters the atmosphere at normal highway speeds. There is no friction heating and no heat shield is necessary. This is true both going up and coming down. That covers the second Space Shuttle danger.

There are several lesser dangers in the Shuttle that do not apply to the Space Elevator. They include, but are not limited to, vibration and high gee acceleration. Rockets vibrate violently. The Space Elevator will not have noticeable vibrations. Rockets also accelerate very quickly and can put a severe strain on the human body. That is one reason why there are strict physical requirements to be an astronaut. Astronauts who ride rockets have to be fit enough to withstand both the vibrations and high acceleration of launch. Elevators accelerate like a car or truck. Riding the Space Elevator will feel like riding an elevator in a very tall building. Everyone is familiar with riding elevators in buildings and there is no physical fitness test to do so. The ride in the Space Elevator will take longer than the ride in the Shuttle, but the safety provided by the elevator is a worthy tradeoff. No medical exam will be required of Space Elevator passengers.

Safety On The Ground

Rockets, including all pre-Space Elevator spacecraft, have lower stages or fuel tanks that fall back to Earth. Rockets create a potential hazard of falling objects or air pollution if the falling stages burn up on the way down. The Space Elevator will not have lower stages or fuel tanks to drop. The Space Elevator will not drop things that would cause either of these hazards.

There are some notable instances in science fiction literature of a Space Elevator collapsing and causing havoc to the planet below. Current designs for the Space Elevator ribbon call for it to be constructed of a carbon nanotube polymer. The cable will be wide but paper thin and light. If the ribbon were to be severed, several things would happen.

The section below the ribbon's center of gravity (roughly geosynchronous orbit) would fall towards the Earth. The section above would be pulled outward by centripedal acceleration. Depending on exactly where the tear occurred, most of the ribbon would actually be pulled away from the Earth.

For the pieces falling towards the Earth, most of it would burn up in the atmosphere. However, several thousand miles of ribbon might still enter our atmosphere. Most of that will tear into sections dozens to hundreds of feet long and flutter to the ground with the speed of a falling newspaper or an autumn leaf.

What of the burnt-up carbon nanotubes in the atmosphere? Carbon nanotubes are a constituent of ordinary soot and are actually created whenever one burns a piece of wood. And while exhaustive research studies have yet to be done, the human species evolved breathing the occasional nanotube and will continue to do so even if a Space Elevator ribbon collapsed to Earth.

Falling elevator cars will be as rare as airliners falling out of the sky and hitting your house. This is rare indeed. If an elevator car ever does fall, the elevator car would most likely land in the ocean far from shipping lanes, harming nothing on the ground. As with aircraft, the greatest reasonable safety will be designed into the system. Life is never perfectly safe, but you can be sure of not being hit by a falling space elevator.

The Hazard Of Not Building The Space Elevator

The Space Elevator will allow us to mitigate, alleviate, or eliminate the following hazards: resource depletion, pollution, environmental damage, giant impacts from meteors and comets, over-population, lack of new real estate and the lack of a wide open frontier.

The carrying capacity of Earth is estimated to be about ten billion people. Beyond ten billion, ecological collapse becomes all too likely. We are already feeling the negative effects of over-population, industrialization, and resource harvesting on both the environment and the global economy.

However, the carrying capacity of the Solar System is probably at least ten times larger than that of Earth. Mars, the Moon, the asteroids, the Jovian system and the moons of Saturn provide new opportunities for explorers and settlers. With the establishment of the Space Elevator, we can once again embrace the natural human impulse to explore new frontiers.

The Space Elevator makes all of the above possible on a grand scale. Economic advancement will reduce poverty and environmental destruction. It will expand our economy, our population and, most importantly, our horizons. These are not only worthy goals, but necessary ones as well.

When asking the question, "Is it safe to build the Space Elevator?" one can answer that it is certainly much safer than any rocket-based space access system. This is due to its inherent simplicity compared to rockets. In fact, one may go so far to say it is unsafe to NOT build the Space Elevator. Can humanity afford to carry on without the benefits the Space Elevator will provide? Certainly not.

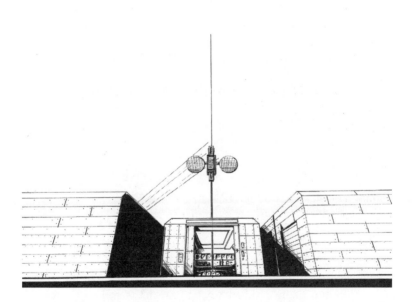

Financial Issues
Preliminary Space Elevator Budgetary Planning
by
Eric Olson

Mr. Olson graduated from Bentley College magna cum laude with a degree in finance. He has earned many accolades for his work in investing and, more specifically, educating young investors. Mr. Olson has been featured in prestigious publications such as Investors Business Daily, The Christian Science Monitor, and the NAIC's young investor newsletter: Young Money Matters. Currently, Mr. Olson is working at Cambridge Associates in Boston, MA as a Private Equity Analyst and plans to pursue a Ph.D. in Corporate Strategy.

Budget Overview

TEN BILLION DOLLARS to build a space elevator, widely considered science fiction before the dicovery of ultra-strong structures known as carbon nanotubes, may seem outrageous to most. Many of us can not even fathom such a large sum of money, let alone investing that amount of money into a project that appears to be very risky. However, one must look at this cost in perspective. NASA's 2005 Fiscal Year budget states that five billion dollars a year will be saved over the next decade because the Space Shuttle is being retired.[1] This means that it costs NASA about five billion dollars each year just to maintain the Space Shuttle. Two years of Shuttle maintenance pays for the Space Elevator. The truth about the Space Elevator project is that it is not as risky or expensive as one may think when carried out using the plan devised by the LiftPort Group.

There are many residual assets, both hard and soft, that will remain even if LiftPort does not achieve its final goal of building the first commercial Space Elevator. These residual assets, which will be further discussed throughout this essay, will come about in three different "phases." These phases will also help to spread out the ten billion dollar total cost across different time periods significantly lowering the risk of the overall project.

Phase I

Phase I will encompass two billion dollars, or 20%, of the total budget and the first five years (2004-2009) of the total fourteen year project length (2004-2018). Phase I will also yield a "go or no go" decision on the project. The emergence of this decision with only two billion dollars spent will significantly limit the risk of the project saving eight billion dollars if the project fails. The two billion spent in Phase I will be used to further develop the intellectual property needed to build the Space Elevator. The major areas that will be researched are carbon nanotubes (for the ribbon), power beaming technology, and robotics (for the lifters).

Currently one of the main problems with nanotubes is their length. The Space Elevator's nanotube ribbon will be about 100,000 km long. Only recently have nanotubes long enough to be made into Space Elevator length ropes become available. Los Alamos National Laboratory reported on September 13, 2004 that University of California students working in collaboration with Duke University Chemists at Los Alamos National Laboratory have grown a world record length 4cm single-wall nanotube.[2] Nanotubes of this size should be able to be made into threads and ropes without any matrix material. Common wisdom is that anything over 4mm is braidable meaning that the 4cm nanotubes would solve the Space Elevator problem if they could be produced in large enough quantities.

As of now, nanotubes cannot be manufactured in amounts large enough to make a Space Elevator ribbon. Tons per day are needed for large scale commercial use. Currently, nanotubes manufacturers can only produce between 25 and 100 pounds per day (source: Carbon Nanotechnologies, Inc.).

The advances that LiftPort will make in nanotubes in the first five years of operations will also yield a plethora of patents. These patents can be licensed so that some of the two billion dollars invested can be recovered. The same scenario will hold true for areas besides carbon nanotechnology, such as power beaming, robotics and solar energy.

Phase II

Phase II will encompass five billion dollars, or 50%, of the total budget and the second five years of the project (2009-2014). In this phase, LiftPort will design and contract production of nanotube manufacturing, lasers, lift systems, and other Space Elevator components. The anchor systems and rockets will also be constructed for the actual assembly of the system.

This phase will also, like Phase I, have a residual value. However, in this phase the residual value will be mainly in concrete assets rather than intellectual property. The rocket, anchor system, and manufacturing facilities developed in this stage can be liquidated should the project fail.

Phase III

Phase III is what some people may call the "nail biting stage." This stage will encompass the final three billion dollars of the budget and the last four years of the project (2014-2018). It is in Phase III that construction of the Space Elevator itself will begin and end.

If Phase III does fail there will still be value left in the company. In the two previous phases, intellectual property and concrete assets were listed as residuals which the company could sell to reclaim some of the money lost if it were to fail. In Phase III the focus will again be on intellectual property. However, the intellectual property developed in Phase III will be of a different variety than that of Phase I.

Phase III will undoubtedly reveal to the world a new and unique method to manage a large project. It will also improve the knowledge base pertaining to high altitude and space construction. While these intangibles are hard to patent and sell, they will still benefit future projects that the public and private sectors may take on which will, in turn, benefit the financiers of the project.

Phase III will also be the phase in which debt will need to be serviced. Part of the three billion dollar budget will go toward this debt servicing. However, LiftPort plans to pursue deals with the public and private sectors to allow use of the Space Elevator. These contracts will provide more and more cash as the Space Elevator nears completion due to different entities using the uncompleted Space Elevator for low altitude tests and other projects allowing LiftPort to service its debt.

Budget Specifics

So far the discussion has focused on the overall price tag of the Space Elevator and the timeline of the project. As you have probably guessed, the ten billion dollar Space Elevator budget will be broken up and spent on the research and building of many different technologies and devices. In this section the discussion will focus on these different technologies and devices and their costs. To make this information easier to digest it has been broken down into ten sections: Launch Costs, Spacecraft, Ribbon, Lifters, Anchor System, Power Beaming, Tracking, Facilities, Admin, and Contingency. (Note: All information in the Budget Specifics section of this essay are from "The Space Elevator NIAC Phase II Final Report" by Bradley C. Edwards, Ph.D. Eureka Scientific.)

Launch Costs:

The total amount budgeted for launch costs is $800 million. This budget will allow LiftPort to purchase four Delta-IV Heavy launch vehicles to place the initial construction spacecraft and ribbon in orbit. Please see the Construction chapter for further details.

Spacecraft:

The initial spacecraft will be of relatively simple design. However, it will be one of the largest systems ever launched. The total amount budgeted for the spacecraft is $294.5 million dollars. This price tag includes the development of all spacecraft components and the assembly of the craft. The purpose of this spacecraft will be to take its cargo (the ribbon) into orbit and deploy it.

Ribbon:

It is difficult to predict the ribbon budget because nothing like it has ever been produced. A completely automated process must be developed to create this ribbon otherwise its construction would be too time consuming and not feasible in any reasonable amount of time. The ribbon production cost also depends on the advances in nanotubes that will take place. The more efficient nanotube production becomes the less costly it will be to create the ribbon. A little over 200 separate ribbons will be built and as of now the budget for the overall ribbon is set at $397 million.

Lifters:

Close to 300 construction lifters will be built. Each lifter will have the same basic design but they will need to deal with ever increasing ribbon sizes. LiftPort would like to design the lifters in a modular form which would cut down on the costs. Based on small spacecraft work, LiftPort believes, as does Dr. Edwards, that $20 million per lifter is a reasonable estimate, resulting in about $600 million in robot costs.

Anchor System:

Using numbers from the similar Sea Launch platform, it is estimated that the total cost of the Liftport anchor system will be about $120 million. However, the Sea Launch system will only provide about half the power needed to operate a 20 ton capacity elevator. Therefore, one or two more power generation systems will need to be constructed. Also, backup systems will need to be in place. These three to four additional power generation systems will add another $30 million to the anchor system's price tag, making the total budgeted cost $150 million.

Power Beaming:

The budget estimate for the power beaming facility is based on a laser beaming system. The total budgeted cost of this facility is $1.65 billion and includes the facility infrastructure, high-power lasers and a large deformable mirror for two power beaming stations. One power beaming station will be located at the anchor and the other will be located on land. Having these two systems in place will improve the overall transmission. A third might be added to speed system deployment.

Tracking:

Tracking will be done with both radar and optical systems. About five new tracking facilities would need to be built along the equator to insure good coverage and to keep the Space Elevator out of jeopardy if one or two tracking facilities go down. The total budgeted cost for the tracking facilities is $500 million or about $100 million per station. However, LiftPort does believe that the cost for each station could easily be less than $100 million due to examples like Berkeley's One Hectare Telescope that only cost $25 million.

Facilities:

On site facilities will be needed for the crew and other people who need to get to and stay on the anchor system. Specifically, LiftPort has budgeted for a floating platform that can house offices and possible sleeping quarters for the crew. The floating platform budgeted cost is set at $200 million. LiftPort has also budgeted $20 million for on-shore offices which will house tracking crew and technicians among others. Therefore, the total combined budgeted cost for worker facilities is set at $220 million.

Administration:

Workers will be needed to build the Space Elevator. The salaries of these workers over the four year construction phase have been inserted into the $3 billion set aside for that phase. However, to make the budget more long term in its' outlook, administration costs for the first 10 years of operations were also determined.

Operating the tracking stations alone will take about $100 million per year according to Dr. Edward's reading of a JSC document. That would amount to $1 billion over the first ten years of operation. Dr. Edwards also estimates that running the Space Elevator will take two platform facility crews (20 per facility), technical staff (30 per facility), support personnel (30 per facility), and administration (10 per facility). That equates to a total of 140 people that will be employed by LiftPort. If the average salary is estimated at $100k and 100% overhead it will yield a total yearly operations budget of $28 million. It should also be assumed that there will be employees back in the US of equal numbers making the personnel budget in total $56 million per year or $560 million for the first ten years. Therefore, the total operations budget for LiftPort in the first ten years will amount to about $1.56 billion.

Contingency:

LiftPort has placed in their budget significantly more money than Dr. Edwards in the area of contingency. In total, LiftPort budgets $3.06 billion for this area whereas Dr. Edwards budgets only $1.4 billion. The reason for this rather high contingency amount is purely to be as conservative as possible. The Space Elevator may only cost $7 billion (total budget excluding contingency) but it is safer to budget with a large safety net in case something goes wrong or an alternative is needed to complete the project. In any large project, especially one that has not been attempted before, there are often times overlooked costs that can creep up at the end of a project when the budget is almost exhausted. The large contingency built into the Space Elevator budget by LiftPort may seem excessive but it aims to address these over-looked costs if they should arise. However, LiftPort does not think they will need most of this contingency to complete the project.

Financing the Space Elevator

Public Financing Piece:

Now that the budget and timeline have been explained you are probably thinking: "Where will this ten billion dollars come from?" And while you may think the Space Elevator is a neat idea, you don't want a new tax to pay for it. Well, you're in luck. Only 40% ($4bn) of the project will need to be funded by public (government) funds.

The four billion dollars will come from a variety of sources that include not only government grants, but also political set-asides and pre-paid contracts. Much of the government funding will come during Phase I and will be used for research. Research on carbon nanotube composites, laser power beaming, long-endurance lifters, and more will have spin-off results useful outside of the space elevator project. Much of the research money (from agencies such as DARPA, NOAA, NASA, the Air Force, DoE, DHS, and DoI) will go to LiftPort research partners. LiftPort hopes to primarily fund this public portion similarly to the way the railroads were first funded. This funding method was alluded to earlier in the description of Phase III: funding through contracts for service.

The transcontinental railroad was a private project just like the LiftPort Space Elevator. Railroad construction was funded primarily by private money but the government did contribute albeit not directly (i.e. through grants).

LiftPort plans to pursue contracts with the government to transport different payloads, such as atmospheric testing equipment, satellites, and other miscellaneous equipment. These contracts will help LiftPort service their debt in the critical third phase of the project allowing the management more time to spend on the Space Elevator's construction. Private sector contracts of the same nature will also be a factor in reducing the public cost.

Private Financing Piece:

The remaining 60% ($6bn) of the project funding will come from private sources, split equally between debt (30%) and equity (30%).

The bulk of the equity funding will occur before the debt funding. The public/private breakdown of funding sources is structured similar to other infrastructure projects.

Very small amounts of equity funding (probably through private offerings) will occur in the 2004-2009 time frame. The bulk of the equity funding will come in during the second stage, in the 2009-2015 time frame. This money will be used for space elevator component design & testing and initial contracting.

Debt financing will be delayed as much as possible in order to maintain a good operating debt ratio for the company. The debt will be mostly used for construction of all the elements of the space elevator in the 2015-2018 time frame. LiftPort will aim to secure cargo contracts (from the government or other sources) before construction begins, and use those contracts as collateral for the debt funding.

Conclusion

The ten billion dollar price tag of the Space Elevator is significant but, as shown, LiftPort plans to break it down and spread it out to lessen the financial burden. Only 20% of the total cost will be incurred in the first five years. With that 20% will come a "yes or no" answer on the project therefore containing the financial blow, if the project were to fail, to only two billion dollars rather than the entire ten billion dollar projected budget. Also, if a "no go" is determined to be the best decision after Phase I is complete, significant defensible intellectual property will remain. This fact is significant because, as mentioned earlier, the intellectual property developed by LiftPort can be licensed to other entities to generate cash for LiftPort, which will recoup part of the two billion dollars spent to that point.

The next 50% of the project budget will be spent creating the physical assets that will eventually help to build, and be part of, the Space Elevator. These physical assets can also be liquidated along with the intellectual property if the project fails in this phase.

The final 30% of the budget will be spent in the construction of the Space Elevator. The Space Elevator's construction will break new ground in many areas including high altitude and space construction. The knowledge developed during this phase will benefit all future high altitude and space construction projects regardless of whether or not the Space Elevator is a success.

This project is not an all or nothing venture. Many lessons will be learned throughout the process that will advance technology and shape the future of the world. In the end LiftPort knows the Space Elevator will be a success because even if it doesn't come to fruition, it will still change peoples' lives for the better in many other ways.

The Business Basics of Space Elevator Development
by
Michael Laine

Michael Laine is transforming a life-long interest in space development into real world results. After starting an Internet technology company in the mid-1990s, Michael Laine consulted for various space-related startup companies. In 2001, he co-founded HighLift Systems to research the feasibility of the Space Elevator. In 2003, he formed LiftPort Group to begin the full-scale commercialization of the Space Elevator project. Mr. Laine is a former United States Marine and studied Business Administration at Boston University.

THERE ARE MANY who question the wisdom of a private company attempting to build the Space Elevator. Some people think surely the Space Elevator is too large a project to be undertaken by anything other than a government entity. However, I could counter this by citing the dozens of projects that have been attempted and failed by government space programs in the past thirty years. While institutions like NASA, NASDA and the ESA have, without a doubt, some of the finest engineers and scientists in the world; they lack the financial, managerial and operational ability necessary to successfully execute the construction of the Space Elevator. I want to be clear on this point: I am not a "NASA Basher." I am, and have always been, impressed and awed by the things these talented and brilliant people accomplish. The simple fact is; all the brainpower and skill in the agency cannot compensate for the systematic shift in the political (and budgetary) landscape in which NASA operates. This handicap is not one of vision or commitment; it is simply the process by which we pay for things in America.

As this book clearly illustrates, constructing the Space Elevator will be much more than just a technical challenge. If humanity is ever going to see the benefits of space activity, it must do so in the era of decreasing space budgets and increasing cynicism towards the huge government space programs of the 1960s. In short, space exploration must be successfully marketed. Specifically, the area of launch services and access to orbit must be commercialized in order to fully open up the space frontier for industrialization, colonization, and entertainment. Only then will the Earth see such wonderful benefits as clean solar energy for the globe, better satellite communications, faster computers, better healthcare, and the possibility for real space tourism.

LiftPort's desire to construct the Space Elevator in the private sector is simple: it's the only way I can think of to accomplish it. One reason for this has already been mentioned briefly: the general public has lost its faith in the government to successfully execute large manned space programs. However, as the recent unmanned Mars rover and X-prize flights have shown, humanity has NOT lost its love affair with space, when it is "done right." In other words: Space travel is worth it only when done efficiently, quickly and safely. LiftPort, by embracing market forces, will avoid the preemptive cynicism the general public feels for large manned space programs. As a high-tech startup, LiftPort will be embracing the best ideals of capitalism, and therefore position itself favorably in the public's eye.

However, LiftPort's desire to be a private company as opposed to a government program is more than just a "public relations move." The Space Elevator is a concept that I believe will radically change the aerospace industry and indeed the entire world. Large government space programs and large aerospace/defense companies (institutions one would think would embrace the Space Elevator) are too entrenched in their current programs to take on anything as risky as the Space Elevator. In many of these organizations, political wrangling and corporate culture would work together to smother something as innovative as the Space Elevator. Along these lines, let me clarify a few ideas. It's not as if these companies could not do it, it's that they should not. They are already in business and are already earning a return on investments for their shareholders. This is the job of the senior managers in these companies; they have a fiduciary responsibility to maximize the outcomes for their investors. It has been suggested that Boeing, Lockheed or perhaps GM or GE should be the "general contractor" of this project. This just isn't practical. Were one of these large, publicly traded companies to try this, they would need a vote of approval from the shareholders. Even if they had that, the company would have to divert substantial parts of its capital away from the company's core product lines. This would drive the revenues and profits down and the expenses up. Their stock would sink like a brick and set the stage for a corporate malfeasance lawsuit.

On the other hand, a company whose founding charter specifically declared the construction of "the first wonder of the 21st century," the Space Elevator, would be immune to these issues. It could also still draw on the expertise of these larger companies by contracting them to manufacture the parts of the system for which they are most qualified. It is my intention to invite these companies to get involved. Their obvious expertise is essential to this project being completed on our set schedule and budget. I believe that only a small startup with "nothing to lose" could successfully construct the Space Elevator.

So the Space Elevator will be built by a small company (which will eventually grow to become a large company), working in the private sector using government and big business partnerships (not subsidies). Still, there are many, many things that need careful consideration in order to successfully build the Space Elevator. Three concepts to keep in mind are the creation of a "first lift" date, the use of "dual-track technology development," and the idea of "the four pillars of infrastructure development."

LiftPort, in order to meet the self-imposed April 12, 2018 deadline for construction, must raise $7-10 billion. But why have a self-imposed schedule at all? The decision to set a date for completion has several motivations. First, it separates LiftPort from many government programs that set deadlines and do not meet them, or worse yet, set no deadline whatsoever. The firm wants the public to realize that we are serious about our Space Elevator development. The countdown clock on our homepage is not a joke or a gimmick, though many are skeptical of us reaching it on time. Secondly, setting a date brings about a sense of urgency within the company. LiftPort employees are constantly reminded that they have "only" thirteen more years to build something the world has never seen before. It reduces complacency and allows the company to meet its milestones faster. Therefore, one can see that setting a date is critical in helping people take LiftPort seriously and motivate our team to work hard towards the end goal of construction completion.

The second main business principle is similarly straightforward. Dual-track technology development requires that LiftPort capitalizes on certain skills that are marketable in the short term, but also assist in the advancement of the Space Elevator in the long term. In this way, LiftPort will be creating revenue while simultaneously enhancing the equipments necessary to construct the Space Elevator. An excellent example of dual-track technology development is the High Altitude Long Endurance (HALE) system being built and marketed by LiftPort and its partners. The HALE system has allowed LiftPort to research prototype lifter mechanics while concurrently creating a marketable system that will lead to significant revenues.

The third main business principle at LiftPort is that of the "four pillars" of infrastructure construction. Besides being necessary for our continued survival and growth, all types of infrastructure share another commonality: they must be built. In order to get food from the farms to the cities, a road must be built over rivers, through mountains and around forests. In order to transmit electricity, power lines must be strung from large steel towers. In order to maintain instantaneous global communication, oceanic cables and satellites must be built and positioned.

All of these major construction projects require approval in four distinct areas. These areas are what can be referred to as "the four pillars of infrastructure development." The pillars are science and technology, finance and business, social and political, and the national and international legal framework. In other words, contemporary infrastructure construction projects must meet requirements in each of these areas in order to be built.

One can use the construction of a hydroelectric dam as an example. A dam is a very large infrastructure project that can provide many services for our society. However, before any serious construction plans may be considered, the sociopolitical requirement for construction must be met. This requirement is not so much a box to be checked off, as it is a campaign of public awareness and acceptance. While a dam has many benefits, it can also have many negative impacts as well. Public perception of a dam's effects can increase the negative image of the project. Therefore, it is the dam builder's responsibility to marshal public support by educating the local community. The dam builder must show that the value of construction outweigh the issues. He must show that any environmental or societal hazards can be overcome. He must also work to dispel any rumors or misconceptions about the project. Thusly, the dam builder can gain social support for the project. By gaining public approval, the dam builder will most likely gain political endorsement as well. Political support is useful in subsequent areas, or "pillars."

Once it is known by the dam builder that the public will support (or at least not violently oppose) the project, the other three pillars of construction can be addressed. The dam must be designed. Civil engineers and surveyors must pick a specific site and design the structure on paper. Contractors and logistical experts must craft a construction schedule. Finally, hydrological engineers must be consulted on the size and extent of the lake to be formed after construction of the dam. All of these experts must work together to make sure the structure is technically feasible. It must be safe, reliable and efficient.

While the engineers are addressing the technical requirement, the dam builder must find a way to pay for the structure. Most major infrastructure projects have significant government backing because they will become a public asset. However, some infrastructure projects are public-private ventures or, rarely, funded entirely from private sources. Whatever the funding mix, financiers must be found; budgets and an amortization schedule must be drawn up and a return on investment must be shown - whether it is privately or publicly funded. With our hypothetical dam, value might be created by the sale of hydroelectricity or irrigation water, by the prevention of flooding or by the creation of a scenic lake for recreation. All of these uses provide value for the public but only some can create value for a private funder. The right mix must be found.

Legal planning will be necessary as well. There is a mountain of construction permits and operating licenses required for a dam to be built and function properly. While it may be technologically possible to build a piece of infrastructure, without legal approval, it simply will not happen. The dam builder would find it prohibitively expensive to hire an army to beat back the hundreds of lawyers attempting to sue him for construction without proper licenses and authorizations.

There is no distinct order for these steps. Their timing and rank of importance will change according to each project. However, every single contemporary infrastructure must meet these four requirements in order to be built with a minimum of expense and societal disruption.

The Space Elevator is essentially a very large piece of infrastructure. It will ferry goods and people to and from orbit. It will provide very clear benefits to society. Therefore, the Space Elevator must meet the four requirements of proper infrastructure construction. We will examine the four pillars of Space Elevator construction.

The question being asked most often today by those interested in the Space Elevator is "Can it even be built?" This is a technical question. Fortunately, technical questions are quickly being answered: Humanity should have the means to build the Space Elevator in the next five to ten years (most likely sooner than that considering the pace of recent nanotechnology developments). Unfortunately, in answering some of the technical questions, more difficult non-technical questions have arisen. These questions are in the realm of the three remaining pillars. It has become apparent that the technical challenges to Space Elevator construction are small compared to the financial, sociopolitical, and legal challenges.

Technical costs of the Space Elevator are predicted to be around six to seven billion dollars. Dr. Edwards, in his initial NASA Institute of Advanced Concepts Report, added another three billion dollars of contingency costs in order to make the total cost of Space Elevator construction ten billion dollars. In the realm of large infrastructure projects that is not an extremely high price, but it is still (needless to say) a significant amount of money to be raised. LiftPort Group plans on using a combination of public and private funding sources over the next thirteen years to complete the first Space Elevator. Obtaining government grants and providing a return on investment will be challenging.

The very large contingency cost budgeted into Space Elevator construction reflects a lack of knowledge as to the cost of the other three pillars of development. Obtaining the necessary legal certification for the Space Elevator will require LiftPort to go to court. There is simply no other way to arrange for the proper documents. In order to make sure the Space Elevator is not infringing on anyone's right, disputes will be settled in court. Quite frankly, the Space Elevator will break new ground in terms of the law and that will not be easy or cheap.

Finally, one of the biggest challenge to Space Elevator construction involves sociopolitical support. The Space Elevator is a concept unfamiliar to many people but can offer the whole world many benefits, such as endless renewable energy via space solar power, and more comprehensive global communication. Many people, however, do not even know about the concept, or worse yet have misconceptions about the idea and what its effects will be.

Therefore, it is the responsibility of the Space Elevator construction company to educate and inform the global public about the promise (both the opportunities and the threats) of the Space Elevator. This is part of the reason why LiftPort pursues an International Public Inclusion Policy and why the firm chronicles their progress on a web log. It is hoped that by spurring grass-roots support for the Space Elevator, political leaders throughout the globe will support the project as well. Having the support of key elected officials in the US and elsewhere will facilitate the successful resolution of funding and legal challenges.

One could argue that the technical pillar is really the only true requirement for construction. During the days of the Pharaohs and Emperors, a few infrastructure projects were completed without the need for "proper authorization" and without public support, but there was always financial planning. However, the Space Elevator is too large a project to be built without considering all these areas. It will not be built without addressing the four pillars. It will not operate without international consensus or proper financial management. Therefore, if we as human beings want to enjoy the benefits the Space Elevator, it is in our best interest to support its construction. It is important that the Space Elevator be built according to the four pillars of proper infrastructure construction in the private sector using dual-track technology development as a catalyst and a deadline as daily motivation. These three basic principles will allow the Space Elevator to be built in a fast, inexpensive and ultimately safe manner.

RETURN ON INVESTMENT:
How the Space Elevator will Pay for Itself
by
Patrick Boake

Patrick Boake is a freelance techno-journalist in Toronto, Canada. On September 10, 2001 Boake took his 20 years of experience in the computer business into Toronto's Centennial College journalism program, graduating in January 2004. While still in school, Boake freelanced for *The Globe & Mail* technology web site globetechnology.com and *Silicon Valley NORTH*, a Canadian high-tech business monthly and still writes for both publications. A voracious consumer of science fiction, Boake enjoys writing about technology and its effects on society.

Blog in Progress:
http://pboake.blogspot.com/

SVN Clippings:
http://www.siliconvalleynorth.com/search/
index.html?qmini=Boake

Globetechnology.com clipping
:http://www.globetechnology.com/servlet/story/
RTGAM.20040303.gtcstrackmar3/BNStory/einsider/caseStudies

IN ECONOMIC TERMS, a Space Elevator (SE) is to rocketry what railways and public transit systems are to automobiles. The technologies to move massive amounts of people and cargo into space inexpensively are coming on stream but the possibility still exists for space to be rendered inaccessible by economics.

There's no question SEs will lower the cost of going to space by orders of magnitude. The question is will the cost threshold be low enough to make a profit for the existing terrestrial industries that will pioneer the space economy and bootstrap whole new industries we haven't thought of yet.

Return On Investment (ROI) will determine when (and possibly whether) humanity will be able to bolster Earth's economy and environment with space resources.

It's clear to Jim Benson, CEO of California satellite manufacturer SpaceDev, why the human race needs to get into space in a permanent, economically viable way. After selling off his software companies Benson was looking for new challenges. He read *Mining the Sky* by Dr. John Lewis of Arizona University and it resonated with his Bachelor of Science degree in geology. His life was changed.

"I was so excited about the book I bought 50 copies and for the next two or three years gave copies away to people I was trying to educate about the abundance of natural resources in space and how easy they are to get to," says Benson. "That was one of my main reasons for founding SpaceDev."

"We don't want to go the Moon or Mars. We want to be going to Near Earth Objects. That's where the wealth and life support and water is."

"I've been saying for a long time that water is the white gold of space."

The problem is getting to those resources in a cost-effective way. A new technology like a Space Elevator (SE) will lower the cost of going to space but Benson believes before it can get off the ground we also need a new way of doing things here on earth. ROI begins in the business model.

"My favorite slogan is 'if we want to go to space to stay, space has to pay'," says Benson. "Everybody knows it costs from US$5K to US$40K per pound [to bring something to space] today. That's just a given."

The reasons for the high cost of leaving Earth are as much systemic as they are practical. Benson is working to change the existing system from within by "bringing the microcomputer way of thinking into space." SpaceDev turns out what it calls micro and nano-satellites designed to reduce the cost of manufacturing and launch.

"When SpaceDev designed ChipSat for NASA there was definitely requirements for the ability to withstand g-forces during launch. I believe it was 10g's in all three axes. That's pretty ridiculous," he exclaims.

"No launch vehicle today generates those kinds of forces. That's typical government fear of failure. There are some expenses to meeting unrealistic requirements like that but it doesn't add that much to the cost. The big cost is simply the launch vehicles [and] the cost of launching itself. That's the heart of the problem."

An SE will shift existing economic paradigms and create whole new ones by making the ride to orbit mundane. Achieving that requires a perceptual shift in those that would build it of a similar or greater extent.

"If a project like this is going to be undertaken it needs to be undertaken by a new company. I really think this has got to be done by a private sector company that's not one of the usual suspects."

"Boeing and Lockheed feel like they're entitled to their share of the military and NASA space budgets.

"They don't know and don't care about doing things in innovative, lower-cost ways because almost everything they do is on a cost-plus, fixed fee contract basis.

"The higher the cost, the bigger the fee so they have no interest whatsoever in doing anything that's innovative or cost-effective."

Benson feels it's time for an entrepreneurial revolution.

"We have to look at everything [and ask] is it profitable? If it's profitable then it's sustainable. Until this point, almost everything in space, except communications satellites, has been government-financed," he says. "There's been no thought given to profitability therefore no thought given to sustainability."

Benson draws on his decades of experience to delineate one of the problems of making an SE project sustainable: "keeping [the SE] from being destroyed by [space] junk" and in doing so comes out as one of the first space environmentalists.

"I think it's inevitable [that we have to] vacuum the vacuum. We've got to stop generating [space debris] and clean up what exists," Benson explains. "People thought the ocean was so big that that it just didn't matter and here we are not only polluting it but depopulating it.

"Most of the satellites and therefore debris are at LEO. [Debris] is a huge consideration. One I don't think they have a good answer for yet."

Benson has but to ask the author of his inspiration, Dr. John S. Lewis, Planetary Sciences Professor at the University of Arizona about the space debris problem. Dr. Lewis sees not only a danger but also a recycling opportunity in the man-made space flotsam orbiting our globe.

"They're not only threatening debris, they are a fairly substantial source of solar cells and metals. You can assume that any spacecraft that's died up there has exhausted its attitude control fuel so you don't really expect to retrieve volatiles," explains Dr. Lewis. "On the other hand you do have the structural metals and solar cells. I'm sure that if you do have a source of any kind of mass up there you'd think of a way to use it if only for radiation shielding."

Dr. Lewis points out that gravitational geographies preclude a geosynchronous SE from use as a launch platform for all but a scant few asteroid mining expeditions but an SE still has practical benefits over blasting into space.

"If you're talking about a geosynchronous tether, it has two main functions as I see it," says Dr. Lewis. "It has the ability to put large masses in GEO and launch science payloads at very high speeds to a wide range of destinations. Those are the clear-cut advantages."

He has no trouble listing several commercial satellite applications.

"Solar Power Satellites (SPS) number one … a constellation of [manufacturing] stations girdling the earth … and orbital hotels," outlines Dr. Lewis. "[The potential of] orbital hotels should not be under-rated. This is a real cheap way to get to GEO and you should be thinking of having tourists up there.

"If you're talking about launching one or more communications or surveillance platforms in geosynchronous orbit this is a great way to do it," Dr. Lewis concludes.

SPSs would concentrate the Sun's energy and beam it to Earth using microwaves or lasers. Unlike terrestrial solar power, SPS's generate electricity 24 hours a day from sunlight unfiltered by Earth's atmosphere.

According to Larry Kazmerski, technology manager for solar energy technologies at the National Renewable Energy Laboratory in Colorado, rocket launch costs are birth control for an SPS industry that has would-be participants already lined up in the waiting room.

"2004 is the fiftieth anniversary of the Bell invention of the solar cell. One solar cell we had back then was five milliwatts of power," says Kazmerski. "Last year the industry shipped out something like three-quarters of a gigawatt, something like nine billion cells. Most of that progress has been in the last 10-15 years. So, if you look 10-15 years ahead, technological progress tends to compress in time.

"Some people think even one SPS up there would be a business, he adds with a laugh.

"I actually served for three years on a NASA panel that looked at the future of space power. They have experts looking at SPSs for Earth still because they said 'eventually we're going to have this.'

"Probably the primary thing right now is delivering those things up to space. The SE does attack a critical showstopper," states Kazmerski. "If you can get this stuff up there cheap, all of a sudden space solar power becomes feasible.

"If you go up [in space] now every near-earth satellite uses dual or triple-junction solar power devices that are on the order of 28% efficient [in zero air mass]. They are not at their limits yet. They could still probably be optimized by adding a 4th junction to bring them up to 40 or 50% efficiency.

"I think right now, if the delivery system were sufficient, [current solar power technologies] would be good enough to start us. [But], right now, it would be difficult to deliver a square mile of photovoltaics up into space."

Solar power isn't the only industry that would be transformed by inexpensive space platforms hoisted into orbit on the SE.

Delbert E. Day, the Curators' Professor of Ceramic Engineering and Senior Research Investigator at the Graduate Center for Materials Research, University of Missouri-Rolla knows who will be happiest when the SE comes on line.

"In the ceramics field it would be those people who are making objects that are difficult to nearly impossible to make on earth," says Professor Day. "In other words, people in the electronics and optical communications fields who know that there are materials out there, which, if they could be made, would find some immediate application."

Ceramics and glasses are made by high-temperature melting of raw materials taken directly from the earth (clay, sand, etc.) and processed materials into inorganic, nonmetallic solids. They are made into everything from spark plugs, glass, electronic components and nuclear materials to abrasives, rocket components, and tableware.

Making any kind of glass means cooling the melted raw material with minimal crystal formation.

"There's been lots and lots of research that hasn't gone anywhere because many of the compositions that have desirable properties tend to crystallize," says Professor Day.

"There are fluoride glasses people know have very good optical transmission qualities which are very difficult, in fact almost impossible, to make here on earth."

An optical fiber made from fluoride glass transmits light over far greater distances than convention optical fiber without the degradation of the light signal found in silicon-based optical fibers. This could have the practical effect of reducing or even eliminating the installation and maintenance of expensive networking hardware enroute.

"One of the advantages of space is, at least from the very limited experiments we've done, everybody's reported that the crystallization tendencies of a melt are lower," says Professor Day. "[If it didn't crystallize] that would be a major stride forward.

"Part of the problem is that we have done so few experiments because of the high cost [of going into space] and limited time available [once there]. I'm confident that if the SE was operational and [transport] cost a hundred dollars per pound, people would do experiments and we would find things we can't even dream of [today]."

Permanently extending Earth's economy into space in an economically and environmentally sustainable way is inspired by dreams but it will have to be achieved by political, business and technical realities that are harsher, colder and as unforgiving as space itself.

The ROI is out there if we can master and marshal our own mental and emotional universes so as to find the courage to change our ways and not simply repeat the mistakes of the past that have cost so much to learn.

TURNING SPACE LAUNCH INTO A BUSINESS
by
Joan Horvath
Executive Director, Global Space League
CEO, Takeoff Technologies LLC

Joan Horvath is the founder and CEO of Takeoff Technologies LLC, based in Pomona, California (www.takeofftech.com). Takeoff is a consulting firm which provides technology management and strategy advice to emerging companies, particularly in the aerospace sector. She is also cofounder and Executive Director of Global Space League, Inc. (www.globalspaceleague.org), a 501(c)3 nonprofit institution based in Frederick, Oklahoma which works to match up student payloads and early-stage flight entrepreneurs. Ms. Horvath has a BS degree in Aeronautics and Astronautics from MIT, and an MS in Mechanical, Aerospace and Nuclear Engineering from UCLA. She resides in Pasadena, California with her astronomer husband, and enjoys figure skating, bicycling and hiking.

Is The Launch Industry Actually A Business?
THE SPACE LAUNCH industry was born out of the American and former Soviet Union defense sectors. Each instance of launch vehicle one-upmanship in the Apollo program and its Russian counterpart was a Cold War surrogate for missile exchanges, not an exercise in scientific collaboration. Like all military operations it encouraged competition and secrecy rather than cooperation, long-term sustainability and commercially useful products. Civilian product development seems almost frivolous in this context. How can one talk seriously about filming commercials in space when the future of the free world is at stake?

Due to this early focus on winning at any cost, performance, not cost-efficiency, was the goal for launch vehicles. Thus it was rare —almost heretical—to say, "This simple rocket system is good enough for this purpose, and it is cheap to operate—let's stop here and start building these." Today, federally-funded scientists compete for launches—not money to *buy* launches—and launch cost for all practical purposes is irrelevant to government-funded users.

No one discusses price of launches except in the odd, largely meaningless metric of "dollars per pound to orbit." If postage rates were compared the same way, a six-ounce FedEx Custom special-handling overnight package between Singapore and Los Angeles would be directly compared with six ounces in a multi-ton Sea-Land shipping container which will take three months across the Pacific. The fact that dollars per pound to "orbit" remains as the commonest metric in the industry is one of the clearest indications that this is not yet a business in any normal sense of the word; new measures are needed and will emerge on a market-by-market basis so that rational competition among bidders for particular missions can arise. Deployment of a Space Elevator would likely make access to some orbits (those which are easier to reach via the system) much cheaper than others, and the nature of the evolution of private markets in space between now and Elevator deployment will likely have an impact on return on investment for Elevator investors, both public and private.

Encouraging private-sector R&D

But what about private-sector research and development for new space products and services? A large profit margin for launch services would imply that there is room for an entrepreneur to enter into the market and make a lot of money based on lower prices. But for this opportunity there must be markets: the inwardly turned aerospace industry's current markets are so small that they do not draw R&D money. Indeed, the large launch companies themselves are relatively small: for a snapshot, consider the situation on October 10, 2004, according to numbers on Yahoo Finance. Lockheed-Martin's market capitalization was $25 billion; Boeing's $42 billion; and Orbital Sciences' $500 million. This means that the total market capitalization of the entire current US launch industry (including all their product lines and divisions, not launch vehicles alone) is around $67.5 billion—barely above eBay ($62 billion) and dwarfed by IBM ($145 billion), Johnson and Johnson ($164 billion), and Microsoft ($305 billion). Wal-Mart's September 2004 sales worldwide were $25.7 billion for *the month*—more than the entirety of Lockheed-Martin's market value. Thus, to have an adequate market to justify significant investments in technology and infrastructure development, new partnerships outside of the dwindling aerospace market must be found and developed to make the investments pay off.

Are other nations better placed to develop a news space business?
After the fall of Communism the newly capitalist Russians were
forced by circumstance to try just about anything to have enough
capital to run their space program. Therefore, they were the first to
take a private space tourist along for a ride and have in general been
rather aggressively capitalist and willing to make deals. Sweeping
change took away too much of their spaceflight infrastructure to
allow them to continue as they were, and now they are becoming a
lean, aggressive, cost-conscious organization quite willing to partner
with American space tourism firms.

Meanwhile, in Britain, Surrey Satellite Technology Ltd., originally a small university spinoff company, has become the power-
house of low-cost high-performance small spacecraft (which they
launch on Russian rockets.) Sir Richard Branson is planning to launch
Virgin Galactic to fly space tourists on a derivative of Burt Rutan's
SpaceShipOne; reportedly at this juncture Virgin has booked 7,000
people at $200,000 apiece, for revenue of $1.4 billion.

Why Surrey and Virgin rather than firms in the United States,
with its longer history of aerospace business? Perhaps in part it is
because there is not a long tradition of competition driven by
market forces among American launch providers. However, from
the American side, export regulations called ITAR (International
Trafficking in Arms Regulations) makes it cumbersome for American businesses to work with citizens from countries other than the
United States. ITAR rules deserve a chapter of their own, but
here suffice it to say that a thorough review of these rules is needed
with an eye toward smoothing international space commerce for
American companies.

High-Risk Space Business Development:
Is There a Role for Government?

Small entrepreneurial space companies, particularly in the United
States, tend to see their funding options as an either-or choice: all
private money, or all government money. However, there are historical analogs for mixed funding and support, and given that the
existing customer base is mostly government-funded researchers,
it is foolish to simply ignore this market and assume it will remain
price-insensitive forever. Historical analogs of the current situation in space may provide some guidance for policy and business
models in this regard.

In the early 1860s, the only real option to get to the gold fields of California was to either take three months to walk across the continent, or to sail around the Cape of Good Hope. Sailing from Europe to California was a shorter trip than from than New York via the Cape (Brands, 2002). There was strong demand to be able to get people and goods to California faster and more safely than was possible at the time, particularly for Sacramento merchants who supplied the gold miners.

To solve this problem and despite (some would say "because of") their lack of knowledge of how hard it would be to develop a railroad across Western deserts and mountain ranges, merchants C.P. Huntington, Mark Hopkins, the Crocker brothers, and grocer Leland Stanford attempted to raise private capital for such a railroad. Initially, a contemporary account reports that the project was "held in such ill repute that it was more than a banker's character for prudence was worth to connect himself with it, even by subscribing for its stock." (Nordhoff, 1873, p. 48). This changed when Stanford became governor of California. Huntington was then dispatched by the others back to Washington (in those days a very long business trip!) and pushed the public/private financing arrangement that became the Railroad Act of 1862. The Union Pacific and Central Pacific hired the best engineers they could find and made it work, always with a business focus in mind and an eye on laying groundwork for eventual markets (some of which were created by the railroad itself). Can this be a model for today's space business?

Consider Oklahoma Senate Bill S720, passed in 1999. State Sen. Gilmer Capps decided that he would try to diversify the economy of his farming and oil drilling Southwest Oklahoma district by bringing in aviation businesses to use abandoned Strategic Air Command bomber bases. To that end, S720 promised transferable tax credits - in essence, matching funds worth around $17 million - for the investors in such companies. Figure 1 shows side-by-side excerpts of the parallels in language to the Railroad Act of 1862 (which granted the Union Pacific federal assets which made it money as the railroad grew). Many rather interesting bidders came to Oklahoma, mostly from California, to compete for the tax credits, which were ultimately granted to Rocketplane Ltd. For investors willing to put private capital at risk for huge endeavors such as a Space Elevator, Oklahoma's S1270—and the Railroad Act—might be interesting models for international grants of "right of way" (perhaps orbital slots or frequency spectrum). Any space "right of way" would require international consensus, which will take time but ultimately might pave the way for high-enough returns to build new global infrastructure.

Figure 1. Two high-risk pieces of technology legislation, 137 years apart

Pacific Railway Act of 1862	*Oklahoma Space Industry Development Act of 1999*
Pacific Railway Act (1862) An Act to aid in the Construction of a Railroad and Telegraph Line from the Missouri River to the Pacific Ocean, and to secure to the Government the Use of the same for Postal, Military, and Other Purposes. *<defines and hereby forms>* "The Union Pacific Railroad Company"; and by that name shall have perpetual succession, and shall be able to sue and to be sued, plead and be impleaded, defend and be defended, in all courts of law and equity within the United States, and may make and have a common seal; and the said corporation is hereby authorized and empowered to layout, locate, construct, furnish, maintain, and enjoy a continuous railroad and telegraph, with the appurtenances, from a point on the one hundredth meridian of longitude west from Greenwich, between the south margin of the valley of the Republican	BE IT ENACTED BY THE PEOPLE OF THE STATE OF OKLAHOMA: This act shall be known and may be cited as the "Oklahoma Space Industry Development Act". SECTION 1. NEW LAW A new section of law to be codified in the Oklahoma Statutes as Section 5203 of Title 74, unless there is created a duplication in numbering, reads as follows: A. Subject to the requirements of Section 6 of this act, there is hereby created for the purpose of establishing commercial and public-use spaceports a body corporate and politic, to be known as the "Oklahoma Space Industry Development Authority", and by that name the Authority may sue and be sued, and plead and be impleaded. The Authority is hereby constituted an agency of this state, and the exercise by the Authority of the powers conferred by this act shall be deemed to be essential

River and the north margin of the valley of the Platte River, in the Territory of Nebraska, to the western boundary of Nevada Territory, upon the route and terms hereinafter provided, and is hereby vested with all the powers, privileges, and immunities necessary to carry into effect the purposes of this act as herein set forth. The capital stock of said company shall consist of one hundred thousand shares of one thousand dollars each, which shall be subscribed for and held in not more than two hundred shares by anyone person, and shall be trans- ferable in such manner as the by-laws of said corporation shall provide.

SEC. 2. And he it further enacted, That the right of way through the public lands be, and the same is hereby, granted to said company for the construction of said railroad and telegraph line; and the right, power, and authority is hereby given to said company to take from the public lands adjacent to the line of said road, earth, stone, timber, and other materials for the construction thereof; said right of way is granted to said railroad to the extent of two hundred feet in width on each side of said railroad where it may pass over the public lands, including all necessary grounds for stations,

governmental functions of this state with all the attributes thereof. B. It shall be the purpose, function, and responsibility of the Authority to plan spaceport systems and projects in this state, to promote the development and improvement of space exploration and spaceport facilities, to stimulate the development of space commerce and education, including, but not limited to, the commercialization of the space industry and the development of space-related industries, to promote research and development related to space and space-related industry, and to promote tourism in connection with the foregoing. In carrying out this duty and responsibility, the Authority may advise and cooperate with municipalities, counties, regional authorities, state agencies and organizations, appropriate federal agencies and organizations, and other interested persons and groups.

SECTION 2.   NEW LAW   A new section of law to be codified in the Oklahoma Statutes as Section 5204 of Title 74, unless there is created a duplication in numbering, reads as follows: Subject to the requirements of Section 6 of this act, the Oklahoma Space Industry Development Authority is hereby granted, buildings, workshops, and depots, machine shops, switches, side tracks, turntables, and, water stations. The United States shall extinguish as rapidly as may be the Indian titles to all lands falling under the operation of this act and required for the said right of way and; grants hereinafter made.

SEC 3. And be it further enacted, That there be, and is hereby, granted to the said company, for the purpose of aiding in the construction, of said railroad and telegraph line, and to secure the safe and speedy transportation of the mails, troops, munitions of war, and public stores thereon, every alternate section of public land, designated by odd numbers, to the amount of five alternate sections per mile on each side of said railroad, on the line thereof, and within the limits of ten miles on each side of said ro1ld, not sold, reserved, or otherwise disposed of by the United States, and to which a preemption or homestead claim may not have attached, at the time the line of said road is definitely fixed: Provided, That all mineral lands shall be excepted from the operation of this act; but where the same shall contain timber, the timber thereon is hereby granted to said company. And all such lands, so granted by this section, which

has and may exercise all powers necessary to carry out and effectuate its purpose, including, but not limited to, the following:
1. Sue and be sued by its name in any court of competent jurisdiction;
2. Adopt and use an official seal and alter the same at pleasure;
3. Make and execute any and all contracts and other instruments necessary or convenient to the exercise of its powers;
4. Issue revenue bonds or other obligations as authorized by the provisions of this act or any other law, or any combination of the foregoing, to pay all or part of the cost of the acquisition, construction, reconstruction, extension, repair, improvement, maintenance or operation of any project or combination of projects, to provide for any facility, service or other activity of the Authority and to provide for the retirement or refunding of any bonds or obligations of the Authority, or for any combination of the foregoing purposes;
5. Acquire property, real, personal, intangible, tangible, or mixed, in fee simple or any lesser interest or estate, by purchase, gift, devise, or lease, on such terms and conditions as the Authority may deem necessary or desirable, and sell or otherwise dispose of the same and of any

shall not be sold or disposed of by said company within three years after the entire road shall have been completed, shall be subject to settlement and preemption, like other lands, at a price not exceeding one dollar and twenty-five cents per acre, to be paid to said company.

(National Archives transcription of original 1862 text - typographical errors retained per original).

of the assets and properties of the Authority;

6. Lease as lessor or lessee to or from any person, public or private, any facilities or property of any nature for the use of the Authority and to carry out any of the purposes of the Authority;

7. Subject to the limitations prescribed by Section 10 of this act, acquire by condemnation land and such interest therein as may be necessary in its determination for the purpose of establishing, constructing, maintaining, or operating a spaceport;

8. Own, acquire, construct, develop, create, reconstruct, equip, operate, maintain, extend and improve launch pads, landing areas, ranges, payload assembly buildings, payload processing facilities, laboratories, space business incubators, launch vehicles, payloads, space flight hardware, facilities and equipment for the construction of payloads, space flight hardware, rockets, and other launch vehicles, and spaceport facilities and systems, including educational, recreational, cultural, and other space-related initiatives...

(Oklahoma Senate Online Archives for 1999 session.)

A case study in developing new markets

We have seen above that the key to private funding of new space vehicles and industries lies in expanding the business base outside its current defense and science core. However, a chicken-and-egg problem arises: if a market is new, how do we know how valuable it will be? How can one try out a space product development without committing vast resources very early on? A key asset as private space markets evolve is access to low-cost flight-testing for vehicles and low-cost flights for prototypes of potential products or services. To that end, I and my associates have founded the Capps Space Science Center in Frederick, Oklahoma. Named for Sen. Capps, the Center is a public-private informal consortium that is intended to make it easy for entrepreneurs to find university partners for needed technology. The Capps Center is working to draw early-stage flight vehicle developers to the site in Frederick to create a pool of test flights, some of which could perhaps carry engineering or marketing prototypes of future new goods and services. An associated 501(c)3 nonprofit, Global Space League, Inc. (www.globalspaceleague.org) arranges for sponsorship of flights of kids' experiments on vehicle test flights. We are hoping to assist Liftport in some of its component flight test down at the Capps Center soon - using assets developed by slightly older startup companies. In time, we plan a suite of flight assets and development services to kick-start development of new commercial companies, leading, finally, to big enough markets in the private sector to end the dominance of government funding for space.

Further reading:

Brands, H.W. (2002) *The Age of Gold.* Random House, NY.

Yahoo Finance: (downloaded 10/10/2004) http://finance.yahoo.com

Horvath, J.C. (April, 2004). Blastoffs on a Budget. *Scientific American,* 290(4), 92-97.

Klerkx, G. (2004) *Lost in space: the fall of NASA and the dream of a new space age.* Pantheon Books, New York.

Oklahoma State Senate online. Text of 1999 Senate Bill S720. http://www.lsb.state.ok.us/1999-00SB/sb720_ccs.rtf

Library of Congress National Archives Online. Text of Railroad Act of 1872.

http://ourdocuments.gov/doc.php?flash=true&doc=32&page=transcript

Nordhoff, C. (1873) *California: for health, pleasure, and residence. A book for travellers and settlers.* Harper and Brothers, NY. From University of Michigan *Making of America Books* archives: http://www.hti.umich.edu/cgi/t/text/text-idx?c=moa;idno=ABA5511

"The Starship Free Enterprise." *The Economist,* (June 26, 2004) p. 79-81

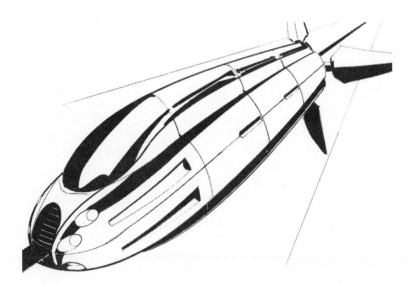

DISRUPTING SPACE:
How the Space Elevator May Affect Existing Industries
by
Robert Brodbeck

Bob Brodbeck works in applications development for the Taxi 2000 Corporation, designers and providers of innovative personalized transit systems. Previously he has worked for a major U.S. jet engine manufacturer as a research and development program planner and controller, accounting and business management systems manager, and has worked independently as a database design consultant. He holds an MBA degree from the University of Cincinnati. Over the years Bob has maintained an ongoing interest in the development of space and has been a member of several space development support organizations. He and his wife reside in Cincinnati, Ohio.

IN HIS 1997 best-selling book, *The Innovator's Dilemma,* Harvard Business School professor Clayton M. Christensen coined the term "disruptive technology" to describe new technologies that replace established technologies. The successful **disruptive technology** usually begins as a new, lower performance, but less expensive product. It starts by gaining a foothold in the low-end and less demanding segments of a market, and then through incremental performance improvements gains a greater and greater share of the market and its segments, and finally displaces the existing technology. Christensen also distinguishes between "**low-end disruption**" which targets customers whose needs are being expensively overserved and "**new-market disruption**" which targets customers that could previously not be served profitably by the existing technology providers.

These existing providers will not want to engage in a price war with a product that is simpler and has lower costs. Thus they will naturally begin to focus more on the high-end segments of the market.

Eventually, as the new technology captures more and more segments of their market, they will be squeezed into the smaller segments, or have to adapt their technologies and services to fill highly specialized high-end segments. Some of the incumbent technology providers, if not most, could be expected to disappear.

Development of the SpaceElevator technology appears to fit Christensen's "disruptive technology" concept, both in terms of comparative cost to the customer and evolution of performance. On the cost side, it has been estimated that the cost of sending payloads into space could be reduced from the current $8,000 to $10,000 per pound down to $400 per pound, and perhaps over time even less, with a Space Elevator. Such a radical change in the cost structure of space launches due to the would clearly make the Space Elevator a "disruptive technology" on that basis alone.

We can map out three business development stages for the LiftPort space elevator project:

Technology development
Early market penetration
Mainstream market penetration

Technology development stage
One aspect of the Space Elevator not described in the "disruptive technology" concept of Christensen directly is the long technology development time period that is required to bring the first operational elevator to market—currently predicted to take around fifteen years. But even during this time frame there will be technology developments disruptive to existing technologies. Indeed, firms developing the system, such as LiftPort Inc. and Carbon Designs Inc., as part of their stated business models and plans, are aiming to profitably commercialize spin-offs from their development of key technologies needed for the Space Elevator. The profits from these development stage spin-offs are intended to help fund the completion of the Space Elevator.

Primary among these potential spin-off technologies is carbon nanotube (CNT) technology, which appears will have numerous uses in a variety of industries. These range from the aerospace, automotive, and construction trades, to sports and recreational products, to name just a few. Being many factors stronger than steel, as well as versatile and extremely lightweight, CNT technology will begin to revolutionize these industries and present new business opportunities as well. It would be to the advantage of businesses in those industries, even now, to begin to investigate the application of CNT to their products. That is, if they want to increase their chances of survival in coming years. Naturally, the current suppliers of materials to these industries that CNT materials will replace have a great need to start thinking and planning to adapt or face shrinking markets or even possible extinction.

There are potentially numerous other industrial sectors that could be impacted by the space elevator development program since it covers a spectrum of needed technologies. Electrical power, for example, will be delivered to the lifters of the Space Elevator wirelessly from the Earth's surface by free electron lasers (or a similar type of laser). The development of such lasers for this purpose could lead to their application in other currently developing areas, such as in powering lighter-than-air high-altitude airship platforms. Such platforms could be used for surveillance and observation, or as wireless telecommunications arrays. Light weight and highly efficient photovoltaic solar collectors, for receiving and converting the laser power beams, will also undergo further development driven in part by the elevator project. These enhanced solar-electric technologies can impact technologies both on Earth and in space.

The construction of the Space Elevator itself, as well as some of the on-board activities both at high atmospheric and orbital altitudes, will require the use of robotic techniques and automated self-assembly of components. The development of these tele-assisted and autonomous operation robotic techniques will undoubtedly help drive enhancements in the field, both for use down on Earth, such as with industrial service and military robots, and for applications in space.

Early market penetration stage

Once the initial Space Elevator is in operation it will most likely serve customers outside of the traditional launch customer base. Primarily, these will be customers who previously have not been able to afford the high cost of launch into orbit. Included may be those with launch needs that are less rigorous or demanding in terms of payload weight, size, security, safety, shielding, and the handling of orbital insertion. Additionally, the payload capacity of the initial elevator is expected to be limited to about 13,000 kg (28,000 lb), which is comparable to NASA's Space shuttle. So initially, very heavy or extremely large payloads will not be able to utilize the Space Elevator (e.g. human passenger ships or very large space hardware).

Current launch customers, such as large telecommunications companies, governments and defense agencies, with highly complex, costly, and often large satellites would continue during this first operational stage to use traditional rocket-based launch services. All manned space launches will continue via conventional means as well during this stage, and for another good reason. The much slower launch velocity of the initial space elevator would take passengers through the Earth's radiation belts much more slowly than by rocket based systems, thus requiring shielding too heavy and expensive.

Therefore the early market will include the launch of low cost and smaller or micro-satellites from smaller organizations that have launched few if any such satellites into space previously. These organizations would include smaller firms, national governments, or educational institutions that, for example, would have satellite applications in the fields of environmental and agricultural assessment, surveillance, private telecommunications networks, medical and materials research and production, among other smaller less expensive payload needs. Essentially the whole market for space launches and the range of space-based applications will make a notable growth spurt, albeit mostly for segments previously under-served or not served at all.

Indeed, even in this early stage, numerous supporting businesses and industries will experience growth driven by the Space Elevator. The system will present expanded business opportunities to the space insurance industry, for example. The demand for the services of the micro-satellite design and engineering firms will expand tremendously, as will component manufacturers. Research and production of very high value materials will begin to expand rapidly, with even smaller corporate and insitutional players now able to afford to get in the game. The Space Elevator and the new low-gravity on-orbit R&D and manufacturing capabilities may well expedite improvements to the materials and components of successive elevators themselves, such as with the CNT ribbon systems.

During this early market penetration stage, although it may last but a few years, traditional launch systems providers and operators will likely feel little if any immediate negative impact on their business. Initially, costs to insure payloads and launches on the Space Elevator will be similar, if not even a bit higher, pound for pound, compared to traditional launch methods.

Mainstream market penetration

During early operation with the less demanding customers, the sub-systems, and the dependability of the elevator itself will be improved gradually, along with enhanced capabilities for handling more demanding customers. The Space Elevator will then enter a period in which it begins to incrementally attract the business of traditional launch customers, even before it becomes human-rated.

As the Space Elevator penetrates the traditional core space market segments, it will begin to displace conventional space launch services. Companies producing the components and providing launch services using ballistic rocket technologies will find their customer base shrinking, perhaps rapidly, as their high-end customers with larger, more complex, and demanding launch needs now shift to the much lower-cost elevator. Prescient rocket launch hardware and services companies will see this as an opportunity, however, because not only will the total market for launches begin to grow rapidly and much larger, but new and much more numerous non-elevator *in-orbit* transfer services will be needed as well. For example, the more complex space-based applications and facilities will need to be transferred, inserted, and assembled on-orbit. All of this in-space activity will require a greater number of rockets, thereby aiding the current space industry. However, the current rocket industry can only benefit from this increased business if they choose to switch from Earth-to-orbit rocketry to in-space rocketry.

Rocket-plane launch companies currently being developed, such as Virgin Galactic, will no doubt by this time be carrying human cargo to and from LEO. They will continue to do so and their market could grow tremendously for some time after the space elevator makes a major penetration of most traditional launch markets for non-human freight. The elevator will lead to the placement of any number of on-orbit manned stations, and some of the greater number of non-manned mechanisms in orbit will need maintenance visits by humans. Once the elevator becomes human-rated, some of their business may drop off, but perhaps only temporarily. Many people are willing to pay a premium for fast travel, and this will likely remain the case for travel to and from Earth orbit. For example, while space tourists may go by rocket-plane to their Virgin Galactic Space Hotel (the components of which were taken up via elevator), the hotel staff will use the elevator to get to and form work. Additionally there will be some increasing occurances, just due to the much larger number of manned facilities in orbit, to have emergency transport to orbit. Eventually, with tremendously expanded space operations, the human traffic to and from space will be many factors larger, and thus even these remaining niches for rocket-plane services will be significant.

The financial services industries will of course expand and diversify into the expanding opportunity envelope created by the rapid growth and commercialization of space related activities. Insurance underwriters will grow in numbers and the cost of their policies will drop. Project financing services will enter in this stage in a big way, with a much greater number of venture funds and investment banking enterprises participating. Governmental sponsored technology development consortiums, at local and state levels, will be assembled to provide opportunities for local firms and institutions to take part in in-space developments. It may even be foreseen that if the Space Elevator services grow quite rapidly and more elevators are quickly implemented, we may see a wave of speculative investment from the full gammut of investment sectors—from individuals to major fund managers. Perhaps we will some day witness a "Space Elevator" bubble—a temporary shake-out.

Stay ahead of the disruptions

Space missions of all magnitudes usually take years of planning, engineering, and preparation. No doubt during the last years of the development stage and increasingly during the early operational stage customers with more traditional launch needs will begin making plans and preparations to utilize the new elevator service to space, pending its successful operational demonstration and empirical data on lower comparative cost.

It behooves the management of the businesses and institutions that may be affected by the coming of the Space Elevator, whether the impact will be felt in the development stage or market penetration stages, to stay informed of the project, monitor its progress, and at the right time to begin planning and preparations for the changes that will disrupt their world.

Standing still is not an option for survival.

Rockets and the Space Elevator
by
Tom Nugent

Tom Nugent brings 12 years of wide-ranging experience in research, engineering, group management, information technology and business administration to his position as Research Director at LiftPort. He holds degrees in Physics from the University of Illinois at Urbana-Champaign and Materials Science from the Massachusetts Institute of Technology, as well as a non-degree certificate in Japanese Language from the University of Pittsburgh. Prior to joining LiftPort, Tom followed his fascination with space transportation by working on liquid-fueled rocket engine development through the MIT Rocket Team, and by researching advanced fusion propulsion at the Jet Propulsion Laboratory. He has served as a consultant to a microsatellite firm, and worked in the Space Development Group at Ishikawajima-Harima Heavy Industry's Yokohama, Japan, research center. Tom currently lives near Seattle with his wife, daughter, and two cats, all of whom remind him why building the space elevator is so important.

MANY PEOPLE NEW to the idea of a space elevator usually assume that large aerospace companies will be against the space elevator based on the belief that it would steal business from them. But this chapter is titled "Rockets *and* the Space Elevator" instead of "Rockets *vs.* the Space Elevator" because rocketry should flourish, not perish, in a world where the space elevator is a reality. We at LiftPort believe that rockets[3] will play a critical part in humankind's future in space. First, there is every reason to believe that the space elevator will increase the overall demand for rockets of various types. Second, the budding sub-orbital space tourism industry will help drive market demand for transport to outer space, thus creating a demand for the space elevator's services.

Getting from Point A to B, and then on to Point C...
What is the point of building a space elevator? The point is to make access to space safer and more affordable than it is now, with more throughput capacity and (drastically) less environmental impact. But "space" isn't a single destination —it encompasses the entire universe!

The space elevator alone, however, can't take you to any arbitrary point in the universe. Riding the elevator can only take you to any point along its length, which will extend in a geosynchronous orbit up to roughly 100,000 km above sea level. You can "let go" at any altitude and you'll fall into some orbit. If you let go at a very low altitude, your "orbit" will intersect Earth's atmosphere and you'll be back on the ground (and burnt to a crisp if you didn't have proper re-entry protection!). Let go at the right height (above 23,500 km) and you can go into an elliptical orbit around Earth, with the apogee at the altitude where you left the elevator. Letting go at GEO (Geosynchronous Earth Orbit, 42,300 km above the center of the Earth) will simply leave you there floating next to the ribbon. And if you let go even higher (above 53,300 km), you could leave Earth orbit entirely. The figure below illustrates the different orbits.

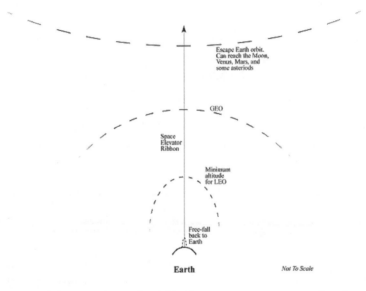

Escape Earth orbit. Can reach the Moon, Venus, Mars, and some asteriods

GEO

Space Elevator Ribbon

Minimum altitude for LEO

Free-fall back to Earth

Earth

Not To Scale

None of these options, though, allow you to get to exactly where you might want to go. Are you trying to deploy a satellite into a nice, circular low Earth orbit (LEO)? That will require an extra "kick" once you've left the space elevator, because your initial orbit will be elliptical, with the low part in LEO but the high part up where you let go of the space elevator, very far above LEO. Right now the only real way to get the needed kick is to use a rocket. What if you're trying to deploy a geosynchronous satellite to an orbital slot over Africa, ut the space elevator is over the Pacific Ocean? Again, you'll need a rocket (whether it's a traditional chemical rocket or the newer electric propulsion rocket) to move your GEO position from the space elevator over to your desired final location.

We can also talk about the longer-term options. If you want to go to the Moon, or Mars, or the asteroids, you can probably get a "free" trip to your destination by letting go of the space elevator at a high enough altitude. But how do you stop and maneuver once you get to your destination, or make course corrections along the way? Rockets, as always, will be the answer.

Currently, ground-to-orbit transportation produces the largest fraction of revenues in the launch industry, and is the main segment of the launch industry that will face significant direct competition from the space elevator. Initially, that segment may encounter decreased launch demand from satellite customers, as the satellite owners discover that the space elevator is safer and less expensive. As discussed below, however, even the ground-to-orbit segment will not totally disappear, and should expect an eventual increase in business.

The other segments of the launch industry (orbital transfer, interplanetary maneuvering, etc.) can all expect significant increases in their market size due to the space elevator. As the cost of getting to space decreases with the creation of multiple space elevators, new types of endeavors will become affordable. The increased traffic will require orbital transfer propulsion systems, i.e., rockets.

Human Safety

The other major customer of rocket services even after the space elevator is operating will be people, at least initially. Space tourists and anyone needing to go to orbit will need to minimize their exposure to radiation while travelling in space. The Van Allen radiation belts (which extend roughly from an altitude of 650 km to 6,300 km) would be deadly for unshielded people climbing at the relatively slow speed of the lifters. The initial space elevator will not have the capacity to carry enough shielding for human passengers, along with their necessary support facilities. Anyone who wants to travel to the space hotel at GEO, or even to space stations at LEO, will initially need to use rockets. (The LEO destination requires rockets because, even though the radiation belts do not begin that low, the "drop-off" point from the space elevator to get to even the lowest orbit is still high up, requiring a trip through the radiation belts). And many people may not want to wait (or may not be able to afford to wait) an entire week to travel to their destination in space, even if the view is awesome along the way. Rockets can get you there in hours, not days.

Luckily, the budding space tourism industry is focusing on improving human-rated rocket safety by a factor of 100 or more over traditional rockets. The use of hybrid rockets (such as in SpaceShipOne) alone should drastically reduce the chances of a rocket exploding. The supplies and cargo associated with human passengers can be sent up via the space elevator, which means that smaller (and potentially safer) rockets can be used for transporting people. Given current commercial projects aimed at creating a space tourism industry, it is reasonable to believe that the rocket infrastructure will exist to safely carry humans to orbit en masse. The cost for sending people to space will go down more than that currently envisioned because the space elevator will be able to loft most of the support infrastructure for orbital space tourism.

Another proposal to increase human safety is to launch a rocket from the space elevator, at perhaps an altitude of 500 kilometers (which is below the inner Van Allen radiation belt). The total energy required to get to orbit is lower at that altitude than for a ground launch, and being outside the atmosphere helps eliminate frictional losses as well. Reducing the required velocity change (called "delta vee") can help make the rocket safer by reducing the acceleration demands. There are concerns about igniting a rocket near the elevator ribbon, but if these can be overcome, then perhaps the space elevator could become stage one of the next two-stage-to-orbit rocket.

Demand for Launch Services

Not only will rockets still be needed once the space elevator is built, they will also serve a vital role before construction of the space elevator begins by helping to grow the market demand for transportation services, thereby increasing the impetus for the creation of the space elevator. The primary source of growth in space transportation in the foreseeable future will be space tourism. As the space tourism industry develops, the demand for putting infrastructure into space will grow.

Virgin Galactic, Bigelow Aerospace, and Space Adventures are some of the biggest players in the developing space tourism industry. Virgin plans to create thousands of astronauts by the end of this decade, and

Bigelow has offered the US$50 million America's Space Prize to encourage development of vehicles to take tourists to Bigelow's planned orbiting space hotels. Space Adventures has already arranged for a couple of millionaires' trips to the International Space Station, and offers other types of space-oriented trips as well. Space hotels will be easier to put in orbit via the space elevator than traditional rockets.

Various market studies have tried to estimate demand and market size for the space tourism industry. At least one study[4] has suggested a market size of one billion US dollars annually by 2021. Once there is a permanent destination in space for the space tourism industry, the need for cargo transport to orbit will increase dramatically. Space hotels will need regular supplies of food, water, orbital hardware, and more, which can be efficiently transported by the space elevator.

Construction by Mega-Corporations

There is one final reason to believe that rational aerospace corporations should not, for the most part, fight the development of the space elevator. That reason is simple: they will probably play a big hand in building the space elevator.

Who else in the private sector has the experience and work force to handle such a large-scale project? Lockheed Martin, Boeing, United Technologies, International Launch Services, Orbital Sciences, Northrup Grumman, Energia, Airbus and others are the types of companies experienced in large-scale aerospace projects. The ocean-based station and the ribbon construction are probably the only pieces of the space elevator in which the major aerospace companies do not have experience. Launch of the ribbon and the initial deployment mechanism, in-orbit assembly of those pieces, construction of vacuum-rated mechanical machinery (the lifters), station-keeping, tracking of orbital debris: these are all areas in which many of the big aerospace companies are perhaps the only ones who can do the work. The space elevator construction consortium should make a specific point of involving the large aerospace companies early in the planning process, both because of their expertise and to help bring them on board the space elevator project.

As mentioned above, the ground-to-orbit segment of the launch industry will likely face an initial decline in revenues as satellites begin to be launched on the space elevator. The aerospace firms involved in the construction of the space elevator may decide that potential losses in launches after the space elevator is built would be offset by the revenues from constructing the space elevator. The construction revenues would, of course, flow in well in advance of any potential business disruption caused by the space elevator.

Evolution of Aerospace Firms

Launch firms will not be the same in twenty years as they are today, whether or not the space elevator gets built. All industries evolve and change, and the aerospace industry has seen consolidation and increased launch competition over the last decade. The advent of space tourism alone will change the landscape of the industry over the next couple of decades.

Whether the new factors in aerospace are space tourism rockets or the space elevator, or both; whether the older aerospace firms act more as contractors to new players or maintain their leading role, change is inevitable. In order to manage that change, aerospace firms should be expanding their current work on electric propulsion systems for orbital transfer customers, and they should also investigate human-rated rockets to compete with the new offerings from some of the Ansari X-Prize teams. If an aerospace firm chooses to ignore or fight the changes, it may be in danger of losing out to those firms which can see the long-term benefits of adapting to new circumstances.

Win—Win for All

As I hope I've shown, the demand for rocketry as a whole will be drastically increased by the use of the space elevator. Much of the construction of the space elevator, as well as future space—based projects, will likely be done by some of the current large aerospace contractors, given their expertise and size.

Although "synergy" is an over-used word in the aerospace world, it aptly describes the relationship between rockets and the space elevator. They will feed off of each other's creation of new space markets and growth of existing ones.

Some aerospace companies may view the space elevator solely as a threat, instead of an opportunity, and may choose to opposed the space elevator out of a short-sighted belief that it could harm their business. However, forward-looking aerospace firms will play a vital role, not only in the construction of the space elevator, but more importantly in providing transportation options to the plethora of payloads which will use it as the first stage in their travels. It is up to the firms themselves to decide whether or not to evolve along with the changing aerospace landscape.

LEGAL and MILITARY ISSUES
Legal Issues Affecting The Erection And Operation Of The Liftport Space Elevator System
by
Keil J. Ritterpusch, Esq. and Mark J. Fiekers, Esq.

KEIL RITTERPUSCH is the managing partner of PIERSON & RITTERPUSCH, LLP.

Mr. Ritterpusch leads P&R's international aerospace, defense and high technology practice, representing clients in a broad range of corporate, contract, and regulatory matters. He is an expert on U.S. export law and regulation and also represents private and government clients in international and domestic contract negotiations. He also has been extensively involved in strategic planning for clients and has represented clients before various executive agencies of the U.S. and international governmental bodies.

Mr. Ritterpusch received his B.A. from Northwestern University and his J.D. from the College of William & Mary. He is a member of the Bar of the Commonwealth of Virginia and the ABA.

MARK FIEKERS is an associate in the firm of PIERSON & RITTERPUSCH, LLP.

Mr. Fiekers advises clients on corporate and securities matters, as well as international and domestic business transactions. Additionally, he helps clients prepare for and comply with the International Traffic in Arms Regulations as well as the Commerce Department's Export Administration Regulations.

Mr. Fiekers received his B.A. from the University of Vermont and his J.D., *cum laude*, from the Catholic University of America. Mr. Fiekers is currently working towards his LL.M. (Securities and Financial Regulation) from the Georgetown University Law Center. He is a member of the bar in New York and the District of Columbia.

INTRODUCTION
As has been discussed in detail throughout this book, the technological hurdles facing the construction and safe operation of LiftPort's Space Elevator are daunting. These hurdles, however,

will be overcome through a combination of ingenuity, persever-ance, and diligence on the part of LiftPort's management, employ-ees, and consultants, not to mention the significant infusion of capital into the Space Elevator program. The legal obstacles to erecting and operating LiftPort's Space Elevator, on the other hand, while numerous and complicated, should not be nearly as difficult for LiftPort to surmount as are the technological hurdles.

Nevertheless, first understanding and then resolving the legal obstacles for the development and operation of LiftPort's Space Elevator will prove to be, in the authors' opinion, just as critical to the successful implementation of the LiftPort Space Elevator as will be the technological hurdles. For, even if we can build the LiftPort Space Elevator from a technological and fiscal perspective, if cer-tain legal implements are not in place before the LiftPort Space El-evator is erected, LiftPort will not be able to safely or effectively operate it.

Herein, the authors address not all of the legal issues that will affect the construction and operation of the LiftPort Space Eleva-tor, but the four areas of the law that the authors feel are the most essential for LiftPort to comprehend and resolve (or at least develop strategies to resolve) early in the development of the LiftPort Space Elevator. For the purposes of this book, the authors note that the discussion of the legal issues affecting the development and opera-tion of the LiftPort Space Elevator is intentionally concise.[5]

In the authors' opinion, the four areas of the law that will have the greatest impact on LiftPort's development and operation of the LiftPort Space Elevator are as follows:

LEGAL JURISDICTION over the LiftPort Space Elevator System;[6]

PROSPECTIVE U.S. LICENSING of the LiftPort Space Elevator System;

APPLICABILITY OF THE INTERNATIONAL LAW OF THE SEAS to the LiftPort Space Elevator System; and

APPLICABILITY OF INTERNATIONAL SPACE LAW to the LiftPort Space Elevator System.

Legal Jurisdiction over the LiftPort Space Elevator System
The LiftPort Space Elevator System will pose an interesting chal-lenge from a jurisdictional perspective. The LiftPort System will include: (1) a comprehensive and permanent sea-based component,

subject to operation in accordance with the International Law of the Seas;[7] (2) a comprehensive and permanent international airspace component, subject to operation in accordance with International Airspace Law;[8] and (3) a comprehensive and permanent "outer space" component, subject to operation in accordance with International Space Law[9] and various national space laws and regulations (which national laws and regulations govern the activities of its citizens in the "outer space" environment). The LiftPort Space Elevator System will not be operated in any territories that are currently subject to sovereign control by a nation-state.

Notwithstanding the lack of direct sovereign control over the territories in which the LiftPort Space Elevator System will operate, the authors strongly believe that the development and operation of the LiftPort Space Elevator System will be subject to U.S. jurisdiction. Specifically, the example of the multi-national space launch company, the Sea Launch Limited Partnership ("Sea Launch") is instructive in the instant case to demonstrate how U.S. jurisdiction extends to the launch activities of non-U.S. entities operating outside of the territorial jurisdiction of the United States.

In the case of Sea Launch, the Commercial Space Launch Act of 1984 ("CSLA"), as amended and as codified in 49 U.S.C. Chapter 701, extended U.S. jurisdiction over the extraterritorial launch activities of the foreign corporation, Sea Launch. Specifically, Section 70104(a)(3) of the CSLA provided (and still provides) that "citizen[s] of the United States" may only engage in launch activities (i.e., to launch a launch vehicle or to operate a launch site) outside the United States and outside the territory of a foreign country if such U.S. citizens first obtain a license from the Associate Administrator for Space Transportation ("AST") of the U.S. Federal Aviation Administration ("FAA").[10] Likewise, Section 70102 (1)(c) of the CSLA still defines a "citizen of the United States" to include an entity organized or existing under the laws of a foreign country, if the controlling interest in the entity is held by a private American citizen or an entity organized under the laws of any of the states of the United States.[11]

In Sea Launch's case, the controlling interest in the Company (40%) was (and is) held by the Boeing Corporation (a U.S. person). Therefore, even though Sea Launch is a foreign entity, because a U.S. corporation holds a controlling interest (40%) in Sea Launch, Sea

Launch's extraterritorial launching activities are subject to the jurisdiction of the United States. The extension of U.S. jurisdictional
control over the launch activities of Sea Launch is merely instructive in the instant case, and not conclusive proof that the U.S. will
be able to exercise jurisdiction over the activities of the LiftPort
Space Elevator system (assuming that a U.S. entity holds a controlling interest in the LiftPort Group). To determine whether the U.S.
would have jurisdiction under the CSLA, it is necessary to determine whether the activities of the LiftPort Space Elevator System
would be considered "launch services," and whether the LiftPort
Space Elevator System would perform any "launches," as such
terms are defined under the CSLA.

Section 70102 (3) of the CSLA provides that "launch" means:

[T]o place or try to place a launch vehicle or reentry vehicle
and any payload from Earth—

in a suborbital trajectory;
in Earth orbit in outer space; or
otherwise in outer space, including activities involved in the
preparation of a launch vehicle or payload for launch, when
those activities take place at a launch site in the United States.[12]

Likewise, Section 70102 (5) of the CSLA provides that "launch
services" means:

activities involved in the preparation of a launch vehicle and
payload for launch; and
the conduct of a launch.

In order to assess whether the LiftPort Space Elevator System
will perform "launches" in accordance with the CSLA or whether
the activities of the LiftPort Space Elevator System will be considered "launch services", we must take the prospective characteristics
and operations of the LiftPort Space Elevator System and assess
them against the CSLA.

As provided above, the CSLA defines a "launch" as the placement or attempt at placement of a "launch vehicle" or "reentry vehicle" AND any "payload" from Earth into a suborbital trajectory,

214   *LiftPort:* The Space Elevator—Opening Space to Everyone

into Earth orbit in outer space, or otherwise into outer space. Thus, the first determination is whether LiftPort's Lifters are "launch vehicles", as such term is defined in Section 70102 (7) of the CSLA. In the alternative, the determination should be made whether the Lifters are "reentry vehicles", as such term is defined in Section 70102 (14) of the CSLA, or possibly both "launch" and "reentry" vehicles. The next determination is if the LiftPort Space Elevator System will transport "payloads" to outer space, as such term is defined in Section 70102 (9) of the CSLA.

Section 70102 (7) of the CSLA provides that "launch vehicle" means:

> a vehicle built to operate in, or place a payload in, outer space; and
> a suborbital rocket.[13]

Since the intended purpose of the Lifters will be to convey cargo and people between the LiftPort base station on the earth surface and the LiftPort(s) in the earth orbit or otherwise in outer space, the Lifters are clearly "vehicles built to operate in, or place ... payload[s] in, outer space." Thus, it is clear that the Lifters are "launch vehicles" within the meaning of Section 70102 (7) of the CSLA.

Likewise, for what it's worth the Lifters are also "reentry vehicles" within the meaning of Section 70102 (14) of the CSLA, because the Lifters are "designed to return from Earth orbit or outer space to Earth... substantially intact."[14]

Finally, Section 70102 (9) of the CSLA provides that "payload" means:

> an object that a person undertakes to place in outer space by means of a launch vehicle or reentry vehicle, including components of the vehicle specifically designed or adapted for that object.[15]

Since the intended purpose of the LiftPort Space Elevator system is to convey cargo and people between the earth's surface and earth orbit or, otherwise, outer space, it is clear that the LiftPort Space Elevator will be carrying "payloads" to outer space within the meaning of Section 70102 (9) of the CSLA.

Based on the foregoing, the authors are confident that the U.S. government will exercise jurisdiction over the LiftPort Space Elevator System and that LiftPort will need to obtain the appropriate license from AST to operate the Space Elevator System as a launcher in accordance with U.S. law and regulation.

Prospective U.S. Licensing of the LiftPort Space Elevator System
As discussed above, the crux of the U.S. federal regulation of commercial space operations is title 49, chapter 701 of the United States Code. This chapter governs all U.S. commercial space launch operations. According to this chapter, all entities which seek to perform commercial launches or to operate commercial launch operations must first apply for and receive a license from the AST. The primary mandate of AST's commercial space transportation licensing program is to ensure that public health and safety is not endangered by commercial launch activities.[16] There are four general types of licenses that a commercial space operator can apply for[17]: (1) launch-specific license authorizations (other than for Reusable Launch Vehicles ("RLVs")) covering one or more launches over a number of years, where each launch has the same general parameters (i.e., launch on the same launch vehicle at the same launch site) and there are a specified number of launches in the relevant period[18]; (2) launch site operator's licenses (other than for reentry operations), covering a maximum period of five years, by which the licensee is authorized to conduct launches from the site within a range of allowed parameters, including the use of multiple launch systems of the same general class and an array of payloads, both of which, as specified in the license application (and as approved in the site license issued by AST)[19]; (3) RLV launch-specific licenses;[20] and (4) RLV site operator licenses, where launches and reentries are authorized and which are valid only for two years.[21]

For non-RLV launches, the licensing process involves: (1) pre-application consultation(s) between the prospective licensee and AST; (2) the submission of the launch license to AST; (3) AST's review of the license to determine whether the proposed launch (or launches) and attendant launch activities present any conflicts with U.S. national security and foreign policy interests or to international obligations of the United States; (4) AST's review of the safety of the proposed launch (or launches) and launch activities;

(5) AST's review of the proposed payloads to be carried on the requested launches, assessing whether the launch of any of the payloads will jeopardize public health, safety, or welfare; (6) AST's assessment of the fiscal responsibility of the prospective licensee, including whether the licensee can cover the costs to third parties for the maximum probable loss ("MPL") by third parties whose persons or property may be harmed by the launch activities; and (7) AST's review of the potential damage to the natural environment that may be caused by the prospective launch activities under the license application (including AST's review of the Environmental Assessment required to be filed with the license application pursuant to 14 C.F.R. §§ 415.101 and 415.103).[22]

For launch site licenses, the same general review as provided for the review of launch licenses applies. However, site operator licenses also require information regarding the specific launch vehicles can be launched from the site, the launch site boundaries, the proposed flight corridors for launches, and a more detailed risk analysis governing complete site operations.[23]

Meanwhile, licenses for RLVs (both launch-specific and site operator license) require the same general review as provided for ordinary launch licenses as stipulated above; however, the FAA applies a different set of risk analysis factors in reviewing RLV license applications[24] and the FAA requires a different showing of financial responsibility for prospective RLV operators as well.[25]

To determine which type of license LiftPort would require, it would thus be necessary to determine whether a lifter is an RLV, and whether the license should be site-specific or launch-specific. This determination would depend on the details of the lifter design and on the frequency and character of the launches. An RLV is defined as "a launch vehicle that is designed to return to Earth substantially intact and therefore may be launched more than one time or that contains vehicle stages that may be recovered by a launch operator for future use in the operation of a substantially similar launch vehicle."[26] It is likely, but not certain, that lifters would be reusable, and thus would qualify as RLVs. A site-specific license would also seem most convenient for a fixed space elevator installation, but launch-specific licenses might be preferable in early stages of operation, depending on the regulations in force at the time of launch.

Applicability of the International Law of the Seas to the LiftPort Space Elevator System

As briefly discussed above, the International Law of the Seas will apply to the comprehensive and permanent LiftPort base station, which is expected to operate in International Waters somewhere in the Pacific Ocean more than 250 miles from any inhabited territories. The LiftPort base station shall use a very similar platform as is used in the Sea Launch program, with two major exceptions: (1) the LiftPort ocean-based platform/anchor will be substantially larger than the platform used to launch rockets by Sea Launch and (2) the LiftPort ocean-based platform/ anchor will operate continuously in the same 5-km radius area in the Pacific Ocean[27], whereas the Sea Launch platform vessel is located at the launch site in the middle of the Pacific Ocean only immediately before, during, and after launch operations. At all other times, the Sea Launch platform is either in transit back to its home base in California or in dry dock at the California home base.

The International Law of the Seas applies to Sea Launch's activities only generally while the platform is operating in International Waters or otherwise in transit between the home base in California and the launch site in the middle of the Pacific Ocean. The applicable law governing these activities is that Sea Launch's use of such International Waters should be free from interference from other users of the same International Waters at the same time. In should be noted, however, that there is a general freedom of over flight over all waters designated as International Waters, despite Sea Launch's general right to use such International Waters freely. Sea Launch would only have to notify the appropriate international body governing the use of the International Airspace above their launch platform regarding the prospective window that launches from the platform will take place, and ensure that the safe, coordinated use of the International Airspace by aircraft and Sea Launch may be accomplished.

Unlike Sea Launch's use of the International Waters and the International Airspace above the Sea Launch platform at the time of its launch operations, which use is temporary, LiftPort's use of International Waters and International Airspace will be effectively permanent (so long as LiftPort can maintain safe operations from the same site in International Waters). The distinction between Sea Launch's temporary use of International Waters and International Airspace and LiftPort's permanent or semi-permanent use is quite significant.

That is, with the construction and continued operation of the LiftPort Space Elevator System from a fixed 5-km radius point in the Pacific Ocean, LiftPort will essentially be establishing a permanent zone of operations in International Waters and International Airspace that are supposed to be free for all to use. There will likely be many nation-states that will react vigorously against LiftPort's operations as an illegal attempt to usurp International Waterways and Airspace that should be reserved for use by all. *This assumption is the main reason for the existence of LiftPort's Policy of International Public Inclusion regarding Space Elevator development and operation.*

Nevertheless, as long as LiftPort is able to operate its Space Elevator System free from interference or damage from other users of the same International Waters and Airspace, then LiftPort may be able to establish international customary law that affords protections to its activities on a permanent basis. However, it must be clearly understood that LiftPort will not have any independent right to the free, permanent use of any portion of International Waters or Airspace for a significant period of time. As a result, LiftPort's operations will be subject to significant potential interference events from other users of the same or contiguous International Waters and Airspace, with little protection afforded under international law to LiftPort's activities.

Despite the foregoing, it should be noted that if LiftPort is able to use the same International Waters and International Airspace exclusively for its activities (including the necessary buffer zone around its operations) for a sufficient period, it may be possible that LiftPort could establish an unprecedented, protected enclave in the high seas that is not associated with sovereign territory. From an international law perspective, however, it would behoove LiftPort to encourage the U.S. government to go through the appropriate diplomatic channels to ensure that the LiftPort Space Elevator System is afforded "protected status," or at least general protections in accordance with general principles of international law and the International Law of the Seas. It is best if LiftPort has the U.S. government perform these lobbying efforts, principally because only nation-states have legal standing under international law.

It might even be possible that the U.S. government would make a territorial claim under international law to protect the permanent area designated for LiftPort's operations (including a reasonable zone surrounding the LiftPort Space Elevator System necessary to protect the Space Elevator from harmful interference). However, the U.S. government will likely only take such position if the U.S. government believes that the safety and security of the LiftPort Space Elevator System is essential for U.S. national security and foreign policy objectives, and that by making such territoriality claim, the U.S. government will not be unduly interfering with the continued, efficient operation of the International Law of the Seas and general principles of international law.

Applicability of International Space Law to the LiftPort Space Elevator System

Ironically, International Space Law is the legal area that is the least critical to the safe and efficient construction and operation of the LiftPort Space Elevator System, considering that the vast majority of LiftPort's future activities should take place in outer space. This is because the current international legal regime governing activities in outer space are woefully inadequate. Specifically, there are four major international treaties that uniformly govern the conduct of nations involved in the exploration and use of outer space. The four treaties were all written by and were the subject of extensive deliberations by a special UN committee, comprised of space-faring and other interested countries, called the Committee on the Peaceful Uses of Outer Space ("COPUOS"). The four UN treaties, the "Outer Space Treaty" (1967),[28] the "Rescue and Return Agreement" (1968),[29] the "Liability Convention" (1972),[30] and the "Registration Convention" (1975),[31] were all signed and ratified by the major space-faring nations over a period of less than ten years, beginning in 1967 and ending in 1976.

Although the major sources of international law governing the use of outer space were ahead of their times when they were first signed and ratified, International Space Law has failed to keep up with the times, and new implements need to be put into place to ensure that commercial operators in outer space can adjudicate claims against third parties that harm their operations (including people and payloads being carried by such operators) into and out of outer space, whether such third parties be governmental or non-governmental actors. Under the current system, claims for harm caused by third parties to operations in space may only be brought in accordance with the general dictates of international law. That is, only nation-states can bring claims against other nation-states under international law. Furthermore, the process by which these claims may be brought (through "international consultations") is extraordinarily cumbersome and inefficient.

Thus, for example, under the current regime, if a satellite licensed by the Republic of Korea were to cause damage to the space-based component of the LiftPort Space Elevator System (likely to be licensed by the U.S. government) the only way for LiftPort to get remuneration for the damage would be to submit a claim to the U.S. State Department. The U.S. State Department would then, if it agreed with LiftPort's claims for damage, engage the government of the Republic of Korea through diplomatic channels in an effort to have the Republic of Korea reimburse the United States for damage to the LiftPort Space Elevator System allegedly caused by the Korean-licensed satellite. No established legal system would govern the discussions and no concrete methodologies would be imposed in assessing the facts of the case and determining fault. Thus, there would be significant uncertainty that LiftPort would receive any remuneration for the damage done to its Space Elevator system in the instant case. Even if LiftPort were to receive remuneration, however, it is highly likely that it would take an unreasonably long time for LiftPort to receive such remuneration in light of the need to involve 2nd parties directly in the discussions regarding the damage to the LiftPort Space Elevator System and the cause of such damage.

Accordingly, it is in the significant best interest of LiftPort to ensure that a system is created for the easier adjudication of claims between parties operating in space when the activities of one party cause harm to those of another. That is, LiftPort should endeavor to work with the U.S. government and other international, commercial users of outer space to develop a comprehensive law of space torts, so that there can be fair and efficient adjudication of claims regarding damage caused by one space actor to another.

In addition to the current, inadequate body of International Space Law, there is a mechanism, in the form of the Radio Regulations of the International Telecommunications Union ("ITU"), under international law that governs the interoperability of satellites operating in earth orbit. Despite popular belief, the ITU does not issue licenses giving the right to use orbital slots to nation-states that ask for such slots. Rather, the ITU merely has created a system, in the form of its Radio Regulations, that govern the use of the outer space earth orbits to communicate using the frequency spectrum. In establishing such rules, however, it has been decided by the ITU that certain orbital spacing between satellites operating in the same frequency bands is required in order to prevent harmful interference by one telecommunication satellite to another. As such, the ITU generally permits the allocation of frequencies to certain orbital locations and potential users of such frequencies can obtain the rights to use particular orbital slots to transmit their frequencies on a first-come, first-served basis.

This system has led many observers to the mistaken belief that the ITU issues licenses for the use of certain orbital slots. In reality, the ITU has merely provided a mechanism for prospective international users of frequency to obtain protected status under international law for their use of the allotted spectrum with the particular satellite system operating with parameters specified by the operator. The ITS Radio Regulations do not, as currently written and organized, offer any rules or guidance regarding the use of outer space by commercial operators for non-telecommunications operations. However, the authors believe that the legal framework of international cooperation underpinning the ITU and the ITU Radio Regulations may provide a fertile base for establishing rules (or at least guidelines) for the shared use of outer space by commercial space actors for non-telecommunications purposes.

Conclusion

While LiftPort has its work cut out for it in developing the technologies necessary for the construction and operation of the LiftPort Space Elevator System, the authors note that the legal hurdles facing the development of the LiftPort Space Elevator System are equally as critical to the future success of LiftPort as are the technological hurdles.

Through detailed consultations with the U.S. government as the Space Elevator comes closer and closer to fruition, LiftPort should be able to work toward the establishment of new international legal implements to ensure that LiftPort's operations are sufficiently protected from outside interference. The development and negotiation of new legal implements to ensure that reasonable protections are afforded to the sea-based, airspace-based, and outer space-based components of the LiftPort Space Elevator System will not be easy. However, without certain legal protections in place, LiftPort's operations will be highly subject to damage and interference from third parties which will, in turn, make prospective investment in the Space Elevator System scarce and the ability to obtain insurance extremely difficult. As a result, it is clear that LiftPort needs to address the legal issues addressed herein as soon as possible.

THE RINGS OF EARTH
by
William H. Keith

THE FIRST THING Davradha Elad noticed about the environs of Rhaddhiannat was how well prayer worked. It always worked, of course, save in the more remote areas outside of Earth's cities, but the quality of the service—the flavor of the foods, the luxury of the rooms, the eye-blink speed with which his requests materialized—was unlike anything he'd known back in Modret Parish, or among any of the cities, towns, or principalities he'd visited in his long journey since. Surely, Rhaddhiannat was blessed of the gods.

It would be, of course. If Modret's Oracle was to be believed, Rhaddhiannat was one of Earth's largest port cities, and one of her oldest. The gods were close, here: close enough, almost, to touch. The joy he felt at being here—and the dread—held him trembling, almost unable to speak. *I'm finally here*, he thought. *Aradye! Beloved! It won't be much longer now!*

He wondered where to begin. Craning his neck, he stared up at the Twelfth Tower, its suspended ramparts, buildings, and terraces pale in the haze high overhead. *That* was where he needed to go.

At no point, of course, did the Tower actually descend all the way to Earth from its foundations among the Outer Spheres. At its nearest tower-tip it might have reached as close as ten *lim* above the gardens and concourses of Rhaddhiannat's High Temple, at the city's heart. A scattering of clouds hung suspended between Tower and Port, lending a sense of scale to the titanic haze and distance-dimmed structure, an inverted hanging city suspended almost directly overhead.

Dav let his eye follow the rising sweep and stack of the Twelfth Tower higher, climbing up and up as it dwindled with perspective until it was lost at the zenith. With a pang, he realized that the Ring itself was completely invisible. *When the Ring at last is lost to view*, the Modret Oracle had declared, *then is it closest, and Heaven is near.*

But the Ring had always been a part of Dav's sky, and he found he missed its comforting presence.

Still staring up into the sky, Dav walked into a priest.

"By the Ascended Adepts!" the man exploded, whirling in a flare of black and scarlet robes. "Watch where you're going, youngster!"

"Uh, sorry, Reverend Master," Dav managed to blurt. "Please, could you possibly—"

But the angry priest turned away and was gone, engulfed by the city crowds.

The great Earthport of Rhaddhiannat was like Modret, but built upon a scale that made Modret seem like a rural cooperative by comparison. Buildings and towers, parks and plazas, archways and concourses and skywalks soared as if to stretch up and touch the pendant reach of the Twelfth Tower, and everywhere, *everywhere* were people of every species and modality imaginable—and quite a few that Dav would never have been able to imagine in the first place. A constant background flicker of new structures coming into existence showed where the prayers of Rhaddhiannat's population was being manifest, or where the actual City was growing and improving itself. The City was alive in every sense of the word, dynamic and constantly changing. Simply navigating this ever-changing maze would take some major low-prayer in itself.

Closing his eyes, he focused his petition. *How do I reach the Twelfth Tower?* he asked. *Who do I see to ask about Ascending?*

Few are permitted an Ascent, a voice in his head informed him. Well, he'd known *that* ever since he'd begun this quest. The Oracle had told him as much. *However,* the voice went on, *a formal petition, cast as high prayer, might be presented to the Most Serene.*

Where do I find the Most Serene? he asked.

At the High Temple.

Of course. Again, he'd known as much. His excitement, and the fear, were making clear thought and focus tough.

Okay. And how do I get to the High Temple?

To your left, the voice replied, as a map window opened in his mind. *Proceed across the Plaza of the Heroes, and look for the entrance to the Skyway Concourse on the other side. From there—*

"Out of the way, bumpkin!" a thin, sour voice said at his elbow, interrupting the internal dialogue. "This is no tourist walk! Rubberneck elsewhere!"

"I—I beg your pardon, Esteemed Sir," he stammered. He was still standing in the middle of a public walkway outside of the hab garden where he'd spent the night, and the foot traffic was parting around him in a steady stream.

"And get yourself new eyes. I am no *sir*."

Dav blinked. The speaker certainly *looked* male, though of a paraspecies unknown to him, three *mets* tall, bright red-purple, hairless and— Ah. That was skin, not a skinsuit, and the lack of external genitals could mean either sex, herm, or neuter. Most humans in Modret wore clothing. He'd reacted to the person's muscular build and lack of breasts, and assumed male.

"Forgive me, Noble Spirit," he said, using one of the more popular of genderless honorifics. But the person, whatever she or it was, had already pushed past and was gone.

People are certainly in a Ring-rounding hurry here, he thought. Turning left, he began following the directions given him by the prayer monitor.

He'd arrived in Rhaddhiannat less than ten hours ago. The tube from Gorreshedhem had deposited him at the Grand Concourse well past Biterise, and, though the High Temple was open all hours, he'd reluctantly decided that he'd needed food and sleep first. The meal had been superb, the room conjured by the hab garden monitor downright sybaritic, the dreams relaxing and lucid.

Now, though, he was ready to embark on the final phase of a quest that had begun nearly four weeks earlier, when he'd decided that the only way he could find happiness was to Ascend to the Ring.

The Plaza of Heroes was dedicated to those legendary personalities who'd actually made the Ascent in the flesh. No one knew the full roster of that company, but the fifteen best-known of the past ten thousand years were here, striking suitably heroic poses, each ten mets or more tall, their faces—or, in one case, their organ clusters—turned to the opened sky. Dav stopped in front of the living statue of Heremgath Sunsinger, sampling the memories played there. Heremgath, of the Era of the Fifth Covenant, was an old favorite of his, one who played the lead in many of his stories.

"Please, most esteemed sir!" a voice cried at his back. "By the Ring's bounty, help me!"

Dav turned. The beggar was disgustingly filthy, naked, with open sores on his scrawny legs and arms.

"What's wrong with you?" Dav exclaimed. He'd never seen anyone in such desperate straits.

"Please—I'm hungry!"

The very thought startled. "If you're hungry, why don't you simply pray?"

"Because I'm an excommunicant!" The man burst into tears.

"By the gods! What did you *do?"*

He shrugged skinny shoulders, then looked away helplessly. "I wanted to Ascend. When my petition was refused, I— I thought I could sneak up the Tower in a shipment of taralyn wood. I thought— I thought the gods would understand. I *needed* to go, needed to Ascend to the Ring—"

Dav had heard of this sort of thing, but never witnessed it first-hand. If the nanotechnic implants in a person's skull were dissolved, he would be unable to access a prayer monitor. The simplest prayers for food or water or clothing would not be heard.

He felt a twist in his stomach. Weeks before, Dav himself had wondered what he would do if his petition for Ascent were denied. He'd thought about stowing away on a Ring-bound cargo hauler. After all, the gods, surely, in their power, in their mercy, would understand.

"Let me get this right," he said. "The gods caught you?"

"The gods? No. It was the priests. I never made it out of the Port cargo docks."

Dav closed his right hand, a gesture of understanding, but he was troubled. He *didn't* understand the man's story, didn't understand how priests of the Ring could deprive a man of his ability to pray. He'd never seen an excommunicant before—not in the far-country parish of Modret at any rate, where crime of any sort was all but unknown. Excommunication was all but a sentence of death.

"Here," Dav said. He fumbled at his vambrace, the plas shell encasing part of his left forearm, plucking at a memory. He handed the chip, the size of his little fingernail, to the beggar. "This might be worth a meal."

The beggar accepted the offering in cupped hands. "Thank you, thank you esteemed sir!"

Dav gestured toward the living statue of Heremgath, looming overhead. "It's a story about *him.* I hope it helps you."

There was no way to know, of course, how valuable a story like this one would be to a prayer monitor here in a major port city, but it certainly should be worth something.

The beggar continued to voice his thanks, until Dav forcibly pulled away and hurried into the moving crowd. The encounter with the beggar had raised for him the specter of failure.

He could not allow himself to think of that possibility.

Once on the skyway, a prayer monitor gave him further directions. He stood on the moving way—a liquid in two dimensions, but solid in the third—and let it carry him and the people and paras around him along at a brisk pace. He looked up through the transparency of the enclosing tube, trying once again for a glimpse of the Ring.

He still couldn't see it, of course. Not here, and not by day. Its absence left him feeling a bit lost.

Through several branchings, the skyway took him at last to the High Temple, a soaring, pinnacled white tower positioned among the gardens directly beneath the Twelfth Tower, as though it were reaching skyward to try to reconnect with the gods somehow. High upon the highest structure was inset the ebon emblem of the Order of the Ring—the disk of Earth embraced by a circle with forty-eight unevenly spaced and disconnected spokes, representing the great Towers. Informational monitors led him to the main entrance, and to the temple's Reception Hall.

He entered the Hall in a daze, overwhelmed by the beauty and majesty of the place. The distant walls were obscured by holographic images of the Earth seen from the Ring, the floor and ceiling both showing radiant starscapes in an illusion so perfect it was like walking on the emptiness between the stars.

"Can I help you, Seeker?" The priest on duty at the dais inside the entrance wore black robes, with the emblem of his order in silver on his left breast, and again, as a tiny hologram, hovering in front of his forehead. The scarlet trim on his sleeves and vambrace marked him as a preceptor of the fifth degree. His use of the term "Seeker" suggested that an information monitor had already told him who Dav was, and why he was there.

"Yes, Reverend sir. I wish to Ascend."

The man gave the ghost of what might have been a smile. "Don't we all? And we will, one day. But, I assume that you wish to Ascend in the body, rather than in spirit alone."

"Yes, sir. My— A friend, Aradye, Ascended in the spirit last year. I wish to join her."

"Hm." For a moment, a vacant, distant expression passed over the preceptor's eyes as he accessed new data. "I see you're from Modret. Surely, the Oracle up there discussed this with you."

"Yes. She told me that very few are permitted Ascension in the body. That I need to wait to join with Aradye again. But—but I can't wait. Not if there's any chance of seeing her again."

"She was right, you know. Some thousands of Seekers come to the port cities around the world every year. None have been accepted since, well, it must have been—"

"Lorin of Tralfallen," Dav said, interrupting. "Over eight hundred years ago, at the Fifth Tower."

"Just so. Your chances of—"

"Sir! I wish to make a high prayer!"

"That is your right, of course, under the Covenant." He pursed his lips, then seemed to be lost in another inner dialogue for a moment. "How would you pay for your prayer?"

"In information, of course." Eagerly, he reached for his vambrace. "I have memories from all over Modret, and from—"

"No," the preceptor said, making the fingertips-opening gesture of negation. "Seeker, you must know that Modret Parish is small and *quite* remote. What memories could you possibly have that would be of interest to a megopolis like Rhaddhiannat? Or to the gods, for that matter?"

Dav opened his mouth, then clamped it shut again. The Oracle had told him as much, but somehow he'd not believed her. After all, she was far from any of the world's megopoli, and might well be out of touch. How could the gods not be interested in all that he'd seen and done?

But the preceptor rubbed his chin, looking thoughtful. "I see you're a Teller."

"Yes, sir."

"You know, we crave another commodity almost as much as information—and that's entertainment. Perhaps you could upload a story or two."

Dav brightened. "Of course! I could tell the Tale of—"

"But not to me. I'll tell you what, Seeker. You may attend the evening meal here at the Temple this evening. Tell your tale then, to the Most Serene, and you will be granted a high prayer."

"Thank you, Reverend sir!"

He raised a cautioning eyebrow. "By granted, I mean that you will be allowed to give your prayer. I can not guarantee a positive answer."

"Of course not! I understand!"

"Good. At the Evening Meal, then, at hour eighteen." He eyed Dav's travel-tired tunic. "In the meantime, you may wish to avail yourself of low-prayer quarters, food, and clothing."

"I certainly shall. Thank you, Reverend sir!"

But the preceptor was already turning away, addressing a woman who'd come in behind Dav and had been waiting patiently for her turn.

It was always a bit of a chance, this gambling on what tales or memories might be accepted as valid currency in any newly visited venue. Still, Dav had been a tale-teller for fifteen years now. In a world where everything from basic necessities to most luxuries were freely provided by civilization's infrastructure, the currency of choice tended to be information, art, or entertainment, or various combinations of the three. Performance art was especially valued. A memory of a legendary story like the one he'd given to the beggar was one thing; to actually stand on the dais and dramatically recite something like the Ascent of Galallel in person was something else entirely. As it happened, Dav had a knack for that sort of thing. His recitations of various hero-cycles, accompanied by memory holos of his own design, had been well received in a dozen different cities across the northern hemisphere, not just in far-off little Modret.

So he would recite one of his pieces for the Most Serene. One of his best, most polished, most acclaimed pieces.

The Ascent of Galallel and the Breaking of Lune would be particularly apt, since it involved a man on a quest for a loved one lost to Death, and his eventual reunion with her in the Third Ring of Heaven.

Yes, that would be perfect.

THE GRAND HALL rang, rocked, *trembled* with the laughter.

Dav stepped back from the center of the dais, stunned. He'd expected his declamation to be entertaining—but not comic. By the Dark Bite, Galallel was a *tragedy*, albeit one with a happy ending. What did they think was so hilarious?

Perhaps a hundred beings—men, women, neuters, embodied AIs, parahumans, and others were present in the Grand Hall, a broad, skylit gallery with long tables which materialized food and drink in response to prayer Perhaps a quarter were members of the Order, the rest servants, friends of the priests, or Seekers like himself, visitors to the High Temple who wanted to make high prayer petitions. Dav's recitation had been placidly received at first, as they politely listened to the death of Lorelen, and Galallel's vow. He threw everything he had into the Telling, as projected holos built dancing images in the air at his back.

The laughter had begun, however, as his telling shifted focus to the story of Lune, the magical Garden of the Gods, and how Galallel had struck a deal with the Guardians of Heaven to build the Ring. Someone chuckled out loud—then another, and still another. He'd pressed on, moving to the most dramatic, most exciting part, at least in so far as he was concerned.

"And so Lune was broken, and the Gods guided the silver fragments down out of the Most-high Heaven, settling them safely into the Third Heaven, the Heaven of the Abyss, which stretches above the Heaven of the Air, and above the Heaven of Radiant Light. Working with Galallel, then, they began to build the Ring from the fragments of Lune, and so transformed the Heaven of the Abyss into the Heaven of the Ring. . . ."

The titterings and chuckles spread, growing louder, and in moments it seemed as though every person throughout the entire hall was laughing except him.

Dav swallowed, took a breath, then pushed ahead. "Only then," he continued, "did Galallel realize that the World's sin was blocking him. Even with the help of gods and guardians, he was unable to complete the Ring, for the emptiness we call the Bite moved endlessly along the Ring's circumference, moving with the night, from east to west, ever opposite the sun, a merging and a congealing of all of Humankind's sin. . . ."

Again, the laughter forced him to stop. Behind him, the holo of the Bite, a vast, dark semicircle cut from the silver of the Ring, wavered, flared, then winked out.

"I am so sorry, Teller," the Most Serene said, leaning back in its chair and wiping its eyes. Talosiad Nedrophilin was a ponderous neuter with deep violet eyes, reclining at the ring-shaped table's center. "Your theology is so— How shall I put it? So quaint."

"I had no idea they still believed such things in the far parishes!" an Adept said. "The Bite is Humankind's congealed sin! Incredible!"

"Tell me," the Most Serene said, heaving its bulk a bit higher on the couch. "Do you believe this tale of yours to be true? Or is it simple entertainment?"

"I—I believe the Hero Legends *embody* truth, Most Serene," Dav said. "I like to believe there really was a Galallel—but whether there was or was not isn't the important thing, is it?"

"No. No, to be sure." The Most Serene chuckled again, shaking its head. "I've heard it said that the deepest truths cannot be told by history; that you need fiction to tell them best."

Dav gave assent by keeping silent. In fact, he'd always thought the Galallel Cycle to be history, not fiction, but he wasn't about to admit that now.

He wondered now, though, if Heremgath Sunsinger had been real, or a truth-telling myth.

"Where are you from, Teller?" the Most Serene demanded.

"Modret Parish, Most Serene."

"Bite! That *is* a long way." Its violet eyes momentarily grew unfocused. "Is it true that the rain actually freezes there? Ice crystals falling from the sky?"

"For part of the year, yes, Most Serene."

"Amazing!" It held out its hand, and a goblet materialized. It took a long sip. "Ah. That is good." A gesture, and the goblet vanished. "So, why don't you show us some of your memories of frozen rain, Teller? And we'll all promise not to laugh."

And so Dav drew upon other of his store of memories, telling them of the far north, and showing holographic images of the Berrinien Mountains, and the great ice fields beyond. His audience seemed most captivated, though, by the images he showed them of the Ring—a titanic arch of pale silver stretching across the southern sky and clearly visible even by day.

And they grew very, very still and silent as he described the nightly passage of the Bite.

"*I'm told, Teller,*" the Most Serene said when he'd finished and the enthusiastic applause had faded, "*that you wish to make a high prayer.*" The words, this time, were spoken in Dav's thoughts, not aloud.

"*Yes, Most Serene,*" he replied in his mind.

"*To the effect that you wish to Ascend?*"

"*More than anything, Most Serene.*"

"*Mm. That would be—difficult.*"

For a moment, Dav felt his world threatening to collapse upon him. If he was refused, there would be no hope—

"Most Serene!" he stammered, aloud.

The Most Serene held up a chubby hand. "We need to think upon this. You will have your answer in the morning. For this night, you shall stay here in the Temple as our guest." It gestured, sharply, with an accompanying thought, and a female figure moved from the shadows at the back of the hall. "A Temple servant will show you where to make your prayers, and will be your companion this night."

"Thank you, Most Serene. Please, may I ask—"

But the Most Serene had already turned to one of its companions, and was talking to him aloud with some animation. The rising babble of conversation, the clink and clatter of place settings and utensils, the intricate weavings of vocal tonings in the background all rose to drown out any further words.

"If you would come with me, Teller?" a voice said at his side. An AI, a gray metal sphere the size of his fist, hovered there, beckoning.

"Are you the Temple servant?"

"*A* servant, yes. Eristhetadinel will be your servant-companion tonight, however. This way, please."

"I CAME HERE about a year ago," Eristhetadinel told him, hours later. She was young—no more than fifty—and full human so far as Dav could tell, with pale silver hair and gold eyes. "And for much the same reason as you."

They'd had sex, a pleasant, nameless coupling, in the palatial sleeping chamber conjured for him by the Temple monitors. Now they walked among the lush, flowering gardens suspended above the Temple grounds, comfortably nude in the warm night air, getting to know one another. The aroma of a dozen exotic plants hung heavy about them; the lights of the terminus end of the Twelfth Tower glowed brightly at the zenith, banishing all but the most brilliant stars from the sky. The Ring, however, and at last, was clearly visible, a brilliant silver thread stretching from horizon to horizon, appearing to run straight through the middle of the Tower hanging overhead. In the west, the Zodiacal Light shone golden by the glow of the long-set sun, bright enough, nearly, to read by.

The Third Heaven seemed very, very close.

"Where did you come from?" he asked.

"Troonde," she told him.

"I don't know it."

"It's in the south, on the Etellenic Coast. Perhaps an hour by flyer or magtube, but it took me months to work my way here, city by city."

"You wanted to Ascend?"

She nodded. "My fastmate had died. Ascended in the spirit, as they say. I wondered if I might see her again, though, if I could travel up one of the Towers."

"So what happened?"

Her gold eyes darkened with the memory. "I was refused. They refuse everyone."

"But—"

"*Everyone*," she repeated firmly. She glanced around, as though looking for eavesdroppers. "But we shouldn't speak of that here. Just try not to be disappointed tomorrow." She tipped her head back, craning her neck to look straight up at the Tower. "Anyway, I never was one for taking 'no' for an answer. I made it *that* far, at least."

"You got up to the Tower?"

She rocked her hand in a gesture of affirmation. "Disguised myself as a Port worker and slipped on board a cargo transport. I think that was the hardest thing I've ever done. I—I can't stand heights. Just looking up that far makes me dizzy, and the thought of looking down—" She shook her head. "I could only make myself do it knowing the lifter's hull would be opaqued. But it didn't matter. They caught me, of course, and brought me back."

Dav thought about the beggar he'd met earlier that day. "Did they— Were you excommunicated?"

She grimaced. "I was given a choice, actually. Excommunication or a life here, as a Temple servant." She shrugged. "I like to eat."

"Oh. I understand."

Her eyes flashed, brilliant in the near-darkness. "Do you? Do you know what it's like to be here, night after night, seeing *that* overhead?" She stabbed a forefinger skyward, at Ring and Tower. "To have come so far—So far—"

She was crying. Awkwardly, he took her in his arms and held her for a long time.

And later, they made love once more, and it seemed to be healing, somehow, for them both.

"TELLER DAVRADHA ELAD," the Adept who met with him the next morning said, "your high prayer petition, while worthy, is refused."

"But Adept!"

"*Is refused,*" the woman, a tenth degree Adept with shifting constellations of light points gleaming in the skin of her bald scalp, said in his mind.

"Adept, I was given to understand by the Most Serene itself that—"

"You were given nothing, Teller, save the generous hospitality of this Temple. The Most Serene suggests that you return to Modret, take a new fastmate, and be content with what the gods have granted you."

"I have tried, Adept. I truly have. But—"

"*Your story last night,*" the Adept said in his thoughts. "*The first one, about Galallel. Do you truly believe it? Believe the story is real, I mean?*"

"*I— I don't know. As I said last night, I think it carries some of the truth.*"

"*How did that tale end? You'd just gotten to the part about the Bite being human sin.*"

"*Well, it goes on to say that ever since the Ring was raised, human sin continues to devour it. The gods follow along behind the Bite, constantly remaking what sin unmakes, but their task will never be complete until a new hero Ascends in the body and offers expiation for human sin. Only then can the Ring can be completed.*"

The woman smiled. "*And do you think that you are that hero?*"

His head snapped back with shock. "*No, Adept! I— I just want to see my Aradye again!*"

"*Do you have any idea how many mortals petition us each year for Ascent?*"

"*I— No. No, I don't.*"

"*You would not believe the number if I told you. And the volume of requests at each of the other Tower ports is similar. Everyone, it seems, wants to Ascend to Third Heaven. If all were granted, what do you think would happen?*"

"*I don't know.*"

"*Earth would be emptied, and the Third Heaven filled. Everything, everything would be thrown out of balance. Earth empty, a desolation, and humans with their greed and their strivings polluting the heavenly realms.*"

"But I wouldn't pollute anything!" The thought was nearly a despairing wail.

"You, alone? Perhaps not. And the legends do say that a few humans have made the Ascent, and even returned to tell of it. But if every person who wanted that petition filled were granted it?" She made the opening, negative gesture with her hand. *"Teller, the gods, in their wisdom, have decreed that mortal Humankind dwell here, on the good Earth they have provided—and that the heavens remain for the gods alone, sinless and pure. Your place, Teller, is here. In a few centuries, you will Ascend in the spirit, and then you will know the wisdom of this."*

"Is there— Is there someone else I could talk to? An appeal?"

"There is not." She said the words aloud, with a death-cold finality. "This audience is at an end."

It was hard to believe that his quest had brought him this far, only to have his goal yanked away from him when victory had seemed so close. The desolation, the despair, seemed to rise up within him and overwhelm all else.

He didn't even remember leaving the audience chamber.

"I TOLD YOU."

They stood again in the temple gardens. It was late morning; the sun vanished behind the bulk of the Tower, which hung suspended overhead like a floating island, in vast, back-lit silhouette. Eristhetadinel had found him there an hour after his meeting with the Adept, still trying to make sense of the sudden reversal.

"I know," he said. "I just— I just thought—"

"That they would make an exception for you?"

He heard the cynicism in her voice. "The Most Serene didn't tell me my petition was impossible! It said it was difficult, but it also promised to think about it—"

"Of course. Do you think it would say no and risk a scene at one of its formal dinners? Besides, this way that Adept you saw can be the villain. Her name is Savarid, and she's well suited to the role, believe me."

Dav stood for a long time staring up at the Tower. Transports and cargo lifters of various designs drifted about the Tower's unsupported base like swarming insects.

Months ago, when he'd first begun his south-bound odyssey, he'd considered the possibility of refusal—and the possibility of finding some other way up to the Tower.

He'd not realized at the time the severity of the penalties of trying to circumvent Temple edict. Losing the ability to connect with prayer monitors for his most basic needs—or spending the rest of his life as a servant, like Eris—no. He wasn't prepared to risk that. Maybe if there was a chance of getting away with it—stowing away or disguising himself, he would have tried it, but apparently the priests were very good at discovering such attempts.

"How do they know when someone is trying to sneak up to the Tower?" he asked.

She shrugged. "There are ways. Many ways. The lifters themselves have AI minds, you know. And the people with access to the Tower are carefully watched at all times."

When minute nanocomputers pulsed through each citizen's circulatory system, maintaining communications linkages with other computers in the area, secrecy and deception both were very hard to arrange.

"There's got to be a way."

She glanced around. They appeared to be alone, and yet—

"Do you trust me, Dav?"

"Of course."

"Not 'of course.' You hardly know me. But can you trust me for a time? Trust me enough to come with me?"

Where was this leading? "Yes, but I—"

Eris touched a fingertip to Dav's lips. "Don't speak. Don't *think*. And most especially, don't pray!"

"But—"

"Not even to ask directions!" She then gestured for him to follow. "Quickly! Before they know I'm gone!"

"JUST WHERE IS it you're taking me?" he demanded.

"Not much farther," was all she would say.

An hour had passed. In complete silence, Eris had led him out of the Temple grounds and into the ever-changing labyrinth of buildings, parks, and skyways that was Rhaddhiannat. He'd followed, thinking at first that she was looking for a private place to speak where they wouldn't be overheard.

Now, though, it looked as though she was leading him out of the city itself. They'd entered a public magtube and taken a car north. Beyond the broad ring of parkland encircling the City's heart, the buildings were older, more permanent, the people slower of pace and more conservative in speech and dress. Dav had the feeling that the outer reaches of the port megopolis had existed more or less unchanged for centuries.

Out here you could see the mountains.

There were mountains back in Modret Parish, of course—high ones forever capped by gleaming sheets of ice—but the city itself was nestled comfortably within a valley between mountains and sea, seeming to have grown from and to be a part of Earth herself. Rhaddhiannat, on the other hand, had been imposed upon the Earth, rising from an artificial mesa created by lopping off the peaks of several mountains and reshaping those nearby. Not until the traveler reached the outer, less technically civilized, reaches of the City could he appreciate the natural grandeur of the surroundings: towering peaks, some ice capped, others brown, in ranks marching down from the north.

"Wait!" he said as they stepped out of the magtube car at its last stop. "Any further, and we're out of the City!" He'd heard stories, even back in Modret, to the effect that Rhaddhiannat was built at an altitude where the air was so thin that breathing was difficult. The City itself was supposed to be constantly adjusting the thickness of the air in its immediate environs, keeping it tolerable for humans and paras alike.

That didn't seem likely to Dav. Air was air after all, pervasive and uniform, not thicker *here* and thinner *there*. Still, some of the hero tales among his memories suggested, strange as the thought seemed, that there was no air at all in Third Heaven—or gravity either, for that matter. He knew the Cities allowed him to take much for granted. If his long journey south had taught him anything, it was that making assumptions about *anything* in the world outside of the cities was less than rational.

Eris was looking around. They'd emerged from the magtube onto a broad plaza extending out over a valley with its depths lost in mist. She stayed well back from the railing at the edge, Dav noticed. Afraid of heights? What must that be like?

On the horizon, Rhaddhiannat appeared to embrace several truncated mountaintops and the valleys between them. The Twelfth Tower hung suspended above the far-off city heart, a column gleaming silver in the sun that went up and up and still further up, dwindling to a point lost in perspective and sunlight directly overhead.

"I think we're safe enough here," Eris told him. "But we need to be careful. The priests hear *everything.*"

He looked around the plaza. It was nearly deserted, with only a couple of neuters gliding past on a slidewalk. "I don't see any priests here."

"You wouldn't."

"Huh?"

She sighed. "Come on." They started walking across the plaza at a brisk, almost urgent pace. "Imagine," she continued as they walked, "cameras the size of motes of dust. Microphones smaller yet, programmed to listen for certain key words or phrases. Monitor nodes wired into each building wall, or adrift on the breeze, invisibly small. They can link with the nanos in your blood so that the City can hear your prayers. But they can pick up other things as well."

"You're beginning to sound just a bit paranoid."

She raised her hands to her temples, rubbing hard. "You would be too, if you'd lived with those—those people for a year. They call themselves servants of Humankind. *Masters* is closer to the mark."

Dav shook his head. Why would they want to be that?"

"Power, of course. They control all access to the gods. That gives them incredible power over everyone else."

The concept was not an easy one to grasp. Why would anyone want that kind of control over others? It didn't make sense. "If their magic is that powerful," he said, "we're not safe anywhere."

"See that up ahead?" She pointed to an enclosed pavilion. "That is our way out."

Still a bit bewildered, Dav allowed Eris to lead him into the pavilion. Steps led down into an underground lobby. Another magtube car waited, hovering silently above its rail.

"What's this?" Dav asked. "Where does it go?"

"Use of this car is prohibited, save to authorized personnel," a voice replied in his head.

"We're on Temple business," Eris replied. Dav caught a burst of code as she transmitted an official travel prayer.

"Very well," the AI voice said in their minds. *"Proceed."* And the tube car's doors slid open.

As they took seats in the comfortably furnished interior, Dav turned sharply on Eris. "What the Bite is going on?" he demanded. "Where are you taking me?"

The hull of the tube car appeared opaque from outside, but inside, the walls were invisible. There was no sensation of movement as the stubby little vehicle moved through an airlock, passing into the hard vacuum of the main transit tube. Seconds later, they were accelerating, still with no sensation whatsoever of movement. The rock walls of the tunnel blurred into featureless grey, then in an instant went black. Dav and Eris sat together in a tiny circle of light, alone in the darkness.

"I hope," Eris told him after a long moment, "that this tube will take us to Ouai."

A strange name. He'd never heard of it before. He began to formulate a prayer requesting information. Eris laid a slim hand on his arm. "That won't work here."

"Why not? The information net extends everywhere."

"And Ouai is not in the data base. Not in one you could access without special authorization."

Stubborn, Dav completed the prayer. A monitor's voice replied a moment later. "There is no information listed for that name."

"Then where is this car going?"

"We are en route to Ouai. We will arrive in twenty-three minutes, twelve seconds."

"Tell me about our destination, then!"

"I'm sorry, but I can't do that. There is no information listed for that name."

AI monitors could be frustratingly obtuse at times. Some were brilliant, but all possessed a certain narrowness of focus, an unwillingness to move beyond boundaries or set parameters.

Dav was only now beginning to realize that the world he lived in was a lot deeper and more complex than he'd ever imagined. The idea that something could be *prohibited*, for instance—

Three principles were the only real laws within a single social structure that had governed Humankind and its offshoots for uncounted thousands of years. *No one can tell another what to do* was the first, which alone made the principles less laws than guidelines. *Complete freedom is balanced by complete responsibility* was the next. *All is permitted so long as you harm none* was the third. Society as a whole retained the right to protect itself from those rare genetic aberrations that preyed upon it, and there was always the problem of interpreting the word *harm*, but with unlimited energy and all needs freely provided, there was no need of any law declaring *thou shalt not.*

And that was what had made Dav's encounter with the beggar yesterday so unnerving. Perfect freedom might be an unattainable abstraction, but to deprive someone of the ability to access the monitors that provided the basics of life itself—or simply to threaten them with that possibility, as had happened to Eris—was so horrific a thought that Dav was still having trouble processing it.

And now, for the first time in his life, a simple request for information had been denied.

"This is—insane," he said at last. "I'm having trouble taking it all in."

"I know," Eris told him. "I went through the same thing myself."

For as far back as historical records existed, society had been founded absolutely upon the joint freedom and responsibility of the individual. A person's freedom was limited, clearly, by the information available to them. And denying anyone basic information, or the means to get it, was almost literally and nightmarishly unthinkable.

He tried changing the subject. "So—what do you know about this Ouai place?"

"Ouai," Eris told him, "is an island in the Western Ocean. I've heard the priests and adepts talking about it, sometimes. There's supposed to be a heretical sect there, a priesthood that serves as a kind of gateway to the Rings."

" 'Heretical sect?' What's that?"

"Priests who don't believe the same things as they do in the High Temple."

And *that* seemed unthinkable—and ominous—as well. Again, he accessed the data net, but received nothing more than definitions for the two words.

"What does *belief* have to do with anything?" he asked, shaking his head. "How could what one person believes be wrong—if it's right for him?"

"That, Dav, is something the Temple would rather you not think about too deeply."

"So, why drag me along? Why didn't you go yourself?"

"That was not allowed. I was given authorization codes for tube travel some weeks ago, when an Adept and I were sent to Gavellerendet on an errand. But that was for two people; I would have been stopped if I'd tried using the code alone."

"You've really thought this out, haven't you?"

"Yes," she said, and he heard the bitterness in her voice. "I just needed to wait for someone like you to show up, someone else who wanted to Ascend, and might want to do it badly enough to break the laws."

" 'Laws?' "

" Directional guidelines enforced by threats or coercion."

"Oh."

"Do you mind?"

"Mind what?"

"My bringing you here. I thought— I thought at least it would give you a choice."

"No, I don't mind. I'm just a little surprised to find things this, um, complicated."

This was supposed to have worked much more simply—a journey to Rhaddhiannat, a high prayer request, and a happy Ascent. Well, the Oracle back home had warned him that things wouldn't be as straightforward as he'd believed. Why, though, hadn't it been able to tell him right up front that his prayer would be denied, and that he'd have to find other means of Ascending?

"Is there another Tower in Ouai?" he asked. "Is that how we get up to the Rings?"

"I don't think so. But the Temple priests talked about another brotherhood there, something called the Order of the Ascended Ones."

"Well, that sounds promising, at least."

"I thought," she told him, "it was worth a try. And I couldn't take the Temple any longer. The lies. The hypocrisy."

"The threats," he added. The abuse of power remained the worst of all that Dav had seen and heard these past two days. He shrugged. "At least we can see what these heretics have to say."

The minutes trickled away, and the car entered a brightly lit portion of the tunnel, coming to a silent and unfelt stop in an airlock seemingly identical to the one they'd left. Dav noticed that not only had there been no sensation of acceleration or deceleration, but there'd also been no feeling of the car tipping down or up, as it must have if it had traveled from the mountaintops to the sea bed, then climbed again at their destination.

Ouai was warm, the air heavy with moisture and the smell of salt. A number of buildings rose from emerald green hills and mountaintops, looking more a part of the landscape than something imposed upon it. It was still midday—in fact, it looked as though the sun might have moved back toward the east a bit. He was delighted, however, to see the Rings by daylight once more, thin and knife-edged, about twenty degrees south of the zenith.

"You've come looking for a way to Ascend, haven't you?"

They whirled at the strange voice. The man—how had he come up behind them so silently?—wore priestly garb, but without symbols of rank, unless rank was indicated by the color itself: a deep and lustrous blue so deep as to be almost black. A symbol did glow in pale light on his forehead, a tiny spiral shape, like a whirlpool of light.

"Yes," Dav told him. "They—They said we couldn't, in Rhaddhiannat."

"No. They wouldn't."

"Who are you?" Eris asked him. "Are you with the heretic order we heard about?"

"Heretic?" He seemed milfly surprised. "I suppose that's one way of looking at it. Not *my* way, of course, but a way. I am a—Watcher. You can call me that."

"Watcher. And— And we can really Ascend? In the body?"

The man hesitated a moment, though whether in thought or because he was accessing information from a local net, Dav couldn't tell. "Yes," he said at last. "Of *course* you can."

"I have memories for exchange," Dav offered. "Stories. Some artistic pieces—"

"Ascent is free to all. That is how it should be."

"Free?"

"Only three things will be required of you," the Watcher said.

"What?" Dav asked. "We don't have—"

"Time," the Watcher said. "Determination. And courage."

"I don't understand."

"The journey requires seven full days. That alone will test your determination—though the fact that you are here at all speaks well of you in that regard. As for courage, well, you'll find out about that. The way to the Rings is— Let's say that it is a very, very old path into space. Ancient. And *not* for the faint-hearted."

For a moment, Dav wondered what was behind the warning. Maybe it was better that he turn back now, while he could.

But he turned and raised his gaze to the Rings, just visible behind a deep blue and sun-brilliant sky.

Of *course* he would go. At least he would make the attempt.

"We've come this far," he said. "We're not backing down now when we're almost at the very end of the journey!"

"Ah. But it's not the end, you see. Your journey is just beginning."

ANOTHER WAVE TOWERED above them, toppled—and for a long moment they were enveloped by a surging, watery blackness. Then the skimmer emerged from the wave, the cabin lit by an angry green-black sky. Rain lashed silently across the dome transparency.

"Can't we just fly this thing straight up to the Ring?" Dav asked, leaning back in the sofa to stare up at the storm. Lightning flared in the distance, though the thunder—like the howl of wind and the crash of rain and waves—was inaudible within the warm, dry circle of the skimmer cabin. "What's the point of going through all of this?"

"That's right," Eris put in. "Back at Rhaddhiannat, there were fliers and cargo lifters that went straight up to the bottom terraces of the Tower."

The Watcher chuckled. "There's a small difference between flying two *li* up to the Twelfth Tower," he pointed out, "and the almost thirty-six *thousand* up to the Inner Rings."

"Thirty-six thousand!" Dav exclaimed. "That's impossible!"

"Not at all. The Inner Ring is in geosynchronous orbit. It circles the Earth once in twenty-four hours, which is why the Twelfth Tower remains precisely above the center of Rhaddhiannat. The mathematics of basic orbital mechanics dictate how far out that orbit must be to match Earth's rotation—35,784 *li* is the exact distance."

Another huge wave broke silently across the skimmer's dome, unfelt save for a slight tremor transmitted through the thick carpeting on the deck.

"Actually," the Watcher continued, "there *are* vessels that can make the trip all the way to Geosynch. A few, anyway; huge ships much larger than this skimmer. Most are in the service of various port Cities, though they rarely see sunlight these days. I believe the Most Serene of Rhaddhiannat owns one, handed down from one Serenity to the next for the gods know how many generations. It doesn't use it, though. None of its Order has gone even as high as the station at the hundred-*li* mark for a very long time. I'm afraid you're going to have to rely on more pedestrian means of Ascending."

For a long time, then, they watched the storm. Dav had endured storms, of course, during his trek south from Modret, but he'd never seen one like this, driving such a wild and angry sea. The Cities, he knew, planned their weather better than this.

"Why wouldn't the Most Supreme want to Ascend?" he asked after a time.

The Watcher shrugged. "Why should he? He has everything he needs in the Temple, including, specifically, power."

"Power? I don't understand."

"Control over the population. By controlling the information accessible over the various City nets, he controls the people. Do you see?"

"No."

"Don't worry about it. The point is, if he Ascended, he would be just another god. If he stays where he is, he can imagine he controls the lives and destinies of several million souls."

Dav was having trouble taking this in. "Why would he want to do that?"

A shrug. "It's what he wants. But that brings us to another issue. You two—why do you want to Ascend? You told me back in Ouai only that you wanted see Ascended loved ones."

Dav nodded. "Her name is Aradyeferalenn. She Ascended in spirit last year. An accident, while hiking in the mountains outside of Modret."

"Ah. I'm sorry. And you?"

"My fastmate, Kerellien. She Ascended almost two years ago. She was piloting a small wind-craft at sea, and there was a storm—"

"I'm sorry for both of you. Fatal accidents can seem so—random. And it's always hardest for those left behind."

"But we'll see them in the Third Heaven," Dav said. "Isn't that right?"

The Watcher took a long moment before answering. "No," he said. "Not really."

"You're lying!" Eris cried.

"No, Eris. I'm not. The gods can choose how long they wish to live—but mortals, I'm afraid, die. Not from disease so much any more, but from accidents, old age, or a chosen passing."

"What's 'disease?' " Dav wanted to know.

"A sickness or an imbalance in the body, caused by stress, tiny organisms, or by genetic mischance. It's almost unheard of now, with nanomedical prophylaxis, but it used to be quite common.

"But people still die in accidents, as with your partners, or, more usually, when their organic bodies wear out after a few centuries and they choose to pass. I'm sorry to have to tell you this, but they do not Ascend to the Rings."

The news struck Dav like a blow to the stomach. "Where do they go, then?" he asked.

"That, I'm afraid, I can't tell you."

"But they're still alive!" Eris cried. "They—Their spirits continue. Right?"

"I don't know. There's some reason to believe that's so, and most of Humankind has believed that they do throughout our species' entire span. But we don't know. All I can tell you with any certainty is that you will not find them in the Rings."

"No!" Eris slipped forward off the sofa, dropping down to her knees, head back, wailing. "*No!*"

"I'm very sorry," the Watcher said.

Dav joined Eris on the deck, his arms around her. "I know," he whispered. "*I know.*"

AN HOUR LATER, they had their first sight of the Ribbon.

Liftport, as the Watcher called it, was a floating city, three *li* across, its buildings rounded and streamlined against wind and wave. It was anchored, they were told, to the sea bed, though once, long before, it had been able to move as much as several *li* in a day in order to avoid impact from orbital debris. At first, the Ribbon was invisible with distance and behind gray sheets of falling rain, but as the skimmer approached the huge marine complex, they could make out a thread-slender line connecting the largest of the city's domes and the low ceiling of angry clouds overhead.

The city, unlike the colorful pastels of Modret, or the wildly imaginative diversity of shapes and colors of Rhaddhiannat, appeared to be cast entirely in a single mass. The structure looked like it was carved from dark gray rock, and as they came closer Dav could see pits, craters, and a broken-ground roughness to the surface.

"It looks—old," Dav said, peering out into the storm, trying to see.

"It is. It may be the oldest of all of Earth's cities, though the city we see now is constantly regrowing and repairing itself. Most of the outer surface is seacrete—a kind of artificial stone accreted from seawater by electrolysis. But even that would erode after a millennium or so of exposure to the elements."

"No lights," he observed. "Or air traffic."

"That's because it's uninhabited."

"No people?"

The Watcher shook his head. "AIs and robots, yes. But no people." He grinned. "Would *you* want to live way out here?"

"Why is it here at all?" Eris asked. Her voice still shook a bit and her face was pale. The news about her fastmate had hit her hard.

"Because Liftport was our first step, Humankind's first *real* step, off of the planet. It's a kind of memorial now."

"But I've never heard of it," Dav protested. Memorials were the stuff of song and memory-telling, like the monuments in the Plaza of Heroes.

"No. Not many have on Earth. But the gods remember."

As the skimmer neared the structure's rim, a portion of the nearest dome melted away, revealing a dark cavern. As they entered, lights came on, illuminating a vast cavern filled with dim shapes and structures, a shadowy forest of supports and titanic gantries. The opening closed up behind them as if by magic, shutting out the tumult of the storm.

"It's so empty," Dav observed.

"Once, thousands of years ago," the Watcher went on, "Liftport *was* inhabited. "And some day, it may be again. Would you like a closer look?"

They stepped out of the skimmer and rode a slidewalk through empty passageways. Compared to the lively bustle of a port city, the cavernous emptiness of Liftport seemed as lifeless as a sepulcher.

At last they came to a large, domed interior space that lit up as they entered. The roof turned transparent. "That, the Watcher said, pointing, "is the Ribbon. That's your road to space."

The Ribbon, jet-black, as thick as Dav's hand and as wide as he was tall, emerged from the floor of the dome, passed through an unusual device that appeared to be clinging to it, and passed on through the dome's ceiling. Beyond, in the storm, it was stretched taut between dome and sky, its edges fluttering wildly in the stiff wind. It looked impossibly fragile against the violence of the storm.

"Woven carbon-nanotube fiber," the Watcher explained. "The original Ribbon stretched for over sixty thousand *li*, from Earth to a counterweight positioned well beyond geosynch. CNT was the first material strong enough and light enough to support its own weight across that kind of distance."

Dav's attention was drawn to the device resting on the dome's floor—a gleaming, upright cylinder clinging to the Ribbon with what looked like two sets of paired rollers. To either side, massive dish antennae aimed at the sky.

"That's the lift vehicle," the Watcher said. "Colloquially, the Crawler. As you see, it's attached to the Ribbon—there, and there—and uses microwave energy beamed down from the Rings for power. Originally, it was solar powered, and a lot slower. Once it gets moving, this unit will manage 200 *li* per hour, so it can make the trip, one-way, in 180 hours—or about seven days."

"Seven *days*?"

"The earliest versions took four or five times that long. The Ancients weren't interested in speed. They needed a reliable, low-energy, cheap, and safe way to get to geosynch. And this was it."

"Safe?" Dav said, looking up past the dome transparency and watching the Ribbon flutter in the wind. "That doesn't look safe!"

"Well, consider that the very first humans to leave this planet did so atop enormous towers made up almost entirely of high-explosive chemicals. The partially controlled detonation of those chemicals hurled them and their equipment into orbit, and even to the Moon."

"What's 'the Moon?' "

"A natural satellite of Earth. It was disassembled thousands of years ago in order to create the Rings."

"Lune!" Eris cried. "Like in your Memory, Dav—"

"Using an explosion to throw yourself into space is not exactly what you could call 'safe,' " the Watcher continued. He spread his arms wide apart, indicating a large amount. "And it took *this* much explosive"—dropping his arms, he indicated a tiny amount with thumb and forefinger—"to boost *this* much mass just a couple of hundred *li* into orbit. Those first star-sailors gambled their lives just to reach low Earth orbit and, believe it or not, the energy available to them was limited and costly. It wasn't until humans learned how to weave the Ribbon that they could get into space in large numbers, and begin building an infrastructure there on a large scale."

"By 'infrastructure', you mean the Rings?"

"That didn't happen for thousands of years. They started out small at first, using the Ribbon to place packages of scientific instruments in orbit, then to build small space stations and orbital factories. With that first tiny foothold, they were able to put up more Ribbons. At one time, we're told, there were hundreds of Ribbons in place along the Equator all the way around the planet."

"Hundreds!"

The Watcher nodded. "But this one was the first. The others were all taken up as the first of the Towers were built. This one was preserved as a memorial, the place and means by which Humankind took Tsiolkovsky's Step."

"Tsiolkovsky?"

"One of the Ancients. Almost prehistoric, in fact. A pre-space philosopher. We know little about him, but he's remembered for something he said. 'The Earth is the cradle of humanity, but mankind cannot stay in the cradle forever.' "

Dav was having a lot of difficulty following what the Watcher was saying. Some of the concepts and language were simply too foreign—"space" and "orbit" and even "chemical explosives." All he really understood was the Watcher's claim that that unlikely-looking device attached to a thread of woven fiber was supposed to be his means of crawling all the way up to Third Heaven.

"You say it's safe?" he asked. "That we can use it to reach Heaven?"

For the first time, the Watcher appeared less than sure of himself. "You can try. Safety—I cannot promise that. The priests are trying to stop you, you know."

"What? How?"

He nodded at the angry sky. "That storm, of course. Serious storms rarely occur in equatorial waters. This one is artificial."

"So—the priests know about the Ribbon?"

"Of course. Many of them have wanted to destroy it for a long time, because from time to time people *do* find their way here, and up to the Rings. Not often, but it's happened."

Lightning forked from the clouds. By the glare of the flash, Dav saw several high, slender towers in the distance, rising out of the waves, seeming to absorb the skyfire.

"Liftport has defenses," the Watcher went on. "Especially against lightning strikes. But a high enough wind *could* snap the Ribbon. That's what they're trying to do now."

"Let me understand this," Eris said. For several minutes now, she'd been silently staring up at the flutter of the Ribbon overhead. "That—That little pod crawls up that black sheet of fabric? And we're supposed to *ride* it?"

"That's the idea." The Watcher seemed cheerful enough, but there was still that undercurrent of doubt. "C'mon. Have a look inside."

A portion of the pod's silvery hull above steps rising from the deck vanished at their approach, and the three of them entered— Eris with visible reluctance. The capsule's interior measured perhaps three times Dav's height from one wall to another, and much of the deck space was taken up by the circular couch that encircled all but the wall-space occupied by the door. It was cramped, but not uncomfortably so. The walls faded to transparency as they entered, and that helped to banish any claustrophobic feelings.

"The Crawler has an on-board AI," the Watcher told them. "Tell it your needs, and it will provide you with food, water, toilet facilities. Nothing very fancy, I'm afraid. This is pretty ancient technology. There is one manual control." He pointed at a large, bright red disk set into one of the armrests, just across from the door. "That was called the panic button," he said. "If you find yourself in trouble— real trouble—and you want to abort, press it."

"What happens if I do?"

"The capsule jettisons from the rest of the Crawler," the Watcher said. "Kicks you clear of the Ribbon."

"And how does *that* help us?"

"Well, if you're above a certain altitude—about 24,000 *li*—you'll be dropped into orbit. How high an orbit depends on how far up you are when you abort, but it should be possible to recover you. If you jettison below that altitude, however, you'll fall. The capsule has a re-entry system. You'll be slowed by a parachute."

Dav didn't know what a parachute was, but he was concerned by the expression on the Watcher's face, and the hesitation behind his words. "So, you're saying we'll come back down. But we'll be safe, right?"

"You'll come back down, yes. But the higher up you are when you jettison, the farther from Liftport you'll be when you touch down. You *could* find yourself on the other side of the planet, or far out at sea. There used to be an elaborate recovery and rescue service in place for just that eventuality—but that hasn't been available for, oh, thousands of years, now."

"Oh."

"There *is* danger, my friends. This is very, very old equipment. It's maintained and repaired automatically—has been since the beginning—but something could go wrong. And, well, the High Temple would rather you *not* Ascend. They're going to extraordinary lengths to stop you. They might succeed."

Dav felt a shudder transmitted through the deck of the lifter. Eris jumped, startled. "What's that? What's happening?"

Outside the dome, the water was rising.

No, it wasn't that. The city, all of Liftport, was sinking.

"A safety mechanism," the Watcher told them. "When the storm becomes severe enough to pose a threat to Liftport, the entire structure submerges."

"Then it's too late! We can't go?"

The Watcher seemed distracted, as though he were listening to something else. "No, Ascent is still possible. For a time, at least. But we must hurry. *You* must hurry."

Water surged and boiled silently overhead, closing off a last circular glimpse of the storm-wracked sky. Moment by moment, the light filtering down from overhead dimmed as Liftport sank deeper into watery darkness. Dav could no longer make out the Ribbon above the dome's transparency.

"What do I have to do?"

"Decide, both of you. Now. Do you want to go? The choice *must* be yours."

"Then we'd better get started," Dav said. Damn it, he was not going to let the Temple priests block him!

But Eris took a step backward, shaking her head. "No. No. I can't do that."

"What do you mean?" Dav said, suddenly angry. "You're the one who brought us here! If we have to climb the Ribbon to get to Third Heaven, that's all there is to it!"

"You don't understand. I can't. Not in *this*!" She looked around at the capsule's transparent bulkheads. Then she whirled back to face

Dav. "Besides! What's the point? You heard Watcher! Your Aradye—
and Kerellien. They're *gone!* We can't see them. Not in Third Heaven.
Not *ever!*" Turning suddenly, she lunged for the capsule's entryway,
and scrambled back outside.

"But Eris!" Dav said. She was leaving him to Ascend alone?
"Wait!"

"Forget it, Dav! Crawling all the way up a piece of cloth to the
Ring? Thirty-six thousand *li?* It's *crazy!*"

Angry, now, she stormed away from the capsule. The Watcher
turned to him. "And how about you, Dav? What's your decision?"

His fists clenched hard at his sides. The idea of riding this capsule to Heaven didn't exactly appeal to him, either, and the thought
of confinement for seven days alone was terrifying. And yet—

"I'm going," was all he said.

But Eris's words still burned. It *was* crazy. But he was still going.
He just wasn't entirely sure why.

ONCE HE'D MADE the decision, things happened swiftly. "Remember," the Watcher told him, "If you need anything, just ask the pod
AI. You'll need to state your request aloud, rather than by silent
prayer, because it's not attuned to your thoughts. But it'll provide
whatever you need."

"How about advice?"

"That too, up to a point. But you'll need to make your own
decisions."

"Okay." He took a deep breath. "Okay! I'm ready," he lied.

"Good luck."

The Watcher stepped through the entryway, which sealed after
him. For a moment, Dav saw the two of them, Eris and the Watcher,
standing outside, arms raised in silent farewell. Then they hurried
from the chamber and, moments later, it began filling with water.

He could see very little once the dome was completely filled,
but he did feel a muffled lurch after a few minutes, and a dropping
sensation in his stomach as though he was moving. Odd. The capsule, apparently, was not screened against inertial forces.

The Watcher *had* said the technology was primitive, but Dav
hadn't expected anything quite like this. Already he was beginning to
have second thoughts. His eyes strayed to the red panic button. *I can
always abort*, he told himself.

Water exploded around him—and suddenly he was again bathed in the greenish light of the storm. The capsule was struck by the full force of the wind; the pod wasn't shielded from sound, either, and he could hear the wind and rain howling just beyond the thin, transparent bulkhead. He could feel the pod shuddering and trembling like a living thing, and a sudden jolt from a strong gust tore a scream from his throat. He gripped the armrests on the couch, terrified.

The climbing mechanism to which the pod was attached blocked part of his view, and he couldn't see the rollers taking him up the Ribbon, but he could see the spray-streaked surface of the water swiftly receding below him with alarming speed. A moment later, the capsule's bulkheads turned a dark and murky grey. At first he thought they'd opaqued, possibly in response to his fear, but, as the murk thickened, he realized the truth.

He was passing through the clouds.

"Pod AI!" he called out.

"Active," a neuter voice said from somewhere overhead.

"How high up are we?"

"Two point four *li* above sea level," the computer replied. "Climb rate now 157 *li* per hour."

Which meant that he was already higher than the bottom levels of one of the Towers. The thought thrilled—and helped to steady him. He'd made it this far up, and the priests hadn't been able to stop him!

Or not yet, at any rate. The vibrations in the pod's hull were growing more and more violent, and seemed to match the pounding race of his own heart. His breaths came in short, shallow gasps.

Two *li* down, 35,782 to go, if the Watcher's figures were accurate.

Light pulsed within the cottony shroud outside, followed almost instantly by a raw, booming blast of thunder, dragging another startled exclamation from him. Close!

He hoped the Watcher had been accurate about protection from lightning, too.

After a time, the murk outside began lightening somewhat, becoming a pearly, swiftly-thinning mist.

His sudden emergence into daylight was even more startling, more stunning than his escape from the ocean. Sunlight blasted through the transparent bulkheads, too brilliant to look at directly.

"Pod AI!" he cried, shielding his eyes with an arm. "It's too bright!" When there was no response, he added, "Can you dim the light from outside?"

The transparency darkened slightly, and the light became tolerable.

Minutes passed, and the cloud tops dropped away beneath him. Even with the polarization effect, the clouds were dazzlingly bright, while the sky overhead, from horizon to horizon, appeared as an unfathomable, infinitely deep and radiant blue. *The Second Heaven*, he thought. The legendary realm of air and light and pure energy. He put his hand out to touch the bulkhead. It felt neither cool nor hot. And—comforting thought!—the vibration was less intense now, too, and seemed to be dying away as he continued the ascent. If only because it was impossible to maintain the physical symptoms of terror indefinitely, Dav's heart rate was slowing and his breathing becoming deeper and more relaxed.

It took a few more minutes to be sure, but he thought— Yes! The knife-edged line between clouds below and sky above was actually *curved*. The memories, the old songs and stories, even the emblems worn by the priests, all described Earth as a sphere circled by her Rings—but Dav had never seen direct proof of this. The Earth felt flat, within the limits imposed by mountains and valleys, of course, and the realization that he really did live on the surface of a huge ball rather than on an infinite plane was a bit overwhelming. He watched, fascinated rather than terrified, as the curve drew more and more distinct. The sky was darkening, too, the blue growing deeper and deeper until it blended imperceptibly into black.

The blue, he saw, was still there, as a thin band just above the white of the cloud deck, but that was dwindling as he watched.

Overhead, the sun shone in unimaginable brilliance, alone in a velvet black sky. He tried to spot the Ring, and finally succeeded. It was a slender, silver thread rising from one horizon, vanishing as it approached the sun, then reappearing as it descended to the opposite horizon. The sun was so bright it was hard to see—and the stars, which he would have expected to see against a night-black sky, were quite invisible.

Looking down, he was now aware of more than the featureless upper surface of the clouds. The cloud deck had taken on a definite form and dynamic: a vast, swirling whirlpool of white overlaying a gorgeous, watery blue. Though frozen motionless, he had the impression that it must be rotating quite rapidly: he could see a kind of dimple or well at the center of the cloud mass. Looking straight down, he could see the Ribbon dwindling swiftly to a thread then vanishing against the clouds. It took him a moment to make the connection.

That cloud spiral below him was the storm.

That spiral shape was so distinctive—solid at the center, trailing into ragged arms at the rim. Where had he seen it before?

Then he remembered. The design the Watcher wore picked out in tiny skinlights on his forehead.

And no wonder. That vast spiral, reaching almost from one horizon to the other, was inexpressibly beautiful.

And as the minutes passed, he became more and more aware of the Earth below as *Earth*, not as a sheet of abstract white cloud. In the direction the sun told him was east, he could see the mottled greens and browns of land, and even make out the wrinkled texture of mountains. And was that a *Tower* reaching from black sky to mountaintop, like a straight, vertical silver line drawn against the black of the sky?

Quite possibly, he realized, that was the Twelfth Tower. If so, the port city of Rhaddhiannat was invisible with the distance.

North, beyond the sweep of the storm, he could see patches of emerald against the blue, a chain of several of them, each mottled in various greens and edged by vanishingly slender wisps of white. Ouai, perhaps? He shook his head. He had to admit to himself that, from here, he couldn't be sure *what* he was looking at.

Isolated clouds drifted here and there, each with a bit of shadowed darkness immediately beneath. Those alone gave some measure of scale to what he was seeing.

For the first time, he was glad that Eris had decided not to join him. If she was afraid of heights— He had to move back from the transparency, had to sit on the couch and breathe deeply. He was not normally affected by heights, but he could definitely feel the tug of vertigo.

"Pod AI," he said. His voice cracked, and he had to try again. "Pod AI! How— How high?"

"Ninety-five *li*," the voice replied. After a pause, it added, "We will reach the one hundred *li* limit in another ninety seconds."

"One hundred *li*? What happens at one hundred *li*?"

"That is the Karman Line, the arbitrary transition point between Earth's upper atmosphere and space, a limit accepted since ancient times. There is no absolute end point to the atmosphere, which has been steadily thinning ever since we began our ascent, but we are currently well above over 99 percent of the Earth's atmosphere. The Karman Line is a convenient way to mark our entry into space."

But Dav was more interested in the news that they were above most of Earth's atmosphere. "Does that mean there's no air outside?"

"There are traces, but from the biological point of view, you are correct."

Again, he placed his hand on the transparent bulkhead, trying to imagine such a strange concept as an absence of air—a *vacuum*. He'd heard that a vacuum existed within magtubes underground, but had never quite believed in the possibility.

They passed the Karman Line without further comment from the AI. Dav felt almost relaxed as the minutes continued passing—and then the hours. The horizons of the world fell away, seeming to close in on themselves, and soon Dav was very aware that the Earth was, indeed, a sphere—a dazzling blending of swirling white clouds and emerald greens and impossibly beautiful blues—hanging in space.

And as hour followed hour, the Earth dwindled, shrinking so slowly he wasn't aware of the movement, but definitely noticeable over the course of each five minutes or so. As still more time passed, the rate of shrinking appeared to slow. He thought perhaps the capsule was slowing in its ascent, and again panic gripped him—until the AI's reassurances convinced him that the effect was one of perspective and scale, not, as it felt, of the rising capsule slowing to a halt.

The sphere, he eventually decided, was not perfectly round. In the east, beyond the wrinkle of the mountains, the panorama dropped off into darkness and, before long, the darkness had enveloped the mountains as well. *There* was Rhaddhiannat—a smear of pale white light hugging the mountains.

Nightfall was advancing in the east while the sun was still well above the white curve of the western horizon.

He asked the AI for something to drink, and got water. He tried asking for a Modret-vintage wine, but was politely refused. The only available beverages were water or a hot, water-based beverage the

AI called caff. When he asked for food, still later, what appeared on the armrest at his elbow was bland and unappetizing but edible and, presumably, nourishing. The toilet facilities that unfolded out of the deck were equally utilitarian, even Spartan but, so far, at least, his Ascent seemed to be unfolding pretty much the way the Watcher had said it would.

Except for how impossibly *beautiful* that vista was. The Watcher had not tried to describe the view, and Dav could understand why. No verbal description, not even a visual memory, could have come close to the reality—and if it had, Dav would not have believed it. Slowly, as the hours passed, more and more of the planet below slipped into darkness until, finally, the sun slipped behind the sharp curve of the Earth in a flare of radiance and sunset colors compressed into a narrow arc at the horizon. The stars had been appearing for some time, now, the brightest ones first and, as the polarization of the capsule's hull switched off, the entire sky was filled with them in a crowded tumble never seen from the bottom of Earth's turgid atmosphere. Above the western horizon, the Zodiacal Light shone like a vast, hazy spray of golden light, with the Rings a solid thread of silver knifing through, up, over, and around to an eastern horizon now visible only where the mass of the Earth blotted out those astonishing clots of stars.

Even the night side of Earth held beauty. He could see the vast cities along the coastline to the east, and glowing filaments, like spider webs, connecting them. A pale light throbbed silently from time to time, muffled within the depths of storm clouds—the silent flare of lightning discharges.

Was that Modret, far to the north? He'd thought he knew his geography well, but he still had trouble identifying what he was actually seeing from this perspective.

More time passed. He was fascinated by the clarity of the Ring in the night sky—and especially by Biterise. He recognized the Bite at once, despite the fact that he was seeing the Rings edge-on as a thin, brilliant thread, rather than as a sharply angled surface as was visible from Modret. At the Bite, the Ring-thread simply vanished, to begin again a little further on.

"Pod AI?"

"Active."

"What is the Bite?"

"I do not understand the question."

"Uh—can you see?"

"I can see."

He pointed. "That emptiness in the Ring. Where it looks like a section is missing."

That is where Earth's shadow falls across the Rings," the voice told him. "With magnification, you can see the city lights there. Would you like magnification?"

"Sure!"

Instantly, that part of the hull transparency shifted, the darkened segment of the Rings becoming suddenly much larger, much closer. Sure enough, he could see something like stars within the gap—but stars too neatly ranked and ordered to be natural.

Part of him, he found, was disappointed, as though some of the mystery had just been lost. But part, too, felt a profound relief.

The Bite, after all, was not the result of the accumulated sins of Humankind. It wasn't even a void.

Dav slept. Woke. Drank. Ate. Earth continued to dwindle, more slowly than before, it seemed. Experimentation with the Pod AI showed him he could also render the pod's deck transparent, so that it was as if he sat on the partial ring of the sofa in empty space, looking down upon the tiny circle of the world at his feet.

He watched the passage of another day across the hemisphere of the planet facing him. He watched the artificial storm track eastward, swing north, and begin to break up in a spray of curving cloud patterns.

The priests' attempt to bring down the Ribbon, evidently, had failed. Or possibly they'd meant only to frighten him into not going.

Dav wondered how the Watcher and Eris were—Especially Eris.

He missed her.

He was surprised to find he was bored.

Was it possible to be jaded by such beauty? Somehow, that didn't seem possible, but he also found that indulging too long in the sensory riot of color and unfamiliar sights overloaded him after a while, made it impossible to take in any more.

At his request, the bulkheads opaqued, and he found he could display upon them the text and images of various stored memories—dramas by Malor and Dorate and Brokatheledrei, an operetta by Lammeserethedieg, and even a recitation of his own *Heremgath's Ascent*. He ate, drank, and slept again. And again.

But after the passage of another two days, the claustrophobia began to wear at him, and he asked again for a view of the stars, and the dwindling world at his feet.

He found the wonder fresh once more.

Sometime on the third day, the ascending capsule jerked to a halt.

"What is it?" he cried, aware by the surging sensation in the pit of his stomach that upward motion had ceased. "Pod AI! What's happening?"

"We have stopped our ascent."

"Why? What's wrong?"

"The Ribbon above us is obstructed."

"Obstructed? By what?"

"Unknown at this time."

"Can you show me?"

The transparency directly overhead shimmered, then enlarged. At first, nothing appeared to have changed. He could see the Ribbon receding seemingly to infinity, swallowed by the night, and the keen, straight-line silver scratch of the Ring against the firmament.

Then he realized that the Ring had been broken at the point where the Ribbon should have joined it. No, the Ring wasn't broken. Something was obscuring it—and that something was growing larger moment by moment as he watched.

"Pod AI! It's coming down the Ribbon straight toward us! Do something!"

"What do you wish me to do?"

"How do I know?" He screamed. *Think*, damn it, *think!* "How high are we?"

"We are currently 18,927 *li* above sea level."

Almost nineteen thousand? That put them a little more than halfway to the Ring.

It also put them below the critical distance the Watcher had mentioned before his departure. If something went wrong above 24,000 *li*, and he was forced to abort, he would be thrown into orbit.

Below that altitude, he would fall.

He looked down through the transparent decking. Earth appeared terribly small at his feet. For an unpleasant moment, he felt a terrible vertigo clawing at his gut. Such a long way to fall.

So many of the hero tales, of Heremgath and others, spoke of being weightless beyond the bounds of Earth. He flexed his knees experimentally. He still had weight. He felt—odd. A bit lighter, as though gravity had released a fraction of its hold, but *only* a fraction. It was difficult to be sure.

He looked at the panic button, and licked dry lips. He would fall. All the way to Earth, he would fall and fall, and there was no way of knowing where he would come to rest. He thought again of his trek south from Modret, of the cities he'd seen, the people, the varied geographies. His adventure might just be beginning.

He thought of the power of the wide and endless ocean, and realized his adventure might be about to end.

Then he looked up again and there was no time to think, no time for *anything*. The object was now showing a visible body even without magnification. It appeared to be the lower surface of a slightly convex disk, constructed of some mottled gray material. A pair of white lights on the rim winked steadily, as though keeping time for its precipitous descent. The Ribbon vanished into a slot passing directly through the thing's center.

A tangle of confused thoughts vied with one another for dominance in his mind. A gibbering of rising panic—the need to tell the pod AI to reverse direction, to communicate with the descending object, to find out what it was, the fear that it was some sort of barrier or weapon put there by the gods, or something put there by the priests of the High Temple, the terror that he was about to be swatted like an insect for his presumption in Ascending—

What won out was the need to hit the abort button. Collision was imminent, and a scant handful of seconds away. If he hit the button, the capsule would jettison from the Ribbon and fall. The gods alone knew where on the shrunken Earth he would end up, but at least he would avoid that massive, falling disk. Turning and leaning over the sofa, he raised his hand, hovering above the fatal red button—

And stopped. The architects of this transportation system had designed well. Amazingly so, for so fragile-seeming a device to have endured the ages. He'd trusted them to bring him this far in safety, slender as this path to Heaven appeared. He knew he could flee the unknown—or he could stand still and accept it, even embrace it.

He withdrew his hand, stood, and looked up through the transparency overhead.

He could no longer see anything of the Ring, which had been blotted out by the descending object. Something like a mouth or a door was yawning wide as if to swallow him.

When the Ring at last is lost to view, the Modret Oracle had declared, . *then is it closest, and Heaven is near.*

Dav hoped that was true as the object engulfed him, and sun and Earth alike vanished.

THE DESCENDING OBJECT, his pod AI told him moments later, was a repair spider, a robotic mechanism that repaired and maintained the Ribbon. Periodically, it moved down the Ribbon's length to reweave sections that had become worn with age or suffered micro-impacts.

Unseen mechanisms grappled with his pod and moved it into a—place, a room filled with light and unidentifiable mechanisms. There was no sensation of movement, but the AI was able to tell him that it was in communication with the spider's AI, and that they were now moving up the Ribbon at a considerable rate of speed.

They completed the voyage, rushing upward across the almost 17,000 *li* remaining in a little less than three hours, where it had taken him three *days* to travel that distance so far.

And when the pod's door dissolved open, he stepped out into a much larger world than any he could have imagined. A woman, nude save for an opalescent glow that seemed to emanate from her form, was waiting for him with a radiant smile.

He could find no words, none at all, not at first. The space he'd just entered was vast—large enough to hold all of the High Temple and its gardens twice over with room to spare—and the sense of scale and scope was staggering. There were buildings, arches, gardens, towers, and even forests—many appearing to drift unsupported in the sky. The whole was enclosed in some sort of curved transparency. Beyond, and to one side, he could see the sweep of the Rings— myriad Rings in band after band, some apparently solid, others composed of what seemed to be sparkling flecks of golden dust compressed into slender circlets. In the other direction, Earth hung against the star-filled backdrop of clouds, three-quarters full, and apparently held at the hub of a web of descending silver threads—the forty-eight great Towers. The sun was visible, bright and shedding warmth, but not too bright to look at, its light somehow dimmed to a bearable brightness without masking the stars. He could see the full glory of the golden Zodiacal Light, as though the sun himself were imbedded in a Ring of trillions of golden dust motes.

Beneath his feet lay a huge spiral of light, similar to the spiraling storm, but apparently made out of uncountable masses of stars instead of lightning-shot clouds. It took a moment to realize that this was not something hanging in the night outside the Rings, but a kind of map or decoration glowing within the deck.

Was it the storm he'd Ascended from? Why did they have its image frozen here?

And the people! He was aware of throngs of them, some standing, most floating in the air against the background of fantastic, soaring architecture. Many wore elaborate costumes or skinsuits of radiant color; many were nude, save for light. They took many forms, machine as well as organic. Perhaps most predominant were beings with supple torsos and smiling faces that betrayed their human ancestry, but with a second pair of arms in the place where legs should have been. These floated about him in uncountable numbers, watching him with large and smiling eyes.

The shining woman approached. A tiny spiral of light glowed on her forehead, identical to the one worn by the Watcher. Reaching out, she placed something like a circular fabric patch the size of a fingernail on the bare skin of his arm. Second by second, he felt an opening of his awareness. *Information*, and the ability to connect with it, expanded within his thoughts. The patch, clearly, had injected him with new and highly sophisticated nano.

"*Welcome, Davradha Elad*," she cried, her voice sounding in his mind. "*Welcome to the Rings of Earth!*"

"Th-thank you, Goddess," he stammered, scarcely able to find his voice. He found himself sagging then dropping to his knees. He knew he was in the presence of the gods. The honor, the sheer sense of mind-numbed awe—

He felt the woman's warm, liquid laughter more than he heard it. Reaching down, she took his arm and drew him to his feet. "We are human, Dav, just as you are. And today it is *we* who honor *you*."

"Me! Why?"

"Because you are one of the Ascended Heroes, of course. Because you braved the unknown and the danger and came here to meet us. Because you dared to bridge the gulf between Earth and Sky."

And then the throng about him was cheering, applauding, and joined in chorused singing. He felt the warmth and the genuine joy of their welcome, and only the woman's hand on his arm kept him from falling.

Bits and pieces of information flickered through his awareness as his questions, apparently, elicited rapid-fire downloads of data from the Rings' net. Those four-armed people were, indeed, descendents of Humankind—*Homo extraterrestrialis agravitus*, though they were called humeans. What he'd known as the "Zodiacal Light" around the sun was actually a cloud of artificial habitats—habitats and cities and worldlets numbering in the hundreds of billions. Earth's total human population might number as high as a billion. The population of the Rings, however, was closer to a trillion; and that of the entire solar system numbered in the tens of trillions, with a hundred trillion more living among the worlds of other stars.

That spiral in the deck was no storm, he now knew, but a kind of map of the entire Galaxy—and as soon as he wondered what a galaxy was, he knew the answer: a throng of hundreds of billions of stars stretching across a hundred thousand light years, home to hundreds of other species besides Humankind, all commingled in a growing, thriving galactic cooperative.

Once again, the sheer scale of what he was experiencing threatened to overwhelm him.

"Do you know why we honor you, Dav?" the woman said, smiling into his mind.

"N-no. I'm no Hero." Not like Heremgath. Or Galallel. Or any of the others of the tales among his memories.

"Because you are like the Heroes of your tales. You follow in the footsteps of others, just as they did. The Ribbon you Ascended, frail and slender as it is, was—even more than Humankind's first step on the Moon of the Ancients—an evolutionary step that led from imprisonment and ultimate extinction upon the Earth to this." She gestured with her free arm, taking in the entirety of the vista about them. "To our maturity as a species. To immortality. To a vitality and a creativity and an expansion of horizons you can scarcely imagine now, but which you will soon experience for yourself."

"It's— It's all a little hard to take in all at once."

"I know. But you'll have time. And help. You are not alone."

Had she been reading his thoughts?

"I can—I can stay here? With you?"

"Yes. If you wish."

He sensed a hesitation, however. "What is it?"

"Dav, like all Heroes, you face a choice. You needn't decide immediately. You may stay as long as you wish. But you will face it."

"What choice?"

"You will need to decide whether you remain here for the rest of a very long, very comfortable life—one nearly eternal by your present standards—or returning to Earth."

"Return?"

"Earth's inhabitants are held in slavery, Dav. A gentle slavery, with light chains, but slavery nonetheless. The chains are their isolation from information, an isolation imposed by those who rule them."

"The priests."

"Yes. And others behind the priests. But the Temple controls access to the Towers, and has done so for many thousands of years."

"Of course! If everybody wanted to Ascend—"

"No, Dav. There was a reason for that restriction on emigration once. In the time of Galallel—no, earlier than that—when the Ribbons first were raised, the bulk of Humankind lived on Earth. Those of us residing in the Solar System lived within a somewhat fragile ecology, one utterly dependent on the world that gave our species birth.

"The Ribbons changed that. They gave us our evolutionary leap forward to a new kind of life, and a new way of thinking, without limits.

"But Earth continues to exist within a philosophy of limits, of *want*. Only so much is available to any one person; there is not, there *cannot* ever be, enough for all.

"Among the rest of Humankind, there is no want, and no need of limits. We could accept the entire population of Earth here within the Rings alone, and feel no crowding."

"*Everyone?*"

"Everyone. Not every person would want to emigrate, perhaps. But all who wished to do so could, and that is what is important. To make that day possible, though, some would have to go back down and share what they know. Give them new memories.

And new ideas. New ways of thinking that do not require limits—or priesthoods."

Back to Earth? Back to Eris. And the promise of Ascending once again.

A new thought asserted itself. "But can't you just go down the Towers and set things straight yourselves? Why would you want someone like me?"

"Dav, what is the first principle of freedom?"

"That no one can tell another what to do." Realization struck him. "Oh—"

"Exactly." She smiled into him again. "You don't need to make a decision now, Dav. As I said, you have all the time for which you could wish.

"And there's something more. Before deciding, you will need to know the dangers such a return would entail. People do not give up privilege or power without struggle. And freedom cannot be won without cost. Heremgath and Galallel, recall, both returned to Earth in the tales, and both were martyred. What made them Heroes was their willingness to return for others, despite the fate awaiting them."

"I know." He closed his eyes, momentarily shutting out the thronging glories of the Third Heaven gathered around him. "I know."

But he also knew what his decision would be.

DEFENSE OF THE SPACE ELEVATOR AGAINST THREATS OF VIOLENCE
by
CDR Michael Breslauer

Commander Michael J. Breslauer, "Mumbles," graduated from the United States Naval Academy in 1989 with a B.S. in Aerospace Engineering. After earning Naval Flight Officer wings in Pensacola, Florida in 1990, he moved to Whidbey Island, Washington to fly the EA-6B Prowler.

CDR Breslauer was selected for the NPS/TPS Cooperative program, earning a M.S. in Aeronautical Engineering from the U.S. Naval Postgraduate School, and graduating from the Naval Test Pilot School, Patuxent River, MD.

CDR Breslauer has made three carrier deployments, participating in Operations Southern Watch, Noble Eagle and Enduring Freedom. He has accumulated over 2000 flight hours in tactical aircraft, and flown over 25 different aircraft types. His current assignment is as Fleet Project Team Lead for the ICAP-III weapons system upgrade to the EA-6B Prowler.

WHILE FREQUENT DISCUSSIONS and significant amounts of thought have been put into dealing with threats originating from the space environment, a question routinely arises concerning the possibility of intentional threats of violence to the space elevator. The social, political and economic significance of an operational Space Elevator may seem to make it an inviting target. Looking closer, the origin of the possible threat falls into two distinct categories; an act of terrorism from a rogue group, be it religious, political, economic or ecological terrorism, or a nationalistic threat as an act of war. For threat from either a violent organization or nation, the form of attack could be either external armed attack or internal sabotage. Although some organization may possibly become a future threat, there are reasonable steps that can be taken to reduce the likelihood and effect of any form of attack.

Location, location, location...

A recurring theme to the defense of the space elevator is location. The current space elevator design uses an anchor station operating in international waters near the equatorial Pacific. At any one time, the anchor platform could be several hundred kilometers north or south of the equator, and have the ability to travel east or west over one thousand kilometers. And this "box," in addition to being nebulous in terms of outer boundary, is approximately 1500 kilometers from the nearest populated land. The equivalent distance is roughly from Seattle to Los Angeles. The anchor platform operating area is away from most sea traffic lanes and commercial air routes. It is off in a corner of the world by itself. No roads, no signposts, just open water. That isolation is a significant defense for the space elevator.

External Attack

Threat of an armed attack on the SE anchor station or ribbon has often been stated as easily accomplished. "Why couldn't someone hijack a jetliner and fly it into the ribbon?" A more likely form of terrorist attack would be a small boat firing rocket-propelled grenades or attempting to attach a contact explosive to the anchor station. Either a governmental or terrorist/pirate attack could take the form of a commando assault on the anchor station. And a state level attack could entail a warship employing naval gunfire, surface or air launched torpedoes or anti-ship missiles.

Fortunately for us, any overt attack would require the attacker to sail or fly thousands of kilometers, detect the presence of the anchor station, and bring appropriate weapons or forces to bear. Commercial aircraft typically possess a weather-detection radar, and if hijacked, would not be capable of conducting open water surface search. The radar detection range of a boat is limited by the curvature of the Earth and the antenna height, and would reduce the probability of finding the anchor. The reconnaissance capabilities to find the anchor station amid hundreds of thousands of square kilometers of open ocean are significant, more typical of those possessed by a nations armed forces, not a rogue group. The distance involved and uncertainty of location of the anchor station make successfully launching an external attack unlikely.

So what if, by successful search, insider information or prior knowledge, the attacker knew of the anchor station location, and mounted a surprise attack? This is a Pearl Harbor or September 11th scenario. For a limited scale attack, the anchor station would have a good chance of survival. Requirements in terms of physical size and extreme on-station time for the anchor platform will contribute to its inherent passive survivability. Being big and well built in order to survive a long time at sea also makes it hard to damage and very tough to sink. The lowest portion of the ribbon, while being potentially fragile, represents a very small profile (meters wide and paper-thin) and would require a good deal of luck or high degree of precision to successfully attack.

For a dedicated, large-scale attack by the armed forces of a hostile nation, the anchor station would be vulnerable and likely be sunk. But the political magnitude and repercussions of such an attack place it outside the boundaries of planning for the engineering of the Space Elevator. By way of comparison, one could ask what would have happened if a foreign government shot down a U.S. Space Shuttle in orbit, if someone dropped a depth charge attempting to implode the middle of the England-to-France Chunnel, or even attacked a modern commercial super-container ship in international waters? An attack by an opposing nation on the Space Elevator would be an act of war. The nature of the organization that deployed the space elevator, be it a single country, a commercial entity, or a consortium, would affect only slightly the international condemnation and resulting onset of hostilities against the aggressor. It is difficult to see how intentional destruction of a Space Elevator would be in the long-term interest of any nation.

Several early statements have been made that a fleet of U.S. warships and aircraft would provide protection for the Space Elevator by surrounding it continuously to counter possible attack. While some of the proponents of the system may consider a long-duration fleet deployment appropriate to their estimation of the importance of the Space Elevator, such deployment would only take place if it were in the U.S. national interest. Perhaps, if there was a credible threat to the system, either after the onset of hostilities during wartime, or from a known organization, some form of protection could be extended. However, armed forces would better be used to eliminate the threat at the source rather than face an extended deployment thousands of kilometers from the nearest land. And U.S. protection assumes that the U.S. will be involved in construction of the Space Elevator, a fact not presently guaranteed.

But that is not to say that the anchor station need be defenseless against external attack. Self-protection capabilities should be included on the anchor station. Passive resistance and tolerance to damage, mentioned earlier, should be maximized during the design process. External access should be limited to reduce the chances of unapproved entrance, with redundant layers of access restriction features surrounding operationally important spaces. While the level of large armaments the anchor station may be allowed to carry may be determined in no small part by the characterization of who builds the Space Elevator; governmental or commercial, there are other defenses. A security contingent can be maintained on board the anchor station to defend against small boat attack and intruders. With basic training, the crew equipped with small arms could be a realistic deterrent to boarders. Even a fire hose can defend against protest level political attacks or unsophisticated boarding parties.

The anchor station should have an extensive suite of radar and optical sensors for tracking space objects and detecting/warning approaching air traffic, which can be used as part of the defensive system. This sensor suite will notify the anchor station crew of any approaching contact. Possible political efforts to establish a no-fly safety zone around the elevator ribbon would assist that security buffer and improve the effectiveness of the sensor information. Innocent contacts penetrating the buffer and approaching the anchor could be directed clear. For unknown or uncooperative contacts, the advance warning given by the sensors will permit the anchor station crew to maneuver and prepare for possible aggression.

Internal Attack

The second form of attack to be anticipated would be an internal attack. It could be sabotage during the ribbon manufacturing process, explosive devices directed against the anchor station ribbon or cargo handling system, explosives inserted in a cargo shipment, or some form of beacon in a cargo shipment to aid guidance of a weapon to target the ribbon itself. The threat varies only as much as the imagination of the potential attackers. And there could be little or no warning of the approach of an internal threat.

But this situation is nothing new to many large-scale industrial organizations, among them the commercial aircraft industry, nuclear power plants, chemical and petroleum manufacturing and all mega-engineering projects. The key is access control and security. Quality assurance on the ribbon and anchor station manufacture, controlled transportation of all personnel, material, and cargo to the anchor station, and background checks on all personnel should be considered as a baseline. Strict security measures should be implemented on everything from food and fuel to lifters and cargo. Each and every cargo shipment should be inspected by the Space Elevator organization to prevent both illicit cargo and dangerous objects. Inspection facilities at both the shore shipping terminal and anchor station, including a large capacity clean room, should be included in the requirements process. The result of a customer not complying with the required inspection routine should be denial of elevator service. There is a wealth of experience and expertise on how to provide security for high-value projects, all of which should be fully utilized. Internal attack is not an idle threat to the Space Elevator, but it can be defeated through a dedicated, disciplined security program.

Sophisticated Attacks

There are other complicated methods of attack that could sink the anchor platform and/or cut the ribbon. Examples include nuclear/biological/chemical attack, submarine torpedo, mine or anti-ship missile attack on the anchor platform, high-power laser or orbital satellite attack on the ribbon, or ICBMs targeted against either the anchor or the ribbon. Each requires a level of sophistication beyond the capabilities of a rogue individual or terrorist group. Each are national level capabilities, which, if employed, would result in war, just as discussed for direct assault.

In order to illustrate this point, a short story about two men camping. One wakes up to see the other frantically putting on his running shoes.

"What are you doing?" he asks.

"There is a bear coming," replies the second.

"You will never be able to outrun the bear," says the first.

The second camper's reply says it all, "I don't have to outrun the bear, I only have to outrun you."

The moral here being that any government, group or individual in possession of such sophisticated weaponry could find more lucrative targets to attack. This concept applies across the entire spectrum from simple planted explosives to nuclear weapons, but for complex and expensive weapons of mass destruction, employment against a Space Elevator anchor seems a significant mismatch. The Space Elevator does not need to be invincible, just harder to target and attack than possible alternatives.

A Realistic Perspective

There is no reason to believe the Space Elevator must be a target. Open diplomatic relations with all concerned governments and access to all customers willing to live within the security guidelines will reduce the number of potential adversaries. The elevator can be a major benefit for all of mankind. By sharing the fortunes it may bring, we can eliminate jealousy and envy, and greatly reduce the potential that any attacks ever materialize. But there is no guarantee that all adversaries can be eliminated.

To deal with possible threats, there is no complete set of precautions that will make the Space Elevator invulnerable. An opposing government, organization or individual, with enough dedication, could find a way to make an attack. Appropriate design and operational measures should be taken to make attack as difficult as possible and safeguard the system in case violence is directed towards the Space Elevator. And any measures to make an attack more difficult or less likely to succeed will reduce the chance that the Space Elevator will ever become a victim of hostile actions.

The Space Elevator may at first seem an attractive target. But through open diplomatic and financial partnerships, we can reduce the number of possible adversaries. Through location, structure and operational regimen, we can reduce the possibility and probability it will be victim to successful attack. If the technical challenges related to building a Space Elevator can be overcome, there is every reason to believe that prudent measures will allow us keep the elevator safe in a chaotic, uncertain world.

SOCIOPOLITICAL ISSUES
An Historical Overview of the Space Elevator Concept
by
Monte Davis

Monte Davis has been a science writer for thirty years. He helped to launch *OMNI* magazine as interviews editor, and *Discover* magazine as a staff writer. His work has also appeared in *Psychology Today*, the *NY Times Magazine*, and other publications.

Since the mid-1980s he has also been a communications consultant and speechwriter for Fortune 500 corporations including leaders in information technology, communications, pharmaceuticals and heavy engineering. He lives in suburban Philadelphia with too many computers, and is working on a book about the end of the first space age—the expensive one, with all the rockets.

THE HISTORY OF ideas leading to a space elevator can be traced in five steps so far:

> The recognition of geosynchronous/geostationary orbit (GEO)
> The idea of a structure making use of GEO's properties
> The idea of a *tension* structure; its properties and dynamics
> Next-century conceptual designs and deployment scenarios (massive)
> A next-decade design and scenario (minimalist); beginnings of engineering

Don't let the steps suggest an inevitable sequence. The actual history is a more interesting tangle of multiple independent discoveries, partial insights, and most recently the role of CNTs in bringing the ideas down to earth.

Geosynchronous orbit
Every rotating, spherical body has one "special" equatorial orbit that keeps a satellite over the same point on the surface. Newton, Laplace, Lagrange and many others may well have noticed that as a curiosity, but synchronous orbit didn't become part of the common coin of orbital mechanics for two hundred years. That could be because a

primary's rotation is an arbitrary "given," and doesn't figure in orbital calculations using point-mass approximations. Also, astronomy provided no natural example of a synchronously orbiting satellite, as it did of synchronous rotation in Earth's tide-locked moon.

As far as we know, the first to draw attention to synchronous orbit was Konstantin Tsiolkovsky in *Dreams of Earth and Sky* (1895). He calculated the synchronous distances for five planets and the sun —and did so in the context of reaching space and *putting* things in space, a context he was creating as he went.

A structure to (or at) GEO
Tsiolkovsky wrote:
"As we ascend a tower, gravity gradually diminishes; and, if this tower is built in the equator of a planet and therefore rotates rapidly with it, gravity also diminishes not only because of its gradual departure from the center of the planet but also because of the increase in the centrifugal force which is proportional to this recession… At an altitude of 34,000 kilometers it vanishes completely, and higher up appears again with a force proportional to the removal from the critical point, but in the opposite direction…"

Tsiolkovsky knew perfectly well that no material was strong and rigid enough to support itself against gravity to such a height. Such a tower was a gedanken (thought) experiment, like Maxwell's demon or Einstein's rider on a beam of light. But the idea opened the way to speculation: by climbing or riding an elevator to geosynchronous altitude, gaining transverse velocity as the tower turned with the earth, one could attain orbit *slowly*. So a would-be spacefarer could use an everyday form of action/reaction (feet on a stair, drive wheels on a cable) instead of hurling away mass at high speed. That would avoid the curse of Tsiolkovsky's own rocket equation: the high propellant fractions and high acceleration that chemical rockets would need.

A tension structure

This was the most important step toward reducing the mass (and increasing the plausibility) of a space elevator. It happened independently several times, twice in a form that identified what we now see as the key properties.

In 1957, Leningrad engineering graduate student Yuri Artsutanov heard about ultra-strong graphite whiskers. He was told that a sufficiently defect-free whisker could support its own weight for 400 km. Artsutanov would write Arthur C. Clarke in 1979:

"I thought that at such a height the gravitating force is less and consequently the length could be enlarged. Then it became interesting for me to calculate the strength of the material to prolong the vertical rod made of it to infinity... Some months later [presumably with Sputnik I] the cosmic theme became very popular..."

Now that people *were* putting things into space, and GEO was being discussed for prospective communications satellites, Artsutanov conceived an application for this self-supporting tension structure as an alternative to rockets. It appeared in *Pravda*'s youth edition in July, 1960, as a popular-science article titled "To the Cosmos by Electric Train." It seems unlikely that Artsutanov or his editors were familiar with the idea in Tsiolkovsky, who by then was celebrated as the forerunner of Soviet space technology; if they had been, surely his name would have been mentioned.

Although non-technical, the article incorporated a number of ideas still central to today's scenarios: deployment up and down from GEO, the trade-off between length and counterweight mass, a tapered elevator to match strength and load, multiple threads to minimize the damage from meteor impact, "bootstrap" reinforcement in place from a weak initial thread, and the use of the cable beyond GEO as a sling.

Most of the same ideas—and more, including capturing energy from loads descending the cable—occurred independently to aerospace engineer Jerome Pearson in 1969-1970. "After years of fighting with reluctant editors," he recalls, they reached print in 1975 in *Acta Astronautica* as "The orbital tower: a spacecraft launcher using the earth's rotational energy." This was the first quantitative and engineering-oriented treatment, although the elevator was still far out of reach:

"To construct a tower [using perfect graphite crystals] with a base cross-sectional area of 50 cm^2 and a taper ratio of 10, about 24,000 flights would be required of an advanced space shuttle with thirty times the payload of the presently proposed shuttle."

Pearson was the first to investigate the dynamic stability of a space elevator against deflections and oscillations caused by the moon, wind loads, and climber movements. In subsequent work he extended that analysis, proposed space elevators for the Moon, and helped stimulate others in aerospace to consider a wide range of uses for space tethers.

Others had taken up the idea along the way. John McCarthy had thought about a tapered "skyhook" in the early 1950s, but dismissed it after doing the math for steel, and never published. Oceanographer John Isaacs and his colleagues proposed an impractically thin paired wire in *Science* in 1966. (That prompted a letter to the editors that for most Western readers was the first news of Artsutanov.) In 1977, Hans Moravec recalled McCarthy's work, reviewed the field to date, and added the concept of the rotating non-synchronous tether or "rotavator" and the free-space skyhook. Both extended the idea of slinging payloads from a fixed elevator to a general scheme for exchange of momentum between incoming and outgoing payloads.

Next-Century Designs and Scenarios

In 1979, Arthur C. Clarke's *The Fountains of Paradise* and Charles Sheffield's *The Web Between the Worlds* —both influenced primarily by Pearson's work —began spreading the idea of space elevators to a wider audience.

Through the 1990s almost everything written about space elevators took for granted that even if the strongest materials were used, the cable would be massive (and thus far in the future). Kim Stanley Robinson's 1991 novel *Red Mars* envisioned a Martian cable of six billion tons, made of "carbon — and helical [synthetic] diamond." Like Clarke's and Sheffield's, it was fabricated from a carbonaceous asteroid whose remnants served as counterweight. But 1993's sequel, *Green Mars,* refers in passing to carbon nanotubes. Early estimates of CNT strength were hinting that the new material could bring space elevators much closer to reality.

A 1999 NASA study directed by David Smitherman, Jr. was still closer in spirit to the grandiose science-fiction treatments than to today's version. Although it took into account CNTs, there was still an asteroid counterbalance. The massive cable, rising from a 20-km tower, supported multiple high-speed trains on superconducting guideways. Construction presupposed a vast fleet of advanced heavy-lift rockets. Little wonder that the only ETA mentioned was "the latter part of the 21st century."

A Next-Decade Design and Scenario

What happened next was not a new idea so much as a new attitude. In a 2000 report for NASA's Institute for Advanced Concepts, Bradley Edwards took a minimalist approach. How light could a CNT-based space elevator be and still take tons to orbit at much lower cost than rockets? How could it be bootstrapped from an initial narrow tape to reduce the launches required for deployment? How much of it could use existing or credibly near-term technologies?

What had been back-of-the-envelope conceptual engineering took on detailed masses, budgets and timelines. The numbers were encouraging enough to initiate a virtuous circle: the lighter and less expensive the design became, the more Edwards and then others took space elevators seriously as something that might be feasible *soon*—and the more ideas they came up with to reduce launch mass, cut costs, and identify issues to be tackled for specific subsystems.

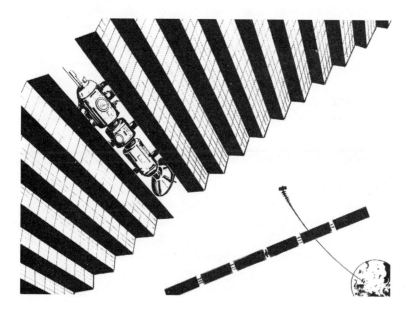

WHY INTERNATIONAL PUBLIC INCLUSION IS IMPORTANT
by
Piotr Jagodzinksi

Mr. Jagodzinski is a native of Warsaw, Poland and is the third of three children. Mr. Jagodzinski studied International Relations at the Uniwersytet Warszawski. He is a novelist, essayist, and sometimes a translator. He has traveled extensively and is interested in Eastern philosophy and, of course, the Space Elevator. Send him email at pantografus@wp.pl

HUMANKIND HAS EXPERIENCED some turning points in its history. Mostly these were inventions concerning some parts of our life, discovered by brilliant individuals. Yet the revolutionary ideas didn't come "ex nihilo", they were always derivatives of some earlier thoughts.

Today a new revolution is in sight. A privately held corporation, the LiftPort Group, is striving to build a Space Elevator (SE) in 15 years. They are trying to convince us that by creating a 100,000 km long ribbon with one end attached to the Earth's surface and the other end to a counterweight in space, they would open up broad-based access to Earth orbit and the inner solar system. This self-confidence goes even further: the plan is to create this mass transportation system from private funding rather than governmental patronage.

Then again, what did Alexander Graham Bell think when he tried to convince others that they could have long distance calls?

Why should the SE be an international project?

Such an ambitious concept like the Space Elevator requires substantial steps. That's why LiftPort Group (LPG) has adopted a policy of International Public Inclusion. The question remains: why would a small company from United States of America appeal to the international community with such a statement? What kind of support does LPG expect? Should anyone from around the world believe in such an incredible idea?

Any serious businessman, from any country, having extra money to spend, would tell you that motivation is the key to success. Give me an idea, a good and moneymaking idea, and I will give you my credit, he might say. Looking at the Space Elevator from that perspective one might agree that this would break the monopoly of the government-dominated rocket industry. If everything goes well, you are a rich man. How simple is that? Well, there aren't many businessmen with over 10 billion dollars of extra money. The anchor station has to be placed somewhere near the Equator, and the Elevator itself needs many potential clients, not just from the US. The ribbon created from CNT composites is not going to develop itself; researchers and scientists are vital for develop such a cable. If someone would think that one company from US could manage these problems, he is surely mistaken.

But do we even need a Space Elevator? Yes, no doubt about it. Humanity as a whole yearns for broad access to Earth orbit. Think of the possibilities; completely new space related markets, a chance to go to Mars, the Moon, and much more. With the operating Elevator every nation on Earth would feel the consequences. There would be repercussions in the form of increased employment, rising markets, new pharmaceuticals, new inventions, progress in power industry, and the list goes on and on.

What about international government cooperation?
LiftPort Group wants to involve the international public in this project. It is very clear that one company cannot do this without the help of the rest of the world. Should it be an inter-governmental project like, for example, the International Space Station? I wouldn't advise such a step. It is not that political support is irrelevant; on the contrary, LiftPort should strive for international consensus concerning the locale of the Elevator (maritime law), and also in the space law arena as well (probably on a wider forum, including perhaps a specific UN resolution). Yet this is not a governmental project, and for good reason. Projects like this shouldn't be dependent on the political will of one or a group of countries; the Space Elevator (or SE), in order to be built, needs to be free of politics.

I could assume that US government involvement is necessary, especially in terms of defense of the SE. However, the Congress and US Army should not monopolize the SE. Any country should be treated as a potential investor with the same rights as non-governmental corporation. Clear and transparent rules should be made for all. In my opinion, I would let the SE be "patronized" only by the UN, just because it would make an enormous impact on the whole planet.

Why should I be interested in something thousands of kilometers away from me?

Globalization is a fact. A seemingly irrelevant action on the local scale can cause global consequences. Compared to other global-scale projects, the US$10 billion pricetag for the SE is almost nothing. The annual military budgets of many countries exceed that amount. Yet there is no comparison to what the Elevator might bring as a result.

Every single human being caring about the future of the planet should be interested in the development of the Space Elevator. Philosophical issues are simple. The SE will let the human race thrive, expand and explore the Universe. I personally believe that the SE would open the door for the colonization of Mars. Almost everywhere you look, one might see the self-destructing tendencies of our species. Think of a Space Elevator as an opposing force to those tendencies. One might even argue that evolution drags us to colonize space. If this is true, then space should be open for all, not just a few astronauts and a couple of rich guys. The elevator to space is the only way to ensure mass transport into space and an opportunity to provide freedom for generations to come.

However, ensuring that freedom will require involvement from many individuals, not just government leaders or large corporations. Academic institutions, research labs, private investors and private citizens of the whole world should get involved. That's why enthusiasts and volunteers from as many nations as possible are so important for LiftPort. That's why the company created the International Public Inclusion policy, and that is why it encourages and invites anyone interested in an elevator to space to join the LiftPort team. The most important thing you can to do help the project is to disseminate the idea of a Space Elevator to people in your mother country. By creating popular support, translating the website, helping to set up international partnerships or giving LiftPort international contacts you can really play a significant role in the development of the venture. The LiftPort staff could help and guide you on how to get involved.

What are some specific steps I can take to help?

The Space Elevator becomes much more feasible when people across the world support the project. Support can be given not only through funding, or legal help, or popular support but also through world-wide collaborative research. Cooperation in key areas such as carbon nanotube composites, ribbon design, robotics, laser power, ocean platform logistics, and orbital debris clean-up/avoidance techniques is very important. There is no doubt that many questions remain, but with international support it is only a question of "when" the answers will come, not "if" they will come.

It is also important to introduce the concept to your fellow countrymen. Popular support is one of the most important issues for the Space Elevator. Through widespread advertisement of the idea, the Space Elevator community will grow and expand. The book you hold is one of these steps, to publicize this ingenious way of safe, cheap, reliable and universal access to space. However, before the international public can act, it must be aware of the opportunity presented by the Space Elevator. You can help to make them aware.

So, if you are still asking why the world should help LiftPort Group, if you are still not convinced here are some final conclusions. The most important premise is to create a safe, cheap and reliable mass transportation system to space. Which way would you rather choose: the bone breaking, dangerous and immediate rocket ride or the calmer and more comfortable way by elevator to reach a future space station? How much money would you like to spend in getting yourself or your cargo up there? A couple of million dollars or just some 400$ per pound? Do you want to beg and wait in line to get to the kosmodrome in Kazakhstan or would you rather fly to the pacific ocean and get a ride right away? Of course Rome wasn't build in one day, yet these fifteen years might bring so many new inventions on the way that would influence our daily life.

One might say we live in a political world, and that politics may make this project impossible. It is true that we live in a world full of opposing forces; all acting in their own best interest and trying to destroy the competition. However, political forces can also be quite powerful and power ultimately flows from the people. If, through grass-roots action, global citizens clamor for the Space Elevator, all but the most brutal leaders must respond to their wishes if they hope to stay in power. Politics can be avoided, yet it can't be ignored! I surely do not suggest it.

The LiftPort Policy of International Public Inclusion is still a preliminary document. It is imperfect and will require revisions. One might ask if such a policy is even necessary? Try to imagine the US or any other government trying to build the Space Elevator on its own. While it is not impossible it would be very difficult indeed. No international help, no collaborative research or funding, accusations of isolationism, no access to an equatorial anchor station, global enmity towards the builder —the list goes on and on. Clearly "going it alone" is the more difficult path. And while coordinating many international partners may be difficult as well, I feel this challenge is far simpler than having one country build it alone.

Turning points in human history

The Space Elevator represents a golden opportunity for all of Western civilization and the entire human race. Therefore every nation adhering to western values should participate. Then again, the elevator to space project is a global project, having tremendous impact on the whole planet, that's why every single nation in the world should get interested. Politics has nothing to do about it, nor religion nor race, even the profits from operating Space Elevator can not turn contracting parties against each other. It might sound high-flown, not adequate to what is going on in the world right now, but the process of creation is a process of cooperation. Overall it's a simple contract—you build, we help, and we're both using it with surplus on both sides.

WE ARE LIVING in a time I like to call "BC" or "before the cable." After April 12, 2018 the world will never be the same again. As I said in the beginning, revolutionary ideas do not stand alone. They are a compilation of many innovative projects throughout all of our world's history.

The Russian scientist Konstantin Tsiolkovsky first proposed the idea of a tower to stars in the late 1800's. As time passed, the original concept evolved with the work of other SE enthusiasts from many countries. For example: Dr. John McCarthy, Yuri Artsutanov, Arthur C. Clarke, Dr. Bradley Edwards and many more. The Space Elevator is not some new revelation; it is not something that one US company has made up. It is an old idea, in fact, more than a century old. Furthermore, this is an international idea. LiftPort is simply a group of brave and ambitious people from US trying to coordinate this global project. We should support them. This would be in our best interest.

THE SPACE ELEVATOR AND THE ENVIRONMENT
Low Cost Access to Space is Key to our Energy Future
by
Ralph H. Nansen

Ralph Nansen has been involved in space engineering for over 40 years, primarily with The Boeing Company. Key positions at Boeing included Design Manager of the Saturn S-1C fuel tanks, Design Manager for the Boeing Space Shuttle definition studies, and, Solar Power Satellite Program Manager to develop the overall concept under the auspices of the Department of Energy and NASA. He is the author of an advocacy book for the public titled *SUN POWER: The Global Solution for the Coming Energy Crisis*, published by Ocean Press.

Mr. Nansen retired from Boeing in 1987.

Mr. Nansen received a BS in Mechanical Engineering from Washington State University.

AS THE ENERGY demands of humanity grow, the fossil fuels that we depend on to supply that energy are rapidly being depleted. Many experts are now predicting that we are approaching the peak of world oil production. Already we are experiencing rapidly increasing prices for oil. What can replace oil as the world's next basic energy source? There are many alternative sources, but all fall short of being able to meet the criteria needed for a future solution except for one: Space Solar Power.

First, let us discuss the criteria for our future energy source. The first criterion is that it must be unable to be depleted. All of our current fossil fuel and nuclear energy power plants use the Earth's resources at a prodigious rate, and these resources will be very difficult to access sometime in the not-too-distant future. The world demand for energy is becoming so great that we cannot supply it with our finite store of natural resources.

The second criterion is low cost. If the cost is not low, a new source will not be developed and the energy will not be used. This does not necessarily mean it has to be low cost in the beginning if we are willing to make an investment in the future, but it must be low cost over the long term.

The third criterion is that it must be environmentally clean. We can no longer continue to pollute our world without regard to the future. We must stop the damage and start to heal the Earth.

The fourth criterion is it must be available to everyone. We can no longer deny energy to the emerging nations of the world and expect to live in peace. Eventually, abundant energy must be made available to everyone on Earth. This means it must be a vast source.

The fifth and last criterion is it must be in a useable form; otherwise, it will be of little help to us.

None of the energy sources in use today can satisfy these five simple but essential criteria. They all fall short in some way. Fossil fuels are being depleted and they also add to the pollution of the earth. Nuclear power uses a nonrenewable resource and also leaves behind toxic nuclear waste. Hydroelectric power is generated by a wonderful renewable source, but there are very few rivers left in the world to dam and there is growing concern over the impact dams have on the fish population. The other hope held out over the years is nuclear fusion. For the past 50 years, it has been touted as the energy source of the future that is "only 20 years away." Tens of billions of dollars have been spent on research, and nuclear fusion is now farther in the future than ever before even though it is still being pursued.

Terrestrial solar power can come close to meeting our criteria, but, due to the intermittent nature of sunlight on the Earth, it will always be too costly for massive, base-load electricity uses. Even as the cost of solar cells comes down, terrestrial solar power retains some inherent problems. The sun goes down at night, clouds occasionally block the sun, and the atmosphere filters out some of the energy. As a result, terrestrial solar systems must be greatly oversized and have additional energy storage systems if they are to provide continuous energy. However, these problems disappear when we go to space to collect solar power.

In fact, space-based Solar Power Satellites are the only solution that meets all our criteria. Solar Power Satellites will be giant satellites in geosynchronous orbit that will convert solar energy to electricity and then convert the electrical energy to radio frequency energy. This benign radio frequency energy will be beamed back to central receivers on Earth 24 hours a day. The ground-based receivers will convert it back to electricity for transmission to our homes and industries. This is possible because of the fact that at geosynchronous orbit the satellites will be in the sunlight for 99% of the year and they are always over one position of the earth. They will be similar to hydroelectric power plants in that there is no cost for the fuel. There is five times more sunlight per unit area at geosynchronous orbit as there is at the best location on the earth. The cost of power is the capital cost of building the satellites plus the cost of maintenance and operations. The satellites can be positioned at any location around the world so that clean non-polluting energy can be delivered to any nation on earth.

The reason that Solar Power Satellites have not been developed is because of the high development cost of the space infrastructure required and the cost of space transportation to launch both satellites and assembly equipment.

The development of the Space Elevator will change all of that. It would make the development of Solar Power Satellites well within the capability of private commercial companies. Paired with a low cost space transportation solution, Solar Power Satellites would be feasible and even quite profitable. However, in order to build Solar Power Satellites, we need a low cost space transportation system that is fully reusable. The development of fully reusable rocket system is very expensive and, without a very large market potential, is not economically practical. Today's launch costs are in the range of $3,000 to $10,000 per pound of payload. Some of these launches only go to low earth orbit. The cost of geosynchronous orbit transportation is on the high side as the energy required is much greater. In order to make Solar Power Satellites practical the cost of transportation to space must be reduced by two orders of magnitude. In addition, the total mass to be placed in orbit is very large. The launch of the satellite hardware would occur in two steps. First the satellite is launched to a low earth orbit base using a reusable rocket system and then it is transferred to geosynchronous orbit using a different system. The mass of a five thousand megawatt satellite studied for the Department of Energy and NASA in 1980 was 50,000 tons. The weight of the same sized satellite today would be much lower as a result of technology development that has occurred since then, but it will still be enormous. The number of such satellites required to meet future world needs is in the hundreds or more.

The potential of the Space Elevator completely changes the prospect of low cost access to space. It has the capability to transport satellites directly to geosynchronous orbit where they can be deployed. This eliminates the need for a low earth orbit transfer station. The only additional energy required for transportation is the small amount needed to move the hardware to the desired orbit location. The Space Elevator has the potential to reduce the cost of transportation to geosynchronous orbit by three orders of magnitude. With this reduction in transportation cost, the cost of building Solar Power Satellites will be reduced to a level that will make them the lowest cost source of electric energy available.

The market potential that would be created is enormous. The world market for electricity is over a trillion dollars a year today. Solar Power Satellites providing clean electricity from space will eventually replace our dependence of ground-based fossil fuels. For this to happen the market potential for the space elevator will grow in proportion. The lift capability will need to become very large. Optimum payload size will increase as the number of satellites grows.

Development of the Space Elevator makes the prospects for the earth's future much brighter as it could be the way to solving the world's evolving energy crisis by providing low cost access to space.

WILL A BRIDGE TO THE STARS SAVE THE STARFISH?
by
Derek Shannon

A doctoral student in astrobiology at the University of Southern California's Department of Earth Sciences, Derek hails from the Magic City of Minot, North Dakota. He earned his undergraduate degree in geobiology in 2002 from the California Institute of Technology. As a founding member of the Mars Society and a Mars scientist, he has participated in multiweek human Mars mission simulations, explored the Mars polar regions using Mars Global Surveyor, and studied the Allan Hills Martian meteorite for signs of past life. When not scanning for nitrogen biomarkers, he investigates alternative avenues for space elevator development, such as a family of SE-inspired transit concepts called Ribbon Rider that stemmed from his frustration with Los Angeles commuting! Derek is also the author of a Mars-themed children's book, *Qahirah's Kayak*.

ESCORTING STUDENTS ON a recent oceanography field trip, I was struck by the stark differences between the unsheltered tide pools and the aquarium exhibits we had viewed earlier that day. Hiking across the wave-battered basalt and inhaling an occasional whiff of the hydrogen sulfide still bubbling up naturally from below, we spotted pale white mats of sulfur-oxidizing microbes, a few feisty crabs, and even an anemone or two. But where were the giant predatory starfish? The tube snails and limpets? The whizbangs and frumpets?

You're right—Those last two are imaginary. But for all intents and purposes, so were the starfish and snails. Responsibility for the absent abalone lay with the visitors who had come before us. Life guards were quick to tell tales of pilfered periwinkles. With thousands of visitors each collecting just one or two souvenirs, combined with a few economically disadvantaged individuals harvesting by the bucketful, these Earth rocks looked in places as biologically barren as the asteroids.

So what might the solution be to this too-human thoughtlessness? What should we do to return the missing mussels to their cozy pools? We must build a space elevator, of course!

You're right again, if you realize I make the above statement in jest. The space elevator itself could end up a joke, if claims of environmental salvation become so outlandish as to defy the realities most people see every day. The space elevator will be an amazing tool, with the potential to create a new reality for humankind. But for now, we must make it happen with the realities at hand.

The Environment in Flux

Those realities can be stark, indeed. Stepping away from our tide pool microcosm, the general consensus amongst those without a financial interest in saying otherwise is that the Earth's environment is in serious trouble. A coalition of the world's eight largest environmental organizations recently offered a refresher course: Temperatures in sensitive Arctic regions rising at rates twice the global average. An expected ninety-five percent of the world's corals left as bleached as Death Valley skulls in just a few decades time. And even with Russia's ratification putting the Kyoto Protocol into effect, the treaty will wither on the wind without participation by the US or developing countries.

We may wither a bit, as well. World Wildlife Federation director-general Claude Martin warns of a tipping point at just two degrees Celsius above pre-industrial global temperatures: "*Everything* must be undertaken to ensure that we do not pass beyond the two degree threshold of global warming because the results will be absolutely devastating, not just for nature but the whole of humanity [emphasis added]."

If Martin is sincere, there may be hope for our hermit crabs yet, for surely "*Everything*" must include the space elevator.

The Space Elevator as a Renewable Energy Enabler

Could the elevator act as our radiator into space, shedding the Earth's increasingly excessive heat? Well, no. But by piercing the sky itself, the elevator could enable new energy sources that beat back the blanket of carbon dioxide threatening to suffocate our environment.

These energy sources include space solar power (SSP), an idea that's been kicking (and kicked) around for a while. If SSP is such a brilliant idea, why did Peter Glaser's 1971 patent on the concept expire without so much as a whimper?

The idea of what to do in space—make clean energy—was and is a winner. The ways of getting to space in the first place were not. The space elevator changes that, making the "space" part of space solar power incidental. Instead of an exotic, unreachable locale, space becomes just the best place to put solar panels. The relatively minor transportation costs of the space elevator would make the location decision between Earth and space as easy as the one today between Alberta and Albuquerque.

The elevator may offer SSP the economic leg up that out-competes Middle East oil, but the options don't end there. At least at this early conceptual stage, the space elevator is a dream-enabling machine. If you are a scientist who dreams of fusion research in the perfect vacuum of space, the space elevator will make it happen. If you want to scour the lunar regolith for Helium-3, so that your unlimited fusion energy can be virtually waste free, the space elevator will make it happen.

The space elevator could even put within reach the dream of a green and vibrant Earth, where gulls can snatch at pil bugs instead of discarded McNuggets.

But back to reality for a moment, where gulls will snatch McNuggets until the sun goes dim. Even infinite energy does our world no good if we don't have a way to use it. For a shift away from potentially dangerous overuse of fossil fuels, for humankind to step back from the rapidly approaching two degree threshold, the space elevator must be just a small part of entirely new energy distribution systems. Sure, space solar power might be pretty easy to dump into our existing and planned electric grids. But unless you're among the few to drive an electric car that fact doesn't help you get to work every morning.

The Space Elevator and the Hydrogen Economy

In this way the space elevator is not immune to the broader issues facing the so-called Hydrogen Economy. In this emerging energy paradigm, hydrogen and other clean energy sources replace not just our power plants, but the fossil fuel in our vehicles, as well. Any proponent of this new paradigm can tell you, this is where the march to clean energy becomes enmeshed in debate and development as intimidating as a tangle of carbon nanotubes.

The lesson is that the space elevator must work with the proponents of the Hydrogen Economy to build upon each others' strengths. This potential for synergy is especially apparent in the idea of platinum for Earth from space. As SkyCorp, Inc. CEO and *Moonrush* author Dennis Wingo argues, the Hydrogen Economy's demand for platinum as a fuel cell catalyst could quickly outstrip the Earth's supply. New mining on Earth might only be possible at an unacceptable environmental cost. Wingo's solution is to seek out chunks of metal-rich asteroids that have survived their impact on the Moon. A space elevator could be the only way to make such an endeavor economically feasible, especially if traveling all the way to Near Earth Objects and the Asteroid Belt becomes necessary.

Cooperation is the key: The Hydrogen Economy creates the demand for platinum. The space elevator fulfills that need. Or the space elevator supplies the platinum. The Hydrogen Economy then comes to fruition. It is a "chicken and egg" problem, with the primary observation being that both entities are essential.

Getting our Gulls in a Row

If the Earth is drowning in a sea of environmental change, and the space elevator is the lifeline to be thrown from shore, what will it take to get our gulls in a row with full-time environmental crusaders? Why didn't that recent press conference feature a ninth organization, a consortium for the development of the first space elevator?

The answer could be as simple as the space elevator's technology readiness level. With the production of the first SE-grade nanoribbon, environmental groups might take the initiative themselves. In the meantime, we must build bridges to these groups even as we build a bridge to space. This collaboration must be built upon trust and mutual support: Trust in the space elevator to not produce undesired environmental consequences of its own, and support from the space elevator community for near-term intermediate action on behalf of the planet.

Even with such a strategy, the space elevator has its work cut out: A cartoon in one Sierra Club newsletter openly mocked space solar power and other technological solutions for climate change. When asked about their opinion specifically concerning the space elevator, groups like Environmental Defense have declined to comment without much more information, or with the technology in so early a stage. Their failure to rush to judgment can hardly be criticized.

While assessing the views of the Natural Resources Defense Council, Dr. Joe Romm, former Clinton Administration Department of Energy official and author of *The Hype about Hydrogen*, weighed in with measured skepticism. Said Romm, "if someone can build a viable elevator, I'm sure people will make a lot of money and have a lot of applications, but I don't see it as a particularly environmental technology." Fusion, too, was kept at arm's length, given that "it's been fifty years away for the past fifty years."

Romm's concerns extended to small particles of nanomaterial getting into the air, echoing early reports of damage from buckeyballs—tiny soccer balls consisting of roughly 60 atoms of carbon—to fish nervous systems. This concern will have to be countered with health investigations into nanotube materials. Optimism is still in order, however, as nanotubes are much larger than buckeyballs, presumably too large to interact with organisms in a similarly deleterious fashion, and will additionally be bound and neutralized within a protective composite matrix.

Trading one Pandora's Box for Another?

Needless to say, even in international waters the space elevator will have a hefty environmental impact statement. The need to address such issues is illustrated by a recent furor stemming from an analysis of the Hydrogen Economy's effect on the Earth's upper atmosphere. The suggestion by Tracey Tromp and her colleagues at Caltech was that much higher amounts of molecular hydrogen would leak into the stratosphere due to the Hydrogen Economy. These molecules would interact negatively with the ozone layer, threatening the recovery of this UV-blocking shield. Only by addressing this issue head on—for instance through the early development of leakage minimization techniques—can the Hydrogen Economy continue to move forward.

In many ways, the space elevator is far less threatening to the environment. Fears of a ring of devastation around the equator must be addressed, but this can be accomplished simply enough through more complete communication of the most current space elevator concepts.

The space elevator's environmental impact closely resembles that of Boeing's SeaLaunch program, which was not required to file an Environmental Impact Statement because its operations would not "significantly affect the quality of the human environment."

SeaLaunch uses command ships and a converted oil rig platform to launch Zenit rockets from the equator. The space elevator will operate in much the same way, but it is important to add in a few SE-specific details: High-powered lasers consuming large amounts of power and firing off into the atmosphere. Cargo ships carving new sea lanes through previously deserted stretches of ocean. And a completely novel material, carbon nanotube composite ribbon, that will interact with ecosytems and geophysical processes that range in elevation from the ocean depths to the fringes of the magnetosphere. Yikes!

One way to make sure the space elevator meets environmental muster is to make not only its *results* environmentally friendly, but also its very *operation.* For instance, the roughly 20MW required for space elevator power beaming and other operations is baselined as coming from a standard diesel power plant. Consuming tanker-loads of diesel could make it a bit hard to sell the space elevator as the Earth's salvation from fossil fuels!

The Space Elevator and OTEC

Let's see what happens if we address the problem head on. The space elevator anchor platform will float in warm, equatorial surface waters. Yet a few hundred meters below, the ocean currents will run ice cold. While the swapping of anchor platforms over time might complicate this solution somewhat, the space elevator otherwise appears to be an ideal candidate for OTEC, or Ocean Thermal Energy Conversion. Long under development at Hawaii's National Renewable Energy Laboratory, powering the space elevator could be the "killer app" that unleashes OTEC on the broader energy market.

With this improvement, the space elevator has become not just a dream-enabler for space energy, but clean Earth-based energies, as well. The planktonic blooms that take place thanks to OTEC's upwelling of deepwater nutrients can even be used to sequester atmospheric carbon on the sea floor. The space elevator then becomes not just the way to prevent further increases in atmospheric carbon, but to reverse them. Environmental voices of concern could very well become a chorus of support, with one rather substantial caveat.

The Importance of Embracing Intermediate Solutions

This caveat is already causing trouble for the Hydrogen (H_2)Economy. Because the H_2 Economy is still at least as far away as the space elevator, environmentalists have perhaps rightfully attacked "H_2 Economy-only" proposals for ignoring near-term intermediate solutions that would provide much more benefit, sooner.

Support from the space elevator community for fuel economy, energy efficiency, and currently available terrestrial renewables—from the above mentioned OTEC to quickly improving wind power—will assuage fears that a space elevator is just another big business infrastructure project, looking to make a buck now while pushing the real costs onto future generations. By embracing a broader environmental ethic, the space elevator can instead be the means by which we repay future generations for the costs we have already incurred.

The Healing Tree

Pollution, privation, and the Pandora's box of global warming—A space elevator can address all these issues. But such a magnificent and impactful undertaking could do even more by fostering a long-term view towards the potential of humanity. It could be a view that makes a person think twice before snatching a seashell that serves as a hermit crab's home.

As a final illustration, there is an evolving tool for fighting pollution called phytoremediation. It suggests the use of plants—from sunflowers to sycamores—to clean toxins from the environment. Their roots can sop up oil spills. Their leaves can pluck the carbon monoxide from the air. It would be lovely to think of the space elevator as our planetary sapling. If we poison our planet too terribly, it will not grow at all. But if properly nourished, our sapling will grow into a mighty tree. Its branches will transport us to the stars. Its roots could sweep our planet clean.

It all comes down to whether we want to manage our environmental problems, or transcend them. The first space elevator won't stop the terrorizing of the tidepools. But the hundredth? Just might do the trick.

Excerpt from *FOUNDATION'S TRIUMPH*
by
David Brin

The Sinews of Trantor

TWENTY-THOUSAND YEARS after some long forgotten ancestor first set forth across the vacuum of space, humanity now lives upon twenty-five million worlds, spanning a Galactic Empire of several quadrillion souls. An Empire that, for all its flaws, has delivered peace and law for so long that few can imagine a time without it.

Few, that is, other than Hari Seldon, the legendary genius whose new science of psycho-history foretells the Empire's decline, followed by collapse into chaos.

That collapse will start gradually. But, ponderous, devastating, it will be unstoppable.

Helped by an ageless robot, Daneel Olivaw, Hari spent his long life developing a program to soften the blow and shorten the post-imperial dark age, before a new light can emerge. Along with a few mathematician colleagues and followers, he put in motion the Seldon Plan, creating twin "foundations" at opposite ends of the galaxy, laying seeds for new greatness.

Only there are other forces at work. The Old Empire is maintained by elites and servants and technologies that keep the vast civilization going. Some might lash out, still, against the fledgling Foundation. Others might decay too soon. The organs, muscles and ligaments of the parent must hold together for as long as possible, if the child is to survive.

One of those ligaments is the Orion Elevator.

Slender as thread are the cables that lead outward from the Capital Planet, stretching outward, creating a web between the worlds. As Hari travels along this marvel, he worries - will it endure long enough?

Can anything?

ACCORDING TO HIS plea-bargain agreement with the Commission for Public Safety, Hari Seldon wasn't supposed to leave Trantor. He also knew that the Fifty Psychohistorians would never permit a frail old man to go charging off to the stars. Even though he was no longer needed for the success of the Plan, none of them would permit a space journey that risked the life of the father of psychohistory.

Fortunately, Hari knew a loophole that just might let him get away. *You can go quite far without officially leaving Trantor,* he thought, while making the necessary arrangements.

There was very little to pack for the journey—just a few necessities which his ever-faithful aide, Kers Kantun, loaded in a suitcase, plus a few of Hari's most valued research archives, including a copy of the Foundation Plan *prime radiant.* None of it looked out of the ordinary, slung on the back of his mobile chair.

Hari's servant-guardian had argued against this trip, worrying aloud about the stress of travel. But in fact, it wasn't hard to get Kers to obey. Hari realized why.

Kers knows that boredom is the worst threat to my health, right now. With the Plan already launched, and younger, more agile minds in charge of any final alterations, I am simply unneeded. If I don't find something useful to do, I'll just fade away.

This little escapade probably won't amount to much. Space travel is still pretty routine. And meanwhile, I'll be too busy to let myself die.

So the two of them set out from his apartment the next morning, as if on a normal daily excursion. But instead of heading for the Imperial Gardens, Kers steered Hari onto a transitway bound for the Orion Elevator.

As their car sped along, and the surrounding metal tube seemed to flow past in a blur, Hari kept wondering if they would be stopped at some point along the way. It was a real possibility.

Had the Imperial Special Police really been withdrawn, as Gaal assured? Or were they watching him even now, with little spy cameras and other gadgets?

A year ago, right after his trial for sedition, official surveillance had been intense, sniffing each corner of Hari's life and eyeing his every move. But a lot had changed since then. Public Safety Commissioner Linge Chen was now convinced by the cooperation of Hari and the Fifty. There had been no more disruptive news leaks about an "imminent collapse of the Empire." More importantly, the move to Terminus was going according to plan. The hundred thousand experts that Hari had recruited with promises of employment on a vast Encyclopedia Galactica Project, were now being prepared and sent in groups to that far-off little world and a glorious destiny they could not possibly suspect.

Soon the capital planet would be rid of the irritation. So why would Chen keep paying professional officers to watch a dying crackpot professor, when their skills could better be employed dealing with other crises?

Soon a chime announced the car's arrival at the Grand Vestibule. Hari and Kers emerged into a mammoth chamber that stretched twenty kilometers across and tapered vertically toward domed heights that vanished in a misty haze.

Anchored to the ground in the very center was a huge black pillar, more than two hundred meters wide, that reared straight upward. The eye assumed that this mighty column held up the distant roof, but the eye was fooled. It wasn't a pillar, but a great cable, stretching outward through a hole in that remote ceiling, continuing past Trantor's atmosphere, linking a massive space station that whirled in orbit, fifty thousand kilometers above.

Along its great length, the Orion Elevator seemed infested with countless *bulges* that kept flowing up and down like parasites burrowing under the skin of a slender stalk. These were elevator cars, partly masked by a flexible skin that protected passengers against dangerous radiation, and against having to look upon vertiginous views.

At the very bottom of this monumental structure, people could be seen debarking from newly arrived capsules, passing through brief immigration formalities, then moving toward a maze of ramps and moving walkways. Other streams of individuals flowed in the opposite direction, aiming to depart. There were several lines for each social caste. Kers chose one of the shorter queues, clearly marked as reserved for meritocrat VIPs.

In theory, I could use the special portal for high nobility, Hari thought, glancing toward an aisle lined with silky fabrics, where fawning attendants saw to the needs of super-planetary gentry. *Any former First Minister of the Empire has that right. Even a disgraced one, like me. But that would surely attract too much attention.*

They paused at a little kiosk labelled EMIGRATION CONTROL and presented their identity cards. Kers had offered to acquire false papers through his contacts in the black market, but that act would transform this little adventure from a misdemeanor into a felony. Hari had no intention of risking harm to the Seldon Project, simply to satisfy his curiosity. If this worked, fine. Otherwise, he might as well go home and let things settle into graceful, boring decline.

The screen seemed to glare at Hari with its enquiry.

DESTINATION?

This was a crucial moment. Everything depended on a matter of legal definition.

"Demarchia," he said aloud. "I want to observe the Imperial Legislature in session for a week or two. Ultimately I plan to return from there to my residence at Streeling University."

He wasn't lying. But a lot could lay in that word —"ultimately."

The unit seemed to ponder his statement for a moment, while Hari mulled silently.

Demarchia is one of twenty nearby worlds that are officially part of Trantor. There were strong political and traditional reasons for this arrangement, one that's been reinforced by generations of emperors and ministers…. But maybe the police don't look at things the same way.

If Hari were wrong, the computer would refuse to issue a ticket. News of this "escape attempt" would flash at the Commission of Public Safety. And Hari would have no choice but to go home and wait for Linge Chen's agents to come and question him. Worse, Stettin Palver and the other psychohistorians would cluck and fuss, wagging their fingers and tightening their reverent guardianship. Hari would never have another unsupervised moment.

Come on, he urged, wishing he had some of the mental powers that enabled Daneel Olivaw to meddle in the thoughts of both men and machines.

Abruptly, the screen came alight again.

HAPPY VOYAGE. LONG LIVE THE EMPEROR.

Hari nodded.

"Long life," he answered perfunctorily, having to swallow a knot of released tension. The machine extruded a pair of tickets, assigning them to a specific elevator car, appropriate to their social class and destination. Hari looked at one of the billets as Kers picked them up.

Intra-Trantor Commute, it said.

He nodded with satisfaction. *I'm not breaking the letter of my agreement with the Commission. Not yet at least.*

A crowd of uniformed figures milled nearby, wearing polished buttons and white gloves—young porters assigned to assist non-gentry VIP passengers. Several of them glanced up, but they turned back to their gossip and dice games when Kers and Hari refrained from making any beckoning motions. Kers needed no assistance with their meager luggage.

Moments later however, a small figure suddenly spilled out of the crowd of purple uniforms, striding at a rapid pace to intercept them. The girl—wiry and no more than fifteen years old—snapped a jaunty salute at the rim of her pillbox cap. Her Corrin Sector accent was unabashed and friendly to the point of over-familiarity.

"Greets, m'lords! I'll be takin' your bags an' seeing you safely along if it pleases ya."

Her nametag said *JENI.*

Kers made a dismissing gesture, but in a blur she snatched the tickets from his hand. Grinning, the porter nodded with a vigorous swirl of unruly platinum hair.

"Right this way to your chariot, m'lords!"

When Kers refused to hand over any of the luggage, she only grinned. "No need to be afeared. I'll see you safely all the way to Orion Station. Just follow me."

Kers rumbled as the girl sped ahead with their tickets, but Hari smiled and patted his servant's burly hand. In a world of dull jobs and soul-grinding routine, it was pleasant to see someone having a little fun, even at the expense of her betters.

They found the third member of their party at the agreed spot, next to an elevator car with DEMARCHIA flashing on its placard. Horis Antic looked infinitely relieved to see them. The gray bureaucrat barely glanced at the porter, but he bowed to Hari more deeply than protocol required, then motioned toward the gaping door of a waiting elevator car.

"This way, Professor. I saved us good seats." Antic's hand showed some nervous tremors, as when he first told Hari about the mystery he had found out there, tucked between the stars.

Hari took a deep breath as they went aboard and the opening slithered shut behind them.

Here we go. Already he could feel his heart begin to rise.

One last adventure.

UNFORTUNATELY THERE WERE no windows. Passengers could watch the view outside through seat monitors, but few bothered. Hari's car was half empty, since the space elevators were being used much less nowadays.

I'm partly responsible for that, he recalled. Most traffic to and from Trantor now arrived by hyperspatial Jump Ships, which floated to the ground on their own self-generated gravity fields. A growing swarm of them shuttled up and down with food and other necessities needed by the Empire's administrative center. Twenty agricultural worlds had been dedicated to supplying this lifeline—up from a mere eight before Hari became First Minister.

Trantor used to create its own basic food supply in huge solar-powered vats, operated by swarms of busy automatons who didn't mind the stench and grinding labor. When that system collapsed during the infamous "Tik-Tok Revolt," one of his first duties in office had been to make up the difference by multiplying the flow of imported food and other goods.

But the new system is expensive and inefficient. And that lifeline will become a deadly trap in coming centuries. He knew this from the equations of psychohistory. *Emperors and oligarchs will pay ever-greater attention to preserving it, at the expense of important business elsewhere.*

To enhance their loyalty, the agricultural worlds had been joined even closer to Trantor itself, sharing the same "planetary" government, an act that now helped to justify Hari's ruse.

Though he did not turn on the outside viewer, it was easy to visualize the planet's gleaming anodized metal coat, reflecting the densely packed starfield of the galaxy's crowded center—millions of dazzling suns that glittered like fiery gems, making night almost like day. Though many in the Empire envisioned Trantor as one giant city, much of the stainless steel surface was only a veneer, just a few stories thick, laid down for show after mountains and valleys had been leveled. Those flat warrens were mostly used for storing old records. Actual office towers, factories and habitations occupied no more than ten percent of the planet's area—easily enough room for forty billion people to live and work efficiently.

Still, the popular image was accurate enough. This center of empire was like the galactic core itself—a crowded place. Even knowing the psychohistorical reasons for it all left Hari bemused by it all.

"Right now we're passin' halfway point," the young porter explained, playing up her role as tour guide. "Those of you who forgot to take your pills might be experiencin' some upset as we head toward null-gee," she went on, "but in most cases that's just your imagination actin' up. Try to think of something nice and it often goes away."

Horis Antic wasn't much cheered. Though he surely traveled extensively in his line of work, he may never have used this peculiar type of transport. The bureaucrat hurriedly popped several tablets from his belt dispensor and swallowed them.

"Of course most people nowadays come to Trantor by starship," the girl went on. "So my advice is to just keep tellin' yourself that this here cable is over five thousand years old, made in the glory days of great engineers. So in a sense, you're just as well anchored as if you were still connected to the ground!"

Hari had seen other porters do this sort of thing, extroverts going beyond the call of duty while trying to make light of a prosaic job. Few ever had an audience as difficult as dour Kers Kantun and nervous Horis Antic, who kept chewing his nails, clearly wishing the girl would go away. But she went on chattering happily.

"Sometimes visitors ask what'd happen if this cable we're ridin' ever broke! Well let me assure you it ain't possible. At least that's what those super-competent ancients who made this stringy thing promised. Though I'm sure you all know how things are goin' these days. So you're welcome to imagine along with me what might happen if someday...."

She went on to describe, with evident relish, how all of Trantor's space elevators —Orion, Lesmic, Gengi, Pliny and Zul—might break apart in some hypothetical future calamity. The upper half of each great tether, including the transfer stations, would spin away into space, lofted by centrifugal force, while the lower half, weighing billions of tons, would plummet into the ground at incredible speeds, releasing enough explosive force to pierce the metal veneer all the way to Trantor's geothermal power pipes, unleashing a globe-girdling chain of new volcanoes.

Exactly according to the doomsday scenario, calculated by our Prime Radiant, Hari marveled. Of course some stories from the Seldon Group had seeped out to the culture at large. Still, it was the first time he ever heard this particular phase of the Fall of Trantor described so vividly, or with such evident enjoyment!

In fact, the space elevators were very sturdy things, built at the height of the Empire's vigor, with hundreds of times the minimal safety strength. According to Hari's calculations, they would probably survive until the capital was sacked for the first time, almost three hundred years from now.

On that day, however, it would be unwise to live anywhere near the planet's equator. The descendants of Stettin and Wanda would be ready, of course. Their headquarters of the Second Foundation would be shifted well before that time—all according to plan.

Hari's mind roamed the future much as a historian might ponder the past. One of the recordings he had just made for the Time Vault on Terminus dealt with that era-to-come, when destruction would rain on this magnificent world. At that point the Foundation would be entering its great age of self-confident expansion. Having survived several dangerous encounters with the tottering Empire, the vigorous foundationers would then stare in awe at the old realm's sudden and final collapse.

His Time Vault message had been carefully written to fine-tune attitudes among the leaders on Terminus at that point, giving a little added political weight to factions favoring a go-slow approach to further conquest. Too much assurance could be as bad as too little. It would be vital for the secret Second Foundation, made up of mentalically talented descendants of the Fifty, to begin taking a more active role at that point, molding the vigorous culture based on Terminus. Secretly guiding toward becoming the nucleus of a new empire. One far greater than the first.

The Plan beckoned Hari with its sweet complexity. But once again, his inner voice of doubt intruded.

You can feel certain of the first hundred years. The momentum of events is just too great to divert from the path we foresee. And the following century or two should proceed according to calculations, unless unexpected perturbations appear. It will be the Second Foundation's job to correct those.

But after that?

Something in the math makes me uneasy. Hints at unsolved attractor states and hidden solutions that lurk below all the smug, predictable models we've worked out.

I wish I had a better idea what they are. Those unsolved states.

That was just one reason for Hari's decision to join this expedition. There were others.

HORIS ANTIC SAT close to Hari. "I have made arrangements, Professor. We'll meet the captain of our charter ship the day after we land on Demarchia."

By now the young porter had finished her deliberately vivid catastrophe tale and fallen silent at last. She wore headphones, apparently listening to music as she watched their approach to Orion Station on a nearby seat monitor. Hari felt safe talking to Antic.

"This captain of yours is reliable? It may not be wise to trust a mercenary. Especially when we can't afford to pay very much."

"I agree," Antic said with a vigorous nod. "But this fellow comes highly recommended. And we won't have to pay anything."

Hari started to ask how that could be. But Antic shook his head. Some explanations would have to wait.

"Coming up to transfer!" The porter announced, extra loud because of her headphones. "Everybody strap in. This can get bumpy!"

Hari let his servant fuss over him, clamping down the mobile chair and adjusting his restraint webbing. Then he shooed Kers away to take care of himself. It had been many years since he travelled down a star-shunt, but he was no novice.

He ordered a holoview showing Orion station just ahead, a giant medusa's head of tubes and spires that sat in the middle of a straight, shimmering line—the space elevator cable. Only a few starships were seen at the docking ports, since most modern hypercraft could land and take-off using graceful antigravity fields. But Hari foresaw a time when declining competence would lead to a series of terrible accidental crashes below. Then vessels coming to Trantor would be forced to offload their cargoes up here, and these great tethers would have supreme importance once more… till they finally were brought down fifty years later.

For the present, ship traffic was taking over the great bulk of travel and commerce in the galaxy. But a few routes were still covered by another entirely separate transportation system. One that was much faster and more convenient.

Star-shunts.

In Hari's youth, there had been hundreds of wormhole links— penetrating the fabric of space-time from one far-flung part of the galaxy to another. Now only a dozen or so remained. Most of those connected to a single spot close to the orbit of Trantor. According to his equations, these would be abandoned too, in just a few decades.

"Get ready!" the young porter cried.

Orion Station seemed to rush toward the viewing screen. At the last instant, a huge manipulator arm rushed out of nowhere to seize their transport car with a sudden shudder. Amid a whirling sensation, the compact vehicle was plucked off the tether and slipped into a long, slender gun barrel aimed at distant space.

The outside view was swallowed in blackness.

Horis Antic let out a low moan. *Some things you just never get used to,* Hari thought, trying to keep his thoughts abstract, waiting for the pulse gun to fire.

Hyperspatial starships were big, bulky, and relatively slow. But the basic technology was so reliable and easy to maintain that some fallen cultures had been known to keep their fleets going even after they lost the ability to generate proton-fusion power. In contrast, star-shunts relied on deep understanding of physics and tremendous engineering competence. When the Empire no longer produced enough proficient workers, the network entered steep decline.

Some blamed "decadence" or failing education systems. Others said it was due to the damage caused by *chaos worlds*, whose seductive cultural attraction often drew creative people from all across the Galaxy. They featured extravagant bursts of creativity—until each outbreak collapsed in a violent cultural implosion.

Hari's equations told the complex reasons for a fall that began centuries ago. A collapse Daneel Olivaw had been fighting against since long before Hari's birth.

I'd hate to be riding one of these shunts thirty years from now, when the declining competence curve finally crosses a threshold of—

His thought was cut off as the gun fired, sending their car hurtling through a hyperspacial microshunt to a spot fifty light minutes away from Trantor, where the *real* wormhole waited. Entry wasn't especially smooth, and wrenching sensations made Hari's gut churn. He sighed under his breath. *"Dors!"*

There followed a series of rocking motions while they hurtled down the well-traveled maw of a giant cavity in space-time. The seat monitors roiled with mad colors as holovideo computers failed to make sense of the maelstrom outside. This mode of transport had disadvantages, all right. And yet, Hari reminded himself of one basic fact about shunting—the single trait that still made it highly attractive compared to travelling by ship. Almost as soon as any shunt journey had begun...

... it was over.

Abruptly, the viewscreens transformed once again, showing a familiar dusty spray of stars in the galactic center. Hari felt several bumps as the car was relayed by micro-shunt a couple of times.

Then, as if by magic, a planet swam into view.

A planet of continents and seas and mountain ranges, where cities glittered as part of the landscape, instead of utterly dominating it. A beautiful world that Hari used to visit all the time when he was First Minister, accompanied by his gracious and beautiful wife, back in the days when he and Daneel thought that astute use of psychohistory might actually save the Empire, instead of planning for its eventual demise.

"Welcome to the second imperial capital, m'lords," said the young porter.

"Welcome to Demarchia."

THE SPACE ELEVATOR:
A Bridge to our Dreams?
by
Dr. Stewart Tansley

Stewart Tansley, Ph.D., is a Program Manager in the University Relations Group at Microsoft Research, Redmond WA, USA, responsible for Embedded Systems. Before this, he was responsible for Microsoft's production IPv6 software as part of the Windows Networking team. Prior to joining Microsoft in 2001, Stewart spent 13 years in the telecommunications industry in various technical and management positions in network software research and development, focusing on technology transfer. Stewart has a Ph.D. in Artificial Intelligence applied to Engineering from the University of Technology, Loughborough, UK. He has published a variety of papers in artificial intelligence and network management, several patents, and co-authored a book on software engineering for artificial intelligence applications.

WHEN I WAS a boy, like so many others of my generation I remember being hustled in front of the TV to watch some incomprehensible grainy monochrome image about something that my parents assured me was stunningly important. And they were right. At the ripe old age of 6-and-a-quarter, I'd seen Armstrong walk on the moon.

As I got a little older, my best friend at the time had a supremely impressive (to an 8-year-old) 4" reflector telescope. I yearned to have one of my own. (Parents everywhere will quiver like mine must have done.) Fortunately, I'd apparently been a good boy that year and Father Christmas was generous. Today, over 30 years later, perhaps I must still be behaving ok - because my wife tolerates two (much larger) telescopes in our kitchen!

When I first came across the Space Elevator, I was ambivalent. We're asked to believe that pure science fiction can become fact in our own lifetimes. The technical challenges seem enormous. The concept is so wild, it's unintuitive that it could work. Yet I also recall my ancient copy of Gerard O'Neill's "The High Frontier" with its dreamy picture of a Stanford Torus on its cover. This fantasy could finally be within reach, given such an elevator...

And so flooded back all the other fantasies I'd read as a boy and teenager. The solar sails, the asteroid miners, the moonbases, the colonies—all could be realized through the extraordinary breakthrough of a cheap and efficient way to escape the maternal clutches of our Earth's gravity.

When I was invited to write some thoughts on what could be achieved with the Space Elevator, I know they were looking to my technical expertise to bring some novel angle in addition to those of the other contributors. The problem is, the Space Elevator is of such drama to me, such personal import, rooted in the formative years of my childhood, that it's hard not to succumb to the sheer romance of the venture, simply spewing every last sci-fi cliché that we—any of us that have lived on a geek diet of Star Trek, Star Wars and Babylon 5, these past few decades—have been soaked in.

So what novelty, if anything, can I bring to this? Well, as a software engineer with roots in Artificial Intelligence, and a career mostly spent in networking, perhaps I do have something to say from those angles at least. And with current interests in robotics and embedded systems, I know that these will form both key components of the Elevator itself, and all its myriad spin-off applications and entire new industries that its success would spawn. Let's start with robotics.

The elevator itself will be a robot. But I'm sure this will be described elsewhere. There will be many other robots involved though - maintenance bots, service bots, repair bots. All of these will be necessary and useful in keeping the device running smoothly and efficiently, and mitigating the multiple failure modes that will inevitably occur whether through act of God, human error or simple wear and tear. These robots will find roles all over the elevator system, not just the vehicles that climb up and down the ribbon, but also at the terminals at each end and in all the support systems in the entire infrastructure

Beyond the elevator system, such robots will also find diverse applications in space. Because the essential value of the Elevator is to carry mass that would otherwise be cost-ineffective to transport out of the atmosphere, robots can be carried like any other cargo. In fact, they may even be the main cargo that's carried—beyond basic materials. They could outnumber people.

These robots will find roles on the new platforms that the Elevator will realize. Platforms like greater numbers and diversities of satellites, space stations (yes, stations), and other space craft. Robot individuals, robot teams and robot swarms, all working in a space-borne virtual society of machines. They will be transported beyond Earth's orbit to the bases on the moon and asteroids, where they will do work which simply doesn't need to be done by expensive-to-maintain and expensive-to-insure human beings. The Space Elevator may actually spawn the age of robotics - one science fiction enabling other science fictions to become fact.

What will all this space hardware be doing? Some of the things have been tantalizingly within our reach in recent years, but the Space Elevator removes all doubt that they will be achieved. Take for instance, the provision of pervasive low-latency broadband connectivity across the earth—a concept that companies such as Teledesic have strived to achieve at the end of the 20th century, but which have been hamstrung by today's extremely high satellite launch costs. With the Space Elevator, such grand visions as a multi-megabit connection for every square metre on the planet become an inevitability rather than a daring venture for high-risk entrepreneurs. The 21st century could finally see such visions achieved—and thereby, all the second-order visions and dreams of those that just need that not-so-small boost of the Elevator.

Beyond commerce and utility, the Space Elevator's boost to enable high orbit hardware means that space science will be dramatically multiplied. Cheaper launch costs mean that more missions will be possible, with more diverse capabilities. Telescopes can be flown in groups to multiply their resolutions, and large numbers of space probes can be sent on much more specialized, targeted missions to the stranger corners of our Solar System. I see a new wave of scientific discovery in our space neighborhood, probably heralding entire new sciences on a per-world basis as these swarms of probes act as our proxy eyes, ears, noses, and fingers as they tease out the secrets of each and every planet, moon, comet and space rock.

There will be people carried too. All these machines cannot be allowed to have all the fun! But apart from Mars, I don't see great space voyages to every planet like I remember reading in my boyhood Hugh Walters sci-fi novels. Unless some other fundamental breakthroughs occur in such areas as propulsion (which may just happen of course, given the extraordinary possibilities of the new frontiers that the Space Elevator will open up), it just doesn't seem worthwhile to send flesh and blood out so far, to me, given the electromechanical supersense capabilities I see of future robotics. I see tourists in Earth orbit, certainly, and I do think that bases on the moon will become important colonies, fundamentally realized by the lifting shoulders of the Space Elevator.

Time will tell whether such colonies will always remain alien and remote, like say Antarctic scientific bases here on Earth, or will instead be the first steps of a new manifest destiny to the stars. I hope I will be around at least to see these first steps, and will enjoy pondering further on just how far we may go. So I wish the Space Elevator team well in achieving their goal for the commercial, cultural and spiritual benefit of our entire species.

VERTICAL JOURNEY
by
Kevin J. Anderson

TWICE DURING MY college years I packed up the old car and took a drive from my home in Wisconsin all the way across the country. Partly because I was just a student and couldn't afford a plane ticket, partly because I wanted to see the US, I opted for the much slower road trip. It seemed to me that was the only proper way to get a first-hand grasp of the real size of the country.

We've all seen the skewed-perspective maps showing the East and West coasts with towering cities, New York, Boston, Los Angeles, San Francisco, and then a distorted blankness across the middle of America, maybe with a few cornfields drawn in, maybe with a line of Rocky Mountains. (One almost expects to see a scrawled "Terra Incognita" or "Here Be Monsters".) Try driving across the vastness and you'll get a whole new perspective of just how much space lies between Here and There.

The space elevator will do the same thing, giving passengers the same sort of perspective—only vertically.

The cruising altitude of a passenger jet is about 30,000 feet. The space elevator tops out at 100,000 km—more than three thousand times as high. The journey from ground to geosynchronous orbit will take about seven days—plenty of time for everyone aboard to take in the view and draw comparisons.

To a person standing on the ground, the sky seems infinite. Astronauts up in space have remarked on how thin the protective skin of atmosphere appears. But when making an ascent on the space elevator, travelers will pass *through* the full thickness of the atmosphere.

Looking out the windows of the observation lounge, sipping a glass of wine (or at least eating a bag of peanuts for those in coach class), passengers will see the troposphere, the lowest layer containing 75% of the atmospheric mass (and also the zone with most of the turbulence and weather systems). The temperature outside the elevator car drops to about -60°C and then, at twelve kilometers, the temperature gradient reverses for the next 38 kilometers, climbing all the way back up to -10°C through the height of the stratosphere.

That's been your first hour or two en route. Leaving the strato-sphere at fifty kilometers, the elevator carries its cargo through the mesosphere. Outside the temperature plummets again to a hundred degrees below zero (C), but by now the pressure is around a mil-lionth of an atmosphere, so the cold would be the least of your worries. The next part of the journey takes you through the ther-mosphere until you reach the edge of space at 100 kilometers—and you're as high above the surface as the bottom of the Marianas Trench is below it. Almost twelve times the height of Mount Everest.

But even at the edge of space, you can't yet see South America, the nearest continent. It's up another 100 kilometers until you can see the edge of Ecuador. Over the next six days, you will be able to see more and more of the Earth's surface, as the planet that once reached as far as you could see slowly dwindles until it looks roughly the size of an apple held at arm's length. Depending on the elevator design itself, you may even have visited waystations along the way. Rest stops, photo opportunities, gift shops. "I went to 1,000,000 meters, and all I got was this T-shirt!"

The practical and technical benefits of the space elevator are well delineated elsewhere in this book. However, such a mode of transportation offers other advantages, especially in terms of hu-man perspective. Imagine looking down at the growing ozone hole from above. See the gray-brown murk of smog and industrial smoke like a great haze over Mexico City, New Delhi, Tokyo. Look at the bare mountainsides where glaciers used to be, rising water levels, the receding Antarctic coastline; still think global warming "needs more study"? See the blaze of cities on the nightside, or the black smudges across the rainforest.

There's more to this seven-day vertical journey than simply arriving at the top. Most important of all, just look across the continents, the great landmasses entirely unmarked by political boundaries, no maps tattooed across the landscape. Just Earth.

Take enough time for a second look.

ABBREVIATIONS

CNT	Carbon Nanotube
DARPA	Defense Advanced Research Projects Agency
DHS	Dept. of Homeland Security
DoE	Dept. of Energy
DoI	Dept. of the Interior
EELV	Evolved Expendable Launch Vehicle (e.g., Atlas V or Delta-IV rockets)
ESAS	Exploration Systems Architecture Study
FEL	Free Electron Laser
GEO	GeoSynchronous Orbit (~35,800km above sea level)
Isp	Specific impulse
LEO	Low Earth Orbit (~185km to 400km)
LH2	Liquid Hydrogen
LO2 or LOX	Liquid Oxygen
MMH	Mono Methyl Hydrazine
MOS	Merit of Safety
MPD	Magnetoplasmadynamic
MWNT	Multi-wall Carbon Nanotube
NASA	National Aeronautics and Space Administration
NIAC	NASA Institude for Advanced Concepts
NOAA	National Oceanic and Atmospheric Administration
NTO	Nitrogen Tetroxide
OTV	Orbit Transfer Vehicle
PV	Photovoltaic
RTG	Radioisotope Thermoelectric Generator
SDV or SDLV	Shuttle Derived (Launch) Vehicle
SE	Space Elevator
SRB	Solid Rocket Booster
SWATH	Small Waterplane Area Twin Hull
SWNT	Single Wall Carbon Nanotube

Further Information and How to Get Involved
LiftPort staff

LiftPort Group Website —www.liftport.com

Galleries—www.liftport.com/gallery - includes both concept art and photographs of our research, experiments and public appearances.

Forums—www.liftport.com/forums - sound off here about the Space Elevator! Join hundreds of other Space Elevator enthusiasts by asking questions, proposing solutions and chatting about the future of humankind.

Research section—www.liftport.com/research.php - includes an FAQ, a research list and initial research papers. If you are a researcher hoping to contribute to the Space Elevator project, start here!

Progress Reports—www.liftport.com/progress/wp - includes almost-daily progress reports in a "blog" style from various staff members. This will let you get a feel for what happens here at LiftPort on a day-to-day basis.

There is also a press release section, a help wanted section and an investor relations section. The website is constantly being updated and tweaked, be sure to visit often.

LiftPort Group Newsletters
LiftPort Group has a general interest mailing list to which three newsletters are sent once every month. By signing up for the mailing list, you can receive up-to-date information about the Space Elevator. Please sign up at http://www.liftport.com/lists.php. Our newsletters are provided completely free of charge, just tell your friends! The three newsletters are:

General Newsletter —basic updates on all LiftPort-related research, finance, media and staff activities.

The Art of the Space Elevator —monthly releases of Space Elevator art from our in-house artist. Be the first to see what the future will look like!

Comic Book Theatre by Last Kiss Entertainment —LiftPort has partnered with Last Kiss Entertainment to provide a monthly newsletter that will chronicle the 'lighter side' of the goings-on at LiftPort Group.

Shareholders of LiftPort Group can also receive the Investor Newsletter, which provides financial news about LiftPort. This newsletter is only available to current investors and staff.

LiftPort Group Recommended Websites and Newsgroups

The Spaceward Foundation —www.elevator2010.org - a non-profit organization (managed by Ben Shelef and Meekk Shelef) working with NASA to promote the development of Space Elevator technology via contest (similar to the X-Prize). Please read Ben's chapter about Lifters in this book.

Space.com —www.space.com - provides comprehensive news coverage of not only the Space Elevator, but all space-related activities.

Liftwatch —liftwatch.org —provides periodic news updates on the Space Elevator project.

Dangling Participle —www.healthspace.ca/spacebridge - Andrew Price has several interesting articles and editorials regarding the Space Elevator, or "Space Bridge." A must-visit for every burgeoning SE enthusiast.

Blaise Gassend —http://www.mit.edu/people/gassend/spaceelevator/index.html - Blaise is a "leading thinker" in the Space Elevator movement. Be sure to read his chapter in this book and then visit his website.

Space Elevator Wikipedia entry - http://en.wikipedia.org/wiki/Space_elevator —Provides basic information about the concept.

SpaceElevator.com —a resource for watching the developments of the project.

We hope, now that you've read our book, that you have had some of your questions answered. However, if you are like the rest of us that are working on the project, what has probably happened is that you now have more questions than you did when you started. That's all right. Considering the size and scope of this project, we are going to keep coming up with questions and having to research the answers. We appreciate your interest and enthusiasm for the idea and we would like to have your help. Feel free to email us, if there is something you'd like to help with, we have a growing volunteer corp. info@liftport.com

(FOOTNOTES)

[1] "NASA: Summary of FY 2005 Budget Request" by NASA: http://www.nasa.gov/pdf/55524main_FY05%20Agency%20Summary-2.31.pdf

[2] "Laboratory Grows World Record Length Carbon Nanotube" by Todd Hanson: http://www.lanl.gov/worldview/news/releases/archive/04-076.shtml

[3] A note on terminology: I use the word "rocket" to refer both to traditional chemical rockets and to the newer, more advanced electrical propulsion systems which are beginning to be used in space (electric propulsion isn't useful for ground to orbit transportation).

[4] Futron Corporation, "Space Tourism Market Study: orbital space travel & destinations with suborbital space travel", October 2002

[5] **[LiftPort desires to keep its strategies with regard to the resolution of the complex legal issues affecting its enterprise close to the vest in order to maintain a competitive advantage over potential competitors to build the first space elevator.]**

[6] The LiftPort Space Elevator System will be comprised by: (1) the LiftPort base site in "international waters" in the Pacific Ocean; (2) LiftPort base station (or stations) located in the "outer space" environment; (3) the Lifters that will transport payloads and people between the LiftPorts; and (4) the Ribbon that the Lifter will travel on between the sea-based LiftPort and the "outer space" Liftport(s). In addition, the authors note that the jurisdictional tenets applicable to the LiftPort Space Elevator System will also apply to the payloads and people that are transported by means of the LiftPort Space Elevator System.

[7] The "International Law of the Seas" is the short-hand term that the authors use to refer to the legal regime that governs the use of the open seas, specifically the United Nations Convention on the Law of the Sea ("UNCLOS") and the Conventions and other instruments of the International Maritime Organization ("IMO"), the specialized agency of the UN responsible for global maritime safety and environmental management of shipping activities.

[8] "International Airspace Law" is the short-hand term that the authors use to refer to the vast body of international customary and treaty law that has been developed over the years to regulate the use of "international

airspace", which is generally defined as "airspace that is above territory that is not subject to the sovereign control of a nation-state".

For the purposes of this book, the authors have not investigated the method in which International Airspace Law will need to be amended in order to afford sufficient protections to Liftport's operation of the LiftPort Space Elevator System. Since the Space Elevator will operate in a fashion entirely distinct from the civil aircraft that International Airspace Law has been designed for, there will be a need to convince the appropriate international legal authorities to create exemptions to the relevant international airspace rules in order to prevent interference events by the LiftPort Space Elevator System on aircraft operating in nearby international airspace as well as by aircraft to LiftPort's Space Elevator System.

[9] "International Space Law" is the short-hand term that the authors use to refer to the body of international treaty and customary law that has been developed to regulate the activities of government and non-government actors in "outer space". None of the numerous international space law treaties provides a definition for what constitutes "outer space"; however, the authors believe that customary international law has been developed by the actions of the space-faring nations such that the term "outer space" refers to any location outside the Earth's atmosphere or the area starting at approximately 200 miles (or 340 kilometers) from the earth's surface and moving away from the earth's surface.

[10] See, 49 U.S.C. § 70104 (a)(3).

[11] See, 49 U.S.C. § 70102 (1)(c)

[12] See, 49 U.S.C. § 70102 (3).

[13] See, 49 U.S.C. § 70102 (7).

[14] See, 49 U.S.C. § 70102 (14).

[15] See, 49 U.S.C. § 70102 (9).

[16] See in general, 49 U.S.C., Chapter 701; see also in general, the FAA's Commercial Space Transportation Regulations, at 14 C.F.R. §§ 400 - 450.

[17] See the FAA's Commercial Space Transportation Regulations, at 14 C.F.R. Part 413 for general rules applicable to all license applications.

[18] See the FAA's Commercial Space Transportation Regulations, at 14 C.F.R. Part 415 for the specific rules affecting launch-specific licenses.

[19] See the FAA's Commercial Space Transportation Regulations, at 14 C.F.R. Part 420 for the specific rules affecting launch site operator licenses.

[20] See the FAA's Commercial Space Transportation Regulations, at 14 C.F.R. Part 431 for the specific rules affecting the application for and issuance of launch-specific RLV licenses and RLV site operator licenses, which LiftPort Space Elevator System will need to obtain in advance of commencing "launching" and "reentry" operations.

[21] See, id; see also 14 C.F.R. Part 433.

[22] See, 14 C.F.R. Part 415.

[23] See, 14 C.F.R. Part 420.

[24] See, 14 C.F.R. Section 431.35.

[25] See, 14 C.F.R. Part 450.

[26] See, 14 C.F.R. Section 401.5

[27] It is understood, however, that the LiftPort Space Elevator System will employ a number of interchangeable and functionally equivalent platform/ anchor vessels in its day-to-day operations, where the platform/ anchor vessels will be rotated from time-to-time.

[28] Treaty on Principles Governing the Activities of States in the Exploration and Use of Outer Space, including the Moon and Other Celestial Bodies, as adopted in U.N. General Assembly Resolution 2222 (XXI), opened for signature January 27, 1967, 18 U.S.T. 2410, T.I.A.S. No. 6347, 610 U.N.T.S. 205; reprinted at http://www.oosa.unvienna.org/treat/ost/osttxt/html [hereinafter the "Outer Space Treaty"]. See, "STATUS OF UNITED NATIONS TREATIES RELATING TO ACTIVITIES IN OUTER SPACE" at http://www.oosa.unvienna.org/treat/status.html for the detailed list of which space-related legal documents that various countries have signed and/or ratified.

[29] Agreement on the Rescue of Astronauts, the Return of Astronauts and the Return of Objects Launched into Outer Space, as adopted in U.N. General Assembly Resolution 2345 (XXII), opened for signature April 22, 1968, 19 U.S>T. 7570, T.I.A.S. 6599, 672 U.N.T.S.

119; reprinted at http://www.oosa.unvienna.org/treat/res/
restxt.html [hereinafter the "Rescue & Return Agreement"]. See,
http://www.oosa.unvienna.org/treat/status.html for a detailed list
of which space-related legal documents that various countries have
signed and/or ratified.

[30] Convention on International Liability for Damage Caused by Space
Objects, as adopted in U.N. General Assembly Resolution 2777
(XVI), opened for signature March 29, 1972 , 24 U.S.T. 2389, T.I.A.S.
7762, 961 U.N.T.S. 187; reprinted at http://www.oosa.unvienna.org/
treat/lia/liatxt.html [hereinafter the "Liability Convention"]. See,
http://www.oosa.unvienna.org/treat/status.html for a detailed list
of which space-related legal documents that various countries have
signed and/or ratified.

[31] Convention on the Registration of Objects Launched into Outer
Space, as adopted in U.N. General Assembly Resolution 3235 (XXIX),
opened for signature January 14, 1975, 28 U.S>T. 695, T.I.A.S. 8480,
1023 U.N.T.S. 15; reprinted at http://www.oosa.unvienna.org/treat/
reg/regtxt.html [hereinafter the "Registration Convention"]. See,
http://www.oosa.unvienna.org/treat/status.html for a detailed list
of which space-related legal documents that various countries have
signed and/or ratified.

CONTEST RULES

1. Eligibility: This Promotion is open to legal residents of the United States, including its territories and possessions, who are at least 18 years of age at the time of entry. No purchase is necessary to enter or to win. Employees of LiftPort, Inc., or its affiliates, subsidiaries, or agents, and the immediate family members thereof, are NOT eligible to participate ("immediate family members" are defined as parents, children, grandparents, grandchildren, and siblings, whether by blood, marriage, or adoption). All entrants must provide a valid United States residential postal address.

    VOID WHERE PROHIBITED. All entrants are solely responsible to assure that they are in compliance with applicable state, local, and municipal laws and regulations.

2. Method of entry: Entries may be submitted by mail using the accompanying form (or a legible facsimile thereof), or at the LiftPort, Inc., Web site (http://www.liftport.com/contest_form.html). Entries must be received no later than 11:59 PM Pacific Daylight Time (PDT) on October 4, 2006. One entry per household. Entries must be legible in order to be valid.

3. Selection of winners: Winning entries shall be selected by a random drawing from all valid entries received. The drawing shall be conducted on October 11, 2006. Odds of winning shall depend on the number of eligible entries received. At the same time that the winning entries are drawn, an additional five entries ("alternative winners") shall be selected; in the event that a winning entry is found to be ineligible, or a winner fails to collect his or her prize within thirty (30) days of being notified that he or she has won, that prize shall be awarded instead to one of the alternative winners in the order in which such additional entries were drawn.

4. Prizes: Five winning entries shall be selected, and the person who submitted each winning entry shall receive an option to purchase one thousand (1,000) shares of LiftPort, Inc., stock at an option exercise price of one cent ($0.01) per share. Shares have a stated par value of one tenth of one cent ($0.001) each. Options will be subject to execution by the winning entrant only, and are not transferable. LiftPort, Inc., makes no representation as to the actual market value of the options to be awarded, or of the actual shares themselves.

Shares in LiftPort, Inc., are issued pursuant to Rule 504 of Regulation D of the Securities Act of 1933, and as such may be deemed "restricted" pursuant to Rule 144 or other applicable laws or regulations. As such, shares may not be freely alienable. Furthermore, the exercise of options or the reselling of shares may be subject to other federal, state, or local laws or regulations, or to any applicable shareholder agreement. Winners are solely responsible to assure their compliance with any such restrictions, and are advised to seek competent professional advice prior to accepting their prizes, executing any options, or attempting to sell any shares they receive as a result of their participation in this Promotion. Winners shall be provided with all information and disclosures required by law at the same time that they receive their options. Winners are solely responsible for payment of any and all taxes or fees incurred as a result of their acceptance and exercise of options, or of holding or selling any shares.

5. Winner notification and acceptance: Winners will be notified by United States mail, at the address provided by the entrant at the time of entry, such notification to be postmarked no later than October 18, 2006. Winners will be required to complete an affidavit of eligibility, and a liability and publicity release (except where prohibited by law), which must be received no later than November 17, 2006. Failure to sign and return the affidavit or release within the time allowed may, at the sole discretion of LiftPort, Inc., result in the winner's disqualification, forfeiture of his or her interest in the prize, and award of the prize to an alternative winner.

Winners agree to allow their name, likeness, and statements to be used for advertising and promotional purposes in perpetuity in any and all media now known or hereafter discovered and without any compensation, unless prohibited by applicable law. In all other respects, entrants' names and other personal information shall be held strictly confidential except as required by law, or as specifically agreed to by the entrants.

6. General conditions: By participating in this Promotion, entrants agree to indemnify and hold harmless LiftPort, Inc., and its affiliates, subsidiaries, or agents (including, without limitation, their officers, directors, shareholders, employees, and attorneys) for any injury, loss, or damage of any kind that may arise from or relate to participation in this Promotion, to the fullest extent allowed by law. Entrants agree further that all disputes, claims, and causes of action arising out of or in connection to

x.

this Promotion, or any prizes awarded, shall be resolved individually without resort to any class action, and in no event shall any entrant be entitled to any award for punitive, consequential, or incidental damages, or for attorneys' fees. While LiftPort, Inc., will make every reasonable effort to assure that this Promotion is conducted in accordance with these official rules and without error, it shall not be held liable for lost, late, illegible, or misdirected entries, nor for any computer, online, telephone, or technical malfunctions which may occur.

All issues concerning the construction, validity, interpretation, and enforceability of these official contest rules, or the rights and obligations of any contestant and of LiftPort, Inc., shall be governed by, and construed in accordance with, the laws of the State of Washington, without regard to any choice of law or conflict of laws provision that would cause the application of the laws of any jurisdiction other than the State of Washington. In the event that any term or provision contained within these official contest rules is held to be invalid or otherwise unenforceable, these rules shall be construed in accordance with their terms as though the invalid or unenforceable term or provision were not included.

BECOME A PART OF LIFTPORT!

Enter to win one of five chances to receive 1000 LiftPort stock options!

NAME: _daddy_ _____ (Last)

_____ (Fist) _____ (Middle)

ADDRESS: _____

_____

CITY: _____

STATE: _____ ZIP: _____

PHONE: (____) _____

EMAIL: _____

DATE OF BIRTH: _____

Mail this to:
LiftPort Group
"The Space Elevator Companies"
245 4th Street, Suite 508
Bremerton, WA 98337

or visit
http://www.liftport.com/contest_form.html

The following questions are completely optional and have no effect on your chance of winning. The answers in this section will be used independently from any identifying information:

# of people in household: _____

Income range (circle one): < $30,000,

$30,000 - $44,999,

$45,000 - $74,999,

$75,000- $149,999,

$150,000+

# of computers in household: _____

Type of Internet connection: _____

Occupation: _____

_____